Just One Kiss

COURTNEY WALSH

Praise for Novels by Courtney Walsh

Just Let Go

"Walsh's charming narrative is an enjoyable blend of slice-of-life and small-town Americana that will please Christian readers looking for a sweet story of forgiveness."

Publishers Weekly

"Original, romantic, and emotional. Walsh doesn't just write the typical romance novel. . . . She makes you feel for all the characters, sometimes laughing and sometimes crying along with them."

Romantic Times

"A charming story about discovering joy amid life's disappointments, *Just Let Go* is a delightful treat for Courtney Walsh's growing audience."

Rachel Hauck, *New York Times* bestselling author

"*Just Let Go* matches a winsome heroine with an unlikely hero in a romantic tale where opposites attract. . . . This is a page-turning, charming story about learning when to love and when to let go."

Denise Hunter, bestselling author of *Honeysuckle Dreams*

"Just the kind of story I love! Small town, hunky skier, a woman with a dream, and love that triumphs through hardship. A sweet story of reconciliation and romance by a talented writer."

Susan May Warren, *USA Today* bestselling author

Also by Courtney Walsh

Harbor Pointe Novels:

Just Look Up

Just Let Go

Just Like Home

Sweethaven Series:

A Sweethaven Summer

A Sweethaven Homecoming

A Sweethaven Christmas

A Sweethaven Romance

Nantucket Love Stories:

If For Any Reason

Is It Any Wonder

What Matters Most

A Match Made at Christmas

Loves Park, Colorado Novels:

Paper Hearts

Change of Heart

Stand-Alone Novels:

Things Left Unsaid

Hometown Girl

A Cross-Country Christmas

Visit Courtney Walsh's website at www.courtneywalshwrites.com.

Just One Kiss

Edited by Charlene Patterson

The author is represented by Natasha Kern of Natasha Kern Literary, Inc.

PO Box 1069, White Salmon, WA 98672

Just One Kiss is a work of fiction. Where real people, events, establishments, organizations, or locales appear, they are used fictitiously. All other elements of the novel are drawn from the author's imagination.

For information about special discounts for bulk purchases, please contact Courtney Walsh Publishers at courtney@courtneywalsh.com

Library of Congress Cataloging-in-Publication Data

Printed in the United States of America

For my fellow writers who've made this solitary journey anything but lonely.
Katie Ganshert, Becky Wade, Melissa Tagg & Deborah Raney
Thank you for being my friends.

Chapter One

Carly Collins hated running late. She'd carefully calculated the amount of time it would take to drive from her house to downtown Harbor Pointe (eight and a half minutes), but she hadn't accounted for being stopped in the driveway by Frieda Jenkins, who walked her corgi, Elmer, at the same time every single day.

Frieda was sweet and lonely, and she was a talker.

After a long and detailed description of her arthritic challenges, Frieda said, "If you need some help with the yard, my nephew Barry is available. It must be hard to keep up with everything as a single mom." Frieda tossed a disdainful look at Carly's overgrown yard.

"No, ma'am," she said with a smile. "My son and I enjoy taking care of our yard."

Enjoy might've been pushing it.

Frieda raised one thinly lined eyebrow and gave a tug on Elmer's leash. "Best get to it, then, I suppose." She trotted off, Elmer at her side, leaving Carly feeling like a Harbor Pointe pariah, the single mom with an embarrassingly overgrown yard and no real plans to catch up in that department.

Who had time?

As she drove downtown, she glanced at the clock on the dashboard of her Honda Civic, well aware that she was cutting it very close.

Sometimes life was simply too much.

The Memorial Day weekend traffic was, as expected, insane. She'd had the perfect parking place in mind, but as she neared Mulberry Street, she found the road blocked.

I should've walked.

Her phone buzzed.

You're going to miss him! Hurry!

Her sister Quinn's text shifted Carly's nerves into panic mode. Carly's son, Jaden, was riding on a float in the big parade, and Carly didn't want to miss it, though at sixteen, Jaden probably didn't care one little bit if his mom was there. But that was just it. He was sixteen—and Carly knew he wouldn't be home many more years. She'd already moved in to "soak it all up" mode thanks to the nurses she worked with.

Her unit manager at work, Dara Dempsey, made a point to lament the fact that her youngest was heading to college in the fall, leaving her to become a "lonely old cat lady with no social life whatsoever." Dara would always follow up with, "It goes so fast, Carly. Get all the time you can with that boy because he's going to grow up and leave you and then what will you be?"

Actually, Carly didn't say so outright, but she hoped she would be Dara's successor. The woman had announced on Thursday she'd decided to take an in-home private care position that would allow her the freedom to set her own hours, better for visiting her youngest in college.

Carly had immediately thrown her hat in the ring as a candidate for the pediatric nurse unit manager at Harbor Pointe Hospital.

And she thought she had a really good chance of getting it.

Carly had spent the last sixteen years of her life as *Jaden's mom*, ruled by *his* calendar and *his* school events and *his* activities. She didn't want to completely lose herself once he went away to

2

school or, more likely, to train for some big ski competition. A promotion would be just the challenge she needed to make a life for herself now that Jaden was growing up.

And maybe it would keep her mind off the fact that her son was growing up, whether she wanted him to or not.

She shook the thoughts aside as she pulled her Civic into a spot on the grass that was absolutely not supposed to be a parking place.

Desperate times.

If she got a ticket, she'd take it up with her dad. The perks of being the sheriff's daughter.

She locked the doors and rushed out into the crowded street. Memorial Day was the big summer kick-off, the weekend when the seasonal residents returned, bringing with them extra business for the community and extra crowds for the locals. And, for Carly, extra bodies in the beds at the hospital. How many tourists did they treat every summer? And while the increase in revenue was good all around, it was hard for Carly to wish for anyone to be injured or ill.

She pushed her way through the crowd like a salmon swimming against the current, and finally found her family set up in front of the Forget-Me-Not Flower Shop, her sister's business. She spotted an open sling-back chair next to Quinn.

Oh good, they saved me a seat.

Her sister, decked out in red, white and blue attire and wearing a giant firecracker-inspired bow on top of her head, spotted her in the crowd and waved. "I thought you'd never get here. They already started!"

Carly hugged Beverly and her dad, waved to Judge and Calvin and finally dropped her purse next to the chair and sat down, heart still racing from her scramble downtown.

"It's good to see you, dear." Beverly gave her shoulder a squeeze.

Carly squeezed the older woman's hand, and it occurred to her that this unlikely foursome—Beverly, Judge, Calvin and her dad—had become a staple in both her and Quinn's life. A momentary, and delusional, pang of jealousy erupted in her heart.

Her father had a group of friends—life friends—the kind Carly had only dreamed of. And yes, she and Quinn had benefited from their relationships. Calvin had tutored her through biology. Judge had waived a parking ticket or two. Beverly had stepped in and loved them after their mom walked out when Carly was thirteen. Even still, as much as she loved all four of them, they couldn't swoop in and fill the empty places in her heart.

What a bizarre thought. Carly shoved it aside. She wasn't empty. She had Jaden. She had her nursing career. She had an overgrown yard and a nosy neighbor.

As independent as Carly was, some days she had to admit it would be nice not to have to be in charge of *everything*.

"Did I miss them?" She pushed her brown hair back, wondering if she looked as disheveled as she felt. Humidity had never been a curly-haired girl's friend.

Quinn shook her head. "No, they haven't come past yet."

Jaden had worked more hours than Carly would've expected from a sixteen-year-old helping Quinn's boyfriend, Grady Benson, and his brother, Benji, with their float for the parade, which advertised their brand-new indoor ski training center. Jaden had practically become a spokesman for the new business, and while Carly thought it was a little silly for an Olympic gold medalist to open a ski center in mostly flat Michigan, who was she to say so?

Carly had a habit of playing out every possible scenario and finding flaws in every plan. She was trying to be better about that.

Her sister was happy. Grady was happy. Benji seemed happy. And Jaden was certainly happy. She should focus on how much joy that center had already brought into her son's life. Grady had let Jaden in on the planning, the renovating, the dreaming—that ski center was a part of her son. It gave him purpose and kept him busy. She knew a lot of kids his age got into trouble when they got bored. Jaden was never bored these days.

Still, it would be nice to see him once in a while.

"I have to be honest," Carly said. "I'll be glad when this training center is up and running. It's all Jaden has been talking about for months."

Quinn smiled but kept her eyes on the high school band as they marched down the street in front of them, playing "Louie Louie." "Grady too."

"I still think a training center in Colorado or Utah makes way more sense," Carly said.

So far, she was doing a terrible job being better about her flaw-finding.

Quinn seemed unfazed. "Those places already have training centers. What about kids like Jaden who love to ski but don't have anywhere to go to learn?"

Carly couldn't argue with that. If Jaden had his way, he'd be competing with both his ski club and his high school team that winter, with the sole purpose of moving on to bigger races.

Carly, of course, wanted him to focus on school. It had been a major point of contention in the house for months.

Grady Benson was both a godsend and a disaster at the same time. He'd taken such an interest in helping Jaden that Carly felt permanently indebted to him, but that interest had landed her with a kid who had one singular goal: to ski.

She supposed she should be happy he'd found something he loved so much, but what were the odds Jaden would end up being the next Grady Benson? Wasn't talent like that rare? After all, not everyone who loved skiing could dream of competing at Grady's level.

"Grady said Jaden is crazy good, Car," Quinn said, as if she was reading her sister's mind. "And he's not one to blow smoke."

"Really?"

Quinn nodded. "He thinks he will do really well if you let him compete this year. And I don't think he just means locally."

Carly groaned. "Let's talk about something else."

Quinn pushed her hair back and turned away, craning her neck down the block. "I think I see the float!"

"Did you help decorate it?" Carly asked.

Quinn shot her a look. "Apparently flowers weren't part of their design aesthetic."

"Why aren't you riding on it? Or at least in the truck pulling it?"

Quinn shrugged. "I like to watch. Besides, who would you have sat with if I was on the float?"

Carly tossed a glance over her shoulder to where her dad and his group of friends laughed and chatted, and she realized in that moment how pitiful she was. Her dad had a more active social life than she did.

"I would've been fine," Carly said quietly.

As the float approached, Carly realized why it had taken so many hours to put the thing together. They had built a giant snow-covered slope onto a flatbed truck, and Jaden stood at the top in his ski gear, posed like he was about to shoot down the hill. It had been decorated with flags and a series of road signs that showed the address of the indoor facility Grady and Benji were opening.

On the side, a professionally created sign read, *We bring the slopes to you*, and on the top of the slope, behind Jaden, another sign read, *Harbor Pointe's Indoor Ski Training Center*.

"Shouldn't Grady be on the float?" Carly asked as the parade crawled forward. "He is kind of the big draw."

Quinn squinted. "I don't even see Grady."

The music quieted and the float came to a stop in front of them.

"What's going on?" Carly glanced at Jaden, who stood stock-still, the perfect model for Grady's new business venture. Despite the oddity of the parade coming to a halt, she still found herself grateful to God for giving her such a good son. Growing up the way he did, without a father readily available until recently, she'd always worried that somehow the parts of him that a dad was supposed to nurture would fall short.

She knew it was still early and her son was only sixteen, but so far, he seemed to be well-adjusted, thoughtful and kind. She thanked God for answering her prayers that her son would possess those qualities.

"Quinn Collins." The name came over a loudspeaker attached to the float, and Carly's sister straightened.

"What in the world?"

Seconds later, Grady appeared on the back of the float. People had said many things about her sister's boyfriend, but one thing no one could deny was how handsome he was. With his athletic build and just the right amount of facial hair, eyes that crinkled at the corners when he flashed that killer smile, the man had a whole lot going for him in the looks department.

And in other departments too. Quinn was different now that she and Grady were together. She took chances. She smiled more. She'd come out of her shell.

Grady Benson, reckless downhill skier, had actually been good for the reserved owner of a small-town flower shop. Who would've guessed?

"I'm not big on public displays of affection." He spoke into a microphone, his voice echoing down the block. The crowd had stilled. The parade had stopped. Anyone within earshot was now looking at the Olympic gold medalist who'd infiltrated Harbor Pointe only a year before and only because his community service demanded it.

"But I thought I'd make an exception this one time because when you feel the way I do about you, you can't help but make sure the whole world knows."

Quinn covered her face with her hands, and Carly glanced at Jaden, who'd broken character to turn and watch as the guy who'd barreled his way into their lives a little over a year ago hopped off the float. As he approached Quinn, he never took his eyes off her, and Carly wondered if anyone would ever look at her like that. Genuine happiness, tinged with the slightest trace of jealousy, bubbled inside of her.

Quinn had found what most people never do—a man who kept his promises. A man who now got down on one knee in front of her, with a bevy of onlookers whom he seemed unaware existed. A murmur made its way through the crowd as people visibly strained to see what was happening.

"I want you to spend the rest of your life with me," Grady said. He turned to Carly. "Will you hold this?" He handed her the microphone and pulled a small, blue velvet box from his back pocket.

People grew even quieter, as if they could hear what was being said without the assistance of the mic.

"Let's get married." Grady opened the box and set it on Quinn's lap.

Quinn stared at the ring for several long seconds—seconds that felt like an eternity, even to Carly—then she nodded.

"Yeah?" Grady's face lit.

"I thought you'd never ask." Quinn stood and threw her arms around his neck as he picked her up and spun her around. The happy moment ended, as it should, with a kiss that was slightly too intense for public consumption.

Carly's dad, Gus, stood. "Okay, okay, that's enough. You're holding up the festivities." But their father's eyes crinkled into a bright smile.

A smile reserved for his youngest daughter.

Quinn pulled away, but her gaze was still fixed on her new fiancé. "I love you."

He kissed her again, then turned to go back to the float, but as he did, the crowd let out a collective gasp and someone from behind Carly shouted, "Is that boy okay?"

Carly followed the pointed fingers back to the float, expecting to find Jaden still in position, but instead she found an empty spot where her costumed son had been.

"Where's Jaden?" Her heart kicked up. "Jaden?"

"He was just there," Quinn said. "Grady, where's Jaden?"

"We need a doctor over here!" someone from the other side of the float yelled. "This kid just fell from the top of the float."

The world turned to slow motion as anxiety clenched Carly's heart like a vise. She sprung forward into the street and followed Grady around to the other side of the float, where Jaden lay on the ground, motionless.

"What happened?"

Grady knelt at Jaden's side. He glanced up at Carly and shook his head. "I don't know." Then out to the crowd he yelled, "Someone call 9-1-1."

Carly knelt down on the opposite side of her son. Grady had pulled the ski goggles off him, and his cheeks were red. She smacked her hand against his cheeks, shaking him and praying that he would open his eyes, that this was all just a big joke they would laugh about later.

But none of those things happened. He lay there, unmoving, unresponsive, a crowd of people closing in as the sirens from an ambulance wailed in the distance.

And all she could think was *God, please protect my baby.*

Chapter Two

The sun shimmered on Lake Michigan as Josh Dixon stared out over the city from the thirty-second floor of a high-rise. Who would've ever thought he'd end up here? Certainly not Josh.

Once upon a time, it had seemed unlikely that he'd be successful at anything, but software development? Something about that didn't fit and he knew it.

Nobody back home would've ever believed his little side hobby of developing mobile video games would lead to this kind of success. Owning his own business that developed apps for other companies had never been a goal or a dream, but here he was.

He was his hardest-working employee, and he didn't see that changing anytime soon. It didn't matter that one app had been monstrously successful—that kind of popularity was fleeting.

So, he worked on the next thing. Always the next thing.

But it didn't hurt to enjoy where he was in the moment every once in a while, and, well, frankly his office had a stellar view of the lake.

Odd how that same body of water looked and felt so different back home. In Chicago, the lake took on a shiny, silvery, sleek look —the perfect backdrop to all the city promised.

But back home, Lake Michigan was all peace, quiet and one giant exhale.

Not that he would call Harbor Pointe "home" anymore— he'd been away too many years.

He balled up a blank sheet of paper and tossed it into the garbage can.

Rebecca appeared in the doorway. "That's productive."

"What are you doing here?" he asked his assistant-turned-partner. "It's Saturday."

"If you're not taking the day off, I'm not taking the day off," she said. "Though I'm really not sure what to do with myself. It's a holiday weekend."

"You should go home." He left the window and sat behind his desk. "Or better yet, get out of the city for a few days. We can afford to take some time off now."

He'd brought Rebecca on after his first solo-designed app had a modicum of success, but neither of them could've predicted what the second one would do. The free video game with in-app purchases and strategically placed ads had caught on like wildfire among the middle and high school crowd, making Josh Dixon, royal screw-up, royally rich.

And other businesses had come knocking. Everyone, it seemed, wanted Josh and his team to develop their apps. Never mind that "his team" had been only himself and Rebecca until very recently.

Hiring a few other employees had given Josh and Rebecca the breathing room they both needed, but they were still swamped.

He couldn't complain. He'd take this over an open calendar any day.

"Are you going to take some time off?" Rebecca asked.

He leaned back in his chair. "Maybe?"

She shook her head. "I can hear the question in your voice,

which means you absolutely aren't, so neither am I. I don't want you dreaming up the next big thing while I'm not here."

"Really, Becks," he said, "go home. I promise I'm not going to do much today. Just came in to grab a few things." *And I couldn't stand that apartment for one more second.*

Her eyebrows drew down in a tight *V*. "You sure?"

"Have I ever lied to you before?"

"Not that I know of." Her eyes twinkled.

"Go find your boyfriend and spend the day with him," Josh said.

Rebecca grinned. "He did ask if I wanted to go with his family to their cottage up North. Probably one of those little towns like the one you're from."

The sting of memories caught him off guard. "Probably," he muttered.

"Who will you spend the weekend with?" she asked.

His mind produced no viable options, so he tossed Rebecca a look and said, "Will you stop worrying about me? You deserve the time off, so get out of here or I'm firing you."

She raised an eyebrow. "You'd be lost without me."

He responded with his own raised eyebrow accompanied by a smirk. She was right, and they both knew it, but he wouldn't admit it out loud. Rebecca did all the things he hated, like schmoozing investors, talking with clients, marketing and generally anything that wasn't coding or creating.

Plus, she was brilliant—a fact he didn't take for granted.

"All right," she said. "You've convinced me. But you have to promise to call me if you need anything."

"I won't call you no matter what," he said. Rebecca had worked tirelessly during the latest app's launch—she'd been the one to recognize the value in his little side project in the first place. She'd worked with test groups and managed their feedback, taking Josh's little video game idea and turning it into what it now was— an overnight sensation.

The game might've been his idea, and the artwork might've

been his, but the finished product was theirs. And he'd paid her handsomely for her loyalty and her insight. She was so much more than an assistant now.

He'd plucked her out of a programming class he'd taught at a local university, recognizing immediately that Rebecca's mind didn't work like everyone else's. Not only did she understand coding, she understood marketing and she worked well with people—something that wasn't exactly Josh's strong suit.

They were a good team. Never mind that she was ten years younger than he was. He valued what she brought to the table. But she needed a break or she was going to burn out.

"Josh," she said.

"Look, Becks, the last thing I want is for you to end up like me—"

"You mean brilliant and loaded?" she joked.

"I mean a workaholic with no social life." He stood, took her by the arms, turned her around and gave her a push out the door.

"Maybe we should do something about that," she said. "I could hook you up with one of my older sister's friends. They're super needy, but don't guys like needy girls?"

Josh rolled his eyes. "I wouldn't know."

"That's right, because you don't date. Or eat out. Or have friends." She faced him. "I'm actually kind of worried about you."

"I'm brilliant and loaded," he said. "I'm doing just fine."

But the words fell flat, as lies had a way of doing.

She stared at him, and Josh wished Rebecca wasn't so observant. He'd done all he could to keep his personal life personal, but she had a way of paying attention.

Still, he maintained a bit of distance with her—part of himself that he protected from everyone, really. He wasn't in a hurry to make new friends or have deep relationships. After all, he'd found a way to disastrously ruin the ones he'd had.

"Go," he said.

"Fine. But I'm going to call tomorrow to make sure you're not working."

He practically pushed her out of the office and closed the door on her, though it didn't have a solid impact given the fact that it was made of glass.

He watched as she packed up her things and walked out of the office into the hallway, leaving him alone with his fancy new office and his view of the lake.

The phone on his desk buzzed, vibrating off the glass and disrupting the quiet. He looked down and saw Carly's name lighting up the screen.

To his dismay, his ex only called him for one reason: Jaden.

Josh's mind raced. With the launch of the app, and juggling a fair amount of new clients, he'd been so busy, but every promise he'd made to Jaden went into his phone with a special alert so he didn't miss anything. He hadn't missed anything, had he? He'd been so vigilant.

He had to be—he had a lot to prove.

"Carly, hey," he said as he tapped the button to answer. "Everything okay?"

On the other end, he could hear people talking. "Car?"

"Hey," she said.

"Hey."

His heart rate kicked up a notch. Why was she calling? It had been so long since they'd had a conversation. And yet, hadn't he wished for the day she called him just to talk? Even after all these years, he'd never quite gotten over her . . .

"Josh, it's Jaden." She interrupted his thoughts.

"What about Jaden?"

His heart lurched, mind spinning with endless possibilities of things that may be wrong, the stuff his nightmares were made of. Only nightmares were usually fiction—his were filled with real memories.

The screaming baby. The high fever. The day he realized he was more like his father than he cared to admit.

Her voice pulled him back to reality.

"We're in the emergency room. He collapsed during the Memorial Day parade."

"Is he okay? What happened?"

"They're doing some tests now. They aren't sure."

He paused, unsure what to say. He'd always felt so helpless in these situations. He didn't have a way to fix it. What words would make it better?

And Carly had always been the kind of person who had everything under control. Still, he was Jaden's father—he wanted to be there for his son whether they wanted him there or not.

"Is it serious?" he finally asked.

She paused. He could practically picture her, chewing the inside of her lip, her brown hair pulled up into a messy bun on the top of her head. He hadn't spoken directly to Carly in a long time, in spite of his renewed relationship with Jaden over the past year. She left most of the planning to their son, which he supposed was best. But sometimes he wished for a reason to talk to her.

Not this, though. This wasn't the kind of reason he was hoping for.

"It could be," she finally said. "It could be serious. It could be nothing. He could be dehydrated or maybe he overheated. But they mentioned that something could be off with his protein levels. They aren't sure."

"I'm going to head up there," Josh said matter-of-factly.

"No, Josh, don't," she said. "It's not necessary. It might be nothing."

"But it might not be nothing," he said. "And I don't want to take the chance."

Carly sighed.

"You can't seriously think I'm going to stay here while my kid is in the emergency room."

He could practically feel her biting her tongue. He knew what she was thinking. How many other things had he missed over the years? There had been plenty, and he was well aware of that, but he'd made a promise to Jaden over a year ago. He was late to the party, but he was in for the duration.

Carly didn't believe him then, and she didn't believe him now.

I'm going to prove to you that I've changed.

"Can you text me updates?" he asked, ignoring her silence. "I have to run home and pack up a few things, but I'll leave right away, and I can be there in a couple of hours."

She hesitated before saying, "Okay."

He made a conscious decision not to let it bother him. She had a right to be skeptical. Their history wouldn't give her a reason to be anything but.

"But are you actually coming, Josh?"

Her question loomed in the air, pointed and direct. Same old Carly. He'd earned her skepticism. He'd own it now. "Yes, Carly, I'm actually coming."

"Because I don't want to tell Jaden you're on the way if you're not going to make it."

He chewed the inside of his own cheek now, to keep from saying something he'd regret. She was trying to spare their son another disappointment. It was fair. But when would she finally realize he was different now? It had been nearly a year of keeping every promise. Would she ever forgive him?

Would he ever forgive himself?

"I'll be there," he said.

"Okay."

She hung up, but he sat for several seconds with the phone still pressed to his ear.

Memories of everything he'd done, things Carly didn't even know about. Things nobody knew. Would there ever be a day the past stopped haunting him?

Leaving had been the right decision—he didn't doubt that—but the repercussions of it were overwhelming. And while Carly had made it abundantly clear she wanted nothing to do with him —that woman could hold a grudge like a toddler held a kitten, tightly and around the neck—Jaden had been open to the idea of starting over. Almost like his son had simply been waiting for him to finally show up.

So Josh vowed to commit. To step up. To man up. To do what he should've done all those years ago, to become a consistent presence in Jaden's life.

And he prayed he wasn't too late.

Since then, Josh had spent two weekends a month with Jaden, and in all that time, he'd only seen Carly in person once.

But once was all it took. It sent his mind spinning, his regret twisting, his heart lurching. He'd done everything he could to move beyond his failed relationship with his high school sweetheart, but he'd failed at that too.

Never mind she couldn't even look him in the eye she was so angry. Never mind that she was better off without him.

But, oh, how he wanted to change that. Even after all this time, she and Jaden were all he wanted. Maybe it was a case of fixating on what he couldn't have.

Or maybe he knew he was never going to love anyone the way he'd loved Carly.

The way he still loved her.

You're no good for her, man. Get it through your head.

Josh rode the elevator to the sixth floor and got off in the lobby that led to his new(ish) apartment. He'd moved in a few months ago, with Jaden's help, in fact, but he'd yet to unpack. The place was a definite step up, but it was a lot bigger than his last place, which only reminded him how alone he was.

He'd moved, in part, so Jaden could have his own room when he stayed with him. He'd even hired someone to come in and professionally decorate the kid's bedroom in a downhill skiing theme. Jaden had loved it—one of the highlights of Josh's year—but later told him he didn't have to go to so much trouble.

"I'm just happy to spend time with you, Dad," he'd said.

The memory wandered around in his mind as he threw some

clothes in his duffel bag, then moved to the bathroom and packed up his toiletries.

He tried to think through anything he could possibly need, mostly to keep his mind from going to a dark place.

Carly only said Jaden had collapsed. They were doing tests. What did that mean? Would she text him when she found out more? Did she think of him as an equally invested person at this point or did she still think of him as the guy who bailed on them when they needed him most?

If you knew what I've done, Carly, you would understand. Heck, you'd thank me for leaving.

He dragged his suitcase and bags to the front door.

Before he left, he walked into Jaden's room and looked around. Gray walls. Mural of a skier painted behind the metal headboard. Framed posters of Jaden's skiing heroes hung in a neat row along with two personal photos—one of Josh and Jaden at a skiing expo this past winter and another of the two of them with Carly in the hospital the day Jaden was born.

He walked over to the photo, the same one he had in his office. Maybe it had been stupid to frame it, but it was important to him, and it was important that his son knew his parents had loved each other once. He'd been born out of love, misguided though it was.

He pulled the frame off the wall, tucked it under his arm and said a silent prayer that God would keep his son safe.

"I'll do anything, God," he said as he closed Jaden's door behind him. "Just please let him be okay."

Chapter Three

J osh definitely had not obeyed the speed limit on his drive to Harbor Pointe. It should've taken him over two hours to arrive in his hometown, but he made it in under an hour and thirty-five minutes.

That had to be some kind of record.

Now, though, sitting in the parking lot of the hospital, he found himself unable to move. What if something really was wrong with his kid? What if the doctors were about to deliver the worst news of his life?

It would only heighten his frustration that things were the way they were—that they had to be the way they were—and especially, that Carly would never understand.

He got out of his truck and strode toward the emergency room doors. Inside, the waiting room was full, but he didn't recognize anyone, and they didn't seem to recognize him. Once upon a time, Josh Dixon had been Harbor Pointe legend—and not in a good way.

A black mark on his family's good name. If anyone were talking about Josh, it likely was followed by pity for his poor parents for having to put up with such a rebellious and misguided son.

Despite Carly's good influence, his life had gone off the rails right around the time he turned seventeen. The fact that she didn't kick him to the curb back then was a miracle—and look, he'd dragged her right down to the gutter with him.

Being back here was going to be harder than he thought.

He glanced down at his cell phone. Nothing. No phone calls. No texts. Nothing to update him since the initial conversation he'd had with Carly.

Could he blame her, really? The virtual silent treatment was probably all he could expect from her.

He approached the window where a plump receptionist in pink scrubs sat. Her name tag read *Barb* and her hair was a tight blond frizz. She looked up.

"Can I help you?"

"My son was here a couple of hours ago. I just got back into town. I need to see if he's been admitted."

"Name?"

He gave her all the pertinent information, though he had to try Jaden's birthdate twice—that had warranted a major stink eye from Barb.

"They took him upstairs for testing. Second floor. Cardiovascular unit."

Josh frowned. "Like, the heart?"

Her expression turned salty. "Yes, like the heart."

His own heart raced. Why? Jaden was sixteen. An athlete. Why were they testing him in the cardio unit?

She gave him directions, which he half listened to, then sent him to an elevator down the hall.

He must've pushed the necessary buttons and he must've rode up a floor because the doors opened to reveal a giant number 2 painted on the wall. He got out, feeling every bit as dazed as he had the day Jaden was born.

That day would be etched in his memory forever.

He found the signs that led him to the cardio unit and buzzed the intercom on the door. A warbly voice came across the other side.

"May I help you?"

"I'm here to see Jaden Collins-Dixon."

"And you are?"

Josh hesitated. "I'm his dad."

Why was it so hard to say it? Because he'd been a crappy father? Because he'd never done right by his own kid? Because now, faced with a crisis, he wasn't the one they were leaning on?

And he should be.

He drew in a stunted breath and forced himself not to go there. He'd been over this with Jaden. It had been a little over a year ago that his son reached out to him, when it should've been the other way around. Josh had been trying to work up the courage, but Jaden beat him to it.

"Hey, Dad," Jaden had said over the phone. "I'm coming to Chicago for a conference with my church. Thought you might want to meet up with me or something?"

Josh's stunned silence might've caused Jaden to stutter, or maybe it was a little bit of his nerves showing through. He started to backtrack, but Josh quickly cut him off.

"I'd love that, kid."

Turned out, the youth conference was a huge deal—thousands of people were there—and Josh felt completely out of place. The whole night kicked off with music, like a concert, only one in which the words were up on a giant screen and everyone was invited to sing along. Josh looked around, bewildered by the way everyone seemed to throw their hands up and join in like there was nobody else in the massive auditorium.

Some of them sang. Some danced. Some cheered. Some prayed.

And as the night went on, Josh felt more and more like a person who didn't belong there.

Then a man came out and spoke. He wore jeans and a T-shirt and there wasn't a single thing about him that seemed phony. He openly talked about his mistakes and Josh twitched while thinking about his own.

But you didn't leave your family. You didn't bury the truth from them and everyone else. You don't know the things I've done.

As if the man could read his mind, he said, loudly and into the microphone, "It doesn't matter what you've done. Jesus already paid the price for all of it."

Josh tried not to roll his eyes. Jesus hadn't paid the price for *him*. He might've paid it for better men, but not for Josh.

I'm not good enough to be here.

Jaden leaned back in the seat next to Josh, and Josh fought the urge to stand up and run out the back door.

"If you're done trying this all out on your own," the man on the stage said. "If you're ready to give God a chance in your life, if you want to be forgiven for the past and you're ready to let Jesus into your future, I'm going to ask you to pray this prayer with me."

At his side, Jaden bowed his head and prayed the words aloud, but Josh had the feeling he'd already prayed this prayer. He had a feeling he'd been set up by a son who was a little too smart for his own good.

And he had a feeling that everything that man on the stage was saying was meant to break down the wall he'd built around his own heart the day he left Harbor Pointe.

And it worked.

He said the prayer, and he meant it. And he left that night certain that nothing would change.

But *he'd* changed.

He found himself replaying the man's words, wanting what he promised. He found himself curious and desperate to be forgiven.

And maybe that was why Carly and Jaden were on his mind all the time. Maybe they were the one thing he wished he'd gotten right. So while he didn't regret leaving, he did regret the circumstances that forced him to leave—and he so badly wanted to change now.

Where was the time machine when you needed it?

The past year with Jaden had been a second chance—and it wasn't surface-level stuff either. Jaden had this natural, easy way of talking about God. And while Josh didn't know a single thing about religion or Jesus or most of what he'd experienced that night right alongside thousands of other people, he did know he needed his son's forgiveness.

No, he couldn't explain everything to Jaden—maybe not ever —but it turned out Jaden didn't ask for explanations or reasons. He simply said, "Let's start over, Dad."

And so they did.

Nobody in all his years had ever shown him that kind of grace. It had been one of his life's greatest gifts, certainly more valuable than all the money he'd made.

If only Carly had been so forgiving.

Josh's eyes welled with fresh tears at the memory as the woman behind the intercom box buzzed the door open and he walked into the quiet cardio unit. The low hum of the fluorescent lights and the indistinct chatter of medical personnel met him on the other side. The oversized metal door closed behind him, and Josh started down the hallway toward the nurses' station, where the jumbled intercom voice had told him to go.

A nurse looked up as he approached. She smiled at him. He tried to read behind the smile—was it a look of pity, like a "you're about to get really bad news" look?

He couldn't tell. These people had probably perfected their poker faces.

"You're going to want to go down to Room 212," the nurse said. "The waiting area is right outside."

"Am I allowed to go in and see him?"

"You said you're the father?"

Josh nodded.

"As long as they're not doing tests, then, yes."

He thanked her and started off in the direction she'd pointed, looking for Jaden's room and preparing himself for whatever he was about to encounter, whatever news he was about to hear. But how did you prepare yourself for the unknown? How did you brace yourself for the realization of your worst fears?

He rounded the corner and found the waiting area outside Jaden's room, and in it, he found something else he hadn't prepared himself for: Carly's family.

He stopped at the door of the little room, lined with a wall of windows, and found himself standing face-to-face with an older, more white-haired Gus Collins. And Carly's dad was not a fan of Josh.

Maybe because Josh had given him plenty of reasons not to be.

"Josh?" Quinn's surprised expression matched her tone.

Carly hadn't told them he was coming.

Josh faced Quinn, thankful for a reason to break eye contact with Gus. "Hey, Quinn."

She pulled him into a brotherly hug, then stepped back. "It's good to see you."

He'd always had such a light-hearted relationship with Carly's little sister—he hadn't thought about it until later that Quinn probably hated him for leaving too. If so, he was thankful she wasn't letting on now.

"Where is he? Can I see him?"

"They're doing tests," Gus said. "Nobody's allowed back there right now."

Quinn shot her dad a look most likely meant to reprimand, but Gus seemed unfazed.

Josh shifted where he stood. "Where's Carly?"

"She's in the room with Jaden," Quinn said, then quietly added, "you should go in there."

He looked around as if they were sharing secrets and he wanted to be sure no one else heard them. "I should?"

"You're his dad, Josh," she said. "And I think Jaden would want you both in there."

"Is he scared?" The thought of it tied his stomach in a knot. He'd take every bit of that kid's fear away if he could. Jaden didn't deserve it.

Quinn gave a soft shrug. "He fainted suddenly and no one knows why. Wouldn't you be?"

A man whose face Josh recognized from the television walked through the doorway, holding a tray of disposable coffee cups.

"I don't know how good it is, but it's caffeinated," he said. He handed the tray over to Quinn.

"Grady, this is Jaden's dad, Josh," she said, taking the coffee.

Grady stuck a hand out in Josh's direction. He smiled. "Terrible circumstances, but I'm glad we're finally meeting."

Josh shook Grady's hand with a stern nod.

"Jaden's told me a lot about you," Grady said.

Josh tried not to think about the stories Jaden might've told this man about him. Jaden had been forgiving, yes, but he'd also made it clear that Josh would have to earn his trust. There was a difference between forgiveness and foolishness. Apparently his son knew what that difference was.

"He's told me a lot about you too," Josh said. "Thanks for helping him on the slopes. Means everything to him."

"He's a great kid," Grady said.

Josh hated that he could take zero credit for that. "I think I'm going to find out if they'll let me see him."

Quinn squeezed his arm. "She's a little stressed out."

Josh took her words as a warning. Carly might take this whole thing out on him. He told himself to be ready for it. She'd never needed anything but words to injure a person. He'd been on the receiving end of her anger more than once—sometimes justified, sometimes not.

He hadn't always understood how to handle that, but he was older now. Wiser. More confident.

Even someone as independent and controlled as Carly Collins couldn't intimidate him.

But as he knocked on the door to Room 212 and prepared to see the woman who still held his heart, he knew that was one of the biggest lies he'd ever told himself.

And he braced himself for the impact of the tidal wave of emotion that was about to wash over him.

Chapter Four

The knock on the door pulled Carly away from the window, where she'd been staring out over the lake for the last half an hour.

They'd taken Jaden back for more testing, and though her family was gathered in the waiting area, she'd chosen the quiet solitude of this tiny hospital room.

She needed to be alone with her thoughts, and, to be honest, her worry. But in doing so, she'd only given it a special place it didn't deserve, and now she stood here, paralyzed with anxiety.

The what-if questions spun through her mind like sugar in a cotton candy machine. She'd played out every scenario she'd ever heard or read about. By the time the knock interrupted her thoughts, she'd practically put Jaden on the heart transplant list.

The door opened, and she expected her dad or Quinn, but it was Josh's baby blues that greeted her from the other side.

"Josh?" His name came out as a whisper on her lips, and it was perhaps the most honest moment she could allow herself to have with him.

Because Josh Dixon could not be trusted.

Never mind that in that moment, she wanted to crawl inside

his embrace and hand over a portion of her burden, like splitting a brownie in half so they could each share a piece of it.

"What are you doing here?" She begged herself to regain some semblance of composure.

"I told you I was coming." Confusion spread across his face.

"That's right." It felt like a lifetime ago that they'd spoken on the phone, that they'd discussed their son fainting in the street during the parade. He'd said he was coming, but she hadn't believed him. She'd stopped believing him the day he walked out the door.

But here he was, looking lost and disheveled and a little like the kid she'd fallen in love with so many years ago. His hair was shorter and darker now, and he'd let his facial hair grow for at least a day or two. She hated to think it, but it was a good look for him.

Easy, laid back and sexy as all get out. That pretty much summed up Josh Dixon. And none of those things were what she should be thinking about right now.

Untrustworthy, unreliable and unfaithful. That's what she *should* be thinking.

This was why she'd handled their arrangements regarding Jaden via phone or text, doing everything she could to avoid this exact moment.

The moment her body responded to being in close proximity to the person who'd simultaneously given her the best gift she could've ever gotten and destroyed so much of her life.

Because as much as she didn't want to admit it, a part of her was still horribly attracted to Josh. She told herself it was the stupid part and begged her heart to get with the program, but as her pulse quickened and her palms turned clammy she realized she was still powerless where he was concerned.

And powerless wasn't a feeling she enjoyed. It ranked right up there with "out of control." Josh had always cast a sort of spell over her—she thought sixteen years would've been enough to break that spell, but as she stood there, unmoving, she wasn't so sure.

Quickly, she steeled her resolve against him. Josh had no right to her heart, her emotions, or her physical attraction.

"You okay?" He closed the door and walked into the room, standing only a few feet away.

She nodded, but it was a lie. She wasn't okay. But she'd been pretending she was okay for years, so why should today be any different?

"What are they saying?"

Carly still felt like she was living someone else's life. She never would've thought that her strong, healthy son would need tests to see if something was wrong with his heart. How did this happen?

"They're running some tests," she said lamely.

"Everyone keeps saying that." Josh raked a hand through his hair and sighed, eyes flashing confusion. "Can you explain it to me? I don't even know what happened."

Carly relayed what she knew. He'd been on the float in the Memorial Day parade. He'd fainted, which led to him falling off the float and onto the ground.

"The fall didn't hurt him," she explained. "But they want to know what caused him to pass out in the first place."

Josh frowned. "The heat? Dehydration?"

Carly shook her head. "They checked his protein levels and made sure he was properly hydrated. Then they took him away for an EKG and I think a stress test. I don't know, they haven't told me everything."

Josh sat in one of the chairs near the end of the bed. "What are they looking for?"

She was a nurse. She was supposed to have answers to these kinds of questions, but the truth was, she didn't want to think about the possibilities. A heart condition could be serious—really serious—and this wasn't some stranger who'd just become a patient. This was her son.

Her mind spun with medical jargon and statistics and numbers and platitudes, but nothing comforted her. Not when there was even the slightest possibility that something might be truly wrong with Jaden.

She folded her arms around herself and avoided Josh's eyes.

"I'm sure it's nothing," Josh said. "I'm sure he's going to be fine. I mean, he's a perfectly healthy, active kid."

Why did his certainty irritate her? Because he couldn't possibly know that to be true or because she couldn't muster the same assurances on her own?

"Carly?"

"He told the doctor he'd been having some dizziness," she said. "That he sometimes gets winded when he's training."

"That's weird." His shoulders slumped. "You didn't know about this?"

Why did it sound like an accusation?

But truth be told, it was the same question she was asking herself. How was it that she didn't know about Jaden's symptoms? She was a nurse. Was she simply not paying attention? But this question also irritated her—what right did he have to question her about anything?

"He's sixteen, Josh. I can't be with him all the time," she said. And not kindly.

He held up his hands as if that would calm her down. "I'm sure he wasn't in a hurry to share any of that with you."

She looked away, still annoyed. "No, he wasn't. And he certainly didn't want to share the fact that he'd fainted one other time, a few weeks ago."

"You just found that out too?"

She nodded, frustrated by it all, replaying the last few weeks, racking her brain for any signs she might've missed.

"So, those spells and this one led them to think maybe a problem with his heart?"

"Like I said—could be nothing." *Could be something.*

Josh seemed to hear the words she wasn't saying and his mood turned somber, then he grew quiet.

The door to the room opened and a nurse named Alisha

wheeled Jaden through. She met Carly's eyes and smiled, an attempt to reassure her colleague that everything was going to be okay.

But Carly knew smiles weren't promises and words meant to comfort often had no factual basis.

But she had to be strong. For Jaden. It's what she did. It's what she had always done. Even when she didn't feel like it.

And today, she didn't feel like it.

"Hey, kid," she said.

A tired-looking Jaden waved, then turned his full attention to Josh. "Dad, I didn't know you were coming."

Carly avoided her ex's eyes. She hadn't told Jaden she'd called Josh. She didn't want to risk upsetting him, despite what Josh had told her on the phone. Truth was, she didn't believe he'd actually show until he walked through the door.

Alisha wheeled Jaden over to the bed, and Josh moved toward him to help him stand.

"Yeah, I just got here. Had to see what all the fuss was about."

Jaden laughed. "I guess I fainted or something."

Again. You fainted again. How could you not tell me you fainted in the first place?

She kept her thoughts to herself, though she desperately wanted to confront her son for his silence.

Josh helped him up into the bed and Carly pulled the blanket over his legs.

"How are you feeling now?" she asked.

"Just tired."

"He hit his head pretty good when he fell," Alisha said. "We don't think he has a concussion, but we want to monitor him to be sure."

Carly nodded. A concussion she could handle. "What about the other tests?"

Alisha pursed her lips. "The doctor will be in soon to talk through those."

"Alisha, really?" She never realized how maddening it was to be told to wait longer when you'd already been waiting hours for answers.

"Sorry, Carly. You know I don't know anything."

"I know you can't tell me anything," she said.

"Thanks so much, Alisha. We'll wait for the doctor." Josh had moved to the other side of the bed and now stood at Carly's side.

She didn't want to be aware of his body that close to hers, but she was. She found it horribly unfair that he'd only gotten better looking with age while her looks continued to deteriorate like a pear left out too long on the counter.

Not that these were the kinds of things she should be thinking about when her child's health was in question. She couldn't care less what she looked like right now.

Alisha turned her attention to Jaden. "Do you need anything else while you wait for the doctor?"

Jaden shook his head. "I'm great, but thanks."

She glanced at Carly one last time before exiting the room.

"Mom." Jaden's tone sounded like a reprimand.

"What?"

"You can't start snapping at everyone. You hate when people do that to you."

He was right. She did. She always felt terrible when the doctors had to deliver bad news. And she felt even worse when she knew before the people getting that news. And even worse still when the people got angry and took it out on her.

And now she was doing the same thing.

"Sorry," she said. "I'm just stressed."

"I'm fine," Jaden said. "I probably just didn't eat enough this morning. All this heart testing is a little over the top."

But Carly knew that wasn't true. She could tell by the sparse words and concerned looks from the doctors and nurses that they suspected something bigger was wrong with Jaden.

Josh sat down on the end of Jaden's bed and the two of them started talking about some video game they played together over the internet. As much as she hated video games, she was moderately thankful Jaden and his dad had found this common ground.

Never mind that it sometimes made Carly feel left out. Did Jaden remember which one of his parents had been there for him since the day he was born?

But then, Josh had always been an elusive kind of person— the kind who didn't put much of himself out there, which, she supposed, only made people want more.

That had certainly been the case for her.

The door opened and Dr. David Willette walked in. Tall, geekily handsome and intelligent-looking (if there was such a thing), he wore a white coat over a pinstriped shirt and tie.

Carly had never spoken to him, but she'd heard her fellow nurses talk about him, the same way they talked about every doctor they worked with. According to the rumor mill, Dr. David Willette was single, loved racquetball and was very good at his job.

"He's perfect husband material," Justine had said just last week.

"If you like boring men," Sasha had replied.

"Why is he boring? Because he's stable? Because he has a good job?" Justine had just gotten out of a bad relationship. Sasha was barely out of college. The two of them had different priorities.

In that moment, Carly thought his best quality was "good at his job."

"Hello, I'm Doctor—"

"Willette," Carly cut in. "I know."

He smiled. "You work in Peds."

It was a statement, not a question. Did he know who she was?

"Carly Collins," she said. "We've never been officially intro-duced." She stuck out her hand, which he shook firmly with a smile.

"Nice to meet you." He glanced at Josh. "And your husband?"

Carly laughed. "No, uh, no—Jaden's father. Not my husband." She felt Josh's eyes on her. "I'm not married," she added quietly, though she had no idea why. It made her sound like a fool.

Josh stood and Carly could feel her cheeks reddening.

"Josh Dixon," he said, shaking the doctor's hand.

"Nice to meet you."

Josh looked at Carly, and for a split second she could see the injury she'd inflicted behind his gaze. As if it were crucial everyone knew she was absolutely *not* in a relationship with this man.

But it *was* crucial that everyone knew that. At least to Carly. If anyone thought she'd taken Josh back after everything he'd put her through, she'd be mortified. As if she could ever be that stupid.

"How you feeling, Jaden?" Dr. Willette asked.

Jaden shrugged. "Just a little tired."

"You've had quite a day." The doctor smiled.

"What do you think?" Carly could feel herself growing impatient. Josh reached over and put a hand on her arm, as if to say "calm down." She shrugged it off and moved closer to Jaden, leveling her gaze with the doctor's.

"Well, we need to rule a few things out," Dr. Willette said. "Could be nothing, but we want to give you a Holter monitor."

Carly's mind raced through her mental medical word bank. *Holter monitor.* "To determine if Jaden has an irregular heartbeat?"

"Yes," Dr. Willette said. "I also want you to keep a diary of your activity over the next forty-eight hours. Then, Tuesday we'll see you back here, and we can take a look at what we find."

"So we're looking at a possible arrhythmia?" Carly said.

"Just ruling it out."

"So, Jaden, that diary is really important." Carly looked at her son. "You need to record any symptoms you might have and what you're doing when they occur."

"I don't have symptoms," Jaden said.

"Your chart says dizziness, shortness of breath, one other fainting spell," Dr. Willette said.

"Yeah, but that's normal stuff," Jaden said. "Lots of guys have those things."

"Jaden," Carly said.

"I didn't think it was a big deal," he said.

"It probably isn't," Dr. Willette said. "But we just want to be sure."

Lots of people had irregular heartbeats. Probably no big deal. *Could be a really big deal.*

She hated that the voice in her head had turned negative and repetitive.

"Dr. Willette, he's an athlete," Carly said. "A skier. He's training nonstop. Is this going to interfere with that?"

The doctor met her eyes. His smile reminded her of Alisha's. The poker-face smile. It gave nothing away.

And yet, it said everything.

"We'll cross that bridge when we come to it," he said. "So, we'll bring the Holter monitor in and get you all fixed up. Then we'll make an appointment to see you back here after the holiday. Sound good?"

Carly nodded as the doctor exited the room, leaving the three of them alone with thoughts none of them wanted to have.

Chapter Five

After Jaden was fitted with a Holter monitor, a small rectangular device that he could wear around his neck and that would record the rhythm of Jaden's heart, Carly's family (including her dad's friends) flooded the small hospital room.

Josh was pretty sure they weren't supposed to have that many people in a hospital room at once, but nobody seemed to notice. Or care.

They asked questions Josh hadn't thought of or didn't know to ask, and Carly answered like the nurse she was. If she felt emotional over any of this, she hid it well.

But then, she'd always hidden her emotions well, hadn't she?

Slowly, Josh moved to the perimeter of the room, feeling like that was where he belonged, but in his head, he prayed that this whole ordeal left them with good news. That Jaden was fine. That there was no irregular heartbeat.

God, this is one of yours. One of the good ones. That's got to count for something, right?

"What are the possible outcomes?" Beverly asked.

Carly explained them, leading, of course, with the least serious, and as she continued talking, Josh's eyes fell on Jaden, who looked like a prisoner trapped in this room.

The din of conversation escalated, and finally Josh cleared his throat. "Maybe we should give the kid some space."

An awkward hush filled the room as they all looked at him, certainly thinking what right did he have to suggest anything about Jaden at all.

But everyone had thoughts and questions and opinions, and it seemed like Josh was the only one considering his son's feelings at all. He looked at Jaden. "You need some fresh air?"

Jaden met his eyes and nodded.

"Well, we can go," Carly said.

"Why doesn't Dad drive me home?" Jaden asked.

Carly's face fell and the tension in the room rose. But Josh wasn't trying to swoop in here like the hero. He only wanted to do what was best for his son.

It's what they all wanted, right? But maybe they had different ways of showing it.

"Okay," Carly said quietly. "If that's what you want."

"Maybe we can swing by the training center, Grady?" Jaden said. "I'd love to show my dad."

"You should probably go home and rest," Carly said.

"Come on, Mom." Jaden sounded exactly like the teenager he was. "I'm fine. They're monitoring my heart, not giving me a pacemaker."

Carly's frown lines deepened. Josh loved the idea of hanging out with his son, and especially seeing this training center he'd been talking about for weeks. But going against anything Carly said right now was a quick way to land on the worst side of her "bad" list, and he had no interest in doing that.

"Maybe we could do that tomorrow, Jaden," Josh said. "Your mom's right—you need to get some rest."

Jaden groaned. "Fine, but can you still be the one to drive me?"

Josh glanced at Carly, who avoided his eyes. "If it's okay with your mom."

She looked at Jaden, then finally, at Josh. She didn't look angry, like he expected. She looked hurt. "It's fine."

But her tone said otherwise.

"I don't have to," he said.

She found his eyes. "I said it's fine."

Josh could feel pairs of eyes on him, as if everyone was waiting for his next move. Unfortunately, he had no idea what that move should be.

He didn't understand Carly anymore. He'd been away too long. He'd made too many mistakes. It was hard to believe that once upon a time, they'd had such an easy relationship. From the day they'd met in third grade, they were friends. And after just moving to town, Josh needed a friend.

They'd grown up together—went to each other's birthday parties, spent their summers with a big group of friends at the beach. Like all Harbor Pointe locals, they had inside jokes about the tourists. They knew the best places to fish, the most secluded spots on the beach, and that Dockside had—hands down—the best Chicago-style pizza in town. They were the kids all the adults knew by name, which made disobedience next to impossible, at least when they were really young.

Carly was in nearly every single one of his childhood memories. The good ones, anyway.

In fact, she might've been the only reason he had good memories at all.

He supposed at some point, the past was bound to come seeping in. He got older. More withdrawn. Somehow, it seemed only Carly could reach him.

And they couldn't have been more different. Carly was on the straight and narrow. She went to church every week and actually believed what the preacher said. She sang in the choir. She ran for student council representative and worked on the school newspaper.

And on Friday nights, she was in bed no later than eleven.

She was steady and dependable, and maybe that was why he was so drawn to her. That or her big brown eyes—they always seemed to read exactly what he was thinking, and he never had to say a word.

He knew they were different. He sensed that he wasn't good enough for her, but that didn't stop him from wanting her.

Unlike Carly, Josh made poor choices. He had a temper and spent a lot of time in detention. His grades were mediocre, and he was never home by eleven on Friday nights.

But for whatever reason, Carly wouldn't let Josh go.

As they got older, their relationship changed, of course. He didn't know if that was natural or just the way things were for the two of them.

She was an academic. He was barely making C's. She spent her free time at the library. He'd discovered the numbing properties of alcohol.

They ran in different circles, yet somehow, they still stayed connected.

Many nights, he'd sneak out, walking through backyards and darkness to her house, and she almost always met him on her back porch.

On the surface, they weren't friends. Nobody would've believed they talked at all anymore, but the fact was, Carly Collins was the only person in the world Josh trusted.

So when she showed up outside his house one afternoon, in broad daylight, he wondered if this was his chance to pay her back for all the hours she'd sat at his side while he didn't talk, just so he knew he wasn't alone.

Josh had been sitting in the living room, flipping through channels on the television, when he looked up and saw Carly standing on the sidewalk outside their house, her cotton-candy-blue bike with the white banana seat and pink-tasseled handlebars at her side. She met his eyes, and he could see instantly something was wrong. She waved him out, then disappeared, but he knew exactly where to find her.

He hollered to his mom that he was leaving and bolted out the back door without waiting for a response. He plodded up over the sand dunes and found her on the beach sitting on their log—the place they sometimes went when her dad was home at night.

She sat with her back to him.

And she was crying.

Josh approached carefully, aware that he didn't know what to say when girls cried. Heck, he hardly knew what to say when they weren't crying.

But this wasn't just a girl. This was Carly. And whether he wanted to admit it or not, she'd stolen his heart the day they first met on the playground in third grade.

In all the years he'd known her, he'd never seen her cry. Not when she got hit in the face during dodgeball. Not when their choir teacher humiliated her in front of the entire class. Not even when she fell off her bike and skinned her leg so badly her dad took her to the emergency room for stitches.

She was without a doubt the strongest person he knew, so as he sat down next to her and saw her tear-stained face, his heart plummeted.

He reached out and took her hand, hopelessly aware of how soft her skin was. Tears streamed down her face, and as he drank in the sight of her, he could see she was trying not to cry.

Josh would do anything to protect her—anything.

Gus had made his feelings about Josh plain—he wasn't a fan. What if she'd finally agreed with her dad that he was bad news? What if she was about to tell him they couldn't be friends anymore—not even friends who only saw each other under the cover of darkness? How would he survive?

"What's wrong?" he asked quietly, afraid to disturb the peace of the silence between them.

She pulled her hand from his and wrapped her arms around

herself just as a slight wind kicked up, loosening a strand of hair from the tie that held it back.

For a brief moment, he imagined pulling the hairband out and running his hands through her long, wavy hair, pushing it away from her face, and finally—after all these months—kissing her the way he'd been thinking about doing.

"My mom left," Carly said, her voice hitching in her throat. "She's just . . . gone."

He hated that he felt relief in that moment. It was thoughtless and selfish, but if he lost her, he knew he would never recover. "Your mom?"

How was that possible? Her mom was practically a staple in Harbor Pointe. She owned the flower shop. She doted on her daughters. She was even their room mother all the way through the sixth grade.

"I guess she didn't want us anymore," Carly said. "I didn't know where else to go." She buried her face in her hands and Josh felt his fingertips tingle, as if he was being led to respond but not sure he knew how.

He sat in silence for several seconds before finally wrapping an arm around her shoulder. When she didn't move away, he scooted closer.

"I'm really sorry," he said.

She shifted and leaned her head on his shoulder. They stayed like that, in complete silence, until the sun set, and he didn't mind one bit.

"Do you want to go get something to eat?" he finally asked. "We could ride bikes over to Dockside."

It was her favorite pizza place—how could she refuse?

She shook her head. "Thanks, but I need to get home. I have to be strong for Quinn."

He watched her straighten, as if mentally putting herself back together.

"I feel better now."

They stood. If he hadn't seen it for himself, he never would've thought she'd just been crying. Somehow, as if by magic, the redness in her face had disappeared and she'd wiped her cheeks dry.

"Thanks, Josh," she said. She stood on her tiptoes and kissed him on the cheek. "You're the best."

Now, standing in Jaden's hospital room, he wondered how they'd gone from that sweet relationship to this terrible disconnect. And yet, he knew how. Their past was filled with mistakes and misunderstandings. It was filled with heartache and sadness, the kind that overshadowed the good times.

Jaden inched his way to the edge of the bed and stood. "Ready, Dad?"

Josh glanced at Carly, but she wouldn't look at him, unlike Gus, who was staring him down.

"Sure thing, kid."

"Great," Jaden said. "See ya at home, Mom. Thanks for coming, everybody."

After they filled out paperwork and got the all clear to go home, they walked through the hallways of Harbor Pointe Hospital, and all Josh could think was *that probably could've gone better.*

But, as usual, he had no idea how to fix it now.

Chapter Six

C arly didn't like this one bit. Letting Josh take a more active role in Jaden's life had been risky to begin with, but it was always Jaden's heart she was worried about—never her own.

The irony of that didn't escape her.

Now, as she paced her living room waiting for her ex to bring their son home from what had started as a simple ride and turned into a father/son pizza night at Dockside, her mind tumbled.

She looked at the clock. How long did it take to eat pizza? She wanted her son home with her, where he belonged. Especially after the day they'd had.

Jaden acted like this wasn't serious, like it was no big deal. Was Josh simply reinforcing that idea?

Her phone buzzed. She picked it up expecting a text from Jaden but instead found one from her sister.

In case it wasn't obvious, I'd like you to be my maid of honor.

Carly's eyes welled with inexplicable tears. Why was she emotional? Anyone could've predicted Grady would ask Quinn to marry him. They'd been practically inseparable since the day they met, at least once Quinn admitted she actually liked him.

And yet, something about it, about her baby sister finding the love of her life while Carly, four years older, did not currently have a single prospect in the romance department—it had worked her over.

And she didn't like it. She didn't like feeling jealous of the happiness she absolutely wanted her sister to have.

She only wished maybe there was a sliver of it out there for her too.

Pull yourself together.

This was ludicrous. Carly had decided a long time ago that she was the kind of independent woman who didn't need anyone taking care of her. Her sister's impending nuptials changed nothing about that.

And yet, every once in a while, she saw the fleeting image of a faceless someone else helping pay the bills, mowing the lawn, picking up groceries, loosening the knots in her shoulders, saying *I love you*—and those images were hard to shake.

She texted back, *Of course, Q. You know I'm in!*

Good! Engagement party details forthcoming.

And so would begin the parade of wedding festivities that would require a plus one that Carly didn't have. The last thing she needed was a throng of Harbor Pointe matrons asking her when it would be her turn and wasn't it so sad that her little sister was getting married before she was.

The front door opened and she turned toward it. Jaden and Josh stood in the doorway, looking at her.

"Hey." She tried to sound casual, feeling suddenly awkward in her plaid pajama shorts and an old pink Gap T-shirt.

Josh had never been in her house. They'd always met halfway between here and Chicago, and frankly, she didn't want him in her space. It set her off-kilter. She didn't trust him, and she didn't want him poking holes in her carefully constructed existence.

"Hi, Ma," Jaden said.

When she'd become "Ma" she didn't know. Was that one of those things that happened when you weren't looking, like your son's voice changing or falling in love?

"Dad, I'll go get those skis." Jaden rushed through the hallway and upstairs.

"Not too fast, Jaden," Carly called after him.

Josh closed the door and took a step farther inside. She should invite him in—that's what normal people did when someone visited their home.

But Josh wasn't just someone. He was *Josh*. And she was still mad at Josh. She'd gotten used to this anger she carried with her. It was a part of her now.

"Thanks for taking him," she said without looking at him.

"Thanks for letting me."

At least her ex still knew who was in control here. That was important.

"You heading back tonight or staying over?"

Josh looked away. "I want to stay until after we find out what's going on with Jaden."

She frowned. "That could be days."

He shrugged. "Okay."

"You're going to stay here indefinitely?"

"If that's what it takes," he said. "I just want to make sure you guys are okay."

She scoffed but bit back the harsh remark that flitted through her mind. No sense fighting. Not today, not with emotions already on high alert.

Not when she felt vulnerable and he looked like *that*.

Knock it off. Remember what he did to you.

"Can I come to the next appointment?"

She found Josh's eyes, earnest and pleading, and against her better judgment, she heard herself agree.

"Thanks," he said. "I can pick you guys up if that works?"

"I can drive us."

"Might as well all go together."

"Josh, this isn't a family outing," she said, more harshly than she'd intended.

"I just thought maybe it would be good for the three of us to be together right now."

It would've been good for the three of us to be together at Jaden's first birthday, at his baptism, his first ski competition.

She drew in a deep breath. She was letting him come to the appointment, that was plenty of give on her end. "We can meet you there."

A look of defeat washed across his face, but he nodded anyway.

A few seconds of silence held the tension between them.

"Will you stay at your parents' house?"

He shifted. "I don't know yet."

She wanted to ask how things were with his parents. His family dynamic had always been stressful, but not many people knew that. Josh wasn't forthcoming with information about his family life, but Carly knew how bad it was. Carly knew more about Josh than anyone else, or she had at one time.

Did she still? Who did he confide in now that they were apart?

He stood there, looking innocent and kind. Like a person who'd done nothing wrong. Or maybe like a person who was sorry?

But no. Josh wasn't sorry. He'd made his choice long ago, and she wasn't going to get swept back in by her pity for him.

"How did he seem?" she asked quietly, hugging her arms around herself.

Josh drew in a breath. "Okay."

"Really?"

Josh shook his head. "I think he's scared, but he's not saying so. Played it off like no big deal."

"He has to take this seriously. The monitor, the diary—all of it."

"I am taking it seriously, Mom," Jaden said from the stairs. He made his way to the entry, skis in hand. "Dad already gave me that lecture."

"Really?" That was a first. She glanced at Josh, who seemed to be purposefully avoiding her eyes.

"Yeah, Ma," Jaden said. "Document everything—every flutter, every symptom. Dizziness, tingling fingers or toes, shortness of breath and what I was doing at the time. I got it."

Carly looked at Josh. He'd clearly been listening to the doctor, and he found a way to tell Jaden so she didn't have to. She should be thankful. She *was* thankful. And yet, skeptical. With Josh, she was always skeptical.

She half listened as Jaden explained why the skis he'd bought with his Christmas money were "beyond cool," but she noticed Josh seemed genuinely interested in what their son was saying.

Not like one of those dads who secretly wanted their kid to stop talking so they could answer a text or get on a work call.

She knew those dads. She'd interacted with them at the hospital lots of times. Did they think their kids were old enough to handle the medical information on their own?

It both surprised and confused her that Josh was not like these dads. Was this what their weekends in Chicago were like? Were they becoming friends?

Jaden finished his spiel, and Josh stood upright with a nod. "Can't wait to see you using these beauties."

Carly's heart sank and a prayer raced through her mind —*please let him be able to use those skis.*

God knew how much skiing meant to her son. Surely He wouldn't take away his ability to do it, would he?

Jaden had become so devout in his faith. Unlike with many teenagers, God wasn't some far-off idea and religion wasn't something his parents were forcing down his throat.

He'd gone to a youth retreat three years ago and returned a different kid. He'd never given her the details, but she was pretty sure he'd had an encounter with the Lord that she would maybe never understand.

Her relationship with God had been all about checks and

balances. She was a good girl. She did the right things. She tried not to sin and that was that.

The way Jaden lived his life had inspired her to believe that perhaps she'd been doing it wrong for a lot of years . . . but she wasn't sure how to have the kind of encounter that would change anything.

"You want God to be real to you, don't you, Mom?" he'd asked her once.

"Of course I do." And she did—but how? What did that look like? It wasn't like she could take God out for coffee. And besides, wasn't *she* supposed to be the one teaching *him* how to build his faith? When had their roles reversed on this issue?

"Then let go of everything you think you know and go find him for yourself."

She hadn't understood what he was saying then, so why were the words replaying in her mind now?

"You think of church as an obligation. You think of God as a disciplinarian. You think you can work your way to heaven. But it's about so much more than that."

Jaden had her number, that was for sure. But what did it change?

God took things from good people. Like taking her mother before they were ready to live without her. Was He going to take skiing away from Jaden too? Or worse—was He going to take Jaden?

"Well, I should go," Josh said. "But I'll see you at your appointment."

Jaden groaned. "This is really going to cut in on my training time."

Carly wanted to jump in with some important motherly wisdom, but Josh beat her to it.

"It's important, kid," he said. "We need to make sure you're okay."

"I know," Jaden said.

"And I'm sure you're okay," Josh added.

"Yes," Carly said. "But you do need to take it easy."

Jaden rolled his eyes. "Fine. Thanks for the pizza, Dad." He headed back upstairs, leaving Carly to see Josh out.

A shadow came across his eyes as he pushed a hand through his hair and faced her. "I'll see you Tuesday, I guess."

For a second, there he was again—that moody teenager who could stop her heart from beating with a single glance.

She walked to the door, pulled it open and nodded. "Yep."

He started to walk through it but stopped directly in front of her. She squared her shoulders and put on her bravest face as she looked up and met his eyes.

But the second a connection between them was made, her bravery faltered, her legs turned wobbly and her breath caught in her throat.

"You gonna be okay?" he asked.

"I'm fine." She forced the words, but inside, her heart crumpled, the weight of the fear she'd been pretending she didn't have nearly crushing her from the inside out. Tears clouded her vision.

He put a hand on her arm, and for a moment she thought he might hug her and he absolutely could not hug her because if he did, she would come undone and her secret would be uncovered.

She wasn't as strong as she pretended to be.

"You sure?"

"I'm okay," she managed to say.

He squeezed her arm. "I'm kind of scared."

No. No. NO. They could not do this. *She* could not do this. She couldn't have a moment with Josh. She had to disconnect whatever this was because if she didn't, it would only take a heartbeat for her to feel seventeen again, unable to resist her feelings for him. She was older now. Wiser. She knew the truth about this man, and she wasn't willing to risk her heart again.

Fool me once, shame on you. Fool me twice...

"He's going to be fine," she said, not fully believing it. But it was what they both needed to hear in that moment.

He nodded. The tension faded. The moment passed.

Good job, Carly. That was smart.

"Call me if you need anything before Tuesday," Josh said.

As if he would be the person she would reach out to if she needed anything. "See ya."

He lingered for another moment, then finally walked out the door, sucking all of the oxygen in the room out with him.

Chapter Seven

J osh let the engine of his Ford F-150 idle in the street in front of the old white cottage where he'd lived after his family moved to Harbor Pointe when he was eight. Perfect *Leave It to Beaver* family house, and to the rest of the world, that's exactly what the Dixon family looked like.

His mother wore an actual apron when she made dinner.

It was all part of the image his parents had worked so hard to perpetuate the second they crossed the city limits of their new hometown. It was all part of the image Josh had shattered when he was a teenager, lost and rebellious.

See, he knew the truth. He saw through the phoniness.

How many nights had Josh spent in his room wishing he could rub a magic lamp and transport himself out of there?

He hadn't spoken to his parents in weeks, but he hadn't seen them in months. A lot of months. Like over a year. Maybe two years. How long had it been since they'd shown up in Chicago and insisted he go to lunch with them?

His conversations with his mother were always brief and always out of guilt.

She'd leave him a message. He wouldn't respond. Another

message. Still no response. He'd send her a vague text and she'd call again—

"Joshua, this is your mother. You know a text message doesn't replace a conversation. I want to hear your voice. I need to know how you're doing. Call me back, please?"

He'd call out of guilt, keeping the conversation brief and surfacey.

"Oh, is that what you sound like?" she'd say after their initial hellos. "I'd forgotten."

"Been busy, Mom. Lots going on here."

"Just like your father."

Josh cringed at the words.

"Things are ramping up for him right now too."

His father was a city planner, and every year his mother mentioned *this* might be the year he ran for mayor.

But Josh didn't want to talk about his father. And he certainly didn't want her comparing the two of them—they were nothing alike. Josh had made sure of it.

"Oh, Mom, sorry, I'm getting called into a meeting."

"Already?"

"Yeah, I'll catch up with you later."

He'd disconnect, then look around his empty office, wondering if God considered it lying if it spared someone's feelings.

Because if he told his mom the truth—that he'd be perfectly fine if he never spoke to either of his parents again—he knew it would break her heart.

What was he even doing here? It was stupid.

He pulled out his phone and scrolled until he found Cole Turner's number. His old friend might put him up for a night or two. But before he could even dial, the front door of the cottage opened and his mother walked outside. She'd likely been watching him from the second he parked in the street.

She covered her mouth with her hands and then waved.

He was about to get a lot of grief for not calling her the

second he heard Jaden had fainted, but she worried—a lot—and it seemed counterproductive to tell her anything before he knew anything.

Besides, he didn't want to hear a word his parents had to say about his absence from Jaden's life, a popular topic every time he talked to them.

"Joshua? Is that really you?" His mother rushed off the porch and over to the driver's-side door as he opened it and got out of the truck.

"It's me, Mom."

She flung her arms around him and squeezed. "Oh, Joshua. You're home." She pulled back, still holding on to his biceps, but now searched his eyes with her own. "What's wrong?"

Josh moved away from her and opened the back door of the truck. He pulled out his duffel bag.

"You're staying?" His mom's eyes lit up.

He knew this was all she ever wanted—him visiting, sharing his latest news. She wanted to be a part of his struggles and his successes the same way most good mothers did. Why he resisted made little sense to the outside world, but the outside world didn't have the inside view.

His mom had sacrificed everything for their family, so why did Josh resent her so much?

"Just for a few days," he said. "Jaden is having some testing done."

"What kind of testing?" She frowned.

"You didn't hear what happened at the parade?" It was a small town, and his parents were well connected. He'd half expected them to show up at the hospital—not because they actually cared, but because they wanted to look like they did.

Her brow furrowed. "We've been out on the lake. Your father was fishing all day. We just got home. What kind of testing?"

"Medical testing," Josh said, not wanting to get into the logistics with her. The last thing he needed was her questions putting ideas in his head. He was having a hard enough time not worrying as it was.

"You didn't call," she said.

He slung the bag over his shoulder. "I didn't have any information until after I got up here."

"Well, I could've gone to the hospital, been there with him."

"Not if you were out on the lake."

"We would've come in early."

Josh chose not to argue, though they both knew that wasn't true. His father wouldn't have changed his plans. "Carly was there, Mom."

"Carly and her family?"

He sighed. His absence in Jaden's life had been a sticking point, but sometimes Josh wondered if it was only because of the way it painted his parents. Were they concerned about their son, about their grandson—or only about the fact that *they* looked bad and didn't have as much access to Jaden as they would've liked?

"It doesn't matter," Josh said. "They're monitoring his heart, and we're going back after the holiday to make sure everything's okay." He started toward the door, aware that downplaying the situation would never work. Not with Gloria Dixon. The woman had a sixth sense for sugarcoating.

"What are they monitoring?"

"His heart," Josh repeated. "I just said that."

"But why?"

"He fainted."

They'd reached the porch, and Gloria rushed ahead to open the door. "Your father is resting in the living room. Maybe you could help him out with the yard work later? It would go a long way."

Josh's stomach knotted. He didn't care to placate his parents to avoid his father's bad behavior. He'd lost any tolerance for that a long time ago.

"I just need a place to sleep," he said.

"And eat," his mother replied. "I made pot roast. Your father's favorite."

Of course you did.

As if that could ensure a good mood for the night.

Josh stopped at the bottom of the stairs. "You okay, Mom?"

His mom quickly hid her frown with a put-on smile. "Of course, dear."

Why would he have thought anything would've changed? She was still here, pretending they were the perfect family, like a character in an old-fashioned family sitcom.

He nodded, aware that was all he'd ever get out of her.

"Josh?"

Josh turned toward the voice and found his father standing in the entryway. The man, once hulking and intimidating, seemed smaller somehow.

"Oh, did we wake you?" his mom asked.

"Hey, Dad," Josh said.

"We didn't know you were coming," his father said. "Gloria, did you know he was coming?" It had been over a year since he'd seen his father—why had he expected any other kind of welcome than this one?

His mother shrunk back. "No, dear."

"It was a last-minute trip," Josh said.

"He came to make sure Jaden is okay," his mom said.

His father frowned. "What's wrong with Jaden?"

"Do you have your phone?" Josh asked. "I find it hard to believe nobody tried to call you about this."

His father walked over to the entryway table and picked up his phone. He held down the power button until the screen came to life.

"Your father needed a day off, so he let his staff know he was unreachable."

"The day of the Memorial weekend parade?"

"He has people in place to handle things, Joshua."

His father held his phone to his ear. "Three messages. Jaden fainted at the parade." He met Josh's eyes. "None of these messages are from you."

Josh twitched. He was eleven again, standing in the doorway of his bedroom, shrinking under his father's anger.

He'd been caught cheating on a test, and the teacher had called his parents.

"Do you know how embarrassing this is?" His father poked Josh in the chest with three fingers. "You made us look bad, like we haven't taught you right from wrong."

"I'm sorry, Dad," Josh said, tears pooling in his eyes.

"You're not now, but you will be," his dad said, eyes flashing cold.

His mom stood behind his dad, pleading with the man to calm down, but his father seemed not to notice.

"I won't do it again." Josh took a step back into the room.

His father swore and advanced toward him.

"Jim, please," his mother said, pulling at his father's arm.

His dad shrugged her off. "This is none of your business, Gloria."

"He's my son too," his mom said in a rare, if short-lived, display of strength.

"Go downstairs and let me handle this."

His mother looked at Josh, fear flickering behind her eyes. He wanted to beg her to stay. He wanted her to stand in front of him, to at least try to protect him. But she didn't. Instead, she did what she always did and went downstairs, leaving Josh to fend for himself.

But at that age, there was nothing he could do. Nothing except try his hardest not to cry while his father whipped him over and over again—on the back so nobody would see the damage he'd done.

"I know you're not crying, you sissy," his dad yelled as his belt snapped against Josh's skin. "No son of mine is going to grow up to be a weakling, and no son of mine is going to be a cheater. You're an embarrassment, you hear me?"

Josh shook the thoughts away now as his eyes drifted to his father's belt. He could practically hear it snapping across his back.

"He didn't have any concrete information," his mother said in response to his father's looming question.

"Of course he didn't," his dad barked. "Surprised he's here at all, he's done such a good job of staying out of the picture."

"Jim, please," Gloria said. "He just got home."

Josh stared at the wall while his father looked him over then finally walked into the kitchen. "You can come help me in the backyard," he called over his shoulder.

Josh's fingers gripped the strap of his duffel bag, his thumb tapping against it. "This was a mistake."

"No, Josh," his mom said. "He just wasn't expecting you is all."

He faced her then. "When are you going to stop making excuses for him, Mom?"

Her forehead pulled. "What do you mean?"

"My whole life, that's all you've done. He's a jerk, Mom, and you know it, but all you do is explain away his terrible behavior."

"He's my husband, Joshua. And your father."

"And I'm your son." Josh's voice broke as he said the words.

He needed air. He needed out. It was as if the suffocation had started the second he'd pulled up in front of this house and the memories had been slowly squeezing the life out of him ever since.

He pushed past his mom through the entryway and out onto the porch, praying she would just let him go.

"Josh, come back inside." She held the door open but didn't step outside.

He faced her, shook his head. "I'll let you know when we hear something about Jaden."

"Joshua, please."

"No, Mom," he said. "This is your choice—to stay here with someone who hurts you, to make excuses for him—but I can't be a part of it. I won't."

"Don't go," she said.

He looked up, and for a moment he wondered if this was a cry for help. Did she want out? Did she need out? He could only imagine what her life had been like these past sixteen years.

"Come with me, Mom," he said, his voice low.

Her reaction told him that no, that's not at all what this was. This was more about preserving the carefully crafted Dixon façade, and not at all about her safety—or his. "I could never leave your father," she whispered.

And he remembered asking her the same question years ago. Her reply had been the same then too.

How did he help someone who refused to be helped?

"I'll see ya, Mom." Josh moved toward his truck, and the door behind him snapped shut. He opened the rear door, threw his bag behind the driver's seat and glanced back at the house, where his mother now stood on the porch, a picture of perfection for the neighbors who were out mowing their lawns or weeding their flowerbeds.

"Okay, honey," she called out cheerfully. "We'll see you soon!"

He shook his head, got in the truck and drove away, angry with himself for stopping at home in the first place and certain it was the last time he'd set foot in that house for as long as he lived.

* * *

Josh: *Hey, man. I'm in town for a few days. Think Gemma would mind if I crashed on your couch? I'll pay you in pizzas.*

Cole: *Don't think Gemma will mind since she doesn't live here anymore. Guest room is all yours.*

Josh: *Whoa. Sorry. I hadn't heard. What happened?*

Cole: *Long story. Not worth rehashing.*

Josh: *Thanks, man. Appreciate it.*

Chapter Eight

Carly sat in the waiting room outside the cardiology unit of the hospital, knees bobbing up and down nervously.

She found herself wishing for an ounce of Jaden's faith—something more than rules and checklists to get her through the here and now.

Jaden's diary was complete, but who knew what it or the Holter monitor would reveal? Carly hated thinking about it. She'd been up most of the past couple nights stewing, and no amount of talking herself off the ledge had been successful.

Jaden sat beside her, flicking his fingers around on his phone, and, just as she'd feared, Josh was nowhere to be found.

"Have you heard from your dad?" she asked Jaden.

"He'll be here," Jaden said without looking up.

Carly decided not to respond. It made no sense to argue. Besides, she didn't want to come off looking like a Negative Nelly, even though, when it came to Josh, negative was her primary feeling.

Yes, he'd spent a lot of time with Jaden over the past year. They'd gone camping and skiing and talked over the internet while they played video games. But this was different. This wasn't fun.

"Carly, hey."

The voice belonged to Dara Dempsey, whose last day at the hospital was just a couple weeks away. Carly hadn't heard a word about her application for Dara's position, but she did wonder, with small-town politics being what they were, if her soon-to-be-former supervisor had any say in who they hired for her job.

Carly smiled at her. "Hey, Dara."

"Hi, Jaden," Dara said.

She was met with a lukewarm smile and a three-fingered wave that seemed to convey *I can't be bothered to lift my whole hand.* Carly would talk to her son about that later.

"Listen, I know this is probably the last thing on your mind, but I wanted you to know they've narrowed the pool to three for the supervisor position. I probably shouldn't tell you this, but since you're my pick and I'm leaving, I'm giving myself some leeway."

"Wow, they're moving fast," Carly said. She hadn't thought much about the unit manager position since the parade, but it was a lingering hope at the back of her mind.

"They are," Dara agreed. "I think they want to hire someone before I leave so I can train them and they don't have to think about it." She smiled.

"Makes sense."

Dara squeezed Carly's shoulder. "You'd be so great at it, Carly. I'm giving them my recommendation, but I don't know what that'll be worth." She laughed. "Good luck today."

Dara gave them both another smile, then walked off.

"You applied for a new job?" Jaden asked.

Carly shrugged. "It's no big deal."

"It's a promotion, though, right? A step up?"

She nodded, hoping her insecurity didn't show.

"They'd be stupid not to pick you," Jaden said, then went back to his phone.

Huh. She wouldn't have expected a nonchalant compliment

from her son to have such an impact, but her heart swelled at his faith in her.

The door that led to the exam rooms opened and a nurse called Jaden's name. At the same time, Josh hurried into the waiting area, a worried look on his face.

"Hey, Dad," Jaden said.

Carly said nothing.

"Sorry. Way more traffic than I thought there'd be."

"Tourist season," Jaden said. "It's started."

Josh nodded. "I thought Chicago was bad."

They followed the nurse into an exam room, where they crowded in, Jaden on the exam table, Carly and Josh in chairs against the wall. The chairs had been placed so close together that his knee pressed against hers.

She was keenly aware of it.

And she didn't like that she was.

"You finish your diary?" Josh asked.

Jaden lay back on the table. "Yes."

"Anything out of the ordinary?"

"No," he said.

Josh glanced at Carly, who only shrugged.

Thankfully, the door opened and Dr. Willette entered. He radiated competency and kindness, which Carly found herself grateful for.

The appointment was uneventful. The doctor took the diary as well as the monitor, checked Jaden over and told them they'd have results for them in a week.

"What exactly are we looking for?" Josh asked.

Carly didn't want to hear the answer. She already knew what they were ruling out. She knew all about arrhythmias, heart disease and every other possible outcome. What she didn't know she'd researched the night before.

Still, Josh knew nothing about any of the possible conditions, and frankly, neither did Jaden. Was it too much to wish they could keep it that way?

"Maybe I could just fill them in?" Carly suggested.

"I don't mind explaining," Dr. Willette said with a smile.

"We want to rule out anything serious that might be going on with Jaden's heart. An irregular heartbeat, for instance, can be a minor nuisance or it can be potentially dangerous."

"And this monitor will tell us that?" Josh asked.

"If the results are inconclusive, we'll keep digging."

"Isn't it possible he just overheated? Or didn't get enough to eat?" Josh sounded hopeful. As if his saying so could make it true.

"I suppose it's possible, but we'd like to be sure," the doctor said.

"We appreciate that." Josh nodded.

It struck Carly how grown up Josh seemed. That rebellious teenager with the chip on his shoulder had been replaced by a mild-mannered, successful adult. She knew he had money now, but she was fairly certain that wasn't what had changed him.

He caught her watching him, and she did her best to recover. "Uh . . . So what do we do in the meantime?" Carly knew the doctor needed to be the one to give the directives or Jaden wouldn't listen.

"Take it easy," he said.

"The indoor training facility opens this week," he said. "I've gotta be there."

"You can be there," Dr. Willette said. "You just can't train."

Jaden huffed. "You serious? We start conditioning for the high school team next week."

"Jaden." Carly's tone warned.

"I can't sit out, Ma," he said. "We've got a new coach. He doesn't know me yet. If I miss the summer practices—"

"We want to avoid any other problems," Dr. Willette explained, keeping his attention on Jaden. "If you've got an undiagnosed arrhythmia, strenuous activity could exacerbate the issue, increasing the likelihood of a serious episode. Jaden, hopefully it's not forever, but it is for now."

"What do you mean 'hopefully'?"

Dr. Willette paused. "I don't want to get ahead of things here. We should just wait and see what the monitor tells us."

"No," Jaden said. "Are you saying there's a chance I won't be able to ski?"

Carly's heart sank. Jaden's worry was palpable.

"Like I said,"—Dr. Willette kept his tone calm to offset Jaden's rising temper—"we don't have any evidence of anything. It's too soon to jump to any conclusions."

Jaden glared at the floor, clenching and unclenching his fists. Carly knew all her son heard was "hopefully." Beyond that, no other words mattered.

The doctor met Carly's eyes and smiled, but only slightly, as if he knew what she was up against.

"We'll make a follow-up appointment for a week from today," he said.

"Great," Jaden mumbled.

Carly smiled, embarrassed.

"Thanks, Doc," Josh said as the man stood.

"I know this isn't the way you want to spend the first week of the summer." Dr. Willette still focused on Jaden. "But your health comes first. We want to take the best possible care of you."

He clapped a hand on Jaden's shoulder, shook Josh's hand and then turned his attention to Carly. "Call me if you have any questions at all."

She shook his hand and noticed he held on a few seconds longer than she thought he would. She looked up and found his eyes fixed on her. He smiled, then walked out of the room.

"That guy's a creep," Jaden said.

"No, he's not," Carly argued. "He has a really good reputation around the hospital."

"Sure he does." Jaden groaned as he jumped off the exam table.

"You will follow his advice until we know if you have a medical issue," Carly said.

Jaden pulled the door open and Carly followed him into the

hallway, Josh close behind. To an onlooker, they may have looked like an actual family.

They walked past the nurses' station and out into the lobby, where Carly pushed the button for the elevator and they waited for their escape.

"So, I suppose you'll be heading back to Chicago now?" she asked without looking at Josh.

Jaden crossed his arms over his chest and stared at the light above the elevator, which was apparently sitting on the fourth floor.

"No," Josh said. "I think I'll hang out until we get everything sorted out."

"Why?" Carly hadn't intended the question to come out with that horrified tone, but that's exactly how it sounded. "I mean, what about work? Jaden says you work all the time."

"I told you, I want to make sure you guys are okay."

She shot him a look as the elevator arrived and the doors opened. Jaden got in and Josh followed, leaving her standing there alone.

"You coming?" Josh asked.

She hesitated another second, then stepped inside. "I can give you an update, or you could even come back in a week for the follow-up appointment."

Josh pushed the number 1 and the elevator doors closed. "You know, if I didn't know any better, I'd think you were trying to get rid of me."

She crossed her arms over her chest and drew in what was meant to be a calming breath, that did not do its job.

"I was thinking about renting a place for a few weeks," Josh said. "I think it's important that I'm here."

"*Now* you think it's important that you're here?"

The elevator opened to reveal the lobby in front of them.

"Yeah, Carly," Josh said. "Is that okay with you? If I want to make sure my kid is all right?"

Jaden walked out. "This'll be fun."

Fun. Right.

They stepped out of the elevator and Carly put a hand on Josh's arm while Jaden continued toward the front door. "We can't spend the next few weeks fighting. It's not good for him. We need to do everything we can to keep his stress levels down."

"Then stop fighting with me," Josh said. "Let me be here for him if he needs me."

She exhaled a sharp breath.

"I'm not going to flake out on you guys," he said.

"It's not 'us guys.' It's just Jaden. I don't need or want anything from you, got it?"

Josh's eyes scanned hers, something he'd always done, as if he could see straight down into her soul. "Look, Carly, I know you're scared. You don't have to hold it together one hundred percent of the time."

She took a step back. "That's exactly what I have to do, Josh. Because I'm the parent. And when you're the parent, you don't get to fall apart."

He stilled. "Well, you can let me be the strong one for a change."

"Maybe. If you were reliable. But you aren't, and we both know it. So just do me a favor and don't make this whole situation worse, okay?"

He didn't respond, but she could see she'd wounded him.

And as she walked away from him, she told herself not to feel badly about that at all.

Chapter Nine

It turned out having Josh in town wasn't entirely disastrous. Over the next several days, she was able to keep working because he'd volunteered to hang out with Jaden.

Carly might be taking things a little too far, but she didn't want her son to be alone—not until they had concrete answers as to what had caused the fainting in the first place.

"You're treating me like I'm a baby," he'd told her.

Carly shrugged her response and plastered a look on her face that clearly communicated two words: *Too bad.*

So far, Josh had shown up when he said he would.

Carly was cautiously hopeful he would at least get that right.

On Friday, she sat in the cafeteria with Justine and Sasha, eating a salad and drinking a Diet Coke, when their conversation was interrupted by Dr. David Willette, who appeared beside their table as if out of thin air. She'd seen him a few times around the hospital, but never in the cafeteria and never in such close proximity.

All three of the nurses looked up, but he was focused on Carly.

"Dr Willette," she said.

He smiled. "I saw you sitting over here and thought I'd come say hello."

"That was nice of you," Carly said.

Justine nudged her with her knee, and Carly could practically hear the teasing she'd have to endure later. The faintest hint at romantic interest would have them giggling like schoolgirls the rest of the day.

Plus, she'd made the mistake of commenting (out loud) that she wasn't looking forward to tackling the wedding activities on her own. Carly had grown comfortable in her independence, but if she was honest, she was lonely.

How did she reconcile the two?

"Could I talk to you for a moment?" Dr. Willette asked.

Carly glanced at Justine and Sasha, who wore matching raised eyebrows and sheepish little grins. She wanted to set them straight. Dr. Willette was her son's *doctor*. Not someone for them to ogle.

She stood. "Of course."

He walked toward the windows that faced the hospital courtyard.

"Probably something about Jaden," she said to her friends.

"Uh-huh," Justine said knowingly.

Carly rolled her eyes and walked toward the doctor, who greeted her with the same kind smile he'd given her the other day.

Her heart sputtered. What if he had something to tell her about her son? What if it was bad news?

"Is this about Jaden's tests?"

"Oh, no, nothing like that," he said. "Sorry, I should've led with that."

She agreed but didn't say so.

He wore navy blue scrubs and a white coat, and Carly took a moment to look at him. He was handsome in a sort of understated way. Clean, well-groomed, well-spoken—these things went a long way.

But he was her son's doctor. And he obviously wanted to discuss something about Jaden's care.

"I wondered if you might be willing to have dinner with me," he said.

Or not.

She'd asked around about him, collecting information on the man whose expertise would determine what direction they headed in with Jaden. She was duly impressed with Dr. David Willette, and thankful he was there when Jaden needed him.

But dinner? That she hadn't expected.

"We can keep it simple—something low-key, if you want."

She frowned. "You're asking me out?"

He tilted his head to one side and smiled. "I guess I am."

She laughed. A nervous laugh, she realized. "Oh."

"I know it's a bit dicey since I'm treating your son, but I have to be honest, I've noticed you around the hospital, even before Jaden's episode."

"You have?"

He took a slight step closer. "Look at you. How could I not?"

Did he want Carly to list off the ways?

Still, the compliment sent a blush to her cheeks.

"You intrigue me, and I haven't felt interested in anyone since I moved here three years ago."

"Wow, that's a lot of pressure," she said.

He laughed. "No pressure. I'd like to get to know you better is all."

"I'm really flattered," she said. "It's just—"

He held up a hand to cut her off. "You're about to tell me it's a bad idea because we work together and because I'm Jaden's doctor."

She laughed. "I was, actually."

"I understand. It's just, I don't meet anyone outside the hospital. I go to the gym to play racquetball at four in the morning. Do you know what kind of people are at the gym at four in the morning?"

She shrugged. "Crazy ones?"

"Pretty much." He laughed. "Just think it over, okay? You don't have to give me an answer right away."

She didn't respond—what did she say?

"But don't wait too long to put me out of my misery." He smiled down at her. "Can I see your phone?"

She hesitated for a beat, then handed it over. He scrolled around, then typed something and handed it back to her, open to her contacts, where he'd been added as *David*, not *Dr. Willette*.

"So, you've got my number now."

She nodded.

"I hope to hear from you." He walked away, leaving her standing by the windows in a daze. Seconds later, Sasha and Justine were at her side.

"What did he want?" Justine asked.

"He wants to take me out for dinner," Carly said.

"Are you going to go?" Sasha asked.

Carly looked at her, then at Justine, then snapped out of whatever it was that had just come over her and walked back to their table.

"You're going, right?" Justine sat down beside her.

"I don't know. He told me not to answer, just to think it over."

"What is there to think over? He's smart. He's handsome-ish." Sasha shrugged.

"Handsome-ish?" Justine shot her a look from across the table. "Wrong. He's just plain handsome. He's successful and stable and smart and he's obviously got great taste."

Carly took a drink of Diet Coke and shook her cup, which was mostly ice by this point.

"Why are you dragging your feet?" Sasha wanted to know.

"We work together," Carly said. "It seems a little unethical."

"How many times have you actually seen him at work?"

"If we dated and it ended badly, you know I would start seeing him everywhere."

"That's probably true, but what if you dated and it didn't end badly?"

Carly groaned. "He's Jaden's doctor. We're in crisis mode over here. You should never make big decisions in crisis mode."

"You're not in crisis mode," Justine said.

It felt like she was. It felt like they'd been white-knuckling it since Jaden's episode at the parade.

"And this really isn't a *big* decision." Sasha piled her garbage onto her tray. "Is this about something else?"

"What else would it be about?" Carly cleaned up her mess, and they all stood, moving toward the nearest garbage can.

"A certain ex who has recently reentered the picture, maybe?" Sasha tossed her trash and put the tray on top of the can. "I saw him at the hospital the other day. He's hot."

Justine gave her a shove.

Carly rolled her eyes. "That's crazy. Josh stopped influencing my decisions a long time ago."

Sasha raised her eyebrows in that annoying mocking way that said *Uh-huh, sure he did.*

"Josh being here is a giant pain in my neck." Carly walked toward the exit. "But I have zero feelings for him other than frustration."

"Frustration is just a step away from passion," Justine said.

"That's not even true," Carly said.

"I'm just saying—this perfectly nice doctor asks you out after, let's be real, quite a long dry spell, and you have to think about it?" Sasha pushed the glass door open and they walked out of the cafeteria. "There must be a reason."

"She has a point." Justine poked the Up button on the elevator.

"There are reasons, but none of them are Josh," Carly said.

"So, what are they?" Justine asked.

"He's Jaden's doctor. I work with him." Carly shook her head. "Aren't those deal breakers?"

But were they? People dated their co-workers all the time. She was an adult. He was an adult. And Dr. Willette *was* a good catch. He was all of the S's—single, straight, stable and successful. He had a lot going for him, and he was interested in *her*. This wasn't the kind of thing that happened every day.

Actually, this wasn't the kind of thing that happened ever. Her dry spell really had been embarrassingly long.

Plus, he wasn't Josh. And regardless of what her fellow nurses thought, that was actually a huge "Pro" on the list she was making in her mind.

"What's happening?" Sasha's eyes widened. "Your whole expression just changed."

Carly smiled. "I think I want to go on a date with the doctor."

Both Justine and Sasha grinned at Carly as she pulled out her phone and scrolled until she found Dr. Willette's (David's) cell number. Her thumbs hovered over the keyboard and she could feel her friends watching her. Neither of them appeared to be breathing.

She quickly typed *I'm in for dinner*, then hit Send before she changed her mind.

Seconds later, a reply came back.

Good. How's tomorrow night?

Perfect.

She tucked the phone in the pocket of her scrubs just as the elevator arrived. Without looking at her friends, she got inside and pushed the button for their floor.

She had a date.

A wave of nerves rolled through her belly.

Oh. She had a date.

It had been a long time since she'd had to think about date things—what if she'd forgotten how to have a conversation or what to wear or what if they had nothing in common?

Or what if he wanted to kiss her at the end of the night—did she even remember how to kiss anymore?

Breathe, Carly. It's just a date.

She'd tell herself that over and over until she believed it.

Chapter Ten

Josh may not fully understand everything about his son, but he did understand video games, and with Jaden on activity lockdown, that meant the two of them had hours to play.

He wasn't complaining, and so far, Jaden wasn't either. He had a feeling it wouldn't last—his son's being content with hanging out with him and not training. They'd already gone to the indoor training center twice "just to check things out." It was nice to see Jaden so invested in something.

Hard to see him have to hold himself back from it.

Truth be told, Josh had been swatting away a singular thought on and off since Jaden's last appointment—*what if he can't ski anymore?*

If Jaden's moodiness was any indication, he was swatting at the same idea. Too many unknowns sent the mind spinning. He'd already decided that no matter what—one of his main goals would be to try and keep Jaden's spirits up.

For the time being, that meant a lot of Super Smash Brothers.

They were in the middle of a battle when the door opened and Carly walked in. Josh had a pizza on the way, and he hoped that by keeping an eye on Jaden he was making Carly's life a little easier.

Jaden didn't look up from the screen when his mom entered, but Josh did. How could he not? Even after all this time, Carly was his favorite thing to look at.

You'd think that would've changed considering how she felt about him, but if he was honest, it only made him want her more.

"Is this what you two have been doing all day?" She hung her purse on the hooks by the front door as Jaden killed Josh's character and stood to cheer in victory.

"What else are we supposed to do?" Jaden asked, plopping back down on the couch. "Prison's super fun."

"Watch it, mister," she said. "Have you eaten?"

"I ordered a pizza," Josh said. "It should be here any second."

"We're starving," Jaden said. "Smash Bros. is hard work."

Carly shook her head and rolled her eyes.

"Wanna go again, old man?" Jaden asked.

Josh set his controller on the coffee table. "Let me talk to your mom for a few minutes first."

The doorbell rang.

Josh stood and reached for his wallet in his back pocket. "I'll get it."

She looked at him, then looked away. "Thanks."

"'Course."

He paid and tipped the delivery guy, then took the pizza and closed the door. Seconds later, Jaden swiped the box from him and took it into the kitchen.

"Are you staying?" Carly asked.

"Uh, no," he said, only just then realizing that would be awkward for her. "I should probably get going."

"I'm not done kicking your butt," Jaden called from in the kitchen.

Josh laughed. He liked this, probably more than he should. If he let himself, he could convince himself they were a happy family.

"He seems in good spirits," Carly said.

Josh nodded. He wouldn't tell her about the quiet stretches, the times he was certain Jaden was trying to keep himself from going down a mental rabbit hole of negativity.

"You're not going to eat?" she asked.

"Nah," he said. "I'm not really hungry. I'm crashing with Cole for a few days until I can find a decent rental."

She made a face. "Nobody's really seen him lately. Is he doing okay?"

Josh frowned. "He has practice every morning."

"And then what?"

Josh didn't know. He hadn't been at the house during the days. "Because of Gemma?"

Carly's expression turned knowing. "It was bad."

"I didn't even know they split," Josh said, wondering if Carly would judge him for that—he wasn't just a lousy father, he was a lousy friend.

Josh and Cole had grown up together. Played football together. Next to Carly, Cole had been his best friend, but when he left Harbor Pointe, he left his whole life behind, and that included Cole. He regretted that now.

"And you're okay to miss work?" she asked, changing the subject.

He shrugged.

She scoffed. "'Course you are. You're rich now."

He'd increased the amount of money he was sending her, but he'd also socked away quite a bit in a college fund for their son. Carly didn't know about that, but when the time came, he didn't want money holding Jaden back, and he didn't want Carly to have to worry about it.

He didn't want her to have to worry about anything.

"We survived our new launch, and now we wait for people to make those in-app purchases. Passive income and all that."

"Must be nice to be able to take off whenever you want."

He didn't tell her he spent most of his night poring over

emails from Rebecca. He wrote code and worked out some of the kinks his new programmers couldn't untangle. He'd say, all in all, he was running on about three hours of sleep a night.

The business was important—but not more important than Jaden. If she knew any of that, she'd likely try to convince him to get back to the city.

And right now, that wasn't what he wanted.

"I've got a good team," he said absently.

She waved him off. "I don't get it at all, but I'm happy you're successful."

"Thanks." *Maybe one day I'll be good enough to win you back.*

Spending time here, seeing them both every day, it had solidified something in his mind—he wanted another chance. He was older now, more responsible, not a total screw-up like he'd been back then.

Plus, he had faith in something bigger than himself. God had helped him change, maybe even forgive himself a little.

But would that ever be enough? Would she ever let him back in?

"Hey, could you maybe hang out with Jaden tomorrow evening?"

Jaden walked through the entry and into the living room, carrying a plate piled high with at least four slices of pizza. "You eating, Dad? You said you were starving."

He avoided Carly's eyes. Did it count as a lie if he was simply trying to escape unscathed and not put her in the awkward position of kicking him out?

"What time do you need me?" Josh asked. "Tomorrow night, I mean."

She pressed her lips together. "Maybe seven?"

Jaden muted the television. "I thought you were off at three tomorrow."

Carly shifted. "I am."

Both Jaden and Josh stared at her.

"I kind of have a date," she said.

Jaden stopped mid-bite. "A what?"

Now it was Carly doing the avoiding. She walked into the kitchen, leaving Josh and Jaden staring at each other.

"Did she just say she has a date?" Jaden asked.

"Yep." And Josh was staying with Jaden so the date could happen. What a cruel twist of fate.

"Mom doesn't date." Jaden shrugged, then clicked a button on the remote, filling the room with sounds of some YouTuber demonstrating how to play Josh's new video game.

Josh stood still for several seconds, running through his options. Did he act like it was no big deal—like it meant nothing to him if she went on a date with someone? Did he ask her questions about the guy, like he was a friend who wanted all the details (when he absolutely did not)? Did he walk out the door and end this charade that there would ever be a place for him here?

He moved through the dining room and into the kitchen, where Carly stood at the counter, eating a piece of pizza. She must not have heard him come in, because she didn't turn toward him or acknowledge him.

He stole the moment to admire her.

He hadn't thought it was possible for Carly Collins to get any more beautiful than she was in high school, but here she was. And she was even more beautiful.

He'd been doing really well ignoring the longing that seemed to accompany his days and especially his nights ever since he'd purposed to redeem himself with Jaden a little over a year ago. His intention had been solely to repair the nonexistent relationship between his son and himself, and he hadn't counted on old feelings for Carly resurfacing.

But he had something to offer them now. Finally, he felt like he could maybe earn a place in their lives again.

More than anything, he just wanted them to be happy—even if it meant he took a back seat. Even if it meant hanging out with Jaden so Carly could go on a date with someone else.

The thought twisted inside his belly. He didn't want to think about someone else holding her hand, kissing her good night—or more. What if she liked the guy? Or worse, what if she fell in love?

I promise to cherish you. To take care of you. To do what's best for you and to always put your happiness before my own.

The words rushed back, as they often did, reminding him why his actions were necessary. Though he and Carly had never married, he'd made promises to her all the same. The only thing that mattered was her happiness, and now, Jaden's health.

"Hey, I'll come by in the morning so I'm here when you leave," he said.

Carly turned toward him, still chewing a bite of pizza. She nodded, swallowed, then said, "Thanks."

"And I'll stay 'til whenever. Get him out of the house, that sort of thing."

"That's great of you, Josh. I appreciate it."

"Gotta prove I've changed one way or another." His laugh was humorless.

She tossed the half-eaten slice of pizza into the box.

"Is this how you usually eat dinner?"

She shrugged. "Usually."

"Rebecca tells me it's important to sit down and enjoy your food."

"Rebecca?"

"My assistant," he said. "Well, not really my assistant anymore. She's more of a partner now."

Carly gave him a nod.

Why was he talking about Rebecca?

"She's a co-worker. Helped me get the most recent app off the ground." Josh leaned against the doorjamb. "She's usually right about stuff like this, so you should probably sit down and enjoy your food."

"Is that what you do, Mr. Workaholic?"

He shrugged. "No, actually. Almost never. I eat at my desk most days."

She faced him straight on. Man, she was beautiful—but it

wasn't her beauty that took his breath away—it was the way she looked at him. Like she knew him. Like she saw him.

He missed that. He missed her.

Jaden pushed past him into the kitchen and grabbed a Coke from the fridge. "Who's the guy?" He cracked open the soda.

"What?" Carly looked caught.

"Your date. Who's it with?" Jaden took a drink.

Carly's eyes darted toward Josh, then back to their son. "Actually, it's with Dr. Willette."

Jaden frowned. "My doctor?"

"The very one."

Josh's heart dropped. She was going out with *that* guy? He was so buttoned-up. So boring. So opposite of Josh.

"Isn't there some kind of code against that? Is he breaking the law or something by asking you out?"

Carly opened the refrigerator and pulled out a pitcher of water. "No, Jaden. It's not against the law."

"Well, it's not cool," Jaden said. "Now my appointments are going to be even weirder than they are with you two in the same room." He looked at Josh. "You three."

Josh looked away. "I'm gonna get going."

Get me out of here.

"Come back tomorrow so I can kick your butt some more." Jaden grinned, then walked back to the living room. Josh gave him a playful shove as he passed by.

He held on to Carly's gaze as the seconds ticked by, then she finally looked away.

"See you tomorrow," he said.

"Yep."

He walked out, said goodbye to Jaden and as soon as he hit the front porch, he inhaled a sharp breath.

How much more of this could he take?

"Josh?"

Carly's voice from behind stopped him. He begged himself to hold it together. He didn't want her thinking he was upset about her going out with the doctor. He didn't want her knowing he was struggling to sort through his regret, his mistakes, his own idiocy. Not to mention the overwhelming desire coursing through his veins.

The idea of Carly with anyone else—no matter how happy the guy made her—turned his thoughts dark.

But she didn't need to hear that right now. She needed someone strong and solid. Probably someone like that doctor.

He turned. "Yeah?"

"What are you doing here? I mean really?"

His chest tightened. "Do you want me to go?"

"No," she said quickly. "I just don't know what to make of any of this. You're in there being Super-Dad, helping me, hanging out with Jaden—" She shook her head. "I just don't get it."

"What can I say? I'm full of surprises." He shoved his hands in his pockets and stared her down.

"I'm serious, Josh." And the look on her face said as much.

"I told you before, I'm not the same guy I was."

"Because you've got money now?"

"Because I know what's important now." Did he ever. It hadn't taken a life-threatening illness or a brush with death to realize the error of his ways. It had simply taken a taste of success followed by the revelation that he'd left behind the only people he wanted to share it with.

And maybe he was fooling himself. After all, the odds of her forgiving him were slim. He'd made a choice, and it had been the right choice at the time. He'd done what he needed to do.

He had so much to work through back then—he still did. But that didn't stop him from hoping he could win her back. That didn't stop him from wanting to be good enough for Carly and for Jaden.

Was he fooling himself?

"We're not playing house here, Josh. You being here, it's confusing."

"Confusing for Jaden or for you?"

She crossed her arms over her chest. "Both, I guess."

"He's not confused," Josh said. "He's already forgiven me. He knows I want to be here for the right reasons." He grew quiet. "I wish you'd believe it too."

She looked away.

"I'm not going to let you guys down this time," he said. "I'll prove it—just you wait and see." He grinned at her, despite feeling like he'd been punched in the gut.

"Good night, Josh."

"Good night, Carly."

His mind spun back to all the good-night kisses they'd shared on the front porch of her childhood home. Sweet, innocent kisses he wished he had the right to relive.

But not having the right hadn't stopped him from reliving his and Carly's greatest hits over the years, had it? Just over a year ago, their best moments seemed his only comfort. His company's success had been fast and furious—the kind that people called an "overnight" success, even though he'd been working for years designing apps for other people or apps that never quite caught on.

And then everything changed. The free video game he'd only created as a sort of pet project, in his free time, began taking off, and it had landed him a feature in *Wired* magazine, naming him one of the top new tech entrepreneurs to watch.

The night the magazine released, Rebecca organized a party to celebrate Josh and his hard work, something Josh never would've approved if she'd told him about it ahead of time. She had to know that, so she'd kept the party a secret and turned him into the guest of honor.

And while Josh was touched by the gesture, as he walked around mingling with acquaintances and work friends, he found himself at the end of the night terribly alone and desperate for conversation with someone who understood him, someone who knew not only his work, but him, as a person.

He stood next to a giant cake that said *Congratulations, Josh,* scanning the room for a single person who fit that description, but he came up empty.

It had been that moment, the moment of his greatest success, that he recounted his greatest failure and began to wonder if there was a way to make it right. Because success without his family fell flat. The only people he wanted to impress, the only people he wanted cheering him on, were hours away, hating him, or at the very least, not thinking about him at all.

As he walked to his truck, then drove away from Carly's house, he internally set his commitment to them all over again.

He may never win her back, but that didn't stop him from wanting to be worthy of her. How did he prove that after all he'd done? How did he win forgiveness he didn't deserve?

It didn't matter. He'd spend his whole life working to earn her trust. And if it wasn't enough—and it most certainly wouldn't be —at least he would be better for it.

And more than anything, Josh wanted to be a better man.

Because of Jaden. And because of her.

Chapter Eleven

J osh showed up, as promised, ten minutes before Carly had to leave for work.

It had been a week since the parade. A week since she started living in *the land of I-don't-know.* Would things ever go back to normal?

"He's still sleeping," she'd said. "You might get out of here early—he said something about hanging out with Grady tonight, some ski thing."

Josh nodded. "And you're okay with that?"

"Yes. I briefed both Grady and Quinn yesterday, so I feel pretty good about leaving him with them."

"Sounds good."

It was weird, talking to him about their son, as if they were making arrangements for a toddler who needed a babysitter. Truth be told, she'd called Quinn last night and asked if Jaden could hang out with them. The thought of seeing Josh right before her date had her nerves on edge.

Not that she'd told Quinn that was her reason.

That she would keep to herself.

"Hey, how has he seemed to you? His mood, I mean?" Carly

had noticed Jaden was quieter than usual, which was saying something because he, like his father, wasn't a big talker.

Josh shifted. "I think he's doing okay. I mean, it's a lot to take in."

But Josh had given himself away. Most people would've missed the line of worry traced across his forehead, but she'd seen it. It had been fleeting, but it had been there.

"Josh, what if—"

He cut her off with an upheld hand. "He's going to be fine."

"You really believe that?"

He nodded.

"And you think he'll still be able to ski?" Carly leveled her gaze with his. Of course, Josh had no answers for her—why even ask these questions?

"Yes," he said simply. No other explanation. As if it were that easy.

She went through the motions of the day, thankful for the distraction of a first date to occupy her mind. The past few days waiting for the results of Jaden's heart monitor had been grueling, and while she'd tried to keep her imagination from running off without her head (and her medical training), she'd mostly done a bad job of that.

She woke up each morning exhausted after the fitful sleep she'd had, mind filled with what-ifs.

Today, though, the constant low buzzing in her belly had quieted, and her nerves were only pinging around because of her date, not because of her fear.

Funny how anxiety came and went without warning or reason.

Around noon, her phone dinged with a new text message from Josh.

Quinn was just here to get Jaden. He seemed ready for a change of scenery.

Great. Thanks for letting me know.

No problem. Need anything else?

I think I'm good.

K

A few minutes later, another text came in from Josh:

Have fun tonight

There was no punctuation, which made the text read a bit insincere, but Josh wasn't a girl—what was he going to do, put a bunch of exclamation points on the end of the sentence?

She texted back *Thanks* and tried to stop thinking about it.

It wasn't working.

After work, she went home, showered, then stood in front of her closet for a solid twenty minutes trying to figure out what to wear.

She called Quinn and hardly waited for her to answer before she launched in with, "This is stupid. I'm going to cancel."

"No, you're not. Put on that black dress, the one with the ruching around the middle."

"To cover up my belly pouch?"

"Yes, Carly, to cover your belly pouch. I don't want the good doctor thinking you have a baby kangaroo in there." Quinn's tone was like a verbal eye-roll. "It looks good on you. He'll think you're stunning."

"I don't even know if I want him to think I'm stunning," Carly said.

"What? Of course you do. He's attractive and stable and he has a good job."

Everyone kept saying that, and it was true. But still, she hesitated. Why? Quinn was right. Sasha and Justine were right. This man was a good catch, and he was interested in her. She needed to try her hardest. She owed it to herself to at least see if this could turn into something.

Don't I deserve to be happy?

"Put the dress on and send me a picture."

Carly groaned. "I feel like I'm in high school again—and not in a good way."

"I seem to remember not all that long ago you were the one telling me how important it was to take risks."

Carly groaned again. That was true. Before Quinn and Grady started dating, it was Carly who prodded Quinn out of her comfort zone.

"And now look at me. I'm getting married."

"I'm hanging up now," Carly said.

"Fine, but don't you dare back out."

"Fine."

"Let me know when I can bring Jaden home."

"Yeah, thanks for hanging out with him," Carly said.

"Was Josh busy tonight?"

Carly's brief pause was enough of a reply for Quinn to put two and two together.

"Oh, I get it," she said. "You don't want Josh there when the doctor picks you up."

Carly sighed. "Can you blame me?"

"Do you still have feelings for Josh? Is that why? I mean—you could look at this as an excellent way to make him jealous."

Carly plopped on the edge of the bed and caught her reflection in the mirror. She was too old for playing games, and that was part of it—but was there another reason she didn't want Josh to see her with the doctor?

Lord, help. My feelings are a jumbled ball of confusion right now. I don't want to even think about Josh, but for Jaden's sake—I need to be kind to him. How do I do that and still protect my heart? How do I reconcile the fact that I'm still mad at him?

"Carly?"

"Sorry—I got distracted. I don't have feelings for Josh." But it surprised her how easy it was to admit to God that she was still mad at her ex. Didn't that mean she hadn't forgiven him? Shouldn't she figure out a way to do that?

But forgiving him meant letting go of some of this anger. And that, she didn't think she could do. That anger kept her heart safe.

"Why do I feel like you're trying to convince yourself?" Quinn asked.

"I have to go. I have to stuff the baby kangaroo into my dress."

Quinn laughed. "Have fun!"

Carly clicked her phone off and flopped back on the bed, staring at the ceiling. Wasn't thirty-four too old for first dates and awkward new relationships?

Apparently not, because here she was, going through all the motions of getting ready for a first date and preparing herself for the awkwardness of this new relationship.

Another text came in from Josh—*Let me know if you need me to pick Jaden up later.*

She reapplied her makeup and curled her hair, then stepped into the black dress. She slipped her feet into her black pumps—the ones she only wore when she knew she wasn't going to be on her feet for any length of time—then stood in front of the full-length mirror and snapped a picture.

She texted it to Quinn with the caption *Is this stunning enough for you?*

Seconds later, the reply came in—*Are you trying to kill me?*

She frowned as her eyes scanned the top of the screen and horror washed over her. Somehow, she'd sent the photo—and the text—to Josh and not to her sister.

Oh no! I meant to send that to Quinn!

Yeah, sure.

No, I did. I'm so sorry. (And so embarrassed!)

Well, thanks for both making and ruining my night.

???

Making it with a knockout photo and ruining it because I know I'm not the one you're wearing that dress for.

She stared at the screen, trying to decide how to respond, when the sound of her doorbell shot a wave of panic through her. She clicked her phone off, gave herself one more glance in the mirror and walked downstairs.

What was Josh saying? And why was he saying it? Was this a

case of him wanting her only because someone else had taken an interest?

On the other side of the door was a man who wasn't Josh. A man with no emotional baggage that related to her in any way. A man who deserved her undivided attention on the off chance that this could actually turn into a relationship. She had to at least *see*. And she couldn't *see* if she didn't put Josh out of her mind.

She deserved to be happy. She deserved to have someone take care of her for a change.

Didn't she?

She pulled open the door and Dr. Willette gave her a once-over. "Wow. You look . . . really great."

"Thanks," she said. "And you look . . . handsome."

He did, too, in a buttoned-up sort of way. He wore black dress pants, a blue shirt and a tie. He looked like a man who'd paid attention to what he was wearing for their date.

On her first date with Josh, he'd worn jeans and a vintage Pink Floyd T-shirt. Of course, he'd been sixteen—it was hardly right to compare.

"I hope you like Italian food. I made us a reservation at Capri."

Of course he'd picked Capri. It was the restaurant where she and Josh had had their first real date a million years ago. She'd only eaten there a handful of times in recent years, but it was a local favorite—the kind of restaurant that didn't quite know what it was.

With an Italian name, one might expect a strictly Italian menu, but in addition to pasta and chicken parmesan, Capri served a burger and steak fries that were to die for. They also had fried chicken, lobster and steak on the menu.

So much for picking a lane and staying in it. Capri broke all the rules of business, but it worked. People loved it, and it was one of the few restaurants that could do a variety of food well.

"Have you been there before?" she asked, knowing he hadn't grown up here.

"Actually, no. Always hear good things about it though."

She smiled, grabbed her purse and tucked her phone inside. "I hope you don't mind if I keep my phone close," she said. "For Jaden's sake."

"Not at all." He pulled her front door open and motioned for her to go first. He followed her out onto the porch, pulling the door closed behind him.

"How's Jaden doing?"

Carly's heels clicked on the sidewalk as she headed toward his black Audi. "Good, mostly. He's bored. He wants to do more than he should—typical teenager."

"Aren't you going to lock the door?" he asked.

She turned toward him. "It's Harbor Pointe. No one locks their doors."

His eyebrows twitched. "I do."

"I think it'll be okay."

He hesitated a second, then finally moved toward her, looking genuinely worried.

"My dad is the sheriff," she said. "He mostly sits behind his desk drinking coffee and playing Solitaire." She didn't actually know that for sure, but she knew there weren't many break-ins and most of the crime in Harbor Pointe was related to bored teenagers looking for trouble.

He opened her car door and she realized she was having trouble thinking of him as anything but "Dr. Willette." She couldn't go on a date with someone if she couldn't even call them by their first name.

David. His name is David.

She got in, and he closed the door, impressing her with his chivalry. Some women wanted to do everything for themselves, but Carly had been doing everything herself for sixteen years. It was kind of nice not to have to for a change.

She let out a heavy sigh. *Get it together. He's just a guy.*

Seconds later, he was sitting beside her and they were driving toward the restaurant.

They made small talk, and she was proud she held up her end of the conversation considering how out of practice she was. It was a nice change of pace. Her typical nights consisted of her yoga pants, a giant Michigan State sweatshirt and a pint of mint chocolate chip she'd stashed at the back of the freezer so Jaden wouldn't find it.

They pulled up in front of Capri, and Carly refused to allow the memories of a bright-eyed, baby-faced Josh driving her here all those years ago.

She wouldn't think about the way he'd spilled aftershave on his chest, filling the car with a piney, masculine scent. She wouldn't think about the way he stared at her throughout the night, like she was the most beautiful girl in the world. And she most definitely would not think about the kiss they'd shared on the boardwalk as they tried to sort out the change in their feelings for each other.

Carly had only kissed one other boy before Josh, but that one was enough for her to spot the differences between a good kiss and a bad kiss.

Josh had never given her a bad kiss in her life.

And that was all she was willing to remember about that.

She got out of the car, forgetting the good doctor's chivalrous side, and met him in front of the Audi on the way to the main entrance of the restaurant. In the near distance, Lake Michigan sparkled as the sun set.

"I hope you don't mind if our table is on the patio," Dr. Willette—David—said. "It's such a nice night."

Carly nodded in agreement.

They were seated at a table for two on the veranda at the back of the restaurant. It offered a beautiful view, with sailboats in the distance and the sun dropping lower in the sky.

But what did they talk about? Work? Jaden? Harbor Pointe?

"So, have you lived here your whole life?" he asked after they ordered. Shrimp primavera for him, chicken marsala for her.

She nodded. "I'm a Harbor Pointe girl."

He took a drink of his water. "Ever think of moving anywhere else?"

She picked up her napkin and spread it over her lap. "I really haven't. Jaden's friends are here, and now this indoor training center he's so jazzed about. I like my job, and my family is close by." She met his eyes. "Why, are you thinking of moving?"

"I took this job because Harbor Pointe intrigued me, and it was a chance to do something new. But I don't think I'll stay here forever. I like to travel. Seems a shame to stay in one place for too long, doesn't it, when there are so many places to see?"

"I don't know," she said. "I think there's something nice about putting down roots in a place."

"I'm sure you're right." He smiled. It was a kind smile. David Willette wasn't the sort of doctor who was going to raise red flags with his rebellious, but life-saving procedures. This wasn't *Grey's Anatomy*, after all. Rather, he was a textbook doctor, meaning he did everything by the book.

If she had to describe him in three words, they might be strait-laced, buttoned-up and intelligent. But her friends' words rushed back at her—he was also single, straight and stable. These were not qualities that could be overlooked.

Then why did she find herself zoning out as he replied to a question she'd incorrectly thought she wanted to know the answer to?

"That was probably more of an answer than you wanted," he said as their food arrived.

She smiled. "Not at all."

He picked up his knife and fork and began to meticulously cut his food into bite-sized pieces. Even the pasta. She, on the other hand, cut one chunk of chicken and stuck it into her mouth. She only just now realized how hungry she was.

"Do you think Jaden's going to be okay?" The question hadn't been pre-meditated, and now Carly almost regretted asking it. But it was what was on her mind, in spite of where they were and why.

He chewed, swallowed, then smiled. "He's a strong kid. I think he's going to be fine no matter what happens."

No matter what happens.

Her mind raced through all the things that *could* happen. "Do you have any thoughts as to what it might be? Should I be worried?"

"I think we'll just need to wait and see."

Right. Waiting. Something she was notoriously bad at. She let out a silent, internal scream, feeling trapped in spite of the beautiful atmosphere out on the patio of Capri.

The conversation lulled through dinner, and she found herself wondering how Jaden was doing. She knew it was silly to worry so much, but she couldn't help it. Until they knew exactly what they were dealing with, she was going to worry.

Mostly, she wanted to make sure he was following her rules and not doing anything too active.

"Do you mind if I run call my sister quick?" she asked after she finished her meal. David still had half a plate of food, and she knew it was rude of her, but she hoped he'd understand. "I'd like to check on Jaden without him knowing I'm checking in on him."

"Of course," he said. "I'll order some dessert."

She nodded, then excused herself from the table, heading off in the direction of the restroom. The dimly lit restaurant hummed with indistinct chatter. She walked through the bar area and approached the hostess's station as the main door opened and Josh walked in.

Of all the people who could've strode through that door at that exact moment, why did it have to be him?

She stopped and realized she was waiting to see who he was with, as if she had a right to wonder. Why did she exhale as soon as the door closed behind him and nobody else joined him?

She realized she was staring. But then she realized he was staring too.

"Night made," he said.

She frowned.

"I got to see you in that dress, after all."

Carly felt seventeen again. Josh had always had a way of saying exactly what he thought. She'd gotten pretty good at that herself in recent years, out of necessity mostly. She wasn't afraid to confront a teacher who was treating her kid unfairly or to be firm with an uncooperative patient.

The only thing she was afraid to face were her own fears, the ones she didn't talk about out loud. And any lingering feelings for an ex she'd stopped loving a long time ago.

"What are you doing here?" Was he following her?

"Meeting Cole," he said. "How's your date going?" He took a step closer—a little too close, actually. She could smell that same familiar scent she'd always associated with Josh. Couldn't he have switched his body wash to something she didn't recognize?

She straightened. "It's going really well."

"Then why are you in here when he's out there?" Josh peered across the bar area and through the windows, out to the patio, where David sat, slowly chewing his food.

"I was going to call Quinn," she said. "See how Jaden's doing."

"I just talked to him," Josh said. "He's good."

"You talked to him, even though you have the night off?"

Josh frowned. "I'm not his babysitter, Carly, I'm his dad."

She started to reply but stopped herself.

"What?"

"I guess I'm just surprised."

"Like I said, I'm full of surprises." He held his arms out as if presenting himself for her approval. "I told you I'm not going anywhere this time. That's my kid. I love him. I *like* him."

She smiled. "He's a good one."

Josh stilled. "He had a good mom."

But he didn't have a good dad.

The words shot through her mind like a missile and landed

squarely in the spot of her brain reserved for common sense. She took a step back. "I should go."

He nodded. "You look beautiful."

David had told her she looked "really great." It hadn't sent a shiver down her spine. Why was she shivering now?

She didn't respond—she couldn't. Instead, she ducked past him into the ladies' restroom, where she begged her heart to stop racing.

What was happening to her? This was ludicrous—letting herself get worked up over *Josh*.

Get it together, Carly. You're on a date with a perfectly nice man. He's a really good guy. You're having a good time. Okay, a good-ish time. Your alternative is a pajama/Netflix/Ben & Jerry's night, so knock it off and give this guy a chance. You owe it to yourself.

Josh already had his chance.

Chapter Twelve

"We have the results from Jaden's testing."

Carly and Josh perched on the edges of two chairs next to the exam table where Jaden sat. Dr. Willette (not David at the moment) rested on the rolling stool that fit nicely under the desk.

She decided she would much rather be on the rolling stool than in this hot seat. She would much rather be the one collecting information, not giving it. And she would much rather be out of the room when bad news was delivered.

But now, bad news was being delivered to her. She could tell by Dr. Willette's furrowed brow.

"What is it?" Josh asked.

"We believe Jaden has something called Long QT Syndrome," he said. "It's a genetic disorder affecting the heart."

Her mind searched her mental archives for any recollection of this disease. She found none. Hadn't they taught her anything in nursing school? Where was her knowledge when she needed it?

"That sounds bad," Jaden said.

She resisted the urge to rush to her son's side and pull him into a tight hug.

Jaden had his phone out. Was he texting? Now?

"So it's a heart rhythm condition." He glanced up from his phone. Not texting. Googling. She wished he'd been texting.

"Jaden, what have I told you about Dr. Google?" Carly said.

"Can cause fast, chaotic heartbeats, which can trigger fainting or seizure." He mumbled through the rest of the sentence, then added, "Can cause sudden death."

"Death?" Josh grabbed the phone from their son.

"Let's not get ahead of ourselves," Dr. Willette said.

Carly's head spun. Long QT syndrome—a genetic heart condition. Had he gotten this from her? From Josh? Neither of them had any trouble with their hearts.

"This is very treatable," the doctor said.

Josh clicked Jaden's phone off. "What's the treatment?" He shifted and their knees touched. She moved away.

He glanced at her, but she kept her eyes on the doctor.

Her only focus was to figure out how to make sure their son had the best possible care. Josh's feelings were secondary.

"There are a few different options, but the one I'd like to discuss is an implantable defibrillator," Dr. Willette said. "I've asked one of my colleagues, Dr. Roby, to join us this morning to explain it a little better. This is more in his wheelhouse."

Carly straightened. Dr. Errol Roby was the hospital's chief of surgery. He'd been a general surgeon for years—so many years the nurses had a pool going on to predict when the man might retire.

"Implantable? Like surgery?" Josh's gaze stayed on the doctor. He was asking the questions Carly should be asking. Where was her head?

As Dr. Willette opened the exam room door, she glanced at Jaden, whose face had turned pale, and her mind spun with memories of her little boy running around the house in a diaper, dragging behind that raggedy old teddy bear Josh had given him on the day he was born.

How had they gotten here? So much brokenness mixed with so much beauty to create the moments that were their lives.

They weren't the family she'd always dreamed of having, but

they *were* a family, and whether she'd ever admit it aloud or not, she was thankful Josh was here now.

Dr. Roby walked in with a robust smile, as if he were a clown at a birthday party, set to entertain. "Good morning, folks."

Nobody responded. Even Carly couldn't muster a hello.

"Carly, I understand you're one of our pediatric nurses," he said. "I hate that we're meeting under these circumstances, but we're going to take very good care of your boy."

"Thank you," Carly said.

"Jaden, I'm the chief of surgery here at the hospital," Dr. Roby said.

"So, it is surgery?" Josh asked.

Dr. Roby explained that implanting the device was a simple and fairly routine procedure. He concluded with, "Surgery will take somewhere around two hours."

"Then what?" Jaden asked.

"You'll be in the hospital overnight, and then we'll send you home where you can recover. I'd expect that to be another few days, maybe a week."

"But when could I ski again?"

Dr. Willette's eyes darted to Carly's. Dr. Roby's stayed on Jaden. His face softened.

"I don't advise that you continue skiing, son."

"What?" Jaden looked at Carly, then at Josh, as if searching for some support she didn't know how to give.

"Dr. Roby, our son is a skier," Josh said. "It's the most important thing in his life."

God, are you really this cruel?

Dr. Roby's expression changed. "I understand this is difficult, but with Long QT and your ICD—that's your implanted device —it's a big risk. We want to lower the risk of malfunction—we all want what's best for Jaden."

"Right," Josh said. "But what's best for him is to be able to continue skiing."

Tears pooled at the bottom of Jaden's eyes.

"I know it's hard," Dr. Roby said, though Carly was beginning to suspect the man didn't know. How could he be this calm if he actually understood? "But it's Jaden's health we're most concerned about."

"How many of these devices have you implanted?" Josh asked.

Dr. Roby's smile condescended. The man was notorious for his ego, and he did not like to be questioned. Carly willed Josh to stop pushing—she had to work in this hospital. She had a promotion on the line.

But at the same time, she was actually grateful he was asking questions, even if they made the chief of surgery squirm.

"I can attest to Dr. Roby's competence," David said. "You're in great hands."

Could those great hands change the outcome of these tests? Could those great hands make this all go away so Jaden could get back to doing what he loved?

"It's a lot to take in, but all things considered, Jaden, you are very lucky. I don't want to think about what could've happened if we hadn't discovered your disease." Dr. Roby met Carly's eyes. "Do you have any questions?"

Only a million.

Namely, why? Why did this have to happen to her son, who finally seemed happy, who had something in that training center that brought more joy than anything ever had for him before.

A little over a year ago, Carly had been worried about her son. He had a sadness in him she couldn't quite place. He had a few friends through church, but mostly, he was a loner—but skiing changed that. It became more than just a passing fancy—and her son blossomed. He smiled more. He had friends. He'd even been out on two sort-of dates. Was everything going to change now?

"Is surgery the only option?" Josh asked.

Another good question. Why hadn't Carly asked that?

"There are medications used to treat Long QT, but we would feel most comfortable implanting the device. Given what we're seeing in his tests, that would be my recommendation." Dr. Roby stood. "Any sudden burst of adrenaline can put your heart into a fatal rhythm. This isn't something to take lightly."

Carly resisted the urge to ask the man which person in the room seemed to be taking any of this lightly? Did he not see her son's heart was broken—literally?

"We're going to give you some time to discuss," Dr. Roby said. "Just open the door when you're ready for us to come back in."

The two doctors left, leaving the three of them sitting in silence. Carly stood and walked over to Jaden, whose lower lip trembled.

She wrapped him in a hug and forced herself to hold it together.

You're the strong one, Carly. He needs you to be strong.

It didn't matter that she didn't feel strong. It didn't matter that her mind was spinning with worst-case scenario thoughts or that her fear and anxiety were at an all-time high. She had a son who needed her, and he didn't need to see her falling apart.

She could do that later, when nobody was looking.

"It's going to be okay," she said.

Jaden's jaw quivered and tears slid down his cheeks. He quickly wiped them away with a stern *I'm okay* nod.

Beside them, Josh stood, maybe feeling awkward and unsure. But he slid an arm around Jaden's other shoulder and they stayed like that for a long moment.

Carly found Josh's eyes over Jaden's head and he gave her the slightest, almost undetectable nod—a nod that said *We're going to be okay* and she clung to it. She had to believe it.

The knot of anger she'd carried around in her belly for all these years slowly began to unravel, only a little bit, but it was something, and she found herself grateful she wasn't facing this storm alone.

She was the one with medical knowledge, and yet, in this case, that may be working against her. How little statistics meant to her when she constantly saw exceptions to every rule, when she constantly saw that common things weren't always common.

"I can't quit skiing." Jaden wiped his eyes dry with the back of his hand.

Carly looked up to keep from crying. Why was this so hard? She'd been strong for sixteen years of this kid's life—why was she flailing so badly now?

"Look, I know it's not what any of us wanted," Carly said. "But it's treatable. That's what we need to focus on. You get to go on living your life."

"You don't get it," Jaden said. "If I can't ski, I'm not living my life."

She knew that. She couldn't be insensitive to how he was feeling right now. This whole thing just stank—there was no way around it.

"Your health is the most important thing," Carly said. "Let's get that taken care of and then we'll worry about the rest of it."

Jaden's gaze fell to the floor as he tried not to cry.

"We'll get a second opinion," Josh said.

Carly shot him a look.

"I mean, that guy might be great, but he doesn't know everything."

"Josh."

He ignored her. "We're going to explore all of our options. If there's a way for you to keep skiing, we're going to find it."

Why was he saying these things? Why plant false hope—wasn't he listening? But then, Josh didn't know any better because he didn't have real parenting experience. Frustration bubbled inside her.

"You trust us to do that, right?" Josh asked.

Jaden looked miserable, but he still nodded.

"So listen, we'll get the surgery scheduled because that's non-negotiable, but we'll ask around about this Long QT Syndrome. We'll exhaust all of our options. Deal?"

"I'm not giving up skiing," Jaden said, his voice resolute.

Carly looked at Josh, then back at their son.

"And I'm not quitting at the training center," Jaden said. "I'm not bailing on Grady."

Jaden wouldn't have only been training at the indoor facility, he'd agreed to work for Grady and Benji, giving lessons to younger kids, cleaning equipment and doing whatever else his bosses told him to.

"I'm sure you can still work there," Carly said, even though she wasn't sure of anything. "You can still do some of what you planned to do."

"Like what, clean the equipment? That's not what I signed up for."

It *was* what he'd signed up for, actually, but Carly didn't say so.

Her heart was so conflicted. Knowing how much Jaden was hurting was killing her, but knowing his heart needed a device to ensure it kept functioning properly was terrifying.

"Jaden, let's get the surgery scheduled and then we'll figure the rest of this out," Carly said. "Okay?"

"Your health is more important right now," Josh said. "You know that, even though you don't want to admit it."

"I know." Jaden shrugged. "You can schedule the surgery, but tell that old guy I'm not going to give up skiing."

* * *

Josh stood in the hallway at the hospital, waiting for Rebecca to answer his call. *Voicemail*. He listened to the outgoing message, then cleared his throat. "Hey, Becks, looks like I'm going to be here a little longer than I thought. I'm going to email you for some files I need you to get off of our server and put into Dropbox. There are a few things I need access to that I don't have right now.

Let me know how things are going—Dale's got a pile of work on his desk with that new client—maybe check in on him for me? I'm sorry this is taking longer than I thought, but I don't really feel like I can leave right now. Call me back when you get this."

He hung up, turned around and saw Carly standing with Dr. Willette. Jaden had gone off to get a soda, leaving the two of them alone, and they looked to be deep in conversation. His stomach twisted. Being here wouldn't be easy, especially if she kept seeing that guy. But he wasn't going to leave them—not with Jaden so fragile and everything so up in the air.

He'd already made that mistake once.

He'd find a rental so he could get out of Cole's way, though that wouldn't be easy in the summer in a tourist town. He'd get his work situated, maybe have Rebecca come up for a few days to go through anything that needed to be discussed in person. But most importantly, he'd do whatever Carly and Jaden needed him to. He'd prove to both of them he was someone they could depend on.

He was done walking away from responsibilities. He was done not being there for them.

He knew it wouldn't be enough—no amount of penance ever would be—but it was a start.

Carly turned toward Josh, who quickly looked away, as if he could hide the fact that he'd been staring. Seconds later, she was walking toward him.

"I think we're all set. Surgery with Dr. Roby early next week." Carly pulled her bottom lip in, and he saw it for the first time in years—she wasn't nearly as strong as she acted—if he had to guess, she didn't feel strong at all right now.

He wanted to pull her into his arms, to hold her, to tell her everything was going to be okay. He wanted to promise to never leave again—if she'd let him, he'd stay forever.

But she steeled her jaw and gave him a forced nod. "Lots to do to get ready for this."

"You trust that guy?" Josh asked.

"Dr. Roby is one of the best." Carly looked over to where Dr.

Roby and Dr. Willette were standing, just outside the exam room they'd vacated only moments before.

"But you're not sure." He could see it in her eyes.

She shook her head. "I'm sure. I completely trust him to do the surgery."

"So what is it that's bugging you?"

Carly's eyes darted to his, then quickly away. "No, it's nothing."

But it wasn't nothing, and Josh could tell.

Carly turned, and Josh followed her gaze across the room to find the older doctor heading their way.

He gave them a smile. It was meant to calm them, to reassure them, but Josh found it patronizing.

"How's everyone holding up?"

"We're doing okay," Carly said.

"This is all going to turn out just fine," he said.

The guy was seriously deluded if he thought not skiing would ever be "fine" for their son.

"We hope so," Carly said.

"Carly, on a positive note, I'm hearing good things about you around here. I think they're making some important decisions in the upcoming weeks. I know it's terrible timing, but maybe you'll get some good news to help digest all that's happening with Jaden."

Her shoulders slumped slightly and she plastered a fake smile on her face. "Thank you."

Dr. Roby shook Josh's hand before walking away.

"What was that about? Are you up for a promotion?"

She looked away, shyness washing over her. It was adorable. *She* was adorable. "It's nothing."

"It's obviously not nothing."

"It doesn't matter anyway," she said. "Right now I need to focus on Jaden." She let out a heavy sigh and ran her hands over her face. Lines of stress stretched across her forehead. He wanted to rub them away.

"Let me help," he said.

She ran a hand through her hair, shaking it out and leaving it fuller and more inviting than before.

Focus. She doesn't need you fantasizing about running your fingers through her hair right now.

But oh, how he wanted to run his fingers through her hair right now.

"I don't even know what to ask you to do," she said. "My head is spinning."

"For starters, you're going to go ask for some time off of work," he said.

She half laughed. "That's not going to happen."

"Why not?"

She crossed her arms over her chest and stared at him. "Have you forgotten what it's like to pay bills?"

"Of course not," he said. "I'm saying, I'm going to take care of everything so you can take a few weeks off to be with Jaden."

She gave her head a deliberate shake. "No, you're not doing that."

"Why not?" he asked. "Look, Carly, I know we don't talk very much anymore, but I'm doing pretty well now."

Her eye roll was less sarcastic and more amused. He wondered if she was secretly proud of his success. He hoped she was. He'd only ever wanted to make her proud.

Besides, he'd never admit it to anyone else, but it had been nice to prove everyone wrong.

Nobody would've believed that C student and perpetual detention holder Josh Dixon would ever do more with his life than work at a gas station and play the lottery.

He'd shown them, hadn't he?

Success should make him feel better than it had. Somehow, it was always overshadowed by the sins of the past—not only the mistakes he'd made with Jaden and Carly, but mistakes he'd made so many years before that.

"I know you want to be with him," Josh said, forcing his mind to stop wandering.

"Of course I do." Tears welled in her eyes. He could pull her into his arms. He could give her the kind of comfort he used to when she'd had a bad day—no questions asked.

But she took a step away, as if she'd overheard thoughts he would never say aloud.

Point taken.

He stared at her.

"Don't look at me," she said, covering her face with her hands.

"Still the best view I've ever seen." He smiled, despite not feeling like it.

She waved him off. "If I take weeks off right now, I can kiss that promotion goodbye."

"You don't know that. Extenuating circumstances must count for something."

She shook her head.

"Let me do this for you," Josh said. "Let me take care of you guys."

Carly pressed her lips together and turned away just as Jaden stepped off the elevator with a can of Coke.

"Can we go home?" he asked.

"Yep," Josh said.

Jaden turned back toward the elevators, and Josh looked at Carly. "Okay?"

"We'll talk about it later," she said.

"Talk about what?" Jaden cracked open the can of soda and took a drink.

"The schedule," Josh said. "Just trying to work it out."

"I don't need a babysitter." Jaden faced them.

"You're going to need someone to take care of you after surgery," Carly said.

"That's you, right? You're the nurse."

The elevator arrived and Jaden stepped inside and put a hand on the door until his parents entered.

"It's complicated, Jaden," Carly said.

Their son pushed the button for the first floor and they stood in silence as the doors closed.

"She just needs to get some time off work," Josh said.

"Can we afford that?" Jaden asked.

Carly held on to the handles of the purse she'd slung over her shoulder.

"Yeah," Josh said. "It'll be fine."

"How?" Jaden asked.

"Don't worry about it, kid. It's going to be fine." Josh looked at Carly until finally, she looked back. She didn't like this, and he knew it, but she was going to have to accept his help if she wanted to be there for Jaden.

And if she did, then finally—finally—Josh would have a tangible way to prove himself to her.

And while he wasn't thankful for the circumstances that had brought him back to Harbor Pointe, he was thankful he was there. He only prayed he wasn't the only one.

Chapter Thirteen

"Jay, you wanna rematch?" Josh asked as they walked to the car.

A rematch of some video game battle, no doubt. Carly wouldn't be able to think straight if Josh came to their house again. And yet, Jaden couldn't do much else—shouldn't she loosen up a little?

But how? The man turned her insides out, and she was terrified her resolve was crumbling right along with the anger she'd carried for so many years. That anger had kept her safe, a constant reminder of what would happen if she was foolish with her heart.

Without it, Carly was utterly defenseless.

"I mean if it's cool with your mom," Josh said.

Jaden glanced at Carly, then back at his dad. "She's probably got another date with Dr. Doolittle anyway."

"Manners." Her tone warned. Jaden's expression turned sheepish the way it often did when he knew he'd crossed a line. Never mind that Jaden likely viewed David as the enemy—someone who insisted on taking away the one thing that mattered most to him.

She didn't want to think about her last conversation with David, the one in which he asked her to go out on his boat with him once they were through all of this medical stuff. He'd said it as if she could think—even for a second—about anything other than her son.

Maybe the doctor was so accustomed to delivering this kind of news and performing these kinds of procedures that he failed to realize there were real people on the receiving end of what he said.

David might be a nice guy, but right now, she sort of wanted to forget they'd ever seen each other as anything other than doctor/mother-of-patient.

"Do you?" Josh looked at her, his blue eyes drawing her in from feet away.

Carly shook her head.

"Can we go to Dockside?" Jaden asked. "You know, one last hurrah before I'm laid up for a month?"

"You won't be a complete invalid," Carly said. "You still have to keep your room picked up."

"Slave driver." Jaden smirked, a hint of amusement washing over him, then looked at Josh. "She never cuts me any slack."

Josh still stared at Carly. "I bet she doesn't."

Carly tried to think of something witty and nonchalant to say in response, but her head was filled with thoughts she'd never say aloud. Besides, she didn't feel witty or nonchalant.

They'd been through so much, and yet the journey they were walking out now felt bigger than everything that had come before.

Carly's eyes darted from Jaden to Josh and back again. The two of them together—it was hard to get used to—and yet, nothing about their relationship seemed stunted in any way. Jaden had forgiven Josh—no strings. He didn't even seem concerned that Josh might let him down again.

Jaden was young and foolish. Carly knew better.

"Mom?" Jaden snapped his fingers.

"Sorry," she said, shaking off her mental reminders to guard her heart. "I can go pick up pizza if that's what you guys want."

"No, let's take a break. Stay out of the house for a little while," Josh said. "I'll drive."

Carly searched her mind for an excuse—anything—not to go with them.

"Awesome," Jaden said. "I'm starving."

Before she knew it, Carly was sitting in the front seat next to Josh, her mind trying (failing) not to scroll back years and remember their first date and how it had felt to sit in the passenger seat of his car as something possibly more than a friend.

They'd always been friends, but around the time they started high school, things shifted between them. Their chosen paths could not have been more different.

Carly had already begun thinking about college, working hard to get straight A's. She'd run for student council representative—and won. She volunteered after school at Haven House, a home for older kids with nowhere else to go that sat on the outskirts of town. The home was run by a local couple, and while it wasn't something small towns often had, it was something many of them needed. Harbor Pointe always supported the home—it wasn't foster care, but it was safe. And Carly loved helping out in the kitchen or tutoring kids when she could.

Josh, on the other hand, had taken a different route. Sure, he still played football, but he spent his weekends partying with the seniors on the team. While Carly was helping bake fresh bread at Haven House, Josh was twiddling his thumbs in detention. His grades had fallen, and it was obvious his future was the last thing on his mind.

Maybe his rebellion was a way to get back at his parents, to disrupt the perfect façade they'd crafted so well.

As they entered high school, the public divide between them grew, but their friendship was intact whether anyone knew it or not.

How could she turn her back on him now, given all she knew about him? Nobody else knew about the times Josh showed up with bruises and welts on his back or the real reasons he never wanted to go home.

But they kept their friendship to themselves. Hanging out with Carly would've ruined Josh's reputation, but hanging out with Josh would've destroyed hers.

One day, a few months into their junior year, though, things changed between them again.

Carly had just finished packing lunches for her and Quinn when they heard a loud engine rumbling down their quiet street.

When the noise stopped in front of her house, Carly made her way to the front window and looked outside. An old black Mustang was parked in front of the cottage. Her heart sputtered. Her dad had worked an early shift, so she and Quinn were home alone.

But her nerves settled as soon as the driver's-side door opened and Josh got out.

Josh had a car?

She opened the front door and walked outside barefoot. "What in the world?"

He held his arms out and grinned at her. "You like it?"

"You got a car?"

"Yep. No more walking to school for you."

He wanted to drive her to school? What would his friends say?

What would *her* friends say?

"No way my dad is going to let me ride with you."

"I'm a good driver." He feigned offense.

She crossed her arms over her chest and gave him a look that clearly communicated *I don't believe you.* "How'd you pay for that, anyway?"

"Been saving everything I made at the car wash." He strode toward her. "Plus, the guy gave me a good deal. It needed some engine work."

She knew Josh was good with mechanical things, but she had no idea he knew how to fix cars. "Well, it's something."

He'd stopped at the bottom of the steps and looked up at her —not in the same way he usually looked at her either. It was the kind of look that made her feel like she couldn't get a deep breath. "I wanted to ask you something."

"Okay, but can you follow me inside? I have to finish getting ready." She turned toward the door but he grabbed her hand before she could take a step.

She looked at him.

"Will you go out with me?"

"What?"

"I was waiting to ask until I could take you out for real." His face turned shy, and even in that moment she knew things would be different between them, whether she agreed to go out with him or not.

"Like on a date?"

He stuffed his hands in his pockets and shrugged. "Yeah."

"Me and you?"

"Is that so hard to imagine?" He met her gaze.

"Kind of," she said.

His face fell.

"I mean, what about your reputation? People might think you've turned soft."

"I don't really care what people think." His grin turned lazy, and her heart sputtered.

She searched for a snappy comeback, but her mind had gone blank.

"But I know you do," he said.

She studied him for a long moment. He'd grown over the summer and now stood at least six inches taller than her. He'd been working out for football, transforming his body from little-boy scrawny to post-adolescent ripped. She knew his workouts were less about football and more about getting strong enough to protect his mom from his dad's angry outbursts—a fact she found both heartbreaking and admirable.

He rarely talked about it, but every now and then, he'd let it slip that he was planning to get her out of there, as if she was the only one who needed saving. As if his father reserved his anger only for her.

But he didn't know she'd caught a glimpse of an inch of skin just above his belt in the hallway last week when he reached for a book on the top shelf of his locker. He didn't know she saw the deep purple bruise—a bruise that should've been easy to hide.

Did he think she'd forgotten the nights he showed up on her back porch, asking to sleep in her dad's old garden shed so no one would find out the truth about his own father?

It had been years now since that started, but she would never, ever forget. How many times had she noticed him wincing when he moved wrong, accidentally irritating whatever injury had been inflicted upon him? He didn't talk about it, but she knew the truth.

She saw that boy even still, every time she looked in his eyes.

"I think we could be really great together," he said.

She couldn't stop the slow smile from creeping across her face. "Okay."

His eyes widened. "Yeah?"

She nodded. "Why not?"

Josh grinned. "Awesome. We'll do it Friday." His face went pale. "I mean, we'll *go out* Friday."

Her face flushed. "I knew what you meant."

He picked her up on Friday in that old black Mustang and drove her to Capri, a restaurant with menus that weren't made out of paper. He opened doors for her and bravely held her hand as they left dinner, something that hadn't seemed as easy as she would've expected for someone who seemed as experienced as him. After they ate, they went for a walk on the boardwalk, and he didn't let go of her hand once.

"I don't know how I feel about this, Josh," she finally said.

"About what?"

She stopped walking, a full moon spilling light onto the boardwalk, and faced him. "I don't want things to change between us. We've been friends for so long. This is . . . different."

Would she miss their easy-going conversations? Would he still confide in her when things were bad at home? Would he still tease her when she was upset over a B?

He took a step toward her. "Different can be good."

At his nearness, and because of the look in his eyes, she felt something inside her turn. She pressed her lips together and swallowed. "But I don't want to lose what we have."

He reached out and put his hand on her cheek. "You won't. You're just trading it for something better."

Another step toward her.

Her stomach wobbled and her breath caught in her throat. This was Josh—her Josh—so why was she nervous?

Maybe because *her Josh* had turned into a hard-bodied brooder, disastrously good-looking and teetering on the edge of trouble.

Everything about him excited her.

But she was Carly Collins—the girl who made straight A's and never stepped off the straight and narrow.

He took her face in his hands and searched her eyes with such intensity, her stomach turned over. "I have a feeling about us, Carly."

"Oh really?" She tried to keep her tone light, flirtatious even, but her heart raced so fast she was sure everything she said sounded ridiculous.

"A good feeling." As he smiled, his eyes dipped to her mouth. He leaned in closer, and his lips grazed over hers—the softest, sweetest kiss she could've imagined.

He pulled back and searched her eyes, as if waiting for her reaction.

In response, she stood up on her tiptoes and found his lips again, kissing him not softly nor tenderly, but with a kind of urgency she hadn't planned on.

A few minutes later, she pulled away.

"What's wrong?"

She leveled his gaze with hers. "Are you sure about this, Josh? I mean—I'm not exactly your type."

He grinned. "I don't have a type, Carly. I only ever wanted to be with you."

How long had he felt this way and how was it possible she hadn't known this before? Josh had only dated girls who were all the exact opposite of Carly—would he wake up tomorrow and realize he'd lost his mind for a little while?

He picked up her hand and placed a kiss at the center of her palm. "I would do anything for you, Carly Collins. And that'll be true until the day I die."

Sitting here now, quietly zoning out in the passenger seat of a much nicer vehicle than that old Mustang, Carly couldn't shake the memories of Josh's kiss, his piercing gaze, his innocent promise.

She knew better now. She knew things didn't work out the way you wanted them to and people didn't always hold up their end of a deal.

But a very small part of her wished she knew neither of those things, because once upon a time, she and Josh had, in fact, been really, really great together.

"You okay?"

She glanced up and found him looking at her. "Yeah, I'm fine."

"You're quiet."

She tossed a look over her shoulder and found Jaden clicking around on his phone, oblivious. "I'm fine."

He reached over and squeezed her hand and for the first time in a very long time, a tingle worked its way through her body.

Slowly, she pulled her hand away and focused again on the buildings passing by out the window. One thing she could not take was Josh's comfort.

There was far too much history between them. Far too many promises that weren't kept and wounds that hadn't mended.

And that's what she needed to focus on.

She'd let him pay for this month of their life because he'd missed so many previous months, and then, once Jaden was on the mend, she'd welcome a life that was back to the way it was before Josh showed up in Jaden's hospital room only days before.

A life without memories that invaded her mind without permission.

That's what she needed most of all.

Chapter Fourteen

Once Jaden's surgery had been scheduled, Grady and Quinn graciously moved up the date of their engagement party, knowing it would be much more difficult for her and Jaden to attend in the few weeks after his procedure.

It was so thoughtful of her sister, but if she was honest, Carly didn't feel much like going out tonight. She'd finished her final day of work before her Josh-imposed vacation, something Dara hadn't been particularly happy about, and she kind of wanted to go home, change into something comfortable and watch Netflix.

This was becoming a trend. Maybe because she'd gotten comfortable with her life the way it had been? Why was everything so complicated now?

Instead, she was curling her hair and slipping into a red cocktail dress and wondering why she'd asked David to go with her to the party.

Maybe it had been a moment of weakness, of not wanting to show up dateless to her little sister's engagement party. Or maybe she wanted to prove to herself that Josh did not have a monopoly on her heart.

But now, given the nerves dancing around in her belly, she wondered if she'd made a mistake.

Quinn and Grady seemed to be fast-tracking their wedding plans, which didn't really surprise Carly. Quinn had told her they simply saw no reason for a long engagement.

"It's like Billy Crystal says in *When Harry Met Sally*," she'd said. "When you find the person you want to spend the rest of your life with—"

"You want the rest of your life to start as soon as possible," Carly cut in. "I know."

Quinn shook her head. "You're so cynical, big sister."

Carly rolled her eyes. If Quinn had lived Carly's life, she'd understand.

"Don't do that," Quinn said. "Maybe this doctor is the one."

The one. The elusive *one.* Carly didn't believe that there was one person out there for everyone—not anymore. Maybe once upon a time she'd been that naïve, but life had taught her that some people are simply made to be alone.

She just never thought she would be one of them.

"Jaden, you're sure you're okay to meet me at the party?" she called up the stairs.

"I'm sure," her son hollered. "No way I'm going with you and the doctor. That's just weird."

Carly saw David's car pull up in front of the house, and she hurried outside as he exited the vehicle.

He met her on the sidewalk.

"Hey," she said.

He smiled. "Hi. You look very nice tonight."

"Thanks, David."

"Listen, Carly, I wanted to apologize. I realize my invitation to go on the boat the other day may have seemed insensitive. I was thinking it would give you something to look forward to, but I think it came across as a bit callous. I deal with this every day, but I know you don't, and I know Jaden is your son. I'll respect your feelings as you work through everything."

After a surprised pause, Carly shifted. "I appreciate that."

"And I'm glad you didn't cancel on me tonight because of my stupidity."

She forced a smile, feeling guilty about the number of times she'd nearly called the whole thing off.

After all, she hadn't exactly thought this through. She'd have to introduce David to her family. She'd have to answer questions about who he was and about the nature of their relationship. She'd have to stick by his side all night because he wouldn't know many people, and that was the polite thing to do.

How would she focus on Quinn if she was tending to David?

It all seemed like a bad idea now that she was in it. But she was in it nonetheless.

"I appreciate you coming with me," she said. And she did. It was a strange mix of being thankful she had a plus one and being anxious for the same reason.

"Of course," he said. "I'm looking forward to spending some non-medical-related time with you." He opened the car door for her and she got inside.

"I've never been to the Harbor Pointe Pavilion," he said as he restarted the engine.

"It's beautiful," Carly said. "Perfect place for an engagement party. Or a wedding, I guess."

"And your whole family will be there?"

"It's just my dad and sister and I," Carly said. "And then my dad's friends, who are kind of like family, I guess." She told him about Judge, Calvin and Beverly and hoped he asked no more questions.

"And your mom?"

Carly stifled a groan. "She left when I was fourteen."

Indifferent.

"Oh, I'm sorry."

"She has a new family now." Carly didn't care—not really— she'd written her mother off years ago. Quinn was the one who battled feelings of abandonment—at least from their mother.

Though, in those early days when Jaden was a baby, it sure would've been nice to have a mother to rely on.

To have anyone to rely on.

But it was what it was. She was better for it. Stronger. Independent.

At least he hadn't asked about her and Josh. At least that wound could stay properly covered. For now, anyway.

They arrived at the pavilion, exited the car and walked toward the music, the sound of voices filling the night air. The mid-June weather was warm but not hot, the sun, still hanging low in the sky, bathing Harbor Pointe in a glorious orange and pink hue.

The Harbor Pointe Pavilion had an outdoor garden that led into a community building, making it the perfect spot for any event. Quinn had a knack for decorating spaces like this, and if Carly knew her sister, she'd gone all out.

They walked through the arch that led to the outdoor part of the pavilion and Carly drank in the ambience her sister had created.

If I ever get married, Quinn will be my matron of honor and my wedding planner.

White lights twinkled and sprays of every kind of white flower Quinn could've dreamed up decorated the open-air space.

David sneezed. Then sneezed again. "It's a lot of flowers."

Carly's eyes went wide. "Are you allergic?"

He nodded and sneezed again.

Quinn rushed over, her face beaming, looking every bit a soon-to-be blushing bride. "You made it."

"Of course I made it." Carly hugged her sister and David sneezed. "This is David. David, my sister, Quinn."

He looked down at the hand that had just caught his last sneeze and then at Quinn.

"It's okay, I'll pretend you're shaking my hand," she said.

Grady appeared at her side. "Hey, Carly."

"Grady, this is David."

"Right," Grady said. "Jaden's doctor."

David sneezed, his eyes reddening with every second that they stood there. "And you're the snowboarder."

Grady smiled graciously. "Downhill skier."

David snapped. "Right. Skier."

"Do you ski, David?" Quinn asked.

"Not even a little bit," he said. "I can't stand the cold."

Quinn smiled. "And you live in Michigan?"

David laughed. "Hopefully not for too long."

Quinn's eyebrows shot up. "Really?"

David shrugged. "So many places to see."

An awkward pause hung there like something stale in the air.

"Hey, there he is," Grady said as he looked past Carly and toward the archway.

Carly followed Grady's gaze and found Jaden standing behind her, wearing the clothes she'd laid out for him. He looked handsome and grown up in black dress pants, a blue dress shirt and a tie. He tugged at his collar. "This is so uncomfortable."

Grady laughed. "But you look sharp, dude."

Carly had been so grateful for Grady over the last year, though she had to wonder if it was her sister's fiancé who'd encouraged Jaden to give Josh another chance. She didn't know the whole story, but she knew his relationship with his own father had been tense, and maybe he had some regrets.

As it was, Jaden looked up to the man as more than a skiing coach, and so far Grady hadn't let Jaden down.

She prayed he never did, though her son apparently had a higher capacity for forgiveness than his mother.

"You do look sharp," Quinn said.

"It pays to listen to your mother, especially about fashion," Carly said.

"I'd rather be in my track pants, but I'll suffer for you, Aunt Quinn," Jaden said with a grin.

Couples and small groups strode in through the decorated archway, and then, as if parting like the Red Sea, they dispersed to reveal Josh standing at the entrance. He spotted them and waved.

And now he was coming over here.

Carly's smile faded. She looked at Quinn and widened her eyes, as if to ask, *Why didn't you tell me you invited Josh?*

But Quinn's own widened eyes seemed to convey that she had no idea herself. She glanced at David, who sneezed again.

As Josh reached them, Jaden clapped a hand around Josh's shoulder and smiled. "Hope it's okay I invited Dad."

Josh carried a small box professionally wrapped in white and silver paper with a big silver bow. He held it out toward Quinn. "Congratulations."

"You got me a gift?" Quinn looked as surprised as Carly felt.

Josh's expression changed. "Well, it's for both of you." He motioned toward Grady. "Was I not supposed to?"

"Heck no, man, we'll take your gift." Grady reached out and took the box. "I'll go put this on the table." He kissed Quinn on the cheek and walked away.

"Thanks for that, Josh," Quinn said. "You didn't have to do that."

He shrugged. "I wanted to."

Knowing the new wealthy Josh, whatever was in that box was probably really nice. And really expensive. He'd made a habit of spoiling Jaden over the last year and now, paying for all of her expenses for a month? No one could say he wasn't generous with his new fortune.

"Hey, Doc, since you're here, could I have a word?" Josh turned toward David.

David sneezed.

He put a hand on David's shoulder and walked him away from the group. Carly followed. No way she was letting her ex talk to her date without her there.

Josh didn't seem to mind. "I was doing a little research about Long QT Syndrome."

Carly had been doing some research herself. And she had planned to discuss it with David later that night if an opportunity presented itself. Perhaps that was the difference between her and Josh—he didn't wait for opportunities. He created them.

"The internet is an unreliable—*ah-choo*—source of information." David squeezed the bridge of his nose.

"But I've read multiple stories about athletes who are competing with ICDs. It seems like an out-of-date practice—" Josh stopped as David sneezed—"to prevent high levels of physical activities simply because there's a fear the ICD will malfunction. There were no instances where this happened, so most sports allow participation. Do you think that means Jaden might still be able to compete?"

"I'd have to do some checking myself, but Dr. Roby is one of the best," David said. "I'd trust his judgment." Another sneeze.

"Maybe we should find you some allergy medicine," Carly said.

"Actually." David sneezed again. "Maybe I should head out." He looked at Carly through bloodshot eyes. "When it gets like this, nothing really helps."

"Okay," Carly said. "I'll walk you out."

They ducked past Josh and Jaden and walked back out into the flowerless air of the parking lot.

"I'm sorry about that," she said. "We're all just trying to wrap our heads around a world in which Jaden isn't able to ski. It's really become such a part of him."

"I understand, but better to not ski and stay alive, right?" He laughed.

Carly didn't.

They reached his car, and aggravation swirled inside her. David didn't understand. Nobody did.

Except Josh.

"I'm so sorry about all the flowers," Carly said. "My sister went a little overboard."

He sneezed again, then held up a hand. "I'm the one who's sorry. I really wanted to spend the evening with you and meet your family." Another sneeze.

"Another time."

David nodded, gave her an awkward hug and turned away in time for another sneeze. "I'll call you."

She waved goodbye as he got in his car and drove away.

So much for not showing up dateless.

Back inside the pavilion, just outside the community building, a DJ had started the music and a few brave souls were out on the makeshift dance floor underneath swaths of white tulle strung with white lights.

They called this the golden hour for a reason. Everything and everyone looked even more beautiful bathed in the last tinge of light as the sun took its final bow for the day.

"Is he okay?" Quinn asked when Carly returned. "I had no idea he was so allergic to flowers. How sad."

Carly grabbed an appetizer off a tray carried by a server passing by. "Me neither."

"Are you bummed?"

Carly shrugged.

Quinn gasped. "You're not bummed?"

"I mean, I feel like a loser being here without a date." She popped what turned out to be a crab wonton into her mouth and chewed it up. "These are good." She looked around for another server, happy to flag one down. She took two more appetizers from the tray.

"I mean, there's always Josh," Quinn said.

Carly followed her sister's gaze to the other side of the dance floor where Josh sat at a table next to Cole Turner and Wes Thompson, another guy they'd gone to high school with. Josh met her eyes instantly, as if he'd been waiting for her to look over.

"Very funny." She turned away.

"So, you're not having, you know . . . feelings for him, are you?" Quinn's eyebrows popped up in expectancy.

"Are you delusional?" Carly ate another wonton.

Quinn clicked her phone to life, scrolled for a minute, then held it out with the screen facing Carly. "Okay, so how do you explain this?"

Carly took the phone and looked at a photo her sister had pulled up on the screen. Staring back at her was the image of her, Jaden and Josh sitting at their table at Dockside a few nights before.

"Why do you have a picture of us?"

Quinn shrugged. "I've got eyes all over town, big sister."

Carly rolled her eyes. "They wanted to get a pizza after Jaden's appointment." She handed the phone back to Quinn and walked away, toward the outdoor bar on the opposite side of the space from where Josh and his friends sat.

To her dismay, Quinn followed her.

"Pretty cozy pizza," Quinn said. "If I didn't know better, I'd think you were all one happy little family."

Carly groaned. "Don't be ridiculous."

"It's not *so* ridiculous." Quinn leaned against the bar and surveyed the space, eyes landing on Josh and his table of brooders.

"Quinn," Carly said, "this is Josh we're talking about."

Quinn met her gaze. "Exactly." She faced Carly. "All I know is, I see the way he looks at you, and it makes me nervous."

"Because you don't want me to get hurt, I know."

Quinn put a hand on Carly's arm. "You kind of lose your mind when it comes to Josh. He has this strange spell over you."

"He doesn't have anything over me anymore," Carly argued.

"Just be careful is all I'm saying," Quinn said.

"I don't need to be careful. Only a fool would make that same mistake twice. You know how long it took me to get over Josh leaving."

Quinn stilled. "Carly, some days I wonder if you're still not over it."

Carly's jaw went slack as she searched her mind for a proper response to this lunacy, but she came up empty.

"There you are." Grady came up behind Quinn and wrapped his arms around her. "Carly, can I steal her for a minute?"

Carly nodded. "Of course." She leaned against the bar and watched as they walked off onto the dance floor, perfectly in sync, as if they were made for each other. What did Carly have to do to find someone like that?

She could be strong and independent all she wanted, but if she was really honest with herself, she longed for what her sister had.

She kept her eyes on the happy couple for several seconds, marveling at the way they moved, the way Quinn looked so comfortable in Grady's arms. It hadn't been that many months ago her sister despised the man.

Now look at them.

They almost made her believe true love did exist. *Almost.*

The activity in the room kicked up, but Carly didn't move. She couldn't. She was lost in thoughts she wished she wasn't having. Thoughts such as *Will it ever be my turn, Lord?*

"You okay?"

She turned and found Josh on the stool next to her, facing the opposite direction. Her body tensed at his nearness. How had she failed to notice he was right beside her? And how long had he been sitting there?

"I'm fine, why?" she asked.

He shrugged. "You've got your *deep in thought* look on."

"I do not." She stayed unmoving, wishing he would leave her alone. She would be able to think so much better if he wasn't so close.

"You do, actually," he said. "It's nice to know after all this time some things haven't changed."

He was staring at her, she could feel it. Their heads faced opposite directions, but he'd positioned himself so they were very close. Too close. And now his eyes practically demanded her attention.

"I've changed," she said without looking at him.

The bartender slid a soda toward him—which he must've

ordered when she was in her daze—and Josh took a drink, leaning back ever so slightly. "Not too much, I hope."

She turned toward him, which, she quickly discovered, was a big mistake. Now their faces were only inches apart—so close she could feel his breath on her cheek—and his eyes grabbed on to hers and left her absolutely powerless to look away.

She stayed still as he searched her like a detective looking for clues, and she tried—failed—to ignore the thoughts and emotions of the last sixteen years.

Maybe Quinn was right—he cast a spell.

Why did he still have such a hold on her? Where was her carefully cared for anger when she needed it?

You are stronger than this, Carly.

Finally, she pulled her gaze from his and went back to staring at the couples on the dance floor.

Josh pushed back slightly on the stool, leaned in so close his lips nearly brushed across her cheek and whispered, "You're still as beautiful as ever."

And then he walked away.

Chapter Fifteen

J osh had left the engagement party with the image of Carly firmly pressed inside his mind, like a drying flower between the pages of a book.

How was he supposed to function when she looked like that? Smelled like that? Yes, he'd been close enough to inhale the scent of vanilla and stupid enough to go in closer, as if he needed more to survive.

Now, lying barely awake in Cole's guest room, Josh heard the indistinct sound of voices in the next room—Cole's and a woman's.

He rubbed his eyes open and sat up in bed, sure he shouldn't be listening to what was definitely an argument.

"You can't just show up like this, Gemma," Cole said.

"It's my house too," she said.

"Not anymore it's not."

A pause.

"Just get your stuff and go," he said.

"Cole, it doesn't have to be like this."

No response but a slamming door.

Josh's friend had never been one for conversation, but whatever had gone down between him and Gemma had made him even more reclusive and withdrawn.

Josh pulled the guest room door open and walked into the hallway just in time to see Gemma take her wedding ring off, put it on the counter and walk out the door.

He'd overstayed his welcome at Cole's—he was sure the man would much rather be having this conversation with his wife without Josh in the next room. And while most people would like company in times of crisis, Cole wasn't like most people. He did better on his own, and he always had.

Josh should go. Cole would never ask him to leave, but he was in the way. What if Gemma came back? What if they needed space to work through things and he stood in the way of that?

He'd start looking at short-term rentals that day—with any luck he'd find something workable and get out of Cole's hair.

* * *

At six o'clock on the Sunday after the engagement party, Josh arrived, Chinese take-out in hand. Carly pulled the door open and the smell of Kung Pao chicken filled the entry of her small house.

She made a point not to notice the fact that he could make a simple T-shirt and pair of worn jeans look *like that*, focusing instead on what he had to offer.

"Hungry?" He held up the paper bag and gave it a shake.

"Starving," she said. "I've been cleaning all day, getting ready—" But she couldn't say it. She didn't want to talk about Jaden's surgery. She'd been over it and over it and she knew he would be fine, but every once in a while, those niggling what-if thoughts weaseled their way in.

Lord, I don't know how to take control of this situation. I don't like feeling helpless. I don't like wondering whether or not he will be okay—I just pray you protect him tomorrow. No more surprises. Let everything go according to plan.

The prayers had been on a constant stream in her subconscious, as if her spirit was continually praying as she sprayed down toilets and folded laundry.

Josh must've seen the way she shut her thoughts down because his gaze on her was so intent she felt it in her stomach, as if he was asking if she was okay and telling her it would be all in a single glance.

But she didn't need assurances from Josh or anyone else. They just needed to get through the next few months and then life could get back to normal.

"Hey, I found something interesting," Josh said. He pulled a sheet of folded paper out of his back pocket and handed it to her.

"What's this?"

"Read it."

Carly opened the paper and found an article printed off the internet. *Michigan Swimmer Powers Through Heart Condition.* Her eyes skimmed the words on the page. This collegiate swimmer had Long QT and she was not only competing, she was winning.

"Her doctor gave her the all clear," Josh said. "But it's not just her doctor, it's most doctors. If you look it up online, you get tons of articles that say they no longer restrict athletes with ICDs."

"But Dr. Roby—"

"Is an old dude," Josh said. "Maybe he hasn't kept up on the latest developments."

That couldn't be true. Could it? He was older—a lot older—so maybe he'd grown tired.

"If there's even a chance he could keep competing, we should look into it," Josh said. "We promised."

"No, *you* promised." Carly sighed. She couldn't deny he had a point. "Maybe I could call the school and get in touch with this swimmer." She looked at the paper. "Elizabeth Maney."

"Yeah?"

Carly re-folded the paper. "Let's not mention it to Jaden though. I don't want to get his hopes up." *Or mine.*

Josh nodded in agreement.

"You gonna stand out there all night?"

Jaden must've come down from his room in the span of the last ten seconds without Carly noticing. His words tugged Josh's attention, and he moved past Carly, who inadvertently inhaled his familiar scent as he walked by.

Get it together, Carly.

She reminded herself she was angry with him. She reminded herself that this was a man who would not stick. She reminded herself, but her self didn't much want the reminder, it seemed, because when she entered the kitchen and found Josh and Jaden dishing up lo mein, the only thing she could think of was how very much she liked seeing them together.

And that defied all logic.

She shook the thoughts aside. She was just emotional with everything going on. Her head knew the truth.

"What did you do today?" Carly asked as Josh plunked an egg roll on his plate.

He licked some sauce from the end of his finger and glanced up at her. Her eyes dipped to his lips and she turned away.

"I went house hunting," he said.

Her eyes darted back to his.

"Yeah?" Jaden asked. "You moving here?"

Her heart did a two-step. Josh would never move back here— according to Jaden, his life in the city was impressive to say the least. He wouldn't trade an office in a high rise and a professionally decorated loft apartment for a quaint cottage in Harbor Pointe, Michigan. And he'd never consider moving back to the same town where his parents lived, no matter who else lived there.

Would he?

Josh took his plate and set it on the table with a shrug. "Nah, just looking for something temporary."

Her pulse started to slow. *Thank goodness.*

Disappointment nagged at her innermost edges. What was that all about? She pushed it aside.

"Any luck?" Carly spooned fried rice onto her plate as Jaden sat down next to Josh.

"No, unfortunately. Everything is pretty booked. Seems like Harbor Pointe is the place to be in the summer."

"Yeah, lots of tourists nowadays."

The town hadn't always been so desirable for vacationers. Sure, they had their share of visitors, but Josh hadn't been around to experience a truly busy Harbor Pointe summer. They weren't simply being visited anymore—they were being overrun.

Lots of the locals griped about all the extras—extra traffic, extra congestion, extra people on the beaches—but most could appreciate those extras for the good they brought.

Extra revenue being the trump card.

Carly added an egg roll to her plate, then turned around to find both Josh and Jaden sitting at the table, not eating. "What are you doing?"

"Waiting for you," Josh said simply.

She glanced at the plate of food in her hand as a blush crept up the back of her neck. "You didn't have to do that."

"I tried to start," Jaden said. "He made me wait."

"It's the polite thing to do," Josh said.

She looked at the empty spot at the table, directly across from Josh, and it occurred to her how intimate a simple meal could feel —not because they were alone but because they weren't. Jaden's presence made them feel like a family, and that was the notion she couldn't shake.

"You must be tired." Josh stood, took her plate and set it on the table. He pulled out her chair and looked at her. "Sit."

Robotically, she did as she was told, refusing to make eye contact with either one of them.

Josh walked over to the refrigerator and took out a pitcher of lemonade, pulled three glasses down from the cupboard and filled them with the tangy drink.

"Can we eat now?" Jaden asked.

Carly's laugh was less because she was amused and more

because she'd been holding on to a heap of nervous energy from the second Josh walked through the front door. Which was stupid —this was Josh. She shouldn't feel giddy and nervous around Josh.

And yet—this was *Josh.* And Josh had always made her feel giddy and nervous, even when she was most comfortable with him.

Finally, he sat down, which turned out to be even worse for her ailing nerves because every time she looked up from her plate, there were those tragic blue oceans, intently focused on her.

"I had no idea this town had become such a hot spot," Josh said.

She chose not to mention that his own father had been a key player in the rejuvenation of Harbor Pointe. As the city planner, it was often his office implementing the ideas that had led to the growth.

"Did you have a Realtor helping you?" she asked between bites of fried rice.

"Yes, Linda something-or-other," Josh said. He'd never been very good with names. "She talked to me like I was crazy for even suggesting a short-term rental in this market."

"Is Cole kicking you out?" Carly asked.

Josh bit into the egg roll and shook his head. "He'd never kick me out—but I'm starting to feel in the way. You know Cole."

Everyone knew Cole. He was the football coach the town was counting on to get their boys back on the right track. He was also the kind of guy who rarely spoke to anyone unless he had to—it amazed her that he seemed to know just what to say to a team of high school boys but appeared completely lost when it came to any other conversation.

He'd always been a little on the grumpy side, even before he and Gemma started having trouble. She could only imagine what he was like now that they'd split. "How's he doing?"

Josh shrugged. "Doesn't talk about it, but she showed up this morning, and then he spent the rest of the day in his workshop. I'm pretty sure he just needs to be alone right now."

"Are you sure that's good for him?" Carly asked. Cole Turner wasn't the type to do anything stupid, but when someone was hurting, was leaving them alone really the best decision?

"I'll still check in with him," Josh said. "I just don't want to be underfoot."

"What about Grandpa's old fishing cabin?" Jaden shoveled a bite into his mouth.

Carly nearly choked on her food. "What?"

"It's not like Grandpa uses it," Jaden said.

"It's not exactly in the best condition." Carly looked at Josh. "I don't think you're going to want to stay there—it's probably pretty rough."

She didn't actually know that because she hadn't set foot in that old cabin for over sixteen years.

Josh shrugged. "I don't mind."

She frowned. "No." She wouldn't say so, but she was ninety-nine percent certain her dad wasn't going to want Josh there. Besides—she wasn't sure how to reconcile the idea of Josh spending his days (and nights) in that cabin. *Their* cabin.

"A little dirt isn't going to scare me off," he said. "I've slept in worse places."

Worse places like the old garden shed in her backyard.

The image of an eleven-year-old Josh at her back door, face stained with tears and back covered in welts, washed through her mind. "Can I sleep in your shed?" he'd asked. "Just until my dad falls asleep?"

She looked away. She didn't want her sympathy for him to return—it messed with her resolve.

"I'll text Grandpa." Jaden had his phone out before Carly could blink.

"No, Jay." Carly glanced up and found matching blue eyes trained on her. "Maybe I can talk to Quinn—she has a lot of connections around town. I'm sure she'll know of someone with something you can rent short-term."

"What's the big deal?" Jaden asked, still poised to send his text to her dad.

She glanced at Josh, whose expression made it clear he knew exactly what the big deal was—and yet, he made no move to back her up.

She lifted her chin, as if to prove that there was absolutely nothing sentimental about that old fishing cabin. "No big deal. Go ahead and ask."

Jaden clicked Send and set his phone on the table. She picked up her half-eaten egg roll and dragged it through the soy sauce on her plate.

No big deal. She'd just pretend that old cabin wasn't the place where she and Josh would sneak away to when they wanted to be alone, that it wasn't the place where Jaden had been conceived.

A lazy grin spread across Josh's face, as if he'd just been reading her mind.

Unbelievable.

Jaden's phone dinged, and he picked it up, slid it open and read what she could only assume was a text from his grandfather. "Grandpa says it's totally trashed out, but you're welcome to it."

Carly glanced up and found Josh watching her again. Or maybe still. Had he stopped looking at her since he walked through that door?

"And you told him it was me who'd be staying there?" Josh asked, obviously aware of how her father felt about him.

"Yeah," Jaden said. "He might've made some remark about it being about as good a place as you deserve, but he agreed, he said, because I asked." He shoveled the last of his food into his mouth and stood. "Now that that's all settled, we've got a date with a certain game." He started toward the door.

"Hey," Josh called out.

Jaden turned.

"Dishes."

Jaden sighed, took his plate to the sink, rinsed it off and stuck it in the dishwasher. "Happy?"

"I'll be there in a minute."

Carly pushed a pea around her plate with her fork.

"Are you really okay with this? Me staying out there?"

She picked up her plate and walked over to the sink. "Makes no difference to me."

"Carly." And then he was standing beside her, close enough for their arms to touch.

It makes no difference. She'd tell herself that as many times as she had to to make herself believe it.

"But it's not in great shape." A step away from him to calm her racing pulse. "We can go out there tomorrow if you want to see for yourself. My dad never uses it anymore. I tried to convince him to turn it into a rental or to sell it, but Sheriff Gus never does anything that's not his own idea."

"And you're good with it? Me staying there?" he asked.

She fished a container out of the cupboard next to the sink and scooped her leftover chicken and rice into it. "Yep. I'll be fine."

Was she trying to convince him or herself?

"I know you will be," he said. "You always are."

"I mean, you're going to have to let me be the one to clean it up and make sure things are the way they're supposed to be."

His smile teased. "Of course."

She shrugged. "Don't mock me because I know what I want."

A steady hum took hold of her as he forced her gaze to his and held on. "I won't. So long as you don't fault me because I know what I want."

He wasn't talking about the cabin. *Oh, wow. Was he talking about her?*

He cleared the leftovers and cleaned the table, and in a flash the room closed in on her and she struggled for a much-needed breath.

"I'll get this," she said, needing distance from him.

He turned off the faucet and looked at her. "I don't mind helping."

"I know," she said. "But Jaden's waiting for you, and I can get this. Thanks, though."

He leaned against the sink and watched her for too many unnerving seconds.

"What?" she asked.

His lazy smile had returned. "It's just nice to be in the same room with you is all."

"If you're going to be hanging out here after Jaden's surgery, I think some ground rules are in order."

"This should be fun," he said.

She ignored him. "Rule number one: you're not allowed to flirt with me."

"Am I allowed to admire you?"

"From a distance."

He took a step toward her. "How about from here?"

She inched away. "Absolutely not."

He took a step back, crossing his arms over his chest. "But here's okay?"

"You're impossible," she said.

"And you're worth admiring—at any distance."

"Josh."

He held up his hands in surrender. "Sorry."

Nothing about his tone sounded apologetic. "Go."

"All right, I'm going." He backed toward the door.

"What are you doing?" She faced him.

"Admiring from a distance," he said. "Gonna do that every chance I get."

She threw the dish towel at him and turned away.

The last thing she needed was for her traitorous smile to give him the wrong impression. Because she most certainly was not amused. And she did not find his flirting cute. And she did not feel the slightest fracture of the wall around her heart.

I'm in trouble now.

Chapter Sixteen

Dear Elizabeth,

My name is Carly Collins and my son was just diagnosed with Long QT Syndrome. He will have surgery in just a few days to have an ICD implanted. Jaden is a competitive skier, and his surgeon is advising that he stop skiing altogether as a result of his condition and the ICD. We ran across an article about you and your great success on the MSU swim team, so I wondered if we might be able to talk with you about your experience and maybe even get the name of your doctor?

If you have time, I would love to chat at your earliest convenience.

My number is below.

Thank you,

Carly Collins

* * *

Carly sat in the passenger seat of Josh's truck, trying her best not to remember a single thing about that little fishing cabin her dad kept on the edge of town.

The cabin had been in their family for years, and her father swore that even just leaving their house felt like a vacation, regardless of the fact that it was barely twenty minutes away.

"I emailed that swimmer," Carly said, mostly to break up the silence.

Josh glanced at her then back to the road. "And?"

"I just sent it, so we'll see."

"Should we reconsider this surgery?" Josh asked.

As they drove, she kept her eyes glued on a big white farmhouse with four kids out front jumping on a trampoline.

"I think he needs the ICD no matter what," Carly said. "And Dr. Roby really is a good surgeon."

"Should we maybe get a second opinion?" Josh asked.

Carly didn't want to think about it. Dr. Roby had a big ego and a lot of pull at the hospital. If she disregarded his advice and Jaden started skiing, he would certainly hear about it.

And then what? She would look like she didn't trust her own superiors. That didn't bode well for someone wanting to move up the ranks.

But her son was more important than her career. And skiing was important to her son.

"Let's just see what Elizabeth says."

They pulled up in front of the cabin and Josh killed the engine. He'd packed his things into a duffel bag and picked her up promptly at nine that morning, fresh coffee waiting for her in the cab of his truck.

His willingness to bring her coffee when she needed it was rapidly becoming one of his best qualities.

She tossed a quick glance at him, then pretended this old cabin had zero effect on her.

Nonchalant was the word of the day.

Sure, I can be in this place and not think about the stupid things we used to do here when we were kids. I can pretend we didn't play house and act like we were a whole lot older than we really were. Stupid. Stupid. Stupid.

She opened the truck door and made a beeline for the porch.

To the right, underneath a pot of dead flowers, was a single silver key, same one Dad had left there all those years ago.

How they never got caught out here still remained a mystery. Her father's trust in her sometimes shamed her all by itself.

She stuck the key in the door and pushed it open, a musty, dusty smell hitting her nostrils. He came up behind her and inhaled.

"Oh, Josh, I don't know if you can stay here." She looked around the dank space, filthy from lack of use.

"It's fine." He pushed past her and dropped his bags on the floor, dust particles catching the light gleaming in from the window.

"It's not fine."

"It will be when we're done with it," he said. "And I don't mind cleaning this place on my own. You didn't have to come."

"Do you want me to go?"

He tilted his head and looked at her. "It's a little late now."

"I can call Quinn to come get me and drive me home."

"Don't be ridiculous. Besides, we both know you weren't about to let me out here without you supervising every little bit of everything."

That was true. She didn't want to open the cabin and give him free rein until she saw what condition it was in. She didn't like the idea of him staying here at all, but she especially didn't like the idea of him staying here without her checking it all out first.

"You're right, it would make a great rental." He walked over to the bay window in the living room and pulled the curtains open, coughing as the dust kicked up.

"Maybe we should toss those curtains," she said.

He walked from the living room into the adjoining kitchen, stopping at the bottom of a ladder that went up to a singular loft bedroom.

Two bathrooms completed the space, and, of course, the big porch off the back with stellar views of the lake. It was a small house, but perfect for a couple of kids looking to escape their parents.

He turned around and caught her staring. "It's weird being back here." His eyes were full of her, and he seemed perfectly fine that they were.

She, on the other hand, was anything but. "I'll go get the cleaning supplies from the truck." She dashed out of the cabin and used her sternest internal monologue to remind herself that all of these pesky *feelings* were not okay.

That's enough giddiness, Carly Raeanne.

She used both her names when she really needed to get through to herself. But when she fetched the bag of cleaning supplies and spun around to find him watching her from the front porch, she realized her stubbornness was going to be hard to combat.

Why had Josh always been so hard for her to resist?

Maybe it was the way he looked at her—long, deep stares with intensity behind his eyes, like he was thinking thoughts he shouldn't be thinking at the most inopportune times. Or maybe it was the unexpected gentle way he always spoke to her when they were together. Or perhaps the impossible way his brokenness turned him into a walking mystery?

Whatever it was, Josh Dixon made her want to throw out the rules.

From the very second he had asked her out, Carly knew she would never love anyone the way she loved him. It was an innocent kind of love, the kind that comes with first kisses and awkward moments. The kind that stayed innocent for a very long time—a fact nobody would've believed.

Everyone had assumed they knew the kind of guy Josh was, but assumptions weren't facts, and Josh had never pressured her to have sex.

It had even surprised her, if she was honest, and sometimes she wondered if he simply wasn't attracted to her.

When the bell rang at the end of seventh hour the Friday

before junior prom, Carly nearly leapt from her desk and out into the hallway.

Finally. She could focus on prom.

She'd had to twist Josh's arm to even take her to the prom—though he swore his unwillingness had nothing to do with her and everything to do with the fact that he didn't want to get all dressed up and go to a school dance.

Eventually, he'd relented, as he usually did, and Carly's happiness won out over his. Beverly had taken her shopping for the perfect prom dress, and they'd found it. With a pink tulle skirt and a silver-beaded pink bodice, it made Carly feel like a princess. She couldn't wait for Josh to see her.

They'd do all the typical prom things—pictures with gawking Mom-arazzi, dinner at Capri, grand march, dance—but it was the post-prom activities she'd planned that she was most excited about—*The Sandlot 2* was playing at the movie theater, and she'd already bought tickets.

It might seem childish, but it would be the cherry on the top of a potentially perfect evening. *The Sandlot* had been their favorite movie as kids, and while there was no way the sequel would live up to the first one, how could they not see it?

Josh had told her they could do whatever she wanted. And this was what she wanted, so he was happy to oblige.

Now, as she left Mr. Jensen's Honors English class, she practically bounded down the hallway toward Josh's locker, like a prisoner who'd just been paroled.

But as she approached the familiar spot in the hall, what she saw nearly stopped her in her tracks.

Belinda Tipton, dressed in her tiny cheerleading skirt, stood way too close to Josh. They were talking, their heads close together, and the sight of it made Carly's heart sputter.

She'd heard Belinda had a crush on Josh, but this confirmed it. The only question was—did he feel the same?

Bubbly and perky and everything a cheerleader should be, Belinda had a reputation for getting what she wanted. The thought that what she wanted was her boyfriend had Carly's stomach turning cartwheels.

Belinda tossed her head back, laughing much more loudly than she needed to. Josh glanced up and saw Carly standing there, and quickly took a step away from Belinda.

"Hey," he said.

Belinda turned, gave Carly a once-over, then looked back at Josh. "Save me that dance, okay?" She pranced off without a word to Carly, who felt small and plain in the other girl's presence.

"What did she want?" she asked, doing her best to keep her tone light, as if she could pretend she didn't care who Josh talked to, as if she was secure in their relationship, which she had been up until that exact moment.

"You know Belinda." Josh shut his locker and didn't say another word.

Later, Carly's friend Beth told her that Belinda had a bet going with the other cheerleaders that she could get Josh to ditch Carly at the dance and leave with her.

That tidbit of gossip plagued Carly for the rest of the night and the following day right up until Josh showed up at her house to take her to the prom.

She questioned the sincerity of his compliment when he saw her in the princess dress and told her how beautiful she looked. She sat through dinner wondering if Josh would rather be sitting across from Belinda. And when they arrived at the country club for the grand march, she found herself scanning the crowd for Belinda, as if knowing exactly where she was would change anything.

"You okay?" Josh asked as they stood in the long line of couples about to parade up onto the stage and out to the back of the big banquet hall.

"I'm fine," she said.

"You seem distracted."

If she mentioned Belinda, would she sound needy and whiny? The kind of girl she swore she'd never be?

But if she didn't mention her, would it ruin their night? It wasn't like she was doing a good job of forgetting what she'd heard—and an even worse job of forgetting what she'd seen.

"I'm fine," she repeated.

"You keep saying that, but you don't seem fine." He fixed his eyes on something ahead of him, and she saw the annoyance in his expression. She was irritating him. She had to be careful or she'd run him off. She knew that. He had plenty of other girls waiting in the wings, including one of the prettiest in school.

She slipped her hand in his as they stepped up onto the stage. He glanced down and she smiled at him. She was being ridiculous. She and Josh were meant to be—nothing Belinda or anyone else said or did could change that.

But an hour later, Carly exited the bathroom stall to find Belinda leaning against the sink, as if she were waiting for her.

Carly's heart raced. Why was she nervous? It wasn't like Belinda was going to beat her up or something. Right?

"You and Josh are really cute," Belinda said.

"Thanks," Carly said dryly.

"But don't you think you're kidding yourself a little?"

Carly found Belinda's eyes in the mirror.

Belinda smiled innocently. "I mean, it was cute when we were underclassmen, but he's outgrown you, don't you think?"

Carly turned off the faucet and moved past Belinda to get a paper towel.

"Face it, Carly, he's hot and you're a nerd. How long do you think he's going to keep dating you once he realizes it?"

She dried her hands and threw the paper towel in the garbage.

Where was her snappy comeback? Her witty repartee? Why was she frozen in the other girl's presence, as if stringing two words together was too complicated?

She left the bathroom even more worried and distracted than she'd been when she came in.

Josh smiled. "The dance is almost over—what's the plan?"

She reached into her purse and pulled out the movie tickets, but quickly stuffed them back inside. "Nothing, it's stupid."

He frowned. "Let me see, Carly. Come on." He reached across her and pulled out the tickets. "*Sandlot 2*?" He laughed.

She snatched the tickets out of his hand and shoved them back in her purse.

He backed away and frowned at her. "What's wrong?"

"I don't really feel like going to the movie anymore," she said.

"What? You were so excited."

"It's kind of babyish, don't you think?"

He shrugged. "It's an ode to our childhood. I think it's awesome." He took her hand. "What's wrong?"

She looked up into his eyes—ocean-colored and full of kindness—and she knew she had to ask him. She had to know, even if she didn't like his answer. And if he lied, she would know because she always knew when he was keeping something from her.

"Do you like Belinda?"

Josh's forehead wrinkled. "Belinda Tipton?"

"How many Belindas do we know?"

He planted himself in front of her, took her face in his hands and smiled. "You're cute when you're jealous."

She swatted his hands away. "I'm serious, Josh."

"Carly, no. I don't like Belinda Tipton—how can you even ask me that?"

"I hear things."

"You heard I liked her?"

She looked away. She was becoming the exact girl she did not want to be. And while she believed Josh, she also worried that maybe he didn't even realize he was getting tired of his childish relationship with Carly.

Maybe he *had* outgrown her. He'd turned in to the kind of guy who would ride a motorcycle, while Carly would always be the girl at the library on Friday night.

Surely he saw that too.

What if Josh started thinking about Belinda—about what

she'd be willing to give him—about how he really did want what she was offering?

No guy in their right mind would turn her down.

That's what she was thinking when she left the dance. Those were the thoughts running through her mind when she told him to turn toward the old fishing cabin instead of the movie theater.

I'm going to lose him.

Up until that point, their physical relationship had been pretty tame. They kissed (a lot), but not much else. That night, everything changed.

It would've been easy to blame it all on Josh. Everybody would've believed that it was his idea to have sex. After all, wasn't the guy usually the one instigating physicality? But Carly knew the truth. She had pushed the issue because she was afraid he would get bored with her. She was afraid she would lose him, and that thought above every other thought was what pushed her forward.

In the heat of the moment, he'd stopped, pulling himself away from her. "I need a minute."

"What's wrong?" she'd asked, not sure she wanted an answer.

He heaved a sigh, still working to catch his breath. "I just need to calm down."

She pressed her hands on his bare chest and kissed his neck. "Why?"

He pushed her off of him and trained his gaze on hers. "Carly, are you sure this is what you want?"

She replied with a kiss. Then another. Then another. Fueled by the idea that this would make him stay. He would never leave her now.

Afterward, they looked at each other for a brief moment and Carly knew nothing between them would ever be the same again. She had changed everything, as she'd intended to, but nothing felt like she'd expected.

Embarrassment, not boldness, crept up her neck, flushing her cheeks red. What had she done?

She wasn't even sure they'd done it right. Did it count? It had been awkward and a little painful. It had been quick and embarrassing. Was that how sex was supposed to be?

Her heart raced and her head scolded her, and despite her best efforts, she melted into a puddle of tears.

Josh sat up straight, confusion on his face. Of course he was confused. Not two minutes before, Carly had practically thrown herself at him. Now, in the shadow of their decision, she was falling apart, and she knew it was unfair to expect him to put her back together.

He reached for her, but she shrank away. "I think I need to go home."

He sighed. "Carly, oh man. I'm sorry—I thought . . ."

She shook her head. "It's okay. I just want to go home."

He sat still for several seconds, then finally they gathered their clothes, got dressed and left the little cabin on the lake.

They rode in silence, and when they reached her street, he slowed down, as if that might stop time. As if they could turn back the clock and make sense of what they'd done.

"I'm really sorry," he said as he pulled up in front of her house.

She shook her head and wiped her cheeks dry. "It wasn't your fault."

"I thought it was what you wanted."

She looked at him. "Me too, but maybe I thought it would be different."

"Maybe we can go back to the way things were? Pretend it didn't happen? I don't need that right now, Carly."

But she didn't believe him. She knew how teenage boys were. Everyone made it clear they all only wanted one thing. Did it matter that Josh had never made her feel that way?

She looked at her house and thought of her dad, who would be sitting in his recliner, watching old reruns of *M*A*S*H* and waiting for her to get home. "I don't think we can ever go back."

He reached across the front seat and took her hand. "Let's at least try."

She looked at him, and she thought in that moment that maybe Josh actually loved her, that maybe he'd loved her before that night and she'd made this decision without thinking it through, without consulting him. She'd assumed she knew what he wanted, but was it possible she'd misjudged him? What if Belinda wasn't what he wanted at all? What if he'd been perfectly content with the way things were despite their differences?

Or maybe because of their differences?

She touched his face, then leaned closer, kissing him on the lips the way they'd done a thousand times before. "Okay," she said. "Let's try."

But the truth was, they both knew it would never have worked to pretend that night didn't happen, even if everything had gone differently. Their sweet, innocent relationship was different now, and no amount of wishing it weren't would change that.

Now, Carly squeezed the bucket of cleaning supplies. "Maybe I should go home. Jaden's probably awake now, and I don't think Quinn is picking him up for another hour."

Josh stepped off the porch and met her in the yard. "You're uncomfortable being here."

"No, I'm not."

"That's the second time you've mentioned leaving."

She shook her head. "I've been here plenty of times." (With him and not since.) "It's just a cabin."

"Right," he said.

"So let's just work, okay?"

He raised his hands as if in surrender and she pushed past him, anxious to shut herself away, turn her brain off and stay focused on something she *could* control.

Because right now, it seemed everything else in her life had a mind of its own.

Chapter Seventeen

A little after noon, Quinn pulled up in front of the cabin. Josh knew if he wanted to have any chance with Carly, he needed to prove himself not just to her, but to her family.

He'd start with Quinn—Gus was far too much of a challenge at this point.

Jaden got out of the passenger side carrying three grocery bags.

"Got the stuff you asked for," he said as he approached the porch.

"Where's Carly?" Quinn asked, one hand shielding her eyes from the sun.

"She's scouring the kitchen like a madwoman," Josh said.

"She cleans when she's anxious," Quinn murmured.

Jaden peeked inside the open door. "Not bad for a morning's work."

"Yeah, it's not a bad little place," Josh said.

Jaden went inside, leaving him standing on the porch with his almost-sister-in-law, though he and Carly had never married. She seemed to have something to say.

"Go ahead," he said.

Her brow clenched. "Go ahead with what?"

"I know you've just been waiting for the right time to give me a piece of your mind."

She shrugged. "No, I haven't."

He only stared.

"Fine, I have," she said.

"So, bring it on. I can take it."

She crossed her arms over her chest. "I see the way you look at her, Josh." She shook her head. "I don't know what you're thinking, if you've got it in your head you guys might be able to try again, but she can't take it—you have no idea what it did to her when you left."

Maybe he couldn't take it. "I know," he murmured.

"But you don't. She loved you more than anything," Quinn said. "And you just walked away. You don't just get over that."

His heart squeezed. *I'm not over it either.* But he had no right. It was his choice—his actions that had done them in.

"I'm telling you, she seems strong, but she's actually pretty fragile, and with everything going on with Jaden—she's not thinking straight. The last thing she needs is for you to walk in here and make everything even more confusing with your—" she motioned toward his chest—"muscles and your blue eyes and all that nonsense."

A smile tugged at the corner of his mouth, but he quickly put it back in its place. "I never meant to hurt her, Quinn."

"You hurt all of us, Josh," she said.

He thought of all the times Quinn tagged along with him and Carly, the little sister he never had. He'd served as her protector back in those days, and she idolized him—he knew she did. But he'd thrown that away.

"I'm sorry if I hurt you," he said.

"I'm fine," Quinn said. "It's Carly I'm worried about. I know you're a good guy, Josh—just not *her* guy. Stay away from her heart, okay?"

He sighed. He didn't want to make a promise he couldn't keep.

"Okay?"

He nodded dumbly. "Okay."

Later that afternoon, he fired up the rusty grill, cooked burgers and brats and they all sat on the back porch eating and admiring the view. Josh had turned Quinn's words over in his head a thousand times and they still didn't sit well. He didn't want to stay away from Carly's heart. He wanted to deserve her—to prove to all of them he'd changed.

To make right the things he'd done so wrong in the past.

Nobody said a word about what was coming the next day, but Jaden's surgery had a way of looming like the giant elephant in every room.

After lunch, Quinn drove off to the training center with Jaden, leaving him alone with his very quiet, very focused ex.

By nightfall, Carly's hair had fallen from her hair tie and her face had grown tired. But she'd moved from the kitchen to the bathrooms and now vacuumed the loft where Josh would sleep. She'd brought fresh sheets, which were now on the bed, and while all the window coverings were going to have to be replaced, the little cabin felt clean and livable.

Still, she showed no signs of stopping.

It had become clear at some point during the day that Carly was cleaning to work out some of her aggression, so for the most part, he stayed out of her way, turning most of his attention to the yard.

But it was late, and they had a big day tomorrow.

He called up into the loft, but her back was to him and the sound of the vacuum drowned him out. She didn't even stir. He moved up the ladder with ease, his mind spinning back to the days and sometimes nights they'd show up here instead of the movies or down on the beach where they'd told their parents they were headed.

They'd said their first time would be the only time—they'd go back to the way things were. But that one time had set in motion something that couldn't be taken back.

Another way he'd been a bad influence on her, to be sure. No way she would've ever dreamed of breaking into this place or continued having sex if it hadn't been for him.

But their time here hadn't always been about that. Some nights they lay in the backyard on a giant blanket, looking up at the stars and dreaming of a future together in spite of the fact that they were headed on completely different paths.

He called out to her, but she still didn't hear him. He waved his arms so he didn't startle her, but still—nothing. He saw headphones in her ears, so in addition to the roar of the vacuum, he was also contending with her Spotify station.

"Carly!" He reached out and tapped her on the shoulder and she jumped, gasped and clung to her chest.

Exactly what he was trying to avoid.

"Sorry—sorry." He held up his hands in surrender as she hurried to turn off the vacuum.

"You scared me to death," she said.

"I called your name at least six times."

She plopped down onto the bed, clearly trying to calm her nerves. "I didn't hear you."

Obviously.

"I think we should call it a night," he said.

She ran her hands over her face and sighed. "But if I stop, then I'll have to think."

"We could go downstairs and watch TV."

"On my dad's tiny old television?"

He shrugged. "It works okay."

"I remember."

He remembered too. He remembered her laugh when the only thing they could get on that fuzzy old set were reruns of Archie Bunker. He remembered sharing a blanket on the worn-out old couch and feeling for a moment like that was the best possible future he could imagine for them.

Here, it was quiet and peaceful. Nobody was fighting or crying or screaming at him. This old cabin was one of the few places in the world where Josh felt relaxed.

Did she remember the promises they'd made to each other right here in this place?

Man, he missed the simple, peaceful relationship they'd shared. He'd had nothing like it—not before or since.

He looked at her, doing nothing to hide the longing he felt.

"You're right. We should call it a night," she said abruptly, standing and winding up the cord on the vacuum cleaner. "It's getting late and Jaden will be home soon."

He moved out of the way so she could descend the ladder, aware that the good memories from their past had the same effect on her that the bad ones did.

And that was something he had no idea how to change.

Chapter Eighteen

J osh: *I know it's 3:00 a.m. but are you up?*
    Carly: *Yes.*
    Josh: *Me too. Worried?*
    Carly: *Trying not to be.*
  Josh: *I keep thinking of every verse I've ever read in the Bible about not being anxious and God caring about sparrows. Somehow I'm still sitting here begging him to watch out for our son.*
    Carly: *You're praying?*
    Josh: *Feels like the only thing I can do right now.*

* * *

The day of the surgery, Carly woke up early.

They had to be at the hospital by six in the morning, so she'd set her alarm for five, and she was pretty sure she'd only been asleep an hour.

It might seem like her medical training would come in handy at a time like this, but she was finding her knowledge of all the risks of surgery did more harm than good.

She shook Jaden, who wanted no part of being awake, then

headed downstairs to make a cup of coffee when a light rap on the front door startled her.

She pulled her short robe around her body and tied it, then went to the door and peered outside.

Josh stood on the porch, clean shaven and showered, wearing a pair of jeans and an old Michigan State T-shirt she thought she recognized from high school.

She opened the door. "What are you doing here?"

"Brought you this." He held up a to-go cup of coffee from Hazel's Kitchen along with a brown paper bag. "You still like chocolate chip muffins, don't you?"

He remembered? She reached out and took the bag, opened it and stuck her nose inside, inhaling the buttery, chocolatey scent. *Heaven.*

"You didn't have to do this," she said.

"I know. I wanted to. Is he up?"

Carly shook her head.

"Can I come in? I want to see him before we head over."

She clutched the cup of coffee to her chest. "Josh, I think maybe we need to talk about something."

He frowned, but surely he knew what she was going to say.

"Nothing's going to happen here, you know that, right?"

His eyes searched hers, and while she thought she saw disappointment, he quickly recovered, nonchalantly shrugging. "'Course I know that."

"Okay, because you've said some things since you've been here —and then being at the cabin yesterday—"

"Just nostalgia," he said. The sparkle in his eyes flickered. "I know where you stand."

Regret twisted in her belly and she wanted to kick herself. He'd been great since he'd been back—and here he was being more thoughtful than she deserved, and how did she respond? By putting him squarely in his place.

But she needed to make things clear now, before her jumbled-up feelings turned even more confusing. Before it was too late to protect herself.

While she'd tossed and turned last night over Jaden's surgery, she'd also been replaying her interactions with Josh—and the play-by-play had led her to the conclusion that she needed to be very careful.

She needed her anger to keep her safe, and some days, she discovered she didn't feel angry with him anymore. Some days, she remembered why she'd liked him in the first place. He was funny and surprising and when he looked at her, he made her feel *seen*.

But she couldn't let herself forget, not even for a moment, the pain he'd caused her when he broke her heart.

She wondered sometimes if Quinn was right. Maybe she'd never completely recovered.

She'd decided after his late-night text had sent her heart reverberating on an endless loop that her only course of action was to be straight with him. To set those rules up and make it clear—even if it made her feel like a jerk.

Which it had, in fact, done. Especially since he'd shown up with coffee and muffins.

"So, we understand each other?" she asked quietly.

"Yeah," he said. "You want me to stop telling you you're beautiful." His gaze settled on her, and she suddenly felt naked. She wished her hands were free so she could pull her robe even tighter.

"That's a good start."

"Even if you are beautiful?"

She laughed. "I just woke up."

His face shifted, but his body was still. "Yep."

"This is what I'm talking about," she said.

"This is called chemistry." His mouth twitched upward in a slight grin. "Doesn't come around every day."

She took a small step back. Where was her anger now? Where was her suit of armor? Her heart was exposed, like a wounded soldier left behind with no cover in a gunfight.

"Dad?"

Josh looked past her, following the sound of Jaden's voice, then smiled. "There's the man of the hour."

"What are you doing here? I thought you were meeting us at the hospital?"

"Just brought over some coffee and breakfast for your mom." He brushed past Carly on his way inside, the nearness of him sending her senses on high alert. "And I wanted to see you."

Carly closed the door, begging her heart to stop racing.

"How are you feeling?" Josh asked.

Jaden shrugged. "Okay, I guess."

Josh stared at him, and for a moment, it seemed the two of them were communicating telepathically, as if they had their own language that required no words at all.

"You're going to be fine," Josh said, clapping a hand on Jaden's arm.

Josh had no medical expertise whatsoever, and yet, she clung to his words. It was as if she'd needed to hear them herself.

Jaden's shoulders slumped like a deflating tire and he pressed his fingers into his eyes, the faintest sob escaping as he did. "I don't want to do this."

Carly stood frozen, confused—Jaden had seemed fine last night. He'd even been in a good mood. She thought he was handling it so well, so much better than she was. It was as if Josh had known the truth the second he asked how Jaden was feeling, like he had a sixth sense about their son that even Carly didn't share.

It should make her angry. It wasn't fair that she'd been the one to raise him all these years, and Josh had swooped in to save the day again. But anger wasn't what she felt now. Her heart broke as she watched Josh step forward and pull their son, nearly the same height as his father, into a tight embrace.

The kind of hug only a father could give. Strong. Steady. Reassuring.

Was Josh these things to Jaden now?

She expected Jaden to pull away, but instead, he stood unmoving, allowing his father to comfort him.

Josh pulled back and put his hands on Jaden's shoulders, leveling their gazes. "This is just a minor setback. A bump in the road. You get this done, then you can recover and move on—and you'll be healthier and stronger because of it."

Jaden nodded.

Josh glanced at Carly. The cup of coffee grew cooler in her hand, and she'd crumpled the brown paper bag to half its size she'd been holding it so tightly. He reached out and put a hand on her shoulder, the other one still pressed on Jaden's.

"I should've been straight with you from the second I knocked on the door," he said. "I'm still having trouble figuring out how to be a dad and not overstep."

Carly frowned. What was he going to say? Was he going to try and make this day about him—about their past—about his mistakes? This day was about none of those things.

"But I came here because I felt like God told me we needed to pray together before we went to the hospital."

Jaden nodded, as if to agree. As if this were normal. As if he and Josh had had conversations about God before. Carly, on the other hand, felt like she was smack in the center of some strange alternate reality—a world in which her ex, the father of her child, made adult decisions with the wisdom of a real father.

"I hope that's okay, Car," Josh said.

Jaden's bloodshot eyes darted to hers, and once again, her heart nearly cracked in two. "Of course." Her own voice quavered.

Josh bowed his head and closed his eyes, and when he began to pray, he didn't fumble or search for the right words. He had an easy, laid-back conversation that started off by thanking God for their son and ended with asking Him to be with them all that day.

Carly screwed her eyes shut tight as she listened to Josh's heartfelt words float up toward heaven. And she probably would've made it through the prayer without a single tear if he hadn't asked God specifically to be with Carly, to comfort her and calm her mind, to give her the peace that passes all understanding.

His hand slid down from her shoulder to her fingers as he prayed, and he squeezed her hand gently.

A tear slid down her cheek as Josh said "Amen" and she quickly wiped it away.

Jaden drew in a quick breath, wiped his cheeks dry and gave his dad a nod. "Thanks."

Josh nodded, removed his hand from Jaden's shoulder and glanced at Carly. She refused his eyes.

"I'm going to finish getting ready." Jaden disappeared up the stairs, leaving her standing with Josh in the entryway of her house, confused at the way he continued to surprise her.

"I hope it was okay I did that," he said.

She didn't respond. She couldn't respond. Because everything she knew about Josh Dixon had gone into a blender and it had just been turned on to "puree."

He left you when you needed him most.

"I should let you get ready," he said. "I'll see you at the hospital." He moved toward the door, brushing her shoulder with his as he did. Before he pulled it open, he turned back and found her eyes, undoubtedly curious and questioning.

"He's going to be okay," he said.

Carly's lower lip trembled and she bit it to keep from crying.

He took a step toward her, but she took a step back. She could not accept his comfort right now. She was too weary, too vulnerable. Too afraid.

He must've sensed it because he froze in place.

She expected him to turn for the door. To leave. To run. Because that was what Josh did when things got messy. That was what she wanted him to do so she could cry in peace.

But he stood unmoving, waiting for her to meet his eyes, something she absolutely would not allow herself to do.

She stared at the ground, chewing her bottom lip as if her life depended on it, as if it were the only thing keeping the dam of tears from breaking.

He took the coffee and brown paper bag and set them on the table near the front door. Then he reached out and took her hand before she could pull it away.

"He's going to be okay," Josh repeated.

Carly knew he was right. It was illogical to be this worried. And yet, what if he didn't wake up from the anesthesia? What if the implant didn't work? What if it malfunctioned? What if their son's heart condition was scarier and more serious than any of them realized?

How had this happened? And more importantly—why?

Josh inched closer as Carly's mind spun, the lump at the base of her throat doubling in size. His grip on her hand loosened and he slid his hand up her arm, taking another step closer. "Carly," he said.

Still, she wouldn't look at him, but the sob caught in her throat and she realized she'd been holding it together for so very long—it was as if every ounce of fear had pooled inside of her, securely positioned in a little box at the back of her mind, and with every kind word he kicked the box closer and closer to the front of her mind. One more word and he'd knock the lid off and the contents would come spilling out.

He tucked the finger of his free hand under her chin and lifted it until her eyes finally met his.

The box tipped over. Her heart gushed out. Fresh tears streamed down her cheeks.

"I know you're worried," Josh said. "And exhausted." He looked at her so earnestly, so kindly, something inside her shifted. "But he really is going to be okay."

"But you don't know that," she said through her tears.

With his thumbs, he wiped her cheeks dry, then continued to hold her face in his hands. "Maybe not, but I believe it. I believe he's going to be fine. He's going to come through this stronger and better for it. God's got big plans for him, Carly. I know you know that."

She closed her eyes and nodded.

"Right?"

"Right." She opened her eyes to find him still looking at her. "So, we'll cling to that."

Josh stepped closer and wrapped his arms around her, and for the briefest moment she let herself be held.

Chapter Nineteen

W hat was he doing? He might as well plunge a knife into his own chest.

He told God (repeatedly) he did not want to go to Carly's house that morning and pray for Jaden. The thought had popped into his head around two, and he'd tried to push it away. Josh Dixon didn't pray. That's what Carly would be thinking. And she would've been right once upon a time.

But now? Praying had become second nature. Because if he didn't pray, he couldn't keep his promise.

Besides, his regret had kept him paralyzed for years—he would've tried anything to bury it. Instead—and largely thanks to his teenage son—he was trying to forgive himself.

Jaden talked about God like they were old friends. He was different than most religious people Josh knew. He wasn't preachy or judgmental, and while Jaden didn't know everything about his father's past, he knew Josh had made mistakes. Obviously.

One time, Josh had asked his son how he ever found it possible to forgive him, and Jaden said, "God's forgiven me for my sins. We all deserve a second chance."

Jaden would never know how those words had burrowed in,

down to a deep place in Josh's soul. They felt like the answer to prayers he didn't know he'd been praying.

Then there was the church thing. Josh never went. His parents had gone out of obligation and mostly to be seen—they were, after all, the picture of a perfect family—but Josh had only ever viewed church as a place where he would be judged and not accepted.

And he'd been right back in the day. He'd sit by his parents trying not to lean his bruised back against the wooden pew, aware of the side glances and death glares from the good, upright folks of Harbor Pointe.

He didn't belong here—that's what they were thinking.

He was a disgrace to his family with his late-night drinking, the constant trouble he got into at school.

When he stopped doing everything his parents told him to do, church was the first thing he abandoned.

But one Sunday morning after a weekend with Josh, Jaden had woken his dad up with the announcement that he'd found them a church to try. The night of the conference had been impactful, but the kid knew Josh needed something consistent in his life.

Wise beyond his years, Josh thought.

"It's not going to be the answer for everything," Jaden said. "I mean, people screw up all the time. But there's a lot of good stuff about being in a good church."

Josh did his best not to groan; after all, he was still trying to win his son over.

So he went. And he'd gone every week since. And in that time, he'd started praying—not because he was so holy and religious now—but because it filled him up in ways that nothing else ever had.

He felt silly discussing God with Jaden, who had a lot more knowledge on the subject, but his son never made him feel stupid.

It had taken months, but he'd begun to recognize when God

was prodding him to do something. And last night, God wasn't being quiet. He heard it loud and clear—*go and pray for him.*

Maybe it was less about what he was going to say in that prayer and more about his willingness to do it. He knew if he ignored that quiet voice, he'd regret it. So he showed up at Carly's under the guise of coffee and muffins.

But the second he saw Jaden, he understood.

This wasn't about him. It wasn't even about Carly—not really. This was about his son. This was about being a father to his son. And that was the only thing that mattered. Not how foolish it felt with so many mistakes flashing red in his rearview mirror. Not how nervous he'd been to ask Jaden in front of Carly if he could pray for him. And certainly not the inexplicable, undeniable bond that had been created among the three of them the second he did.

Had Carly felt it too? Had Jaden? He may have come to Harbor Pointe to be there for Jaden, but it hadn't taken long for a bigger desire to take hold.

And Quinn was right—he didn't deserve a second chance. His actions had brought Carly to her breaking point all those years ago. How did he make up for that?

But it was different now. He was different now. He wasn't sure how to return to Chicago and go on living the life he'd built. He wasn't sure how to go on living a life Carly and Jaden weren't a part of every single day.

He wanted—needed—to put his broken family back together.

Now, as he stood in the elevator at the hospital, he took note of the quiver in his belly. The way his nerves darted around. He inhaled a deep breath and exhaled a quiet prayer.

Please let him be okay.

Because for all his talk, he needed the same reassurance he'd given Carly only an hour before.

Josh exited the elevator and saw Dr. Willette standing at a counter, looking over paperwork in a folder. The man had been a good doctor, answering all of his questions and keeping his tone professional. But the knot in Josh's belly when he saw him had nothing to do with his skill as an M.D. He'd been genetically programmed to dislike the man who was dating the mother of his child. He couldn't help it.

He exhaled another prayer and moved down the hall, hoping the doctor didn't notice him.

"Josh?"

No such luck.

He turned around and faced Dr. Willette. Carly had sent Josh a text to tell him where they were, and frankly, he just wanted to get there. "Morning, Doc."

"Good morning. I've just seen Carly and Jaden," the doctor said. "Both seem to be doing pretty well."

Josh's lips twitched. "Yeah, I thought the same thing when I left Carly's house this morning."

Dr. Willette's eyebrow quirked, but Josh didn't bother explaining. It wasn't like he owed the guy an explanation. And fine, he wanted to one-up the guy.

"Okay, well, I'll let you get to it," Dr. Willette said. "I'll stop by with updates as I get them."

Josh nodded, walked down the hall and pushed open the door to Jaden's room. He found Jaden on the bed under a thin sheet, wearing a hospital gown. Carly sat in a chair near the window, looking like she could come undone at any minute.

He took a step into the room. "Did they say when they'd be back to get you?"

"Soon. They asked a bunch of questions, made sure I understood what was happening, made me pee in a cup. Good times." Jaden sort of shrugged.

The door opened and two nurses walked in. "It's just about time to take you back," the male nurse said to Jaden. "Any last-minute questions?"

Josh glanced at Carly, who was sitting at full attention, then at Jaden, whose eyes had fallen. His son had plastered his brave face on, but now, looking at him in that hospital bed, Josh was certain this was what he'd looked like as a boy. Vulnerable. Shy. Scared.

Carly must've seen it too. She stood and moved to the side of the bed, putting a hand on their son's shoulder. Jaden looked up at her and said, "You sure we can't back out?"

Something squeezed Josh's heart, and he swallowed the lump at the back of his throat. Tears filled Carly's eyes as she sat down on the bed and took Jaden's hand. "Remember what your dad said this morning. This is a good thing."

Jaden nodded. "Yeah, I know."

"This part totally stinks, but this is what we have to do to get you healthy, to get you skiing again. It's a little speed bump, that's all."

If she had any doubt about what she was saying, Josh couldn't tell. He wouldn't say so, but he had doubts—worries, concerns. Mostly about the skiing. How many elite athletes could compete at such a high level with Jaden's condition? Were they all fooling themselves with their blind faith?

"I'm still a little nervous," Jaden said.

The male nurse took a step toward them. "We've got something we call 'happy juice' to put in your IV. That is going to calm your nerves and make you feel a lot more relaxed." He held up a plastic package that had some sort of syringe in it, then got to work administering it to Jaden.

Within seconds, the kid was completely at ease. Whatever the nurse had given Jaden, it had done the trick.

Josh wondered if he could get a dose of that for himself.

"Feel better?"

Jaden smiled. "I'm feeling good, Rick."

The nurse frowned. "My name's Tom."

Carly laughed as a tear slid down her cheek. She quickly wiped it away. Josh resisted the urge to take her hand.

"Ready to go?" Tom asked Jaden.

Carly reached out and covered Jaden's hand with her own. "We'll be here when you wake up."

Jaden nodded, then looked at Josh. "You'll be here too?"

Josh took a step forward. "Yeah, I'm not going anywhere."

"Promise?"

Josh took Jaden's other hand. "Promise."

Jaden nodded, then spun his finger around in a circular motion. "Fine. Let's do it already."

Tom nodded to the other nurse, and the two of them swooped in, moved a few things around on the bed, then rolled him out of the room and down the hall, leaving Josh and Carly standing, alone.

Carly turned away, wrapped her arms around herself and let out a quiet sob. Josh moved toward her but stopped short.

"Carly—"

The door opened again and Dr. Willette, with his awesome timing, walked in. "Came to check on you both and show you to the waiting room."

Josh had a feeling this wasn't something the doctor typically did. It was more likely that a nurse handled this part, but then Carly wasn't the typical patient's mother, was she?

The doctor strode across the room to Carly, as if Josh wasn't standing a few feet away. He stood in front of her, and she looked up at him. Josh couldn't see her face, but the doctor smiled warmly. "He's going to be fine." He spoke in a hushed tone. "Jaden is going to be just fine, and Dr. Roby is the best."

Carly nodded.

Another smile from the doctor. "Why don't I get you both some coffee and show you to the waiting room? You'll get regular updates on your pager."

Carly glanced down at the device in her hand. It looked like a restaurant pager, but it would be their connection to Jaden while he was in surgery.

Finally, she tossed a look in Josh's direction. He held her gaze, wondering if she was thinking of the way he'd held her that very morning, wondering if it was his arms she sought comfort in.

But no. That moment between them had passed, and Carly had gone back to despising him.

She looked away, back toward the doctor, who led her out of the room. Josh drew in a deep breath. It was going to be a very long day.

Chapter Twenty

About half an hour after they took Jaden back, Carly's family showed up in the waiting room. It wasn't the first time they'd been in the hospital for Jaden—in a way, they all fussed over him as if he were their own.

The television quietly played a *Golden Girls* rerun, and the tension of *not knowing anything* had dissipated. They watched the pager with quiet intensity, until it finally beeped to inform them Jaden had been fully prepped and was heading into surgery soon.

"I thought he was already prepped," Quinn had said.

"I guess he was sort of pre-prepped," Carly explained. "There are more things to do once they take him back—give him anesthesia, insert the catheter, that sort of thing."

Quinn nodded and pulled a deck of cards from her bag. "Euchre?"

Carly shook her head briefly. "Not for me, thanks."

Quinn tucked the cards back in her purse. "Wedding planning?"

Carly smiled at her little sister. "That sounds like a good way to pass the time."

Grady slid into the seat next to Quinn, eyes focused on Carly. "How you holding up?"

She nodded.

"He's been pretty upset lately," Grady said. "All this talk of not skiing."

"His doctor said he's done," Carly said.

"Jaden doesn't think so," Grady said. "He's been reading all these articles about athletes with those implantable devices. He's convinced he's coming back."

Carly wasn't surprised. And she was both terrified and proud at the thought. Her kid was no quitter. And yet, what if Dr. Roby was right?

She told Quinn and Grady about Elizabeth Maney. She'd already decided if the swimmer didn't email her back this week, she'd email again. Or find another athlete with Long QT. Elizabeth and Jaden couldn't be the only ones.

"I think it's smart to get another opinion," Quinn said. "You don't want to count him out if you don't have to."

"Yeah, even though the new ski coach has."

Quinn jabbed Grady in the side.

"What did you say?" Carly asked.

"It's nothing," Quinn said.

"Obviously it's not nothing."

Her little sister sighed. "It's not something to be thinking about today." An annoyed look at her fiancé.

Grady's face apologized.

"Now you have to tell me."

"They interviewed the coach," Grady said.

"Who did?"

"The newspaper, Carly. It was dumb. Not even worth reading. And I counted three typos on the same page," Quinn said.

"Great." Carly took out her phone and searched for the *Harbor Pointe Gazette*. Right there on the front page was a bold headline: *Heart Condition Sidelines Harbor Pointe Ski Phenom.* "This is just what he needs."

"Don't count him out," Grady said. "Josh and I have both

been reading about this. I think maybe your doctor is a little senile."

She shook her head, annoyed that everyone was discussing her son's health. Or maybe that she would soon be faced with a choice: take Dr. Roby at his word or find another doctor and say goodbye to that promotion.

The elevator ding drew their attention and Jim and Gloria Dixon strode out.

Over the years, Carly's family had grown and changed, but her dad, Beverly and Quinn had been a constant.

A little less constant had been Josh's side of the family.

Carly's eyes darted to Josh, who sat in a heap across the room. He straightened at the sight of his parents, and the surprised look on his face brought back decades-old memories of the boy she'd wanted so badly to protect all those years ago.

The Dixon family sure had everyone fooled. If she hadn't seen the cigarette burns on the bottoms of Josh's feet or the bruises across his back, she might never have believed anything other than perfection went on in that house.

But she had seen. And she did know. And whenever Josh knocked on the back door, she walked him out to the shed and made sure he was okay.

He made her promise to never tell.

She knew now that some promises weren't meant to be kept.

As he got older, his stays in the shed grew more frequent. He never said much about what triggered his father or even what horrors he saw at home.

He never said much of anything.

And then one night, in middle school, he showed up more spooked than usual.

Carly fetched a clean blanket and pillow from the spare room and met him in the shed. She turned on the flashlight they'd stashed in one of the buckets and Josh quickly turned away.

"Josh—"

Carly rarely asked questions. She knew better.

But he sat in a ball in the corner, shivering and trying not to cry, and one question raced through her mind—*what happened to you?*

Finally, he looked up, holding on to her gaze as if it was the only thing giving him life. "I couldn't protect her."

Carly's skin turned cold, but she said nothing.

"It's all my fault. Dylan. My mom. What else am I going to ruin?"

Carly stilled at the mention of his brother's name. Josh never brought up Dylan—ever. All Carly knew was that Josh had a brother who'd died before they moved to Harbor Pointe, but the information stopped there.

"I tried. I tried to get him to come after me this time. I thought I could take him—I've been working out. I've gotten stronger." Josh stopped trying to stifle his sobs, pulling his legs up to his chest and burying his face in his knees.

Carly knelt down beside him.

"She told me to run, and I did." He cried softly. "I left her."

Carly's mind spun. She'd never known anyone in this situation before. Her home life was far from perfect, but nobody had ever struck her. Even when her father lost his temper, he wouldn't have dreamed of doing something like this.

"I should've stayed."

Carly slowly pulled him close. He sank into her and cried, staining her pajama top with tears.

Moments later, he pulled away and looked at her, eyes fierce. "You can't tell anyone, Carly. No one can know about this."

Carly didn't want to make that promise. Josh and his mom were in danger—shouldn't someone step in and help them?

"She won't leave him, and if he knows I told anyone, it'll just get worse for her, for both of us."

"How do you know she won't leave?"

"I asked her last week," Josh said. "I begged her to get out of there. She said she could never leave him, no matter what."

"But it's not safe," Carly said.

Josh gently wiped his cheeks dry with the sleeve of his jacket.

"Our life would be so much better if he was gone," Josh said.

They were quiet for a tense pause.

"You can't stay there," Carly said.

Josh waited for her attention. "I can handle it. But nobody can know, especially your dad."

Her dad was the sheriff's deputy. Of course Josh didn't want him to know.

"Promise me you won't say anything, Carly." Josh forced her to look at him.

She didn't respond.

"Carly . . ."

"I promise," she finally said, though she wondered if crossies counted. She couldn't imagine keeping this secret any longer.

"I don't need them anymore," he said. "Maybe I should just leave."

"You don't mean that."

He looked at her. "I do too. I don't have a family anymore— not after tonight."

She wrapped an arm around him and watched as he angrily wiped his tears away. "I can be your family now."

Now, looking at Josh across the waiting room, she could see the same trace of fear flashing in his eyes. It was much more subtle than it had been that night, but it was unmistakable, at least to her.

Carly hadn't completely kept the promise she'd made that night. Twice she tried to tell her dad the truth about Josh's father, but both times, Gus told her that his buddy Jim Dixon had to lay down the law with his son because his son was making bad choices. Tough love and all that.

"I've heard all about it, Carly, and I have to say, if Josh was my son, I'd take a heavy hand to his backside myself."

"This isn't discipline, Dad," she'd said. "It's abuse."

"Carly, you're overreacting," he said. "I know Jim myself, and

I know how much it weighs on him that his son is into so much trouble. He's doing the best he can."

Now, here in the waiting room, Josh stiffened, weariness washing across his face. His jaw twitched as he watched his parents stroll into the room like they belonged there. He didn't get up to meet them. He didn't say hello.

Carly drilled him with her glare, but he refused to look at her.

An awkward tension filled the room.

When nobody moved to greet the Dixons, Carly's father filled in the gap. Probably saw rudeness as another one of Josh's shortcomings.

"Jim, Gloria," Gus said warmly, "good of you to come."

Jim stood tall and thick, wide like a freight train. Josh, by comparison, was muscular and athletic, but not quite as solid as his dad. Even now, Carly had to wonder if the son had a chance at overtaking the father.

"We weren't sure Josh would stick around, so we wanted to be here for Jaden," Jim said loudly. His laugh rippled through the room with no place to land.

Gus looked flustered, but he quickly recovered. "We're all just waiting now. Grady went to get some coffee. You want me to have him get you some?"

Jim lifted a hand with a quick shake of his head. "We're fine, but thanks."

Gus nodded, then took a step back as Jim locked eyes onto Josh like a hunter in the wild.

Carly watched as Josh slowly stood, as if waiting for a heavy blow. He started walking, and for a second she thought he might actually speak to his parents, but he bolted out the door without so much as a word.

Confusion crisscrossed the room, and Gloria quickly piped up. "He's just so nervous this morning," she said, as if she knew anything about Josh.

"Is he okay?" Quinn kept her voice low.

Carly glanced at her. "I'm not sure."

"Go see."

Carly didn't want to care. She didn't want to think about how any of this was affecting Josh when it was so clearly destroying her. She wanted to wallow and figure out how to put everything back together once Jaden was out of surgery. She needed a plan of attack. A checklist. Something she could control.

Emotions were messy and feelings tipped her off-kilter, and ever since Josh had returned, she'd been having all the feelings and fighting all the emotions.

For some perplexing reason, her heart had gone back to high school, and she could only think of the boy who'd slept in the garden shed that night and so many other nights before and after.

Scared. Confused. Devastated. Injured.

That boy had needed her. Did he still?

The pager buzzed.

Surgery has started. Jaden is doing well.

She read the update aloud, then sat for several more minutes, turning over options in her mind.

"Go," Quinn said. "It's okay."

Carly quietly slipped into the hallway, leaving her dad to make pleasant conversation with Jim and Gloria Dixon. She clung to the pager, and for a moment she wished everyone who'd come to show their support would show it by leaving them alone.

Of course she didn't mean it, she was so thankful for her family—but she didn't want any of them to see how scared she was.

And she definitely didn't want any of them to notice the web of confusion in her eyes every time she looked at Josh.

She walked down the hallway to an atrium where she spotted him staring out the window overlooking the lake. The atrium was all glass, and the sunshine poured in, filling the space with light.

What did she say? She couldn't tell him she was a ball of confusion. She couldn't tell him that the second she'd closed the door after he left that morning, she'd slid to the ground and cried for five minutes straight.

And she certainly couldn't tell him that his prayer had nicked the lining around her heart, giving her anger a place to escape.

She knew Josh. She needed to remember that. He was a man who couldn't stick. A man who ran. A man she could not rely on.

People didn't change, no matter how much you wanted them to. Her mother had left them and never returned. She went off and found herself a new family and a new life without so much as a glance in the rearview mirror.

And yet . . . was it wrong to hope?

She shoved the thought aside.

He didn't move when she approached. He didn't move when she slid into the spot right next to him. He didn't move when she let out a tense breath, inadvertently fogging up the window.

Was he off in another world? Maybe a world where he was a kid hiding bruises and making up reasons he couldn't participate in gym class?

What happened to you?

She stared out the window, looking out across the lake, gaze landing on a brightly colored sailboat a little way from the shore.

Her mind spun, searching for something to say. Her relationship with Josh was tenuous, but she was the one who knew the truth about Josh's past. She was the one who knew that he wasn't simply an ungrateful son who didn't respect his parents.

Regardless of what anger she still carried toward Josh, she didn't wish this kind of pain on him.

Be careful.

The words rang out in her head like a warning shot, and she swatted them away, inching toward Josh.

Still, he didn't move, didn't even acknowledge she was there.

Slowly, unsteadily, she slid her hand into his, uncertain if he would respond. Seconds ticked by and she wondered if she'd made a mistake. Maybe he really did want to be alone. Maybe she should go back to the waiting room and let him stew out here by himself.

But then his hand tightened around hers as if to say, *Don't go.*

And it sent a sizzle straight through her spine.

As was often the case all those years ago, Josh said nothing. She said nothing. They simply stood in silence, together, both of them wishing things were different.

Chapter Twenty-One

"Can I show you something?" Carly asked.

He didn't look at her. Couldn't. She knew too much.

"Come on. It's not doing either of us any good to sit around here." She gave his hand a tug toward the elevator. When he followed, she let go.

He felt the absence of her skin on his instantly.

She pushed the Up button on the elevator and waited.

"Where are we going?" he asked, wishing he wasn't depressing and morose at the moment. He'd vowed to be strong for her, but here he was, anything but.

She tossed him a sideways glance. "You'll see."

The elevator took them up, and when the doors opened they were in a glass atrium on the roof.

"A few years ago, someone donated a lot of money to the hospital." Carly exited the elevator, pushed open the atrium door and drew in a deep breath.

He followed her out onto the roof.

"It's a prayer garden," she said.

Josh stood at the end of a path and an indescribable peace washed over him, the kind he hadn't felt in years.

"Think of all the people who've come up here to pray," she said. "We're just standing in the midst of all of it."

The path stretched out in front of him, brick pavers set into pea gravel, and on either side were plants and flowers neatly arranged for the most visually stunning display. Small stone benches lined the path and also had been strategically placed for maximum privacy, hidden in small alcoves surrounded by bushes. Up ahead was a bronze statue of Jesus surrounded by children.

"It's my favorite spot in the hospital," she said.

"You come here to pray?"

She shrugged. "Don't do as much of that as I should."

He followed her out onto the brick pavers.

"Jaden, though, he prays a lot," she said. "At least he did. I don't know how all of this is affecting his faith."

Josh had wondered that too. "He's pretty solid."

She stopped and looked at him. "But he's never faced anything like this. What if . . . ?" Her voice trailed off, the unasked question lingering.

He wanted to wrap his arms around her and tell her everything was going to be okay. Wanted to be the source of strength she needed right now, but something stopped him.

"What if what?"

She turned away. "What if Dr. Roby is right? What if he can't ski after this?"

"I thought we were waiting until we hear back from the swimmer. I'm not giving up on this, Carly."

"You might not be, but everyone else is."

"What are you talking about?"

She took her phone out, clicked it open and scrolled. "This." She handed him the phone. Josh read the headline of an article in the *Harbor Pointe Gazette*.

He skimmed the article, a few keywords jumping out at him. *Career-ending heart condition. Injured players can't compete. Don't want to risk further injury. Won't be a part of the team this year.*

"They interviewed Dr. Roby," Carly said. "Of course he said

nothing specifically about Jaden, but he had plenty to say about Long QT."

His blood curdled. "They're already counting him out?"

Carly looked away. "No coach is going to go against the doctor's advice."

"Don't these reporters do any of their own research? One Google search and I knew there were conflicting ideas about this."

Carly took the phone back and stuck it in her pocket. "His coach is new this year. Doesn't even know Jaden yet. But he's got his mind made up."

"Well, that's not going to happen," Josh said. "He's not sitting out next year. Not if it's safe anyway."

A tight line of worry stretched across Carly's forehead.

"I'll take care of it," he said, thankful for something to focus on—something that gave him a hint of purpose.

He turned back toward the elevators, leaving her standing there at the center of a prayer garden, but before he hit the button he turned back to find her eyes intent on him.

In another time, he might've walked straight back to her, folded her into his arms and kissed her senseless. Instead, he gave her a resolute nod, pushed the button and got into the open elevator without another word.

* * *

Josh hadn't been in Harbor Pointe High School for years, but if there was ever a reason to go back, this was it.

The new coach of Jaden's high school ski team didn't have all the facts, but that hadn't stopped him from making a decision that would severely affect Jaden's recovery.

Josh strolled into the main office and found a heavyset woman with dark hair cut severely at her chin sitting behind the desk. She glanced up and her eyes widened at the sight of him. "Good morning, handsome." She smiled. "Can I help you?"

"Here to see the ski coach. A guy named—"

"Ted Myers," she interrupted. "It's summer around here. Most of the teachers and coaches aren't keeping regular office hours. But I can give him a message."

"Do you have a number for him or something?" Josh asked.

"I'm sorry, sir, I can't give out that information."

The door to the office swung open and Cole strolled in. The woman behind the counter stood. "Hello there, Coach Turner. Been hearing great things about your team this year. And about you."

Josh did a slow turn toward Cole, doing nothing to hide his amusement at this woman's blatant admiration for his friend.

"Thanks, Joni. They're shaping up," Cole said. He stuck a hand out toward Josh. "Saw you through the window. Shouldn't you be at the hospital?"

Josh shook his friend's hand and glanced back at Joni, who clearly only had eyes for Cole. "Got a bone to pick with the ski coach."

"The article?"

Josh nodded toward the door and Cole tipped his ball cap toward Joni. "See ya later," he said, following Josh out into the hallway.

"What do you know about this guy?" Josh asked.

"Nothing," Cole said. "He's new."

"I don't know much, but I know Jaden's pretty good on the slopes. How can he just write the kid off without any facts?"

"Calm down, slugger," Cole said. "Nobody's writing anyone off."

"The article said the coach isn't relying on Jaden to get the team where they need to go this year because with his current medical condition, it is unlikely the former phenom will ever be able to compete again."

"Did you memorize it?"

"Look, the guy doesn't have all the facts. I've done a lot of research, and there are lots of athletes competing with Jaden's condition."

"The doctor said—"

"Doctors can be wrong. Even good ones." Josh shoved his hands in his pockets and caught a glimpse of Joni, inside the office, craning her neck for a better look at Cole. "What's her story?"

Cole glanced at her then back at Josh, moving him farther down the hall and out of Joni's line of sight. "She's got a crush. So much worse now that Gemma left and I stopped wearing my wedding ring."

"I think it's cute," Josh teased.

Cole rolled his eyes.

"I just want to have a little chat with Ted. Do you know where he lives?"

"That's a bad idea," Cole said. "Coaches hate that stuff. Just wait and see how it all plays out."

"Look, I'm sitting over in that hospital staring at the wall. I need to do something. And Jaden needs a coach who believes he'll be strong enough to compete this year."

"It's months away, dude," Cole said. "There's time for all that."

"Just tell me where to find the guy, would ya? I just want to explain a few things that the doctor left out."

"He's in the athletic office," Cole said after a long pause.

"Now?"

"Yeah, we have a fundraising meeting."

"Why didn't you say so?"

"Because you look like you're about to do something stupid," Cole said.

"I just want to talk to the guy—give me some credit." He turned on his heel and walked down the hall toward the gym, where the athletic director's office was.

Josh followed Cole into a small room where three men were seated, one behind a desk. That one stood as soon as they passed through the door.

"Turner," he said. "Good practice this morning?"

"Yes, sir," Cole said. "Boys are strong this year."

"Strong enough for a state title?"

"Think maybe so, sir," Cole said.

The man behind the desk looked at Josh.

"JR, you remember Josh Dixon."

"Josh Dixon—as I live and breathe." JR stuck his hand out toward Josh, then looked at the other guys in the room. "One of the best receivers I've ever seen, this guy."

JR Houston had been a year ahead of Josh and Cole in high school—the quarterback they all looked up to.

"Josh, this is Bilby and Ted." Cole motioned toward the other two guys in the room.

"What brings you back here?" JR asked.

"My kid's having surgery today," Josh said. "Came to talk to the ski coach." He looked at Ted. "That's you?"

Ted stood. "It is."

"You gave an interview in the newspaper. Said Jaden wouldn't be reliable this year—that he wouldn't be strong enough to play."

"With a heart condition?" Ted laughed. "Is that far-fetched?"

"You don't know my son," Josh said. "Or his condition."

Ted's eyes narrowed. "The doctor was pretty clear."

"The doctor was wrong." Josh didn't know that for sure, but at the moment, it didn't matter. He'd decided it was true.

"Josh just wants to make sure you'll give him a fair shake," Cole said. "Jaden's our strongest skier by a long shot."

"Oh, I know all about Jaden," Ted said. "Been training with Grady Benson."

"That's right."

"He's a family member or something? Isn't that right?"

"He's an Olympic gold medalist," Josh said.

"Doesn't matter a bit to me," Ted said. "When we start practice, all the guys are the same. They all have to prove themselves to earn their spot."

"Well, telling the newspaper a bunch of garbage about Jaden's condition isn't going to do much for his morale, Ted," Josh said.

"All I'm asking is you stop talking to reporters when you don't have the first clue what you're talking about."

"Now, Josh." JR stuck out his hand as if to calm him down.

"I had a long conversation with Dr. Roby—".

"Look, Coach," Josh cut in, "skiing is the most important thing in Jaden's life. He plans to get back to it once he's recovered —and quotes like the ones you gave the paper, they aren't going to help. That's all I'm saying."

"That's fair." Ted crossed his arms over his chest. "But the doctor made it clear—"

"He's not the only doctor with an opinion."

"I understand," Ted said. "In that case, I hope Jaden makes a full recovery."

"He will."

But even as he said it, his resolve wavered and an unwanted thought filtered through his mind. *What if he doesn't?*

"We'll keep him in our prayers, Josh," JR said, his words meant to dismiss Josh.

"And keep him out of the newspapers." Josh shot a pointed look at Ted.

Cole clapped a hand on Josh's shoulder. "I'll walk Josh out and be right back, fellas."

Josh reluctantly left the office.

"What was that?" Cole asked when they were in the hallway.

"What was what?"

"You're losing it, man."

Josh pushed his hands over his face and into his hair. "I hate this. I can't fix it. I can't do anything to help."

Cole stood in front of him. "Go back to the hospital and be there for your kid. That's what you can do."

Josh looked away. "He's gonna be okay, right?"

Emotion registered on Cole's face. It was stupid to ask. His friend had even less information than Josh did.

"I hope so, man," Cole said.

Yeah, but right now Josh needed more than empty wishes. He needed to offer Carly and Jaden more than that.

He pushed through the front doors of the high school and out into the parking lot, wondering why God allowed bad things to happen to kids like Jaden—kids who believed so strongly that he was good.

And wondering if he'd ever get used to feeling as helpless as he felt right now.

Chapter Twenty-Two

C arly's phone rang, disrupting the quiet of the hospital waiting room.

She saw a number registered to East Lansing. *Michigan State.*

"Hello?"

"Mrs. Collins?" A female voice on the other side. "It's Elizabeth Maney. You emailed me."

"Yes, hi, Elizabeth. Thank you for calling."

"Is this an okay time?"

"I'm in the waiting room. Jaden's in surgery now."

"Oh," she said. "I can call back."

"No," Carly said, strolling out into the hallway. "I need the distraction."

She pushed the Up button on the elevator.

"I wanted to call and see how I could help put your mind at ease," Elizabeth said—*God bless her.*

Carly explained the situation, including Dr. Roby's advice that Jaden give up skiing completely. "I'm sure you can relate to how devastating that would be for him."

"I can," she said. "And I think things have changed in recent years. Lots of athletes with Long QT are still competing, most with ICDs."

Carly's heart turned a circle.

"They've done numerous studies and found that it's perfectly safe," Elizabeth said. "Otherwise—believe me—my parents would not let me keep swimming." She laughed. "Why don't I text you the name of my doctor? Just so you can get a second opinion?"

A second opinion. An opinion that went against one of the top doctors in the hospital where she worked. Carly's heart fluttered. She should accept what Dr. Roby said—he could easily shift his weight and get her promoted (or not).

But Jaden meant more to her than any job.

"I'd appreciate that," she told Elizabeth.

They chatted a few more minutes about Elizabeth's condition and recovery and then Carly hung up the phone. Seconds later Elizabeth shared her doctor's contact information with Carly via text. Seconds after that, another text came in:

Let me know when Jaden's back on the slopes. I'd love to meet him and you.

Well, that sealed it. Elizabeth Maney was Carly's favorite person in the world.

Because she had single-handedly filled Carly with something she was greatly lacking—*hope*.

* * *

Carly tried calling Josh, but there was no answer.

Where was he?

His voicemail clicked on. "Josh, I just got a page. He's done. The surgery is finished. He'll be waking up soon, and you promised him you'd be there." She paused. "Where'd you go?"

She sat in a small room alone, waiting for the surgeon to come in and give her a full report.

She texted Josh. *Hurry up and get back here, Josh. I'm getting ready to meet with the surgeon.*

Moments later, the door opened and Dr. Roby walked in. He smiled. "Carly." He shook her hand. "He did great."

Carly exhaled all the fear and worry she'd been holding inside, which was more than she'd realized. "Oh, that's so good to hear."

"Everything went the way it was supposed to. The device has been implanted, and that should prevent any other episodes. It'll keep his heart on track."

"And what are the risks now? I read about implanted devices malfunctioning?"

The doctor nodded. "It does happen, but it's rare. We'll go over all of that with him, make sure he knows what's normal— and what's not."

She paused. "Dr. Roby, I've been doing some research." She left out the part about it being on the internet. Doctors hated that. "I've just spoken with a college swimmer from MSU. She has the same condition and device that Jaden has, but she's still swimming."

His brow furrowed. "That's not advisable."

"Well, I've read several articles and the consensus seems to be that it's perfectly safe for athletes with ICDs to return to their sport."

Dr. Roby bristled. "Miss Collins, I understand this is difficult for Jaden—and for you—"

"No, sir, it's not difficult. It's devastating." Carly hugged her purse to her chest. "You don't understand what skiing means to my son. Or how it's changed his life."

"But I do understand that he has a unique condition," the doctor said. "In my expert opinion, Jaden should find something less strenuous to be passionate about." He'd stressed the words *expert opinion* so slightly she almost didn't hear it. It was pointless. He had his mind made up.

She stood. "Can I see him?"

"Yes," Dr. Roby said coolly. "He's in recovery now. The nurse will take you down. I'll be by to check on him in the morning." He walked away.

Carly couldn't be certain, but if she had to guess she'd say all her questions had just landed her at the bottom of the candidate pool for the unit manager position.

She pulled out her phone. No new messages.

Same old Josh.

A frizzy-haired nurse Carly didn't know led her to a large room that had been sectioned off by curtains. "He's just in here." She pulled the curtain back and revealed Carly's still-asleep son on a bed next to a technician who was running some post-op tests.

The tech's name was Aaron, and Carly had met him a few times. He looked up at her and smiled. "Heard we got to work on your son today."

"How's he doing?"

"He's doing really well," Aaron said. "He's going to be groggy, maybe a little nauseous. You know the drill."

She did. She knew some people came out of surgery nauseous and vomiting while others felt tired and run down. She prayed Jaden wouldn't be sick, that he'd bounce back like a champ, and —one more time for good measure—that his father would show up.

He'd promised.

Josh, you promised.

"You can talk to him if you want to," Aaron said.

She set her bag down and took Jaden's hand. Her son lay limply under the covers, slack-jawed and breathing heavily. She perched on the edge of the bed.

"Jaden?"

She almost didn't want to wake him—she wanted to give Josh more time to come through. He'd done everything he'd said he would do the last few weeks—why now, on the most important day they'd had in years, had he chosen to go MIA?

But Jaden stirred. His eyes dragged open and he pulled in a breath. "Hey."

"Hey, kiddo," Carly said with a smile.

Jaden pressed his lips together and made a smacking noise with his mouth. "So dry."

"That's normal, buddy," Aaron said. He clicked around on a machine. "How are you feeling otherwise?"

Jaden closed his eyes. "Nauseous."

Aaron looked at Carly. "We'll get him something for that."

She nodded, then turned her attention back to her son. "You did great, Jay. Dr. Roby said everything went just like it was supposed to."

"Throat's sore."

Aaron nodded. "From the tube. It'll feel raw for a little while."

Jaden nodded slowly, letting them know he'd heard. "Where's Dad?"

Carly's own mouth went dry then. Years of practice should've given her plenty of excuses for where her ex was in that moment, yet she had nothing. No good reason for him to be missing.

She thought back to the way he'd reacted when his parents had shown up in the waiting room. Had something happened to set him off?

Even still, it shouldn't have been enough to make him disappear.

Why do you always leave when we need you most?

"He, um, he left for a bit," Carly said.

Jaden's eyes fluttered open. "Where?"

She squeezed his hand. "Why don't we concentrate on you?"

"Is he gone?"

What was she supposed to say? She didn't know. He'd seen the article and taken off. Carly could only imagine where he'd gone.

"Mom?"

Her eyes clouded. "I'm not sure."

Jaden swallowed slowly. "Something must've happened."

She couldn't mention the article—it would upset Jaden to know his new coach had no faith in him at all.

His eyes were closed, but a tear slid down Jaden's cheek. A lump expanded in her throat at the sight of it, and in that moment, she realized it was back—the ball of anger she'd been carrying around since the day Josh had walked out of their lives.

She wasn't going to give him the benefit of the doubt. Maybe he'd had it out with his father. Maybe he was upset about the circumstances. Maybe he ran for coffee and got sidetracked.

But he'd made a *promise* to their son.

And he broke it.

And that was the bottom line.

"I've got about all I need here," Aaron said. "We're going to take him up to his room now. I'd recommend giving him a little time before visitors show up."

She nodded. Too much commotion wouldn't be good for him.

And she could honestly use the peace and quiet herself.

She sent a quick text to her family:

He's awake and doing well. Doctor wants to let him recover for a few hours before he has visitors. I can call when you can all come back to see him.

Quinn texted back: *Okay, we'll head out for a little while, but let us know if you need anything.*

How about an ex who did what he said he was going to do?

Will do.

* * *

Josh returned to the hospital. He wished he had better news after confronting the coach, but all he had was the hope that the man would keep his mouth shut and give Jaden a fair shake.

Maybe it would be enough to ease Carly's worried mind.

He took his key fob from the drink holder and picked up his phone, which had been surprisingly silent all morning.

He clicked it on.

Oh no.

189

He had two missed calls from Carly, a voicemail and three text messages. He scanned these quickly, eyes settling on the last one.

Jaden's asking for you. Are you coming back soon?

He closed his eyes and let out a heavy sigh.

He'd put his phone on silent that morning at the hospital and forgotten to take it off.

He'd promised he'd be there when the kid woke up—he never should've left. He'd let them down again. Sure, it was a small thing, but to Carly, it was proof that he hadn't changed.

Even though he had. Even though he'd been trying to do something for Jaden. Would she understand that?

He exited the car and strode toward the front door.

Only one way to find out.

Chapter Twenty-Three

Carly was mad. And no matter what Josh said, she was going to stay that way.

She didn't care what he'd gone out to do—whatever it was could've waited until after Jaden had woken up.

There had been fleeting moments in which she wondered if they could be some cobbled-together version of a family again.

But this? Maybe it was the wake-up call she needed. The reminder that Josh had some serious flaws.

These were the thoughts racing through her mind when the door opened and Josh walked into the room. He looked windblown and terrified.

She said nothing.

He glanced at Jaden, who'd just fallen back to sleep, the anesthesia not yet out of his system. "How's he doing?"

A pile of snarky comebacks pelted her mind.

You'd know if you'd bothered to stick around being the gist of all of them.

She must've waited too long to reply because he turned toward her then. "Carly?" He sat on the sofa bed next to her chair. "I'm so sorry I wasn't here."

She stared at him, waiting for an explanation that didn't

come. Her skin tingled, the way it always did when she was angry or anxious or frustrated. She bet her neck was all splotchy too, a tattletale to her emotions.

She never could hide her feelings from him.

He sighed, then raked a hand through his hair. "It was stupid. I shouldn't have left. I just wanted to do something—to fix something."

"Where did you go?"

But before he could respond, Jaden stirred, drawing their attention.

Carly rushed to his side. "Hey, kiddo."

Jaden took a second to swallow, then opened his eyes. Josh now stood a few inches behind her, and Jaden's eyes focused on his father. Carly braced herself for the anger their son was likely feeling, and prepared to tell Josh to go. He was upsetting Jaden and right now, they needed to do everything they could to make sure their son didn't have extra stress.

But Jaden didn't lash out. He didn't even frown. A smile crawled across his tired face. "Dad."

Carly stiffened as Josh moved closer and took Jaden's outstretched hand. "I'm here, kid," he said.

So am I, she wanted to say. *And I have been for sixteen years.*

"I'm sorry I wasn't here when you woke up," Josh said.

Surely Jaden wasn't going to buy this apologetic father act.

But Jaden did buy it. He flicked the air as if to wave the whole idea of an apology away. "Glad you're here now."

And that was it. No punishment. No making his father pay for disappointing him.

Carly pressed her lips together to keep from saying something she would regret. This was about Jaden, and so far, her son seemed perfectly fine with Josh's broken promise.

She shifted away from Josh, who let go of Jaden's hand. "Do you need anything to eat or drink? Can I do anything for you?"

He looked so earnest, as if he really wanted to help, but Carly reminded herself that he could not be trusted.

Trusting him had been one of her life's greatest mistakes.

A barrage of visitors began, including her family, her father's friends, and—thankfully—several members of the high school ski team.

She was so grateful to see so many people there to love on her son, and then Ian Dobson brought up the newspaper article and Carly's gratitude came to a screeching halt.

"You'll show that lame Coach Myers, Jay, don't even worry about it," Ian said. "We all know you're gonna make a comeback."

"What are you talking about?" Jaden asked.

"You know, the article. So dumb. That guy hasn't even seen you ski yet."

Jaden frowned, then looked at Carly, who searched her mind for something productive to say.

"I talked to the coach today," Josh said.

He did?

"Explained a little bit about your condition. He's hoping you make a full recovery."

"He was just going off what your doctor said anyway," Ian said. "Like, that you're done skiing or whatever."

"That's not exactly what the doctor said, Ian—" Josh started to say, but Jaden quickly interrupted.

"My doctor told Coach Myers I can't ski?" Jaden looked like someone had punched him in the gut. "So now Coach thinks I'm, like, an invalid?"

"Who cares what he thinks?" Ian said, then called the coach a name.

"Language," Josh said. "He's still your coach, so give the guy some respect."

Carly couldn't help but think it was strange to hear Josh doling out fatherly advice. Even stranger that she agreed with it.

But the damage had been done. It didn't matter that the doctor hadn't gone into detail about Jaden. It was enough that he'd made his *expert opinion* about Long QT very well known.

Jaden's face had clouded over and his entire mood had changed.

"Hey, Ian, I think maybe we need to let Jaden get some rest," Carly said kindly.

"Sure thing, Mrs. C."

She didn't bother explaining that "Missus" was what you called married women. She was pretty sure Ian didn't care.

He left, and Carly stole a quick look at Josh, who appeared to be just as worried as she was.

"Look, Jaden," she said, "the coach doesn't know much about your condition. Let's not jump to any conclusions."

"You read the article, right?" Jaden's eyes drilled into her.

She nodded.

"They said I'm done?"

"It doesn't matter, kid," Carly said. "I know you've been reading up on this. And your dad and I have been doing some research on our own too."

"And?"

She wasn't planning to tell him anything. False hope and all that. So why did she hear herself say, "I talked to a collegiate swimmer today. Elizabeth Maney. She's also got Long QT Syndrome *and* she has an ICD." Carly could feel two pairs of eyes on her. "And she's still competing."

"Seriously?" Jaden's eyes brightened.

"You didn't tell me that," Josh said.

"You weren't here." Carly snapped the response without thinking.

Josh looked away.

"So, what did she say?" Jaden asked.

Carly filled them in on the details of her conversation with Elizabeth, ending with, "I have the name of her doctor. I already called and left him a message."

"Even if I can still compete, they start training next week," Jaden said. "I'm already behind."

"So, you'll have a little extra work to do," Josh said. "The season doesn't start for months. Isn't that better than not being able to compete at all?"

God, please. Don't take this away from him.

She wasn't sure who her son would be if he couldn't ski.

"I just want to sleep for a while." Jaden closed his eyes, dismissing them.

After about twenty minutes, he was in a medically assisted slumber, and she was in the room alone, with Josh.

"You went and talked to the coach?" she whispered over the beeping of one of Jaden's monitors.

"Yeah." Josh sat down in a shiny leather chair on the opposite side of the bed. "It's why I was late getting back here."

The protective wall around her heart cracked, causing a tiny web of fissures.

"You saw his face," Josh said. "I had to do something." He looked at her. "You talked to the swimmer?"

"Yeah. Really nice girl. I was so grateful she got back to me."

Her eyes fell to her sleeping son, looking a little like the toddler she'd sung to sleep so many times, and she prayed—earnestly and fervently—that this whole thing would be a setback but not a roadblock.

* * *

Carly looked uncomfortable on the makeshift sleeper sofa, but that didn't stop him from wondering how soft her skin would feel underneath his fingers.

Nurses were in and out of Jaden's room, checking his vitals, giving him pain medication and making sure their son was recovering as he was supposed to.

Carly understood everything happening in front of them. It wasn't a surprise to her when Jaden woke up feeling nauseous again and they had to give him more Zofran.

Josh, on the other hand, understood nothing.

He spent the night half-sleeping upright in the chair while Carly dozed softly on the uncomfortable sofa.

Around three in the morning, she rolled over and found him, eyes open, blankly staring at the muted TV screen. He wouldn't tell her he'd also found himself blankly staring at her off and on throughout the night, and every time he did, he begged God to help him figure out a way to make up for his broken promises.

He *had* changed—he knew he had. So why was he still finding ways to mess everything up?

"You're still here," she whispered.

He adjusted the thin hospital blanket on his lap. The light of the television flickered, spilling a faint blue over the room. "Yeah."

"You should go home and get some sleep," she said.

He found her eyes, faintly illuminated, and said, "I'm not leaving again."

A world of weight hung behind those words, and he knew she felt it too.

"One of us should be awake tomorrow," she said.

"Are you having trouble sleeping?"

She inched up on the nearly flat pillow and nodded. "I wake up every time they come in."

"Darn nurses," he said, hoping to lighten the heaviness between them.

Her mouth quirked up in the slightest smile.

He went back to flipping through the channels, loathing cable television and longing for Netflix or Hulu.

Infomercial. Infomercial. A dubbed-in-English foreign Kung Fu movie (that, let's be honest, he would've watched if Carly were still sleeping).

She gasped. "No way."

His thumb hovered over the button on the remote as the familiar image of old Converse sneakers walking across a run-down baseball diamond rolled across the screen.

His eyes darted to hers.

She looked at him and smiled. "What are the odds?"

"All we need is the popcorn."

With the sound off, he could only imagine the song that played under this particular scene. He remembered it well because he'd looked it up as a kid and added it to the playlist on his iPod.

The room went quiet as a posse of baseball players, decked out in real baseball uniforms, rode their bikes onto the shabby field. How many times had they watched *The Sandlot* in Carly's living room as kids?

They'd spent so many years loving each other without even realizing it.

Carly giggled, then whispered the exact insult Porter yelled across the field.

Josh responded with the insult hurled back by the ball-playing bully.

"You play ball like a GIRL!" Carly hissed, then they both erupted in laughter.

They finished out the scene, then the screen blackened and a commercial came on. It felt good to joke around with her, and he wished every drop of tension between them would disappear.

He glanced at her, photographing her smile in his mind. He'd missed it.

She found his eyes and it faded, gone as quickly as it came, as if she'd only just remembered she didn't like him, as if there was no way she was letting go of her anger toward him.

Two steps forward, three steps back.

She looked away.

The light from the TV flickered.

The hum of the machines surrounding Jaden's bed was the only disruption to the silence in the room.

"I'm really sorry, Carly," he whispered. "For not being here."

Slowly, her eyes found his.

He wanted to confide in her. To tell her it messed him up to be back here, to see his parents still stuck in this same holding pattern he'd lived in for so many years. He wanted to tell her he was terrified of something happening to Jaden—to her—something he couldn't control. He wanted to tell her all the real reasons he'd left sixteen years ago, to make her understand why he had to go.

He wanted to, but he didn't. He wouldn't make any excuses for breaking that promise. He'd put his feelings above it, and he knew that was really what stood between them now.

And when Carly rolled over and laid back down, he was pretty sure he'd never get a second chance.

Chapter Twenty-Four

T he following morning, Carly awoke to the sound of Dr. Roby's voice.

The light filtered in through the blinds. What time was it?

Josh stood next to Jaden's bed, showered and in clean clothes. Had he even had an hour of sleep?

After his apology—too heartfelt for her heart to bear—she'd lain awake for at least another hour, reminding herself of how it felt when he broke his promises.

At some point, she'd drifted back to sleep, and now she was late waking up and Josh was here looking like Super-Dad.

He glanced at her. "You're awake."

I'm still mad at you. The Sandlot changes nothing.

Jaden lifted a hand to wave at her.

She stood, wishing she'd showered and changed already.

Dr. Roby was examining Jaden's incision, something Josh, she noticed, wouldn't look at. He'd always been squeamish around blood. Seeing the stitches holding their son's skin together was probably a step above what he could handle.

Carly, on the other hand, had seen these kinds of wounds hundreds of times. She just didn't like seeing one on her own son.

"How are you feeling?" she asked.

He gave her a thumbs-up, but his eyes were still sagged with grogginess.

"Everything looks good." Dr. Roby reaffixed the bandage to Jaden's chest. "I think you're going to get to go home today."

Jaden gave another thumbs-up.

"What does his recovery look like?" Josh asked.

Carly decided not to point out that if Josh had been there yesterday, he would have at least a small idea of the recovery process, and instead chose to let the doctor talk. Truth was, she'd researched every detail of this procedure and in that moment, she'd forgotten everything she'd learned.

"You might have some soreness and bruising today," Dr. Roby said. "We'll give you something for that."

Jaden nodded.

"I know we already discussed this, but it bears repeating," the doctor continued. "No strenuous exercise for four weeks. You're going to want to avoid even lifting your hands over your head for a couple of weeks. You've got to give yourself time to heal."

Jaden blew out a frustrated breath, undoubtedly thinking about the ski team, the coach and a newspaper article he hadn't even read yet.

"I don't want you lifting anything heavy for a few weeks either, so that'll get you out of helping around the house." The doctor's joke fell flat. "Will he have someone to help while he recovers?"

She looked at Josh, trying to ignore the overwhelming feeling of gratitude that he was supporting them for the month so she could be there for Jaden. She didn't like feeling indebted to him, and she easily could've argued that he owed them at least that much, but she knew he didn't have to do that, and she *was* grateful.

She couldn't imagine going off to work while her son was at home recovering.

"Yes," Carly said. "I'm going to take some time off of work."

"And I'm sticking around," Josh said. "I'll get back to Chicago once Jaden's recovered."

"Great. Get him outside. Go on short walks this week. Wait a day or two before showering, and cover the wound completely. He'll be back to normal in no time."

"And then we'll hit the slopes," Jaden said.

Dr. Roby raised a brow. "Son, we've been over this. I'm afraid skiing is not in your future."

"I spoke with a doctor in East Lansing this morning." Josh looked at Carly. "Sorry, he called back when you were sleeping so I answered."

"Oh?" Dr. Roby clicked his pen and stuck it in the chest pocket on his white coat.

"He said it's outdated thinking that ICDs prevent athletes from participating in sports. We've got an appointment with him in a couple of weeks."

"Josh—" Carly could feel her promotion slipping straight through her fingers.

"Very good," Dr. Roby said. "I'll be in touch to check in, and you let me know if you have any other questions."

He seemed to force a smile before leaving the room.

The door opened seconds later and David, dressed in a pair of khakis, a button-down, tie and white coat, walked in. She imagined David standing in front of the mirror at the gym, carefully combing and gelling every hair neatly in place.

Carly ran her hands through her own hair as if that could somehow make her seem more put together and not at all like a person who'd just woken up five minutes ago.

David's eyes jumped from Jaden to Josh to Carly, and then he turned awkward. "Good morning. I came to check on the patient."

Jaden said nothing. Josh said nothing. Carly quickly stood and moved toward him, while Josh took her spot on the opposite side of Jaden's bed.

"That was nice of you," she said. She looked at her own attire, a pair of flannel Christmas pajama pants and an old gray T-shirt. "I look like a mess."

He smiled at her. "You look cute."

She could practically *feel* her son and his father rolling their eyes.

"Do you want to step out into the hallway?" she asked.

He nodded toward Josh and Jaden, then turned and led Carly out of the room, but once they were out there, she realized she didn't have much to say.

"Heard things went well," he said. "I would've been by sooner, but I worked late."

"Oh, that's okay. It's nice of you to come by," she said.

David nodded, seeming to search for another conversation topic, and she didn't fault him for coming up empty. The situation was strange, what with Josh in the next room and her attention now solely on her son's recovery.

"I should probably get back," she said.

"Of course." He took a step away from her. "Should I call you?"

She pressed her lips together and looked up at him. She'd been lamenting Josh's inability to follow through, and she had a feeling that would never be an issue with a man like David. He was, now that she thought about it, the exact opposite of Josh. He was focused and driven and reliable. He could bring much-needed stability to her life, and she couldn't deny she'd been craving that.

Josh, on the other hand, couldn't keep a simple promise and show up when he said he would.

Though, an argument could be made that his reasons were well intentioned. But that wouldn't justify the anger she was so desperately trying to hold on to.

"I'd like that," she said.

He reached out and put a hand on her arm, patted it twice, nodded and walked away, leaving Carly feeling like she'd just been dismissed by a rich uncle.

Chapter Twenty-Five

Text message from Dara Dempsey to Carly:

I'm so sorry, Carly. I'm not supposed to say anything, but I guess they've hired my replacement. They went with someone external. I don't know what happened. I really thought you were a shoo-in.

* * *

The smell of coffee lured Josh from slumber.

His eyes fluttered open and it took him a minute to piece together the events of the night before. He hadn't slept at all in the hospital, so when they got Jaden home and settled in the recliner with a fresh dose of pain meds, it took almost no time at all for Josh to nod off on the couch.

Someone had covered him with a knitted afghan and he couldn't be sure, but he thought he might've fallen asleep with his shoes on. They were now on the floor next to the couch.

He sat up and ran his hands over his face, then saw Jaden, still sleeping peacefully in the chair. At this point, sleep was probably the best thing for him.

He stood and shuffled into the kitchen, where Carly stood in pajamas, hair in a bun on top of her head, her perfect skin practically glowing.

She gave him a once-over. "You look rough."

He nodded toward the coffee. "Did you make enough for me?"

She hesitated, then opened the cupboard and took out a second mug. The coffeemaker beeped, and she poured two cups. "Can you grab the cream from the fridge?"

He opened the refrigerator door and found three casserole dishes, something that looked like a dessert, two Tupperwares and a cake. "What's all this?"

"The neighbors and Beverly," she said.

He had to shift things around to find the creamer, but he pulled it out and handed it to her. "That was nice."

"Your mom brought muffins."

Had he slept through that? "When?"

She shrugged. "It was all in the refrigerator when we got home. I'm thinking Quinn must've organized it."

"Ah."

She stirred cream into both cups of coffee and handed one to him.

"Have you called your mom?" she asked.

He took a sip of the hot drink and wished she hadn't asked that question. Maybe he should've called them, but he hadn't. He shook his head.

"You should call her, Josh."

He inhaled and leaned back on the counter. "Probably."

"Was it hard seeing them yesterday?"

He shrugged. They weren't doing this now. He wasn't going to talk about his parents.

"They show up to things sometimes. Birthday parties, that sort of thing."

"As long as you never leave him alone with my dad."

"I would never," she said. "I promised you that."

There was that word again—*promise.* She'd kept her promises. He hadn't. Was that what she was thinking too?

Josh stared at the mocha-colored drink in his mug. "Does Jaden know?"

He could feel Carly go still across the room. "No."

He looked at her. "Does anyone?"

She shook her head.

After a beat, she picked up her mug and took a sip. "Do you think it's still going on?"

Josh hoped not. All these years he'd been gone, he'd done his best to make sure his mom knew she always had a way out—he'd be her escape. But maybe his father had outgrown his temper? Or maybe his mother had learned how to keep the man from getting too riled?

Maybe Josh had been the source of all their problems to begin with?

Carly had never wanted to keep his family's secret. She'd begged him to come talk to her father, or at least to Beverly, but Josh had refused. He knew nothing would come of it—his father would talk his way around the truth, and then take his anger out on his mom and Josh. It wasn't worth it.

But now, he wondered if he should've told someone.

Of course he should've. Hindsight is always 20/20.

Was it too late for that? Could he convince his mom to leave now? Circumstances had changed—Josh could find her a house or an apartment or let her come stay with him for a while.

"Thanks for letting me crash on your couch," he said, anxious to change the subject.

She looked away. "Thank Jaden. It was his idea."

Josh felt like a tire that had just been slashed, all the air oozing out in a hot, hissy stream. "Well, thanks for not overriding him."

"Maybe you should leave and come back," she said. "Before my neighbors wake up and get the wrong idea."

He smiled. "You want me to sneak out like I'm doing the walk of shame?"

She tossed him a skeptical look, and for a split second he swore he saw amusement dancing behind her eyes.

"Fine, I'll head to the cabin, shower and come back later. Keep your reputation intact."

"Josh, we need to set some ground rules," Carly said.

He frowned. "Didn't we already do that? No flirting. I got it."

She raised a brow. "You actually don't get it, but that's not what I'm talking about."

He'd forgotten how much he liked her. She was smart and funny and a little bit sarcastic. She pushed his buttons and she made him want to be better. A deep sense of longing pulsed through his body.

He just wanted a second chance—to prove to her he could be the man she needed. *God, that's all I'm asking for.*

"If I'm not working and you're hanging around for the next four weeks, we're going to need a system."

"So you can spend as little time with me as possible?"

She avoided his eyes. "That's not what I'm saying." Her tone had turned defensive.

"I was just kidding, Carly," he said, realizing maybe joking with her wasn't the best idea. "What do you propose? I'll do whatever you think is best."

She drew in a breath. "I guess I'm just wondering what you're going to be doing the next four weeks."

"You mean am I just going to be sitting here playing video games with Jaden every day?"

"Are you?" She studied him with cruel intensity.

"I'll be working," he said. "So maybe we can trade shifts or something?"

"You're going to work from here?"

"My work is mobile," he said. "All I need is a computer. I'll have some Zoom meetings to take sometimes—so I can keep my staff on task—and I was thinking about teaching Jaden a little bit about what I do—get his mind off of skiing while he's laid up."

"That's a great idea." She sounded surprised.

"I have those sometimes." He smiled.

Her shoulders went stiff and she refused to smile. Man, he missed the days when their relationship was light and easy. He missed their playful banter, their easy way of joking with each other. He missed *her*.

"Okay, well, I plan to be here as much as he needs," she said, back to business.

"But you need to take breaks too." Josh finished off his coffee, rinsed out the cup and put it in the dishwasher.

"I'd feel better if I was here."

The words were like spurs digging into his sides. Even after all this time, she didn't trust him with their son.

He tried to shake it off. Tried not to remember the day that finally convinced him Carly and Jaden would be better off without him or the day that had put the idea in his mind in the first place.

He tried, but he failed.

It all came rushing back as if the wound only needed to be nicked for the pain of it to begin throbbing again.

Josh had been a father for about a month, and he still felt completely useless. Carly had taken to parenting much better than he had. She seemed to have a sixth sense about what the baby needed—when he was tired or hungry or needed to be changed.

To Josh, the pudgy little human was still a mystery.

Maybe that was why Carly rarely let him help. Maybe that was why when he offered to change the kid, she stood beside him, explaining exactly how to clean the baby, how to affix the diaper, how to get him dressed.

Maybe that was why she was constantly running through a list of instructions, as if she was the teacher and he was the student. She must've known how inept he was—must've seen it on his face or in the way he held their son. Awkward and unnatural.

They were living in the apartment above Mimi's—something that still didn't sit right with the older woman who'd bought the shop from Gus after Carly's mom took off.

"I don't like you two living in sin up here, but you need a place and I've never been one to turn away someone in need."

They'd settled in, mostly, but that didn't mean they were used to having a baby to tend to. Especially not a baby who slept in three-hour stretches.

"You still planning to go out tonight?" Josh asked Carly minutes after Jaden fell asleep.

She shook her head. "No."

He frowned. "Why not?" She could use the break, and honestly—so could he. She wasn't exactly easy to live with these days.

She plopped down on the couch and let out a heavy, tired sigh.

"You should go out," he said.

She leaned her head back and closed her eyes. "I wish." She stretched her legs out on the couch, putting her feet in his lap.

He picked up her foot and started rubbing it. "Seriously, the baby is down for at least a few hours. I can handle things here."

She lifted her head and looked at him. "What if he wakes up?"

Josh shrugged. "Then I'll feed him."

"But he doesn't eat for nearly four hours."

"Then I'll hold him. Or change him. Or burp him," Josh said. "I'll figure it out." *Let me figure it out.*

She closed her eyes again and tipped her head back on the cushion. "I don't think it's a good idea."

"Your friends are only home 'til Sunday," he said. "And you need a break."

"What makes you say that?"

"You're cranky," he said. "Really, really cranky."

Her eyes popped open again. "Thanks."

"You're hardly sleeping. You've had no time alone. It's understandable." He turned his attention to her other foot. "And I think you should let me hang out with our baby for a few hours alone."

"I could see if Beverly could come over," she said.

Josh stopped rubbing her foot and she sat up and looked at him.

"What?"

"You don't need to call Beverly, Carly. I'm his dad. You have to let me help take care of him."

She pulled her feet off him. "Josh, let's be real, you don't know the first thing about babies."

"Neither did you until you had one," he said. "Let me figure it out."

She hesitated, and Josh's annoyance level went up.

"Carly—"

"Fine," she said. "But you have to promise to call me if he wakes up."

"How about I call you if I can't handle it?"

She chewed the inside of her lip, and he could tell she wasn't comfortable with this idea at all, but he didn't care. He was Jaden's dad. How was he supposed to get used to being a father if she never gave him a chance to do anything?

"Okay?" he asked, still waiting for her to agree.

"Fine." She wasn't happy, and he knew it. But Jaden had been asleep all of ten minutes. Odds were, he'd sleep for a few hours and wake up before Carly even got home.

How hard could it be?

Turned out—very hard.

The baby woke up within the first half hour and began crying. Josh picked him up and held him, made sure he was dry, rocked him, bounced him, fed him—but nothing he tried was working. He picked up the phone, but quickly hung it back up—if he called, she would know he couldn't handle this, and he already felt worthless ninety-nine percent of the time.

He set the phone down, stood and walked the length of the small apartment—back and forth—bouncing, cooing—he even tried singing.

But Jaden replied with ear-curdling screams.

After forty-five minutes, Josh started to get frustrated—really frustrated.

"Will you just stop crying?" He'd anticipated a calm, relaxing night at home. He'd worked all day at the car wash, and he never would've encouraged Carly to go out if he'd known his night was going to go like this.

His bouncing had grown more impatient, his mood foul.

"Just go to sleep!" He raised his voice now, as if shouting at a baby would do any good.

He tipped Jaden back and looked at him. The bald-headed baby's face was red and wet and he continued to scream.

"What do you want?" Josh just wanted him to shut up already. He needed a little peace. It had been over an hour, and his blood boiled. The screaming had to be the worst sound he'd ever heard. It delved through his skin and straight to the place that kept him sane.

His temper spiked as he looked at the clock, knowing Carly would be home soon. If she came home and found him like this, she'd know he was incompetent—as if he needed to give her more reasons.

He walked into the kitchen and turned a circle. Feeling like a caged animal, Josh began to think only one thing—*I need to get this baby to stop crying.*

Frustration grew and he glanced down at his son and the thought that flashed through his mind terrified him.

What if I hurt my son like I hurt Dylan?

He hurried toward the crib and set the baby down, spinning around in a circle and heaving out a heavy sigh.

What if I hurt my son like I hurt Dylan?

His face flushed and he couldn't get a deep breath. What was he doing? He palmed his face. He'd been pretending to be something he wasn't—capable.

He had no business—

The door opened and Carly walked in, worry on her face. "I

could hear him screaming downstairs. How long's he been like this?"

Josh faced her. "For a while."

"Why didn't you call me?"

Like a perfect storm, the room began to spin. Carly rushed toward Jaden, picked him up and kissed the top of his bald head, but she drew back almost instantly. "Josh—"

"What's wrong?"

"Have you felt him at all tonight?"

"I've been holding him—he's been screaming for over an hour."

"He's burning up." She had turned frantic.

"He's probably just worked up from all the crying," Josh said.

"I know a fever when I feel it." Carly picked Jaden up and stormed out.

"Where are you going?" Josh followed.

"To the emergency room," she said. "This isn't normal."

Josh's heart raced as they hurried out of the apartment and into the street. She buckled Jaden in to his car seat and they sped off toward the hospital. He could practically feel the barrage of angry words she wasn't saying.

"Carly, I'm so sorry," he said. "I didn't think he was sick." Josh's stomach rolled. He felt like a total jerk for getting so angry that the baby wouldn't stop crying. Why didn't he think Jaden might be sick?

"Just get us to the hospital," she snapped.

He didn't say another word until they arrived at the emergency room. He dropped her off at the door, then went to find a place to park.

Minutes later, when he ran inside, Carly and Jaden were nowhere to be seen. The receptionist promised she'd find out where they'd gone, but as Josh paced the room, his mind turned over the events of the evening.

This is all your fault.

He wasn't any good at this, and it was obvious. Same as his

own father. His thoughts turned to a childhood he'd worked hard to forget. His anger—Josh thought he had it under control, but the night had proven otherwise.

Maybe he was just like his dad. Would he hurt them if he stayed? If Carly knew the truth, she'd force him to go. And she'd be right to.

Carly and Jaden would be better off without him.

The door of the ER opened and Carly's dad and sister hurried in. "Josh—what's going on?"

Josh shrugged. "I don't know. I parked the car and when I came in, Carly had already gone back. They said they were going to find out where they were, but so far, they haven't told me anything."

Gus frowned. "Did you tell them you're the father?"

Josh nodded.

Gus stomped over to the desk where the receptionist sat, on the phone. "I'm gonna need you to hang that up."

The woman looked up. Josh didn't know if it was Gus's police uniform or his intimidating presence that got through to her, but she ended her phone call and gave the man her undivided attention. "What can I do for you, Officer?"

"My grandson came in here a short while ago, and that young man is the father." He pointed at Josh. "I think you were going to get him some information about his child."

"Let me see what I can do," she said. "What was the name again?"

Gus did a terrible job of trying not to seem exasperated. "Dixon."

"Collins-Dixon," Josh corrected.

Gus looked at him. He didn't know Carly had hyphenated Jaden's name. They weren't married yet, so it seemed to make sense. Did that make Gus happy or was he indifferent?

Josh knew Carly's dad was still angry with them. Telling him Carly was pregnant had been one of the worst days of Josh's life.

Clearly, he blamed Josh, and maybe he was right to. Let's face it, Carly's life would be completely different if he wasn't in it.

Gus had done nothing to hide his disappointment. Sure, he'd shown up for Jaden's birth, but other than that, he mostly stayed away. He also seemed hell-bent on making sure the two of them had to face their current circumstances on their own—there was no bailing out happening here.

"I'll be right back," the receptionist said.

Gus turned a circle and heaved a sigh. "Sometimes you gotta get a little feisty."

"Thanks for that." Josh stuffed his hands in his pockets.

Gus nodded at him. "Doesn't change anything. Just don't think you should have to wait around for answers about your own kid."

The receptionist reappeared. "You can come back."

Josh tossed a grateful look at Gus, then followed her through the doors. He found Carly just as a doctor was telling her she was smart to bring Jaden in—his temperature was too high, and they needed to run some tests.

Josh's stomach churned. What if Carly hadn't come home when she did? What if something had happened to their baby while Josh was watching him? He would've never forgiven himself.

His mind flashed with the memory of the moment the screaming overwhelmed him. What if something had happened?

I'm not good for them.

It was too much.

"Most likely we'll give him a round of antibiotics, and he'll be just fine, but we want to rule a few things out."

"What kind of things?" Carly asked.

"Infections, mostly," the doctor said. "It could be a virus or bacterial. We'll get to the bottom of it."

The doctor walked out, leaving them alone in the small exam room. Josh didn't move. His heart raced with thoughts he didn't want to think.

Jaden lay at the center of the exam table, with Carly's hand on his belly.

"This could've been really bad," she said.

"He's going to be okay," Josh offered, though the empty words meant nothing.

"But if I hadn't come home—" She stopped.

She was thinking it too. She was thinking the words she wouldn't say because they were true. If something had happened —it would've been his fault.

He slipped his index finger inside the baby's hand. Jaden kicked and cooed, his eyes focused on the ceiling. He was perfect. Absolutely perfect.

What if Josh ruined that?

The doctor returned and Carly swiped Jaden into her arms. Josh took a step back and before he knew it, he was in the hallway, not a part of the picture at all.

He walked toward the waiting room and he didn't stop walking until he was back home, packing his things into a big duffel bag and leaving her a note.

Carly, I love you, but I can't do this anymore.

—Josh

He left the note on the counter, got into his car and drove out of Harbor Pointe, certain that this was not only what Carly wanted, but what was best for her and Jaden.

Now, standing in her kitchen, he battled those same feelings of insecurity. He hated the way he still doubted his abilities as a dad. He and Jaden had a good relationship now. And yet, here, in Carly's presence, the memory of the past taunting him once again, he had that same strong feeling everyone would be better off if he just left.

He could go home and get back to work. Dive into a new app or figure out new ways to market the old ones. He could help other companies get their apps up and running. Carly could give him updates by text or phone. He could call every night. Maybe it was what was best.

"I'm going to get going," he said abruptly.

Carly stood, years and canyons between them. "Okay."

An invisible thread of electricity connected them, and Josh wished he had the right to go to her, to pull her into his arms, to let her fall apart, because he could see her strong façade faltering behind a mask of strength.

Instead, he turned and walked away.

Chapter Twenty-Six

I
t had been a week and a half since Jaden's surgery, and in that time, Josh had spent nearly every day (and most evenings) with their son—which meant he'd also spent nearly every day (and most evenings) with her.

What did she expect when he said he was staying until Jaden was recovered?

Truthfully, she'd half expected him to change his mind.

So far, he hadn't. And here he was.

Sometimes, she'd stand just outside the living room, watching the two of them—her son and his father—and their quiet, easy-going relationship. Josh brought out a side of Jaden most people didn't see. And on the days he acted depressed and moody over being laid up, it was Josh who got him out of the funk.

And while she'd never say so, some days, he got her out of her funk too. More than once he'd noticed her mood was foul, and somehow, miraculously, he found a way to turn it around. It was as if he still held the key to a secret door to her soul. Like he still knew her better than anyone else.

Twice, he'd caught her crying in the kitchen, and both times he'd comforted her with exactly the right words. "He's going to be just fine." As if he had the power to make it so.

These brief encounters were working her over. Something had to be done. Put more time, more space, more distance between them. Josh wasn't her husband, and he shouldn't act like it. That meant the schedule they had in place needed to be followed. As it was, he'd all but ignored it. Instead of working during his designated work times, he hung out with Jaden. Instead of giving her space in the evenings, he'd made them dinner.

Bits of him were beginning to show up around the house— his shoes by the front door. His newly purchased rain jacket hanging by the back door. His piney scent lingering in the hallway.

It messed with her resolve.

Maybe she'd simply remind him of their schedule? Ask him to honor it a little better?

The coffeemaker had just beeped when she heard Josh coming in the back door. She reminded herself that he had been kind. She didn't need to injure him. She would be kind, but firm.

Set boundaries. Stick to them.

It sounded easy enough.

His footfalls grew closer until he walked through the kitchen door, dressed in jeans, a faded red T-shirt and a baseball cap she swore he'd had since eighth grade. He leaned against the doorjamb and smiled that lazy, sexy smile at her.

"Morning," he said.

His skin had miraculously turned bronze, probably on his walks to and from his truck, considering he browned right up in a literal minute. Carly, on the other hand, still looked translucent in certain light.

Unfortunately for her, the suntan only made Josh more attractive.

That and his eyes were a recipe for disaster.

"You're up early." She looked away.

"So are you." He was probably smiling. He seemed to know how his smile affected her. "Hey, look at this."

He plopped a stack of paper onto the counter.

"What's this?"

"I've been talking with that swimmer's doctor—Dr. Carroll."

"The appointment isn't for a few more weeks."

"I know," Josh said. "But I didn't want to wait."

"And?"

"He sent me some research. In your hand is every study they've done in recent years suggesting that our son should be able to return to skiing in just a few short weeks. The swimmer was right—if he wants to ski, he can ski."

Carly could practically feel her own heart double in size. "What?" She looked at the pages in her hand—

Long QT No Longer Benching Athletes

Overcoming Long QT to Win Olympic Gold

Cleared to Play

Josh nodded. "Good news, right?"

Tears sprang to her eyes. She leapt forward and threw her arms around him. "Great news." Quickly, she pulled away. "Sorry."

He smiled. "Don't apologize to me."

"Josh, I think we should talk." She pulled the schedule she'd created from the refrigerator. It neatly outlined when Josh would be with Jaden, when he would be working, when he would be out of her hair.

Had he even looked at it?

"Ah, your schedule." He walked farther into the kitchen, stopping about a foot from where she stood. He reached up and took a mug from the cupboard, then poured himself a cup of coffee.

Every move he made felt deliberate, and he'd yet to break eye contact with her.

"So you are aware of its existence."

He smiled in reply.

"We have a schedule for a reason." She looked away.

He grabbed the bottom of her shirt, then gave it a tug. "You have a schedule. I'm much more spontaneous."

She took a step back, releasing his hold on her, aware of two things: 1) He was flirting with her, and 2) It was working.

"Josh," she said sternly.

He grinned. "I'm just messing with you. I'll stay out of your way today. I've got a plan."

"What's your plan?"

"Is your garage open?"

She frowned. "Yes, why?"

"I'll be back in time for my shift, boss."

He grinned at her—the kind of grin that took her straight back to high school.

It was getting more and more difficult to stay mad at him.

She liked him. She'd always liked him. He'd gone from sweet, wide-eyed kid to rebelliously attractive teenager to this kind, self-less man who'd become more successful than anyone would've ever guessed. Under Josh's photo in the yearbook, it said *Most likely to end up in jail*. It most certainly did not say *Most likely to become a tech mogul*.

And of course, he was still disastrously good-looking—and she suspected he knew it.

Yeah, she liked him.

But not liking him had never been the problem.

If she didn't stay angry with him, she risked falling for him all over again, and that she could not allow.

Why was he making it so hard?

He walked off the porch and around the side of the house.

She closed the door and went back inside.

"What's Dad doing?" Jaden asked from his spot in the recliner.

"No idea," she said. "Need anything?"

"A life?" he said dryly.

"Funny. Here's a little light reading for you." She set the stack of articles on Jaden's lap and walked into the kitchen, where she spotted Josh out back with her old lawn mower. Jaden usually mowed the lawn, and he must've noticed it had been neglected.

Josh gave the cord a tug , and the old mower sputtered. He went back into the garage and reemerged with an empty gas can, which he threw in the back of his truck. Seconds later, he'd started the engine and driven away.

And it wasn't until that moment that she exhaled.

"Mom, for real?" Jaden was in the doorway with the articles. "You're going to let me ski?"

She smiled. "We still need to go to the appointment with Dr. Carroll, but those are from him and not from the internet, so yes. It sounds promising."

He threw his arms around her, the same way she'd thrown her arms around Josh, which, she had to admit, made her momentary lapse in judgment seem a little less troubling.

"It's still going to be work," she said when he let go of her.

"Work doesn't scare me," Jaden said with the same grin as his father. "Bring it on."

Thank you, Jesus, she thought. *For answering this prayer.*

Dr. Roby might not have understood how important this was to Jaden—to all of them—but God sure did. She would never tire of the fact that he knew them all so personally that the things that mattered to them mattered to him.

Her heart nearly burst with gratitude.

* * *

Later, while Carly was cleaning up the kitchen from the pancake breakfast she'd made, Josh returned with what she assumed was a full gas can but turned out to be a brand-new lawn mower. She squinted as he pulled into the driveway, killed the engine, tugged the tailgate down and lifted the mower out and onto the ground.

She dried her hands and walked outside barefoot, crossed her arms and glared at him. "What is that?"

"It's your new lawn mower."

Her raised eyebrows demanded an explanation.

"Yours is old and broken."

"It was out of gas."

"Trust me, Carly, it's junk."

She eyed him. "You mow a lot of lawns in Chicago?"

He pulled the old mower into the garage, then pushed the new one toward her. "This one is state of the art. It will practically mow the lawn itself."

"I don't need a state-of-the-art lawn mower, Josh."

"Well, now you have one, so you're welcome."

She groaned. "This changes nothing."

He waved her off. "I know. You're still mad at me."

"No, I'm—"

But he yanked the pull cord and the engine roared to life, drowning her out. He grinned, and she rolled her eyes.

He waggled his eyebrows at her as he walked by, taking his first pass on her lawn.

He bought me a lawn mower.

Unbelievable.

Josh spent the entire morning in the yard. Mowing, weeding, raking. By the time he finished, Carly's house was ready for the Lion's Club Garden Walk.

And Carly couldn't utter a word of complaint.

* * *

Later that night, after her shower, Carly changed into pajama shorts and a tank top, eager to get downstairs where her pint of almond praline Ben & Jerry's had softened to the perfect texture on the counter.

It was the first night Jaden was sleeping in his room since his surgery, and Carly had already decided to stay up late watching *Friday Night Lights.*

She was standing in the kitchen, fishing through the dishwasher for a spoon, when she heard a soft knock on the door.

"What in the world?" She flipped on the outside light and found Josh standing on the porch.

She pulled the door open and stared at him. "I thought you finished hours ago."

He'd showered and changed out of the clothes he'd mowed in, and was out of breath, like he'd been running.

"Are you okay?"

How many times had he shown up on her back porch, in need of help? Now, a grown-up version of that young boy stood before her, and her feelings warred with each other. That boy had won her heart a million times over—but this man had broken it just as many times.

How did she reconcile that?

She shoved aside thoughts of years gone by and focused on him now. Why was he here?

"Josh?"

"No, Carly," he finally said. "I'm not okay."

She quickly surveyed him for cuts and bruises. "What's wrong?"

He raked his hand through his hair, then met her eyes. "It's you."

She frowned. She hadn't done anything wrong. "What about me?"

He shook his head. "I thought I was over this. I thought I'd gotten it in my head that I was here for Jaden and for no other reason, but every day it's becoming clearer that's not enough."

"What do you mean?"

"I mean, seeing you every day. Seeing you here, now, with your hair all piled on top of your head and wearing those shorts."

She felt suddenly self-conscious.

"Or the other morning making coffee."

"What about that?"

He seemed not to hear her. "Or when I saw you out at that restaurant in that dress with that doctor guy and . . ."

She stilled. "And what?"

"And I didn't like it." He turned in a circle but snapped his attention back to her. "I hated it, actually."

"Josh, I—"

He held up a hand to silence her. "I know. I don't deserve a second chance. Not even a little bit, but I'm still standing here asking for one, Carly, because—" His eyes, filled with every earnest and genuine thing, met hers. "Because I've never stopped loving you."

"Josh—" What was he saying? Why was he saying this now? This was the last thing she needed. As if things weren't confusing enough.

"I don't know where things stand with you and the doctor, and if you decide that this guy is right for you, I will step aside. I've spent my whole life believing you were better off without me, and that's probably true, but I don't want it to be. I'm different now. I've had enough time away to realize I don't have to be that guy I was back then."

She watched as his breath finally slowed and he took a step back.

"I want you more than anything, Carly. I can't stop thinking about you." He moved toward her, so close she could feel his breath on her skin. "You and me and Jaden—we're a family. Let me at least try to make this right. Give me a second chance."

Her knees wobbled as she forced herself to look him in the eyes. "Josh, we tried. It didn't work out. It would be foolish to think anything has changed."

He touched her face, then dipped his forehead to hers. "We were really good together. I know you remember."

She hated that her eyes clouded over. Traitors. She closed them and drew in a deep breath. She did remember. Despite all her trying to forget, she remembered. And he was right—they had been so good together for a while.

And then they weren't. She opened her eyes and pulled away.

"I do remember," she said, forcing herself to be colder than she wanted to be. "I remember you leaving. I remember you choosing to go. I remember raising our son by myself."

"And I've lived with that for years."

"And so have I," she said.

"I know you don't believe me, but I promise, Carly, I *will* make it up to you."

She couldn't look at him. She feared that he might see straight through her.

"You can't tell me you haven't thought about it." He moved closer. "Just one kiss, Carly. Let me prove that what we have between us isn't over."

She faced him, the overwhelming desire to give in washing over her. "Josh—" She forced herself to take a step back, and his face fell.

"I'm not going anywhere. I'm going to earn a second chance." His eyes locked on to hers. "I'd wait a lifetime for that kiss."

Her eyes fell to the slats of the porch below her bare feet.

"That's all," he said. "That's all I came to say."

"Okay," she said dumbly.

"You should water the lawn in the morning." He walked off the porch and out to his truck, leaving her standing there in a daze, wondering when the world had gone sideways.

* * *

The following day, Grady and Quinn showed up to take Jaden to the indoor training center for a few hours.

"You cannot let him do a single active thing," Carly warned in her most threatening voice. "You and I both know he will try."

They all looked at Jaden, who shrugged. "I'm fine, you guys. I don't know what the big deal is."

"The big deal is that you have a device sending electrical currents through your body and we need to make sure it stays in the right place," Carly said. "Plus, it hasn't even been two weeks since your surgery, so don't argue and do what you're told."

"Fine," he said. "I just need to get out of the house." He skulked off toward Grady's Jeep, and Quinn's fiancé followed behind. Quinn hung back and gave her an *I'm worried about you* smile. For a fleeting moment, Carly wished she could tell Quinn everything—the jumble of feelings that had gotten so mixed up in her mind, how Josh had shown up last night professing his love. How he'd bought her a lawn mower. How he'd already been there that morning to turn on her sprinklers and keep the grass from dying.

But of course, she couldn't. Talking about it only made it real. If she kept it to herself, there was a chance these feelings would up and walk away.

Besides, she didn't need Quinn's reminders of all the ways Josh had let her down. She was well aware, *thank you very much.*

"You okay?" Quinn asked.

Carly sighed, then nodded. "I'm hanging in there."

"Yeah?" She reached over and took Carly's hand. "Because you look terrible."

Carly's eyes widened and Quinn burst into laughter.

"Seriously, what is happening with your hair?" More laughter.

Carly yanked her hand away and swatted her sister on the shoulder. "Thanks a lot."

"You should go shopping," Quinn said. "Buy something nice for yourself, even if it's chocolate. Or go see a movie or something. Take yourself on a date—unless your doctor is free."

Carly wrinkled her nose. She hadn't thought of David in days.

"What? Trouble in doctor paradise?"

She shrugged. "No, he's fine. He's a perfectly nice guy. I should like him, shouldn't I?"

Now Quinn shrugged. "I think you should feel about him however you feel about him. I don't think you should force yourself into anything."

She sighed. If only it were that easy.

"I think you need a break. Do you want me to come with you? I have some wedding shopping we could do?" Quinn practically beamed every time she brought up the wedding.

Her excitement must've turned Carly's mood around because

suddenly shopping for her sister's wedding seemed like the best idea in the world.

"I'd love that," Carly said.

"You trust Grady with Jaden?"

"Maybe it'll be good for Jaden," Carly said. "He seems a little down, to be honest."

"I think so." Quinn smiled.

"Does Grady know the rules?"

"You wrote them down on a piece of paper, texted them and sent us a video last night. He knows." Quinn raced back to the Jeep, told Grady the new plan, kissed her handsome man on the lips and ran back toward Carly.

"Let's go shopping!"

Chapter Twenty-Seven

I t had been a long time since Carly and her sister had had a normal conversation. After all, Carly's life right now was anything but normal.

"Before we leave, I think you should change your clothes," Quinn said.

Carly looked down at her cut-off jeans and black tank top, then looked back up at her sister. "Why?"

Quinn made a face. "We're going to all the nicer boutiques and stores, Car, and you look like someone who only shops at Walmart."

"I *do* shop at Walmart."

"Right, but you shop at other places too." Her expression shifted. "Don't you?"

"I'm not changing. My kid just had surgery, my ex is back in town, and this is the first time I've been anywhere besides the grocery store in weeks. I have no desire to get dressed up."

Quinn grimaced. "Okay, but what about the hair?"

"I'm about to leave you here."

"Fine," Quinn said. "Hope we don't run into anyone we know."

It was a ridiculous thing to say because they knew everyone in town, but Carly didn't mention it. Obviously a last-ditch effort to try and convince Carly to make herself more presentable.

But she didn't have the energy. She'd put on a little bit of mascara and some lip gloss—that was plenty for today.

She was tired. If she was smart, she'd go inside and take a nap.

Instead, she and Quinn hopped into Carly's Honda and drove toward town.

"You're quiet," Carly said after a few minutes.

"Am I?"

"Yes. Don't you have updates on the wedding?" She stopped at a red light.

Quinn looked at her. "I wasn't sure it was appropriate to talk about it considering all you're dealing with."

"Are you kidding?" The light changed and Carly stepped on the gas. "Please, let's talk about something other than me."

"Well, we have a date and a venue and yesterday I booked our honeymoon." Quinn stared out the window, eyes glassy. "It's like a dream, really."

"Where are you going? Wait—let me guess—Utah? No, Colorado?"

She shook her head. "We're going to Paris. Grady doesn't want to ski on our honeymoon. He said he wants it to be about me."

Carly reached over and squeezed her little sister's hand. "Have I told you how happy I am for you both?"

Quinn squeezed back. "No, but you've been a little busy."

"Well, I am." Carly pulled her hand back, thankful she could say those words and mean them. "I love Grady—we all do."

"He's pretty great." Quinn angled her body toward Carly. "But what about you?"

"What about me?"

"It's just, Jaden's getting older. I hate the thought of him going off to school—or training, whichever—and you being here alone."

Carly shrugged. "I'm a big girl, Q. I can take care of myself."

She forced a smile, but her throat had tied itself into a knot. She *was* perfectly capable of taking care of herself—and another human being—so why did the thought of being alone settle so poorly on her shoulders now?

"I know you can," Quinn said. "But it would be nice if someone else took care of you for a change."

Yes, it would.

Carly pulled into a parking space in front of Hazel's Kitchen and looked up at the ceiling to keep from crying. She couldn't allow herself to entertain the idea. She couldn't let herself think of Josh mowing her lawn, weeding her flowerbeds, buying her a new *state-of-the-art* mower. She hadn't said so, but that old mower was one she bought secondhand and it was always a crapshoot whether or not it was going to start.

He'd obviously known that. And he hadn't asked—he'd just done what needed to be done.

Why couldn't you have done that for the last sixteen years?

It didn't matter. Carly had spent her whole adult life becoming the woman who needed nobody but herself. Nothing had changed.

And yet, everything had changed.

It was as if Jaden's diagnosis and treatment had shone a spotlight on her own fragility. Was it possible she wasn't as indestructible as she thought she was?

They each opened their car doors and stepped out. Quinn was telling her about the Parisian flower markets when she stopped mid-sentence. "Is that Josh?"

Carly followed her sister's gaze across the street, where she spotted Josh exiting Dandy's Bakery with a leggy blonde.

The woman was young, slender and clearly spent a lot of time in the gym. And she was beautiful.

And all at once Carly wished she'd taken Quinn's advice and changed her clothes. Fixed her hair. Put on some makeup.

She grabbed Quinn's arm and pulled her into the hardware store.

"Who is *that*?" Quinn's eyes followed Josh and the blonde as they walked down the street in the opposite direction. They stopped in front of the fudge shop and went inside.

"I have no idea."

"Is he dating someone?"

Carly pretended not to care. "Beats me."

Maybe he was. Maybe this woman loved Josh and wanted to marry him. Maybe she'd surprised him because he'd been gone too long and now he was doing the polite thing and showing her around his hometown.

But then that meant he'd been lying to her. Had everything he said last night on the porch been a lie? And why did it matter? It wasn't like she wanted those things to be true.

"We came here to shop," Carly said. "Not to spy on Josh."

Amusement washed over Quinn's face. "Okay."

"Can I help you girls?"

They spun around to find portly Ed Delancey, owner of the Harbor Pointe hardware store, staring them down. He wore a plaid shirt, denim overalls and work boots, same thing he wore every single day, Carly suspected.

Once when they were kids Quinn had swiped three root beer barrels from the candy counter and their dad made her bring them back in and apologize. Ed Delancey had been suspicious of them ever since.

"We're good, but thanks," Carly said, pushing Quinn toward the door.

Quinn giggled as they went back outside.

"All right, little sister," Carly said, needing a distraction. "What's left to be done for this wedding of yours?"

Quinn linked arms with Carly and gave her a squeeze. "Well, there is the small matter of my bridal shower."

Carly gasped. "Oh, Q. I'm supposed to plan that, aren't I?"

Quinn shrugged. "Knowing Beverly, it's probably mostly done. She was going to get started because she didn't want you to be stressed about it, but I don't want you to feel left out."

"I'll call her," Carly promised. How could she have forgotten one of her main duties as maid of honor? She'd always thought she'd make such a wonderful maid of honor—obviously she'd mentally exaggerated her own abilities.

"Good. She told me at Sunday dinner she'd been searching online for shower games and she found one called 'Put a Ring On it.'" Quinn shot her sister a look. "Please don't let that happen."

Carly laughed. "I promise. I won't. I much prefer the one called 'Lady Marmalade.'"

Quinn pulled her arm away. "You're hilarious."

"It sounds like you have everything all figured out," Carly said, willing herself not to so much as glance at the fudge shop.

Quinn stopped. "Not everything." She'd stopped directly in front of Ever After, the only store in Harbor Pointe that carried formal gowns. Nearly every homecoming, prom, bridesmaid and wedding dress was purchased here, and Carly hadn't been inside since high school.

Before she could reply, she saw the door to the fudge shop open out of the corner of her eye, and the leggy blonde walked out onto the sidewalk.

"Great," she said, shoving Quinn through the door of Ever After.

The building, like all of the buildings downtown, had a brightly colored exterior, eclectic and charming at the same time. The brick on the outside of Ever After had been painted Pepto-Bismol pink, with large display windows on the main floor. The second story was lined with tall, skinny windows encased in thick white molding. The words *Ever After* had been painted on the front window in a beautiful hand-lettered font.

The store was charmingly old with an equally charming (and equally old) owner named Dorothy Mischief. Carly had a theory that the old woman had made up that name years ago, but she had no proof.

Dorothy, or "Dot" as her friends lovingly called her, had been a Harbor Pointe staple for as long as Carly could remember, and her store, small and quaint, actually did quite well.

As soon as the sisters strolled through the front door, Dot clapped her pudgy hands together and gasped. "Girls! Look who it is."

She rushed out from behind the counter toward them, and Carly looked around the empty store, wondering who Dot had been shouting at. She leaned toward Quinn and whispered, "Are you famous now?"

Quinn shushed her and smiled at Dot. "Mrs. Mischief, I bet you know why I'm here."

"All those weddings you've worked on this past year, and now it's finally your turn." Dot took Quinn by the shoulders and gave her a shake. "It's about time you married that hunky Olympian."

Quinn's cheeks pinked. "I was just waiting for him to ask me."

"Well, I already started a list of dresses I think would look stunning on you," Dot said. "Polly!" She called out the name as a round girl with dark hair emerged on the landing above them and Carly couldn't help but feel like they'd entered the letter shop in *Mary Poppins*. "Can you pull the dresses for Miss Collins?"

Quinn beamed. "That was so thoughtful of you. Thank you."

Dot glanced at Carly as if she'd only just that second realized she was standing there. "And we haven't seen you in here in ages, Miss Collins. I assume you're the maid of honor?"

"I am," Carly said. She didn't melt when people talked about weddings. She didn't swoon or sigh or even care much about the pomp and circumstance. A wedding, to her, was secondary—it was the marriage she craved most.

The thought startled her. Not that she'd had it—she'd always known she wanted a real family, and a husband was required for such a thing—but because she'd had it so openly. Typically she was better about deceiving herself.

"What colors are we thinking?" Dot glanced at Quinn. "Teal? Peacock blue? Aqua? Something in that family."

Dot brought her hands to her lips and squealed. "So beautiful. Let me see what I can do."

She led them to the back of the store where the changing rooms were. The only problem? The changing rooms had no mirrors. Carly assumed this was a sales tactic on the part of sneaky Dorothy Mischief. After all, if a bride exited the changing room to all the oohs and aahs of her adoring friends and family, wouldn't that make the dress all the more appealing?

Within minutes, a rack of white dresses had been positioned just outside the dressing rooms. Some were beaded and elegant. Others were puffy and princess-like. One was short and another sleeveless, and no two dresses were the same.

Now Quinn was the one swooning. "They're so beautiful." She pulled one off the rack, the one with a tulle skirt that would make it impossible to hang back up. "Don't you love it?"

Carly didn't know when she'd stopped wanting to look like a fairy princess— maybe when she'd realized fairy tales didn't come true, and the dress didn't appeal to her at all. Still, there was no way she was bursting her sister's wedding bubble.

"It's really pretty," she said.

"It's stunning," Dot said from behind them. "Absolutely stunning."

Quinn reached over to the rack and pulled out another dress, this one the exact opposite of the first. "Here." She shoved it toward Carly.

Carly took a step back. "What do you want me to do with it?"

"You can't just sit there while I try on all of these dresses." Quinn stared at her, wide-eyed.

"You want me to put this on?"

"Yes, Little Miss Grumpy. I do."

Carly shoved it back. "No way."

"Carly, come on, at least pretend you're having fun." Quinn pouted the way she did when they were kids. It had never worked —Carly couldn't understand why she still did it. "I'm only going to get married once."

"You know this is not my thing, Q," Carly said.

"Today, pretend like it is." She shook the dress out toward Carly. "For me?"

Carly sighed. "You owe me." She snatched the hanger from her sister and scowled.

"When you get married, you can force me to do something I don't want to do."

"Like let me elope?"

Quinn gasped. "That's not even funny."

"Not everyone has been planning their wedding since they were a little girl," Carly said.

"I haven't even done that," Quinn said. "But now that I met Grady . . ." Her voice trailed off and she turned wispy and weird. "I can't explain it. I just want everything to be perfect."

Carly stared at her, waiting for her to snap out of this fantasy.

When she finally did, Quinn shot her sister a look of annoyance. "Try it on. And you have to come out here in it to prove you actually did."

"Fine."

In the quiet of the changing room, Carly hung the dress on the hook and stared at it. It really was beautiful, the kind of dress Carly would've loved to get married in. If girls like her got married.

She ran a hand over the simple A-line, fingering the beaded belt and the tiny details that likely only the bride and groom would be able to see. It was exquisite.

She undressed, then slipped her feet into the sleeveless dress with an elegant line of sparkling beads outlining the high neckline and zipped it up.

Was this the kind of dress she would've worn if she'd accepted Josh's proposal all those years ago?

People said a lot of things about Josh Dixon, but Carly knew he'd at least try and do right by her. But she had it in her head that they were too young, and she didn't want her pregnancy to be the only reason they got married.

"It wouldn't be," he'd said. "We'd get married because we love each other."

They were sitting on the top of a sand dune, overlooking the lake, and she'd just told him about the pregnancy test. Seeing a positive result had nearly knocked the wind out of her—she'd run to the car wash where Josh worked and pulled him out before he could even tell his boss where he was going.

He'd taken the news better than she had, but then, reality probably hadn't set in. Suggesting marriage before high school graduation was ludicrous. And yet, shouldn't they get married? Wasn't that what good Christian girls in her *situation* did?

"The offer stands," Josh said. "It'll always stand."

"We can't get married, Josh. We're kids."

Kids who shouldn't have had sex. That's what their parents would say.

Oh no. Their parents. Her father. How were they going to tell them?

"What's going on?" Josh said. "You just turned pale."

She blinked and tears streamed down her face. "My dad is never going to speak to me again."

"He will," Josh said. "Just maybe not for a little while." He stood and walked a few steps away, then turned back to face her.

"You're freaking out," she said.

He pushed his hands through his hair, eyes wide. "A little."

She screwed her eyes shut, pressing the heels of her hands into them. "This is a disaster."

Quickly, he was at her side. "No, no. We'll figure it out. I promise. We'll figure it out together."

She looked up into his eyes and he used his thumb to wipe another tear away. "You promise?"

He kissed her forehead. "Always."

"Carly?" Quinn's voice pulled her back to the present, where she found herself standing barefoot in a wedding dress.

Of all the ridiculous . . .

"Come out!"

She let her eyes graze the long, white satin, and she couldn't help but wonder when everything had gone upside down. What made him decide to break his promise? She and Josh had been young, yes, but they did love each other.

Didn't they?

She pulled back the curtain and found her sister standing on the other side, wearing the poufy princess dress with a tight beaded bodice. Carly couldn't believe how stunning it looked. On the hanger, the dress had looked borderline silly, like something a Barbie doll would've worn.

But on Quinn? It was perfection.

For a brief moment, she forgot she was wearing a wedding dress too.

"You look gorgeous," she said.

Quinn's eyes brightened. "I haven't looked yet. I was waiting for you."

"It's stunning. If you don't get it, you're bananas." She smiled at her sister.

"Nobody gets the first dress they try on," Quinn said.

"That's not true," Dot piped up. "Happens all the time."

Quinn grabbed her hand. "Let's go look."

Carly pulled away. "You go look. By yourself. This is your day —I'm just here for your amusement."

"But, Carly, you look so beautiful it makes me feel like crying." Quinn's eyelids fluttered, as if blinking back tears.

"Well, don't cry," Carly said. "I'm not even a real bride."

The bell on the front door jangled, pulling Dot's attention. "Oh, girls. I'll be right back." She shimmied off, leaving them alone at the back of the store with nothing to do but go stand in front of a three-way mirror.

"Here I go," Quinn said.

Carly moved back as her sister stepped up on a small platform, admiring her reflection for several seconds before spinning around. "It really *is* beautiful."

"*You're* beautiful," Carly said. "The dress is just icing."

Quinn smiled. "It's going to be hard to beat such a knock-out dress."

"And to think, I thought it was truly hideous before you put it on."

Quinn gasped. "Mean!"

Carly laughed.

"Get up here." Quinn stepped off the platform and motioned toward it, as if Carly should be overjoyed to take a turn peering at a future that would never be.

She groaned. "This is so incredibly silly."

"Well, you might've given up on finding Mr. Right, but I sure haven't." Quinn tugged Carly's arm. "He's out there, and when you find him, you're going to be a stunning bride, even in that plain old boring dress—"

Carly gasped as Quinn pushed her up onto the platform.

"That you somehow turn into something only royalty would wear."

Carly faced the mirror.

"One more thing." Quinn pulled the hair tie out of Carly's hair and her long, chocolate waves tumbled over her shoulders. Quinn stood behind her, eyes shining. "You're like something out of a fairy tale."

Carly stared at the way the dress showed off her curves, the way it cinched at the waist, making her look slender and small. It was simple and maybe a little plain, but to her, it was perfect.

Inexplicable tears sprang to her eyes, and she willed them away with sheer stubbornness, same as she'd done a thousand times before. She knew the truth about fairy tales, after all.

They didn't come true.

I will not cry. I am strong. I am independent.

"It's okay to dream, big sister," Quinn whispered.

Carly's eyes found Quinn's in the mirror, and she did a quick about-face. "Sorry, kiddo. This is just not my cup of tea. You know me, jeans and tanks and ponytails." She stepped off the platform, still willing away the emotion that had formed a tight ball at the back of her throat.

It wasn't fair for her to feel this way, not when she had so much going on. Not when so many things in her life didn't make sense. She had no room in her life for fairy tales.

"I'll stick to the bridesmaid's dress—and only because you're forcing me to." She spun around and faced the front of the boutique, wholly unprepared to see Josh staring at her, the leggy blonde at his side.

"Carly?" His face turned pale.

She raced into the solace of the changing room, cheeks hot with humiliation, and one word echoed at the back of her mind.

Always.

Chapter Twenty-Eight

J osh took a step back and nearly ran into Rebecca.

Why was Carly wearing a wedding dress? Were she and the doctor more serious than she'd let on?

He looked up and found Quinn staring at him. She glanced at Rebecca, then spun around and disappeared into a dressing room.

Carly in a wedding dress. A dress that hugged her body in a way that sent his mind straight to places it shouldn't go.

She looked like a goddess, like something out of one of his dreams.

Without thinking, his hand found his wallet, safe and secure in his back pocket—what was inside, a touchstone for times like this, times when his head couldn't keep his emotions in line.

They'd never gotten married, but he had made her a promise. A few promises, in fact. The kind he didn't take lightly. The kind he'd never forget.

Seven months pregnant and an emotional train wreck, Carly had begun the "freaking out" stage of pregnancy, and one night, Josh found her collapsed in a puddle, fear written all over her face. She leaned against the wall in the living room of the apartment above the flower shop—a place they could only afford because Mimi let them stay for free.

She looked up at him, then buried her face in her hands. "Don't look at me. I'm a mess."

He sat down next to her, put a hand on her knee. "What's wrong?"

She wiped her wet cheeks with the sleeves of her sweatshirt, which he only just that second realized was actually *his* sweatshirt, then turned toward him. She was red-faced and splotchy, and he couldn't help but smile.

"Are you laughing at me?"

"Are you kidding? I know better than that."

She frowned. "Then why are you smiling?"

"You're cute is all." He shrugged. "Even when you cry."

She gave him a shove. "You don't even know why I'm crying. It could be something really serious."

"Or it could be because you feel fat and unattractive." He watched her as she looked away.

"You think I'm fat."

"I think you're pregnant, and I've heard you say you're fat every day for the last two months, and every time I've told you I think you're beautiful." He picked up her hands and held them for a few silent moments. "Or did you forget?"

She didn't respond.

"Scared?"

Her face crumpled and her voice broke.

He pressed a gentle kiss on her forehead. "You're not alone, Carly. I told you."

"That was months ago. Look at me now—you really want to have a wife who looks like this?"

He felt his jaw go slack. "A wife?"

"Or whatever." Her cheeks turned pink and she looked embarrassed.

"Does that mean you changed your mind?" He leaned back

and took her in. "Because we can go to the courthouse tomorrow."

"Are you crazy? I can't get married like this. I look like a barn." Her voice cracked and tears streamed down her face again.

He told himself not to laugh—she'd likely throat punch him if he did, but she was so adorably pathetic, it was a struggle to hold it together. "I think you look beautiful." *Please let that be the right thing to say.*

She shot him a look that said, *Whatever. I don't believe you.* Rolled her eyes and looked away.

He slid his arm up to her shoulder and squeezed. "Carly, I've never known anyone as amazing as you."

She sniffled, then wiped her nose on her sleeve. He made a mental note to let her keep the sweatshirt.

He stood and looked around the room until his eyes landed on a plain one-subject notebook with a blue cover. He opened it and began writing.

"What are you doing?"

He shushed her.

After several minutes, he reread what he'd written, tore the page from the notebook and faced her. He knelt down in front of her. "Carly Raeanne Collins—"

"Josh—"

He held up his hand to silence her again. "I promise to love you the way I loved you the first time I ever saw you when we were kids. To remember the way my heart jumped the first time we held hands. To reinvent ways to kiss you like it was the first time we ever kissed. I promise to be faithful to you, to protect you, to listen to your advice and sometimes even take it." He glanced up and found her smiling through tears that he hoped had turned happy.

"I promise to cherish you. To take care of you. To do what's best for you and to always put your happiness before my own. I promise that in all things you will forever be my *always.*"

A tear streamed down her cheek, and he reached over and

wiped it away with his thumb, letting his hand rest in the crook of her neck.

"You really mean it?" She looked up at him, eyes wide and uncharacteristically insecure.

"More than anything." He leaned in and kissed her, the kind of kiss that made their problems melt away. Suddenly they weren't two kids about to have a baby, they were Carly and Josh—two people who loved each other even though it made no sense.

"Maybe we have to wait to get married, but to me, it's a done deal. These vows are the proof. This piece of paper makes it official." He handed it to her, wishing it looked a little less like a high school English assignment and a little more like something worth framing, but it was heartfelt and that had to count for something.

Carly took the paper and pressed it to her chest. "I think this is the best gift you've ever given me."

The memory of that night, coupled with the vision of Carly —*his Carly*—in *that* dress, had taken his heart out to the shed for a good and honest butt-whooping. He wasn't sure when, or if, he'd ever recover.

"This is such an amazing shop." Rebecca seemed not to notice the exchange that had just happened or the reaction it had drawn out of Josh, and that was probably for the best. The woman was notorious for poking around in his personal life, and he'd become a master at revealing nothing. He'd like to keep it that way, though he realized asking her to come to Harbor Pointe was probably not the best way to do so.

To Rebecca, Josh was a sad, slightly older man who seemed lonely and bored. How many times had she mentioned "a friend she could set him up with"? How many times had he refused?

Josh cleared his throat. "We should go."

But Rebecca shot across the store with her face full of wonderment, her eyes wide and bright. She picked up a veil. "I absolutely love this."

"You can get all this stuff in the city," Josh said.

"For three times the cost." She tossed him a look. "Aren't you supposed to be selling me on this little town of yours?"

He turned a circle, raking a hand through his hair, feeling trapped like a rat in a cage.

The curtains on both changing rooms opened, as if the two sisters had been rehearsing their entrance in a musical. Josh might as well have had a mouth full of cotton. He tried—failed—to swallow around the dryness.

The little old woman who'd greeted them when they walked in bustled over to Carly and her sister. "Girls, you aren't leaving?"

"Sorry, Dot," Quinn said. "We're kind of in a hurry, but we'll be back. I wonder if you might be willing to hold this one for me?" She held up the dress, and Dot smiled.

"Of course I will, dear," she said. "It was truly beautiful on you."

"Josh, what do you think of this?"

He turned and found Rebecca holding up a lacy white garter with blue flowers on it. Once she had his attention, she grinned. "Just kidding. How much do you hate this store?" She'd whispered the last part—thankfully—or the old woman might've been offended.

Rebecca put the garter back, then spun toward him. "We can go now if you want. I can tell you're bored." Her eyes traveled across the room to where Carly was standing. She squinted. "Hey, isn't that . . . ?"

"Rebecca, don't."

She looked at him, but she rarely listened. "It's Jaden's mom, isn't it?" She smiled. "Finally, I can get the dirt on you." She flounced over to Carly like they were old friends who hadn't seen each other in years.

Seconds later, Carly looked up, horror on her face. Her eyes darted to Josh then back to Rebecca, who was just . . . about . . . to . . .

"You're Carly," Rebecca said in her usual bubbly tone.

Quinn's eyes widened. Carly froze.

"I recognize you from the picture in Josh's office."

Josh hurried toward them, silently begging Rebecca to stop talking.

"He has my picture in his office?" Carly asked.

"It's from the day Jaden was born," Josh said, imagining it. It was the same one he'd had framed for Jaden's room in his apartment. The same one he'd thrown into his duffel when he left for Harbor Pointe a few weeks before.

Carly practically glowed in that photo, snapped only seconds after Jaden had arrived. It was the only photo he had of the three of them. And if his office caught on fire, it would be the only thing he grabbed on his way out the door.

Carly watched him with eyes so intense it set him off-kilter.

"I'm so glad we ran into each other like this. I have so many questions," Rebecca said.

"Who are you?" Carly asked in a not-quite-unfriendly-but-not-quite-friendly-either tone.

"Carly, Rebecca," Josh said, motioning to each of them as he said their names. "Rebecca, Carly."

"We work together," Rebecca said. "I'm the real brains of the operation." She winked.

Josh tugged her arm. "Becks, we should go."

"Josh is on a mission to convince me it's a good idea to make this cute little town our company's new headquarters." She smiled. "I gotta say, after sampling the fudge across the street, I might be on board."

"You're moving back?" Carly's eyes darted to his, but he quickly looked away. He wasn't ready to discuss the crazy idea that they should move here—not yet. He didn't know if it would lead to anything, but Rebecca seemed to think everyone on the planet needed to know the innermost thoughts in his mind.

"I'm just exploring options," he said.

Rebecca rolled her eyes dramatically. "He gave me the hard sell the second I got out of my rental car. Now I just have to convince my fiancé."

"Your fiancé?" Quinn asked.

"Kyle." Rebecca did that wide-eyed, *I'm so in love* thing girls do and Josh tried not to shrink under the weight of Carly's glare.

Why hadn't he told her he was considering moving back? That's what she would want to know.

Because he was afraid of how she might react to the idea.

"We're going to meet Jaden at that fancy new ski training center," Rebecca said. "Maybe we'll see you there?"

"Uh, maybe," Carly said.

Josh tried to shake the image of her in the wedding dress, but so far he was failing. He couldn't unsee something that beautiful.

"Okay, see you later, then," Rebecca said. She leaned in and kissed Carly's cheek. "So glad to finally meet you."

Carly didn't move or respond. She only stared at Josh, who gave them a lame wave and walked away.

Chapter Twenty-Nine

After their unfortunate run-in with Josh and beautiful Rebecca, Carly didn't feel much like shopping anymore. Quinn sat across from her in their favorite booth at Hazel's Kitchen, waiting for their lunch to be delivered and obviously waiting for her to say something.

Carly had nothing to say.

"What's going on?" Quinn asked.

Carly knew lying to her sister was not an option—she'd always been able to see right through her. But telling her about the jumble of emotions was not an option either.

"Let's talk about the wedding. Paris for the honeymoon, huh? What will you do there?"

Quinn frowned. "I will only talk to you about my wedding when I have your undivided attention."

"You do."

"I most certainly do not," Quinn said. "And I'm not leaving here until you tell me what's bugging you."

She frowned. "It's nothing."

"Is 'nothing' also known as 'Josh'?"

Carly sighed. Told her about the lawn mower. Told her about

the porch confession. Told her that her stomach still wobbled when he was around.

And to her surprise, Quinn didn't try to talk her out of anything or tell her what a fool she was. She simply listened. Nodded at the appropriate times. Covered her hand with her own and smiled sympathetically.

"You and Josh were really good together once," she finally said after Carly had gotten it all out.

"That was a lifetime ago," Carly said. "And he broke my heart."

Quinn nodded. "I remember. And I don't want to let him back in either."

Carly found her sister's eyes. It had been hard for Quinn too, when Josh left. She'd loved him like a brother.

"But he is making some good choices," Quinn said. "What if he has changed?"

Carly shook her head. "You can't start talking like that, Q. I'm already floundering over here."

"I know. It's just—"

"What?"

"I saw the way he looked at you in that dress."

Carly stilled. "Attraction was never our problem."

Quinn shook her head. "It was more than that. He loves you, Car. Whether or not he's capable of loving you the way you deserve though, that remains to be seen."

Carly's heart teeter-tottered in her chest.

"But every time we open our hearts, it's a risk."

Carly turned her water glass around in her hand, the condensation wetting her skin.

"If you decide to give him another chance," Quinn said, "I'll support you completely."

Carly looked at her through cloudy eyes. "You will?"

Quinn nodded. "I just want you to be happy. And if Josh makes you happy, then I'll be happy for you both."

Carly couldn't believe they were even having this conversation, but somehow it settled her nerves.

At least one person in town wouldn't think she was crazy to give Josh a second chance.

* * *

After they left the diner, Carly and Quinn drove toward the training center to pick up Jaden.

"He's probably had enough activity for one day," Carly said as they arrived. She was a little surprised he'd lasted this long.

They walked in the large, nearly empty space and found Grady sitting at the front desk, on the computer.

"Place is looking great," Carly said.

He looked up and smiled. "Just about ready for our grand opening."

"Where's Jaden? Did you watch him like a hawk?"

"I did until Josh got here." He raised an eyebrow. "Who's the blonde?"

"Just someone he works with," Quinn said, widening her eyes.

Carly shrugged. "Even if she was more than a co-worker, that would be fine because Josh and I are not a couple."

"Yet."

Carly ignored her. "Where are they?"

"Just through there." He pointed down a hallway and off Carly went. As she walked away, she heard Quinn say, "I might've found my wedding dress today."

She smiled at the thought.

Down the hall and around to the right, Carly knew she would find the main attraction—a large, indoor slope that worked a little bit like a treadmill, but for skiers. According to Jaden, it could be adjusted depending on skill level, and it wasn't an arcade game—it was serious training.

She knew it was breaking his heart not to be up there, trying it out for himself—the machine hadn't been ready until after Jaden's diagnosis. He could hardly wait to get out there himself.

Or not.

She followed the sound of laughter around the corner and through the doors, but when the machine came into view, she found Jaden—not sitting on the sidelines, but on the slope, wearing a pair of skis and cheering as he and Josh—what? Raced? Was this a simulated race?

"What are you doing?"

The laughter cut out as abruptly as a recorded track on an old sitcom.

"Mom!"

"You know the rules!" Carly glared. They were making her look like a horrible, mean, un-fun ogre—and in front of Rebecca. But really? What were they thinking?

"It's on the easiest setting, Mom," Jaden said. "And I've got my monitor on—my heart rate hasn't changed a bit."

"You know the rules." She glared at Josh. Good old, fun, *unreliable* Josh. "And so do you."

He stepped off the machine and shook his head. "Carly, I'm sorry. It really isn't strenuous at all, and he was dying to try it out."

She narrowed her eyes. "I can't believe I trusted you." Then to Jaden—"Get your stuff. We're going home."

She stormed out, and Josh followed her, though it was a bit tricky considering he was still wearing the skis. "Carly, wait."

She didn't stop. "I'll be in the car. Jaden, you better hurry up." She rushed past Quinn and Grady and out onto the sidewalk, the warm June air stifling and humid tonight.

Or maybe that was simply her situation constricting her lungs.

Josh ran out, barefoot, as couples walked by—tourists most likely—on their way to the boardwalk, a restaurant, the beach. Normal people who didn't have piles of baggage and a million years between them.

She was jealous of those people.

"Carly, you know I would never let him do anything that might hurt him." Josh rushed toward her car.

She stopped before opening the door. "How would I know that? From your stellar track record?"

People were staring. She could feel their eyes. She didn't care. She shook her head. "And to think, I almost fell for it."

"Fell for what?"

"Your little speech last night. How you deserved a second chance—what absolute garbage. You're with him alone for five seconds and you're breaking all the rules again."

"It wasn't garbage—will you let me explain?"

"No, I'm done listening to you, Josh," she said. "You confuse me. I can't see straight when you're around."

He took a step toward her, but she stopped him with an upheld hand.

"Just leave me alone, all right?"

He lingered there for a long moment, and she could tell he wanted to say more—but he didn't. Instead, he turned and disappeared inside the training center, leaving her standing on the sidewalk with pairs of touristy eyes trained on her.

She wondered if any of them had filmed her outburst. Would she see herself on Twitter later that night?

She pulled the door of her Civic open and got inside, plopping down into the beautiful solitude of the vehicle. Only then did she look up and straight into the eyes of Dr. David Willette, standing only a few feet away, a witness to her glorious outburst.

Well, great. She supposed now he would do what he should've done weeks ago—run as far away from her as he could.

Chapter Thirty

Carly got out of the car and met David on the sidewalk. So far he wasn't running in the opposite direction, though it was highly likely he was contemplating it.

What could she say to smooth over what he'd just seen and heard? She didn't deserve someone like him and she knew it. She'd always known it.

"David, I'm sorry you had to hear that." She rushed after him, away from the curious onlookers watching through the windows from inside the restaurant. How could she lose her cool like that? Where was her ever-present, carefully controlled, level head?

Her father was right—Josh did bring out the worst in her. It's what he'd said when she told him she was pregnant. He blamed it on Josh, the troublemaker, as if he'd been the one who'd twisted her arm. As if it hadn't been her idea for them to sleep together in the first place. As if she'd protested the several times they'd been together since the junior prom.

Sometimes she regretted not standing up for Josh. She'd let her dad believe what he wanted to believe because she was so afraid of what he'd think of her.

Why had she been such a coward?

Why was she still such a coward?

David turned and faced her. "No, I'm the one who's sorry. I obviously inserted myself into a very complicated situation."

"There is no situation," she said.

But the expression on his face told her that was hardly true.

"Okay, maybe it's a little confusing right now, but Josh and I, we're ancient history." If she didn't believe that before, she certainly did now that she knew he couldn't be trusted.

"Sounds like there's still a lot to work through," he said. "And I'm going to give you some space so you can do that."

"David, no."

"I'm not saying this is over between us, just that maybe we should put it on pause." He was pragmatic and measured. He would never show up on her porch late at night, out of breath and needing to profess his love. David might not be passionate, but he was a good man. And good men were hard to find.

But when she boiled it down, they had very little in common, and truthfully, she couldn't see herself with him for the rest of her life, which made her the worst person in the world, she knew.

"I'd like us to still be friends, Carly," he said matter-of-factly. "If you want."

"Of course," she said.

"I know you don't share my feelings," he said. "And why would you? You're smart and beautiful and independent. I sneeze every time I'm in the same room with a bouquet of roses."

She smiled. "You're a great guy, David."

"Oh, I know," he said with a smile. "But maybe not *your* guy?"

She studied him. "I don't think I deserve you."

He pressed his lips together and smiled warmly. "I think you deserve the moon, Carly. And I also think you deserve a fresh start."

She frowned. "What do you mean?"

"I've been offered a position in Denver," David said. "And I accepted."

Carly took a step back. "Oh."

"There's something wonderful about starting over. Maybe you should consider it for yourself?"

"Moving?"

"Why not? I think getting out of Harbor Pointe could be good for you."

"What about Jaden—his friends—the training center? He would never leave."

David shrugged. "Maybe he would. The skiing is better in Colorado. Or if not there, somewhere else. It's a big world."

That was true. Maybe . . . but what was she thinking? She couldn't leave Harbor Pointe. She'd never lived anywhere else. This was where all her memories were.

And yet, maybe that was exactly why she needed to go.

"I care about you, Carly," David said. "You deserve to be treated with respect. You deserve to be happy. And I'd be glad to be your friend for as long as you'll let me, but I'd be lying if I said I'd stop hoping for something more."

It was refreshing to have an adult conversation. She definitely did not deserve this man. After all, wasn't she the one who'd just caused a scene on a busy sidewalk?

"You're not mad?"

"Why? Because you led me on?"

She frowned. "Don't say that."

"No," he said. "Because I really don't believe even you realize you still have feelings for Jaden's dad."

"But I don't—"

He held up a hand to silence her. "It's okay. I get it. There's a lot of history there."

"You've misunderstood, David. We're honestly so over. We couldn't be more over if we were the Civil War."

A perplexed look washed across his face.

"That made more sense in my head."

He smiled. "Think about Denver. It could be good for you and for Jaden."

"I'll think about it."

He leaned down and kissed her on the cheek, treating her with far more kindness than she deserved.

He started off down the street in the opposite direction of the training center, and when she turned back, she found Josh standing on the sidewalk, hands in his pockets, staring at her.

And she turned and walked the other way.

* * *

After far longer than he should've taken, Jaden got in the car and slammed the door.

"Do you care to explain yourself?"

"That's what Dad was trying to do," he said.

"This isn't about your dad."

"Really?" He gave her a dubious look.

"I left specific instructions, Jaden," she said. "I made it all very clear. And your dad ignored them. Why am I surprised? That man cannot be trusted."

"Mom, he called Dr. Carroll," Jaden said. "The swimmer's doctor. He's got his cell number."

"What?" Carly tapped her thumb against the steering wheel, a wave of *oh no* rushing over her.

"He called the doctor on his cell, interrupted his dinner on some yacht somewhere, but the guy didn't even care."

"Why would he do that?"

"To make sure it was okay for me to go on the simulator."

She could feel him staring at her. A car behind her honked, and only then did she realize she'd stopped in the middle of the road. She stepped on the gas. "He called the doctor?"

"Yep."

"And the doctor said it was fine?"

"Yep."

"But how did Dr. Carroll know what you were actually doing?"

"FaceTime," Jaden said.

And Carly felt like an idiot.

"He said I could do it as long as my heart rate didn't spike, so we kept it on the lowest setting, which was smart anyway because Dad kind of sucks at skiing."

He called your doctor?

She'd instantly thought the worst of Josh, as if she was just waiting for him to mess up.

How would she ever face him again after that humiliating display?

"So you should probably apologize to Dad," Jaden said.

She groaned. "I'm such an idiot."

"Why? Because you're still in love with Dad, but you pretend not to be?"

Carly gave Jaden's arm a smack. "I am not in love with your dad."

"Yeah, okay." He opened the door. "Keep telling yourself that." He slammed the door, leaving Carly alone in the quiet of her car.

"I am not in love with your dad," she whispered, as if saying it made it so.

Chapter Thirty-One

It was one of those nights. Tossing. Turning. Mind racing. She'd had more of these nights since Jaden's diagnosis than she'd had in her entire adult life, but tonight, her thoughts weren't filled with worry over her son's health.

She rolled over for the thousandth time, flipped her pillow to the other side and stared at the ceiling.

She hated that she'd made a scene—a public scene! It was so unlike her. Cool, collected Carly flew off the handle. What was wrong with her? She rarely took a step without first analyzing all possible outcomes.

She hated that Josh still had this crazy hold on her, as if there was no way of escaping his lips, his eyes, the way he saw straight past her façade to all the things she would never say aloud.

Josh didn't buy her strong, independent act for a second, did he?

Sure, she put up a good front, but inside, she was crumbling. He saw that now. Everyone saw that now.

She'd avoided her phone all night long, then hid out in her room, and now—she lay here, willing herself to sleep so she could pretend, at least for a few hours, that everything was back to the way it was supposed to be.

Wishing she hadn't felt the unmistakable pang of jealousy the second she spotted Josh and Rebecca in town together. She *did* think they were a couple. She *had* been relieved when he explained she was a co-worker. She'd been downright *overjoyed* when Rebecca mentioned her fiancé.

That Kyle was one lucky guy.

And suddenly she wondered about the women Josh had dated over the years. Had he loved any of them? Why hadn't he gotten married? Had he whispered *I love you* through intimate, stolen kisses the way he'd done with her so many times?

And again, she was back to wondering why she cared.

You're still in love with Dad.

Jaden's words rushed back and she swatted them away as if they were angry gnats at a summer picnic.

She most certainly was not in love with Josh. He'd left her, after all. She'd raised their son alone for fifteen years. Did he get a free pass simply because he seemed to have figured out he'd made a colossal mistake?

Sigh. Still. She might owe him an apology. She hadn't even bothered to ask—she'd assumed. Jaden was up on the simulator. Josh was right beside him. They *must've* thrown out the rules like thoughtless morons. They must not have cared one bit about the risks.

What an idiot!

Slowly, she crept out of bed and pulled on her favorite gray sweatshirt. Once upon a time, it had been Josh's sweatshirt, she realized now, remembering how she wore it throughout her pregnancy with Jaden. Remembering sweeter, more tender moments between the two of them.

They'd been so in love. Crazy about each other. Josh wasn't only her boyfriend, he was her best friend—the person who knew her better than anyone else in the world.

And then he left—and that love inched over the precipice into hate, and that's where it had remained.

Until he showed up here and bought her a lawn mower and

helped take care of their son and hugged her when she needed (and didn't want) to be hugged and told her everything would be okay.

She shuffled downstairs quietly, so as not to wake Jaden, then walked outside into the darkness, started her car and drove toward the old fishing cabin.

He wouldn't be awake, of course. It wasn't like he was going to lose sleep over her public display of ridiculousness.

But when she pulled up and parked across the street from the small, shingled house, she saw the blue light of the television flickering through the bay window at the front. He'd probably found her father's old VHS movies. Maybe he'd fallen asleep in a recliner or on the couch. She glanced at the clock. It was nearly two.

What am I doing here?

Wide awake and fully aware that she wouldn't sleep until she got a few things off her chest, she hopped out of the car and strode toward the front door.

"God, if this is a mistake, please stop me," she said aloud. "Let a comet fall out of the sky or put a giant sinkhole right here in front of me before I make an even bigger fool of myself."

When neither of those things happened, Carly pressed on until she found herself standing on the porch of the little cabin that held so many memories.

She stood, unmoving, for several seconds, contemplating what she might say if Josh opened that door. She didn't even know what she wanted from him—they obviously couldn't get back together. She obviously wasn't still in love with him. He had his life and she had hers, and now she was even considering a move across the country. Okay, maybe that was something of a fleeting thought, but it was still there at the back of her mind. She'd lost her promotion, after all.

Why am I here?

Her mental Olympics were cut short when the outside light came on and she felt like a criminal caught in a police search light.

She froze as the door opened and there he was.

His hair was mussed, looking darker than usual in this light. He wore sweats and a T-shirt, and he stared at her with curious eyes filled with such an intensity it was a wonder her knees didn't buckle under the weight of it.

"Is everything okay?" His brow furrowed, laced with concern.

She nodded, unable to find words. How did she apologize to the man whose apology she'd been waiting for all of sixteen years?

"Jaden's okay?"

Another nod. "Everyone's fine."

He looked around the dark neighborhood, then back to her. "Did you want to come in?"

"For a minute maybe?"

He stepped out of the way so she could pass, though she was drawn to his body on the way through the door like a magnet to a sheet of steel.

Inside, she turned a circle. "It looks good in here."

He pushed a hand through his already messy hair. "I don't sleep much."

She squared off in front of him and lifted her chin. She might have to eat crow, but she wasn't going to grovel. She'd get it over with quickly, before she could talk herself out of it. "I made an idiot of myself today."

He leaned against the doorjamb, and even in the faint light from the lamp outside, she could see that lazy smile had returned. "Nah, you?"

"It was out of character, I admit, but Jaden told me you cleared it with the doctor," she said. "I think I've just been extra emotional because of the surgery and everything."

"Is that what you're blaming it on?" He pushed himself upright and took a step toward her.

"It's not a giant leap," she said, inching away, as if putting any distance between them could sever the attraction. "It's been an emotional few weeks."

"It has." He moved closer, and she realized she'd backed

herself against the wall. "Why are you really here at two in the morning?"

Well, when he put it that way, it did sound a little dire. And insane. She'd gone insane. "I came to ask for a truce."

"A truce?"

"Yeah, you know, like waving the white flag?"

He stood directly in front of her now. Inches from her. If she shifted, their bodies would be touching. She studied his eyes, searching them for answers to questions that had kept them apart for years, but in them, she only found more questions. She was sure of nothing in that moment except that the air between them sparked, filled with tangible electricity, the kind that kept her glued in place.

"I was never at war with you, Carly," he said, his voice husky and low.

Slowly, she tipped her chin up and latched on to his gaze. There, she saw unmistakable desire—so thick it pinned her to the wall. She forced herself not to hold her breath, drawing in air and willing it to calm her racing heart.

"I'm sorry I thought you were careless with our son."

Josh tucked a stray hair behind her ear. "I would never be careless with him." He inched closer, then took her face in his hands.

Carly searched his eyes. This was crazy. What was she doing here? Did the darkness make her more susceptible to stupidity? Did it make her bolder? Less afraid?

She could deny it all she wanted, but nothing in her life had felt this right in a very long time. When she inhaled, her breath mixed with his, as he brought his forehead closer to hers, a hand at her chin.

"I need to kiss you," he said, voice charged with urgency.

"This is a bad idea." She pushed herself back against the wall, but barely moved, and the second his lips met hers, her doubts fell away. His kiss wasn't soft or gentle or tentative, it was as if she was filling his lungs with air. Her hands found his chest, then slid upward and laced around his neck, drawing him closer as he deepened the kiss.

His tongue grazed her bottom lip, sending a shiver down her spine, then all at once he pulled back, resting his forehead on hers. "You have no idea what you do to me." His hand rested on her shoulder, still wrapped gently at the side of her neck, and his skin on hers awakened something inside her that had been lying dormant for more years than she'd realized.

"This is crazy," she said.

He shook his head. "It's just crazy enough to be right." He kissed her again, this time softer, gentler, sweeter, as if savoring every part of her in this moment.

"I told you," he said.

"Told me what?"

"It would just take one kiss to prove this isn't over."

She didn't argue. Instead, she pulled him closer, her kisses so intent they proved his point.

She'd forgotten the way his lips tasted, distinctly and uniquely *Josh*, the way he inhaled her as if drinking her in made the whole experience that much richer. She'd forgotten how it felt to rest in the strength of his embrace, and how he made her believe she could do anything simply by the way he looked at her—like she'd hung the moon.

With his body pressed against hers and his hands searching for a safe place to land, Carly took a fleeting moment to savor him as if this all made perfect sense. In her kisses, she unleashed the fire of passion she'd forgotten she held and let herself fall deeper into the warmth of him.

Were David and Jaden right? Did she still love Josh?

His kisses turned hurried again, and she responded to the height of his desire, wishing they could stop time, wishing away the pain of a past that had hung them both out to dry.

He pulled away, and in the absence of his lips on hers, she covered her mouth with her hand and watched him inhale—

exhale—then inhale again, as if it was impossible to catch his breath.

He took a step back, then met her eyes. "You're so beautiful, Carly."

She looked away. "I bet you say that to all the girls."

He tipped her chin up with his hand, forcing her gaze. "There haven't been any other girls."

She frowned, a nervous laugh escaping through her lips, but when she steadied her eyes on his she saw he wasn't kidding. "What do you mean?"

"There's only ever been you."

He'd never loved anyone else?

He walked over to a small table in the entryway and picked up his wallet, opened it and pulled out a folded sheet of what looked like notebook paper. He unfolded it and handed it to her.

Her eyes fell on the page and the familiar words he'd written so many years ago came into focus through her clouded eyes. "Is this . . . ?"

"I made you a promise."

She looked at the paper in her hand. "I don't understand."

"I promise to cherish you. To take care of you. To do what's best for you and to always put your happiness before my own." He recited the words steadily from memory. "I promise that in all things you will forever be my *always*."

She shook her head. "You mean there's been no one serious?"

That made sense. She'd dated, after all, but none of those short-lived relationships had turned into anything. Perhaps it was the same for him?

"No, Carly." He took her hand and kissed her palm. "I mean there's been no one."

She pulled her hand away. "This doesn't make sense." Her heart pounded through her chest now. She spun around, walking toward the blue light dancing in the living room, simply to put distance between her body and Josh's.

He made her feel things she shouldn't feel. As if all the

sleeping places inside of her had suddenly awakened, quickening her pulse, spinning her mind. And now this? What did he mean there had been no one else? How was that even possible?

Josh likely had been propositioned on a weekly basis, more so since his app took off and he'd grown wealthy—no way he'd resisted this whole time.

"It's pretty straight-forward. I haven't been with anyone else —" He cut himself off, folding the sheet of paper and tucking it back in his wallet.

"Why do you have that?"

He met her eyes from across the room, and she saw the hurt he didn't even bother to try and hide. "What do you mean?"

"I mean you left—why would you keep the vows you wrote? You broke them." Her mind worked to wrap itself around the idea that Josh might've been faithful to her in his absence, as if they were legally bound, as if he owed it to her.

But no, he'd made his choice. He walked out on them. His actions had broken those vows ages ago.

"I didn't." The words were clipped. "I've cherished you. I've put your happiness before my own—don't you see that?"

She shook her head. "No, I don't."

He pushed his hand through his hair, an exasperated sound escaping his lips. "I left so you and Jaden would have a shot—so you'd be happy."

"What?" Disbelief worked its way through her mind as she struggled to understand.

"I know it didn't exactly make sense, but I did what I thought was best."

"Josh, you walked out on us."

"You don't understand." His words were spiked with frustration. "I left because it was better for you guys."

"No," she snapped. "I don't get that at all. Do you know how hard it was raising a baby by myself?" Her voice caught in her throat and she struggled to swallow, struggled to speak. "I was eighteen. I had no idea what I was doing."

"You had everything figured out from the start, Carly," he said. "You didn't need me. You didn't need anyone."

"What does that mean?"

"I tried to help you, but I never did anything the right way. I always felt like a screw-up."

"And that's my fault?"

He sighed. "That's not what I'm saying."

"You are. You're saying I made you feel like you didn't know what you were doing."

"Well, you did!" He shouted the words, his anger flaring. "And then you make these assumptions about me like you've got everything all figured out, just like you did today."

Carly's jaw went slack. "It was an honest mistake, and unlike you, I apologized."

"You get these ideas in your head, Carly, but you don't know the whole story. You don't know—" Again, he stopped short of saying what she could only imagine was something very important.

"What don't I know?" She knew everything—didn't she?

"Forget it." Josh stared at the floor and drew in a slow breath. "I don't want to fight with you."

"How can you not see how hypocritical this is?" she asked, not willing to let it go. "You pull these vows out like I should be impressed you haven't slept with a bunch of women—"

"No, Carly. I haven't slept with *any* women. Only you."

The words hung there, filling the space between them.

"For me, it's always only been you."

"Then why did you leave?" Tears sprang to her eyes and she willed herself not to cry. "Don't you regret it at all?"

He moved across the room, eyes locked on to hers, and when he reached her, he stopped, almost as if he didn't dare touch her now. "I regret that I wasn't the man you needed."

A tear slid down her cheek. "But you don't regret leaving?"

His gaze dipped to her mouth then back to her eyes and he

shook his head ever so slightly. "I did what was best for you and Jaden."

She stepped back on wobbly legs, eyes filling with fresh tears she would not let herself cry. "This was a terrible mistake."

He reached for her, but she yanked her hand away.

"Carly—don't."

She started for the door but stopped in the entryway and looked back at him. "I never thought my heart could feel as broken as it did the morning I realized you were gone. But I think this is even worse—so congratulations, Josh. You're the only man who's ever broken my heart twice." She wiped her cheeks dry with the sleeves of the tattered sweatshirt. "And I'm the fool who fell for you all over again so shame on me."

His eyes had turned glassy, but he said nothing.

And Carly walked out the door, certain that, at long last, things between her and Josh were officially over.

Chapter Thirty-Two

J osh stared at the empty space in the entryway, the memory of Carly's kisses so fresh in his mind they brought him physical pain. How good it had felt to hold her, to explore her body with his hands, to taste her lips on his tongue.

He wanted her—every part of him wanted her. But more than that, he loved her. How could she not see that? How could she doubt for a second that he'd done the right thing—he'd vowed to put her happiness first. If she knew the things he'd seen, the demons he battled—she would thank him for leaving when he did.

Wouldn't she?

He sank back onto the couch where he'd fallen asleep hours before she came. It had been a fitful sleep, interrupted and frustrating, and when he saw her standing at the door, for a moment he thought he was dreaming.

Now that dream had turned into a nightmare.

He loved her—was God really going to make him let her go —again?

He clicked the television off. Maybe it was time to tell her the truth, the secrets he'd spent his whole life keeping.

But what would she say if she knew the real reason why he'd

left? There would be no coming back after that. He'd lose her for good.

He tried to sleep. He tried focusing on nothing, but the image of his little brother's face kept creeping into his mind.

Dylan.

He didn't talk about Dylan. Nobody talked about Dylan. The only reason Carly even knew Dylan had existed was because she saw a photograph of Dylan and Josh, the one Josh still kept in his desk.

She'd asked about Josh's little brother, but he hadn't been forthcoming with the details.

"He died when I was younger," he'd said. "I don't like to talk about it."

And he didn't.

They'd moved to Harbor Pointe to escape the memory of what happened with Dylan. Why was it coming back now—as if it had happened yesterday?

The details had always been a thick fog at the back of his mind.

"It was an accident, Josh," his mother had said. "Try not to dwell on it."

But how could he not? It was his fault. His actions had caused his brother's death.

They'd grown up in a neighborhood with boxy houses and small yards, so all the kids played at the park down the block. It was a neighborhood park with swings and a slide and a merry-go-round. Sometimes in the summer, they spent their entire day on that playground.

That day, they got there late. The sun was setting, and it was a strange time for them to be at the park at all. They hadn't had dinner, and Josh's stomach growled.

He rolled over, trying to shove the thoughts aside. He worked to fill his mind with the image of Carly instead of the image of Dylan—with his dark, curly hair and big blue eyes. With Dylan being the typical tag-along little brother, the two boys were inseparable. Josh liked being admired, and Dylan looked at his older brother like he was a celebrity.

What happened next?

His thought bank was empty.

But then he remembered. The ambulance. The sirens. The paramedic picking up Dylan's limp body and putting it onto a stretcher.

One of the other kids had run home to fetch their parents, but Josh stayed frozen in the spot where Dylan had collapsed, right next to the merry-go-round, which had gone eerily still.

His parents rushed through the yards and into the park, arriving moments before the ambulance pulled up.

"What happened?" Josh's mom knelt down next to Dylan, whose eyes were closed. She gave the boy's cheek three quick, but gentle, slaps. "Dylan, wake up." She looked at Josh, her eyes wide. "What happened?"

"They were rough-housing again," his dad said. "Isn't it obvious?"

Shock and fear prevented Josh from speaking.

The ambulance screamed in and two paramedics raced toward them. Gloria moved aside to give them space to check on Dylan as a small crowd of neighbors gathered.

"Do we know what happened?" one of the paramedics asked Josh.

"He—" Josh started.

"They were messing around, you know, being boys, and he hit his head on the merry-go-round," his father interrupted.

Josh looked up at his dad, who quickly met his son's eyes. "I'm always telling them not to push each other, but they don't listen."

"So you pushed him and he fell?" the paramedic asked, eyes steady on Josh.

But Josh couldn't speak.

He couldn't speak because he didn't remember. He didn't know what had happened to his brother. All he knew was that one minute he was fine and the next, he was on the ground, unconscious.

"Josh, answer him."

Josh's eyes filled with tears. "I don't know. I don't remember."

The paramedics lifted Dylan up onto the stretcher. "One of you can ride in the back with us." They rushed off and Gloria ran to catch up, leaving Josh sitting on the ground in the dirt under the heavy weight of his father's glare.

"You better pray your brother is okay," his dad said.

Josh struggled to understand. Why didn't he remember?

"What happened, Josh? You were mad at Dylan earlier because he took your Game Boy. Were you fighting? Did he make you mad enough that you hit him? Pushed him down?"

Josh shook his head. "I don't know."

His father frowned. "Get up."

Josh stood, expecting the full weight of his dad's anger, but there were people around, and that was the only reason his dad let him walk home without a scratch.

"I'm going to the hospital," he said when they reached the driveway. "You go inside and start praying your brother is okay."

Josh ran up to his room, flopped onto the bed and cried for an hour straight, praying—begging God—that his brother would be okay.

But when his parents came home later that night, it was clear by his mother's tear-stained face and the emptiness in his father's eyes that God hadn't heard Josh's prayers.

Dylan didn't make it. He had a brain hemorrhage as a result of being struck on the head.

"Josh, some people are going to come by tomorrow and ask you some questions," his dad said.

Josh frowned. "About what?"

"About what happened on the playground."

His mother cried quietly.

"But I don't remember," Josh said. "He just fell down."

His father shook his head. "Don't start making up stories. You'll sound like a liar."

"I'm not—"

"When they get here, you tell them the truth. You were playing. You pushed your brother. He fell and hit his head."

Josh looked at his mom. Why wasn't she saying anything? Was that what happened? Why couldn't he remember?

"Sometimes we get angry, and sometimes our anger makes us do things we don't mean," his dad said. "We know you didn't mean to hurt your brother."

Josh choked back a sob. "I didn't—"

"Stop lying!" his father barked. "The doctors said he had to have been pushed, Joshua. He was pushed and he fell and hit his head."

Josh dropped to the ground. Tears streamed down his face as sobs took over his eight-year-old body.

His brother was dead—and it was all his fault.

The following day, he overheard the police talking to his parents after their short interview with Josh. He'd told them exactly what his father said he should. They'd been playing. He pushed Dylan. Dylan fell and hit his head on the metal merry-go-round.

But there were questions they'd asked that Josh couldn't answer.

Blank spots in his memory that didn't make sense.

"We have some concerns," one of the officers said. "It sounds like he might've blacked out during some of the argument with his brother."

Josh wanted to tell them there wasn't an argument, but he couldn't say that for certain, could he?

"What does that mean?" his mother asked in a tone so hushed he was surely not meant to overhear.

"We think you should take him to a child psychologist," the officer said. "If he has fits of rage that lead to blackouts, that's cause for concern."

"He could be a danger to himself or, really, anyone else."

"But Joshua is such a mild-mannered child," Gloria said.

"Just have him talk to someone," the officer said.

"We'll have more questions," the other officer said. "We can't exactly piece together what happened, but we need to keep an eye on your son."

They moved toward the entryway and Josh raced away from the door. Was what they said true? Was he a danger to the people he loved? How had this happened—was something wrong with him?

A month went by and his parents never took him to a child psychologist. The police spoke with him two more times, but nothing ever came of their questions. Another month passed and Josh's father moved them to Harbor Pointe—to escape the rumors, he'd said. They needed a fresh start.

When he met Carly that first day in town, she'd been like a beacon of light. It was as if somehow he knew that she was the life preserver that would keep him from sinking.

Even at that young age, he'd been so drawn to her, but even she knew nothing about Dylan. She didn't know Josh's fit of rage had led to his brother's death. Every time she talked about what kind of monster Josh's father was, all he could think was *I'm that same kind of monster.*

If she knew that, she'd be horrified. He'd lose her forever.

But now, years between that day and this, he thought perhaps it was time to tell her the whole truth. She'd be horrified, yes, but would she finally understand why he'd left? Why he didn't regret it? Would she see, once and for all, that in leaving, Josh had saved them?

And as he drifted off to sleep, he thought maybe it was a chance he finally needed to take.

Chapter Thirty-Three

Carly and Jaden hadn't been to Sunday dinner in a couple of weeks, and as they were leaving church, it was clear they weren't going to get out of it again.

She'd sat through the message thinking the kinds of thoughts that made her blush, replaying her short-lived make-out session with Josh. She'd felt like a teenager all over again, and for a few delicious moments, their past hadn't mattered.

He'd gotten his one kiss. She was mortified to think he'd almost convinced her he was right.

She told herself to think about what had happened after the kiss, the fighting, the harsh words they'd spoken, but the memories of his soft, full lips kissing her with such urgency kept creeping in.

"You're coming to Dad's," Quinn said.

Carly held back a groan. "I have a lot to do, Q."

"I don't care. You can't keep avoiding family dinner."

"Dad's just going to lecture me."

Quinn raised a brow. "And why would he need to do that?"

"He doesn't." Carly slung her purse over her shoulder as Beverly wrapped an arm around Quinn's.

"You girls ready for ham and potatoes?"

"I'm ready," Jaden said from behind his mother. "I'm starving."

Beverly smiled, then reached over and squeezed Carly's hand. "It'll be good to have the whole family together again."

Carly sighed as the older woman walked away.

"Now you have to come," Quinn said.

Carly wished she had Quinn's easy-going relationship with their father, but the truth was, she'd been the great Collins disappointment. After their mother left, Gus had raised the girls the best he could, but Carly hadn't turned out the way she was supposed to. She'd made the kinds of mistakes that publicly humiliated her dad, practically proving he wasn't fit to raise a teenage daughter on his own.

She'd embarrassed him, and he was ashamed of her.

And Carly was ashamed of herself, sometimes even still.

She'd suffered through weeks and months and years of family dinners, and it never changed. She always left feeling just on the underside of accepted.

How much worse would it be today—with news of her outburst outside the training center spreading throughout the little town? Not to mention her flushed cheeks over her encounter with Josh last night.

Nobody even knew about that, but if they found out . . .

What they must think of her.

She and Jaden drove in silence until they reached the neighborhood where she and Quinn had grown up.

She could practically see herself as a child, chasing Josh and some of the other kids down the sidewalk on the way to the park.

"I invited Dad." Jaden stared out the window.

"You what?" She spun sideways and faced her son.

"He probably can't make it," Jaden said. "Said something about going to his own parents' house today."

Carly turned back to the road, aware she was frowning. Why would Josh go to his parents' house? Her pulse kicked up a notch at the thought. What if Josh did something stupid? She'd always marveled at the fact that he seemed nothing like his own father, and yet, he did have a temper—what if he lost it?

What if he finally faced all those old demons?

"What's wrong?"

"What?" Carly had absent-mindedly put the car in Park and now stared out the window. "Oh, nothing."

"You seem distracted," Jaden said.

Carly waved him off. "You know how I feel about Sunday dinner."

Jaden rubbed his stomach. "I feel hungry." He grinned. "I'm going to eat everything." He exited the car, leaving her sitting alone, conflicted feelings racing through her mind.

She pulled out her phone and scrolled through her messages, found the last one she'd gotten from Josh—something about Jaden—and started typing.

Josh, I know things aren't great between us, but I'm still here if you need to talk. She sent it, then looked to see the message had been delivered.

She waited a few seconds, then typed: *Don't go to your mom and dad's.*

He didn't respond, and she didn't expect him to, but that didn't stop her from worrying. Just the way he'd reacted to seeing his parents at the hospital had been enough to prove Josh struggled with being back here.

She closed her eyes and prayed for the man who'd infuriated her and broken her heart. "God, I don't pretend to know what he's been through, but keep him from doing anything stupid today."

The knock on the window startled her. She turned and found Quinn standing on the opposite side of the window, holding a pie. Carly opened the door and got out.

"What are you doing out here?" Quinn asked.

"Nothing," she said. "Just pulled up."

She followed her sister inside, where they found Gus, Beverly, Judge and Calvin standing in the dining room around a beautifully set table. Hellos were exchanged, questions about Jaden's health were answered, and she did her best to ignore the nagging thoughts about Josh and his parents.

After dinner, Quinn fetched the apple pie she'd made and Beverly added her famous frosted brownies to the table. Everyone heaped desserts onto their plates, oohing and aahing and discussing the sugar content, the calories and how none of that mattered at Sunday dinner.

"You're quiet, Carly," Beverly said warmly. "You've been through so much." She looked at Jaden. "We've missed you."

Sometimes Carly wondered if Beverly said all the things their father didn't say, as if she could parent them by proxy, as if she could lead by example. But if that was true, Gus had never picked up on any of her cues.

"It's good to be back," Carly said, telling herself it wasn't a lie. The food was good. Did it matter if her insides were spinning?

"You and Josh get things worked out?" Gus stuck a bite of pie in his mouth and peered at Carly down the table.

What has he heard?

Her stomach dropped with a thud. She didn't want to discuss Josh—not with him. He had strong opinions on Jaden's father, and it had taken her a long time to convince him to keep them to himself—for the sake of his grandson.

The image of her body tangled with Josh's the night before raced through her mind and she forcibly removed it.

"I'm not sure what you mean," she said. "Everything's fine."

Jaden had stopped chewing. "Dad wanted to come today, but he had other plans."

"Mm-hmm." Gus shoved another bite in his mouth, and Beverly placed a calming hand on his arm.

Carly pushed a brownie around her plate with her fork.

"I'm sure he's got lots of people to see while he's here," Quinn said, obviously trying to keep things from turning awkward, though Carly thought it might be a little late for that.

Carly looked up and caught the confused expression on

Jaden's face. Was her dad really going to put her son through this? Was it too much to ask for him to keep his opinions of Josh to himself?

"And just how long is he going to be here?" Gus gave Carly a pointed look.

"He's thinking about moving back," Jaden said.

Gus let out a wry laugh. "Is that right?"

Jaden's face fell. "Yeah. His business is mobile, and he said he wants to be closer to us."

"Us?" Gus asked.

"Me and Mom." Jaden set his fork down. "What's the big deal, Gramps? Dad's just trying to do what's right."

"Is he now? After all these years?" Gus glowered.

"There's no expiration date on second chances," Grady said.

Wise words from a man who knew a little something on the subject. Still, Carly wasn't convinced Josh deserved any such thing.

Gus turned his attention to Carly. "Heard about your little show outside Grady's training center yesterday."

"It wasn't a show," Carly said.

"Gus, please," Beverly interjected.

"I heard about it too," Judge quipped. "Always knew you were a feisty one, Carly Rae." His laugh boomed, and Grady smiled, but the air hung like a tense cloud above them.

Once upon a time, the relationship between the two men had been tense at best. Judge had been the reason for Grady's long stay in Harbor Pointe.

One might argue that Judge could be to blame for all of Grady's happiness—Judge certainly thought so.

"It was a misunderstanding," Carly said.

"Oh, we know," Gus said. "Ruth Nelson told us all about it. She's very concerned that history might be repeating itself."

Carly dropped her fork with a clang. "Why is it any of her business?"

"It's not," Quinn said. "I was there. It wasn't that big of a deal."

"My question, Carly, is why are you getting so worked up over Josh?" Gus eyed Carly with his familiar disapproval.

"I'm not," she said.

"You sure?" he asked. "Seems like you are."

"Oh, Gus, leave the girl alone," Judge said from his end of the table. "You know there's history there. Some of it is bound to come back up."

"Nothing is coming up," Carly said. "Josh and I are fine. And there's nothing going on."

"So long as you're sure," her dad said pointedly. "Remember, people don't change."

"I did," Grady said quietly.

Carly glanced up and met her future brother-in-law's eyes. Quinn reached over and took his hand.

Grady turned toward Gus. "Because of you."

Gus swallowed and took a drink. "That was different."

"Why? Because Quinn and I didn't have history?" Grady glanced at Jaden.

"This kid loves his dad, and far as I can tell, Josh is doing a good job with him. Maybe we should give him a second chance. Don't we all deserve that?"

The words hung in the air and Carly tried to knock them away, but she couldn't. Did Josh deserve a second chance?

"He's my dad, Gramps," Jaden said. "And he loves my mom."

Carly faced Jaden. "What did you say?"

"He told me. He's never stopped loving you."

Carly's breath caught in her throat, and she struggled for air. The room seemed to be closing in. Josh had told her the same thing, but she had no idea he'd discussed it with Jaden.

"And you love him too, so what's the big deal?" Jaden pushed his chair away from the table. "I'm going out to shoot some hoops."

"Be careful," Carly said.

"I won't even break a sweat."

"It's not anyone else's place to get in the middle of your relationship with Josh," Quinn said simply. "Not even yours, Dad."

"I disagree," their dad said. "When I see one of my daughters heading for disaster, you better believe I'm going to steer them the other way."

Anger welled up inside of Carly, and she thought she might explode. "But how would you even know if it's a disaster? You don't even know Josh anymore. You never really did."

"I know plenty," Gus said.

"Because you're buddies with his dad?" Carly's words were as dry and sarcastic as she'd intended them to be.

"Well, yes, if you must know. Jim has told me stories over the years—two fathers trading battle wounds."

"Battle wounds." Carly threw her napkin over her plate. "That's rich. If you knew what that man—" She stilled. Josh didn't want anyone knowing about his father. It wasn't her place, no matter how her silence made Josh look.

"That man, what?" her dad asked.

"Forget it," she said.

"I don't know why you're defending him," Dad said. "Clearly you've blocked out the pain of the last sixteen years."

Carly stood. "My last sixteen years haven't been all pain, Dad. I got a great kid out of the deal. My life wasn't ruined, and Josh didn't destroy me. He made me stronger. He forced me to become the person I was meant to become. I've forgiven him for leaving. And if I decided that I love him, I would expect you all to accept that and stop having an opinion about it." She looked at Beverly. "Thank you for dinner."

"Carly, don't go," Quinn said.

She looked at her dad. "Of course you aren't willing to give Josh a second chance—you haven't even given your own daughter a second chance. What more can I say? I screwed up. I let you down. I disappointed you. But you can't hold it against me for the rest of my life."

She didn't expect him to follow her—her dad was too proud for that—but she did hope he'd at least consider what she said.

Inside the quiet of her Honda, she let out a heavy sigh. She'd been holding that all in for years—why had she chosen today to let it all out?

She glanced at Jaden as he slid into the passenger seat and found him staring at her, the faintest hint of a smile on his face. Wow, he looked like Josh. Same dark hair. Same strong cheekbones. She'd stopped thinking so years ago, but with Josh back in her life, the similarities were hard to ignore.

"What are you smiling at?" she asked.

He held his hands up in mock surrender. "Nothing."

She started the car.

"Except you just totally defended Dad in there."

"So?"

"Told you you still love him."

She groaned and pulled away from the curb. "Don't read anything into it."

"You said you forgave him, Ma," Jaden said.

"You weren't supposed to be listening."

He shrugged.

"Besides, I told you that a long time ago."

"Yeah, but this time you meant it."

Did she? She did a quick gut check and noticed that little ball of anger that she carried with her wasn't there anymore. How was that possible given her exchange with Josh the night before? They'd left things poorly—not even on speaking terms. How could she even suggest she'd forgiven him? "Just because I don't want your grandpa talking about your dad in front of you or anyone else doesn't mean I'm still in love with him."

"Yeah, okay." Jaden stared out the window.

"Jaden, listen. I know you think your dad is a great guy—and he is, in his own way—but there's no future for him and me."

"You don't know that."

She slowed to a stop in front of a streetlamp. "Yes, I do."

"But you said you forgave him, and that's a huge step, Ma."

"I can forgive him without repeating my past mistakes."

Jaden scoffed. "So everything you said in there—all that stuff about second chances—?"

"Was true," Carly said.

"But you won't give Dad one. I get it."

"He's in your life, isn't he? Isn't that enough?" Carly stepped on the gas again and turned toward home. "I don't have to get back together with him in order to prove I've forgiven him."

"He loves you, Mom," Jaden said.

Carly tapped the steering wheel with her thumb. "But sometimes love just isn't enough."

Chapter Thirty-Four

J osh stared at his childhood home, not a trace of nostalgia in his mind.

His memories of the house were filled with angst. Tiptoeing around his dad. Watching his mom walk on eggshells. Finally getting tired of it as an older teenager and fighting back.

It occurred to him that you could never tell the truth about what went on inside a home when looking at it from the outside.

The perfectly manicured yard, the clean porch, the welcome mat under the door—it all suggested something that didn't exist.

A happy home.

He didn't know why he was here. He hadn't seen or spoken to his parents since he left the hospital that day. He had words bubbling at the back of his throat. Truth he'd held on to since he was young—was today the day he finally said it all aloud?

The memory of a day years ago crawled up the back of his brain, begging for attention.

Hadn't he proven he was just like his father? Angry. Violent. Ill-tempered?

Hadn't he shown that beyond a shadow of a doubt?

He shoved thoughts of Dylan out of his mind.

No. That wasn't who he was. Not anymore anyway. He hadn't had a violent outburst in years. But the details of that day were still so foggy, floating in the space just outside his memory. And the threat of it had been enough to drive him away for a very long time.

Robotically, he opened his car door, strode across the street, up the walk and onto the porch. He lifted his hand to knock on the door, but it opened before he could.

His mother's face brightened at the sight of him. "Joshua."

"Is Dad here?"

"He's in the backyard," she said. "Do you want something to eat? Or some coffee?"

"No, Mom."

"What is it, Joshua?" his mom asked. "You look upset."

Josh stuffed his hands in his pockets and studied her, over-whelmed with one thought—*get her out.*

"I've got money now, Mom."

"I know, dear," she said. "We're so proud of you."

"No, I mean—you don't have to stay here anymore."

Her face fell. "Joshua." She leaned in closer, lowering her voice. "What are you talking about?"

"Let's cut to the part where we stop pretending things are okay," Josh said.

She frowned. "Things are fine, Josh. You haven't been home in ages—everything is fine."

"Everything is not fine, Mom," he said. "He's still the same controlling, abusive loser he always was. You don't have to live like this."

His mom tossed a glance over her shoulder, as if to check to be sure his father couldn't hear. "It's fine, Josh. This is the life I chose."

"You're not safe."

"That's not true. He's not like that anymore," she said.

"Why? Because you do whatever he says?" Josh knew his volume made his mom uncomfortable, but he didn't care. She needed to understand the seriousness of the situation—how could she not? How could she still, after all that had happened, pretend everything was fine?

"I don't." She smoothed her shirt. "We've just learned how to live with each other."

"You can't tell me you're not scared, Mom," he said.

"I'm not scared," she said simply. "We hardly even argue anymore."

"You don't even see it," he said. "You're so blind. You know what he's done. How can you just pretend you don't?"

From behind her, a shadow passed through the entryway and his father appeared in the kitchen doorway. He glared at them, eyes locked on Josh.

"Gloria?"

His mother's face went pale, and Josh could see that despite what she said, she was terrified.

"Mom." Josh spoke softly, hoping his dad wouldn't be able to hear. "Come with me. I'll put you up in a nice house. I can support you. I'll make sure you're taken care of."

Her lower lip trembled and her chin dipped, eyes on the ground—meek, just the way her father had trained her to be. "My home is here," she whispered.

"What are you saying to her?" His dad made quick work of the distance between him and the front door.

His mom spun around. "He just came over to give us an update on Jaden, honey."

He pushed her aside, and Josh moved into the entryway.

"Don't touch her," he growled.

"Or what?"

Josh drew in a deep breath. *One—two—three.* He forced his mind to calm. He unclenched his fists. "You don't get to do this anymore."

The older man laughed. "That's where you're wrong, son. You might think things are different because you have money now, but you're mistaken. This is my house." He pointed at Gloria. "And she's my wife."

"Joshua, please. Let's have some lunch. It's Sunday so I've made—"

"Fried chicken and coleslaw. Dad's Sunday meal. I know." He kept his eyes firmly on his father.

His mom laughed. "Am I that predictable?"

"No, Mom, you're that brainwashed. He's trained you to do everything just the way he wants it done—or else."

His dad shoved Josh in the arm. "Don't talk to her like that."

"Don't pretend you care," Josh spat.

"You're not going to come into my house and disrespect my wife."

"No, but I am going to get her out of here," Josh said.

The wrinkles in his father's forehead deepened in confusion. "What are you talking about?" He looked at Josh's mom. "Gloria, did you tell him to come here?"

"Of course not."

"She might be too scared to stand up to you, but I'm not." Josh took a step between his parents, positioning himself in front of his mom. "I'm not going to let you bully her anymore."

His dad scowled, eyes flashing anger. "What are you going to do about it?"

Josh planted his feet. "I'm going to stand here while she packs a bag, and then we're going to leave."

"That's not happening, sonny boy."

The words ignited something inside Josh, and once again he had to draw in a calming breath. His anger would not get the better of him today.

I am not like you.

"You cost me everything, Dad. Everything. I've been so afraid of turning out just like you that I left my family—and you just watched it happen. What kind of father does that?"

"Don't you blame me for your mistakes. You're the loser who got that slut pregnant."

Josh's face heated. "Don't you dare talk about her like that."

"Both of you, that's enough," Gloria said, moving from behind Josh. "We haven't been together as a family in ages. Let's go eat dinner."

"Shut up, Gloria!" Jim shouted.

"Mom, enough is enough. Get outside."

Get outside. Get outside.

The words wrestled in his mind. He looked up and found his father locking his sights on Gloria, eyes angry, breath rushed.

Get outside, Dylan. Run!

Josh looked up as his father growled. "She's not going anywhere." He lunged toward Gloria, but Josh stepped between them again. His father swung a beefy arm back, striking his mom with the back of his hand. She fell to the ground with a shriek.

"Stop it!" Gloria yelled.

"Mom, get outside."

His dad circled Josh, positioning himself between his son and his wife. He gave her a backward kick with his heel.

She cried out in pain.

"Leave her alone."

Leave her alone!

"Get up, Gloria. Stop whimpering," Jim snarled. He spun around and faced Josh. "Come on, sonny boy. Let's see what you're made of!"

Josh's mind spun back decades. He was young—only eight.

Come on, sonny boy. Let's see what you're made of!

Dylan, get outside! Run!

He brought his hands to his head as his father shoved him backward.

Josh swatted his father's hand away, mind still whirling, trying to settle on what was true, trying to peer through the fog of memories he'd worked so hard to forget. He stumbled toward the kitchen, the image of his little brother flashing through his mind.

Feisty and rambunctious, Dylan had been full of life. Full of spunk.

That night was like most nights.

Their parents were arguing. Angry words lit the air, and Josh raced upstairs, determined to wait it out, just as he'd always done.

But Dylan—he was younger, but he was braver. Dylan left the hiding place inside the window seat in the upstairs hallway and ran downstairs, shouting the whole way.

"Leave her alone!"

Josh could hear his tiny voice echoing through his safe spot.

"Get out of here, boy!" their father shouted.

"Dylan, get outside! Run!" Gloria shrieked the words.

The sound of a smack reverberated through the walls.

"Leave her alone!" Dylan yelled again.

Josh pushed the window seat open and raced downstairs, hollering for Dylan the whole way.

"Dylan, get outside! Run!"

He reached the door of the kitchen seconds before his mother grabbed on to his father's arm—a failed attempt to keep him from injuring their youngest son. His dad reared back, and his mom fell onto the floor, but as his dad righted himself, he flailed again, this time seeming to lose control of his large, muscular arm, knocking Dylan backward—hard—into the corner of the counter.

Josh screamed.

Gloria screamed.

Dylan fell to the ground, head bloody in the back, and crashed onto the tile with a thud.

Josh raced over to his brother while his father stood upright, hulking over the two boys.

"I said get out!"

"Go, Josh," his mom said. "Get outside. Go to the park."

Dylan's eyes fluttered open and Josh tugged him closer to the doorway. "Let's go. We have to go."

Now, standing in the kitchen—not unlike the one in that house in another small town—Josh heaved a heavy breath.

What happened next?

He spun around, away from his father, away from his mother, memories seeping in like water through cracks in a wall.

"It was you," he said. His eyes slowly crept from the floor to his father's angry face. "You said it was me."

"What are you talking about?" His father growled.

Josh's eyes darted to his mother, who stood, unmoving—a look of panic on her face.

Josh stumbled backward but stopped himself from falling with a hand on the counter. His eyes searched the air, as if the answers were there, waiting to be captured and clung to.

Images raced through his mind like an old home video, but quickly, the images turned into Josh's worst nightmare. His father's arm swung back, hitting Dylan with such force, the boy fell into the corner of the counter and then onto the ground. Their mother lay in a quiet heap, unable to help.

Josh picked Dylan up, helped him to his feet, and together they raced off to the playground. The wound wasn't gushing blood, so Josh thought his brother was okay—it would heal, like a scab on a skinned knee.

He covered his head with his hands, unable to escape the memories.

"We'll wait here until dark and then we'll go back home," Josh had told Dylan as they sat on the merry-go-round, slowly pushing it in circles with their feet. "We'll wait 'til he's asleep."

"My head hurts." Dylan touched it gently.

"I know, Dyl," Josh said. "It'll get better soon."

But it didn't get better. As they spun, Dylan started to fade. His eyelids seemed too heavy to hold open and then, in a flash, he tumbled off the merry-go-round and onto the ground.

There were only two other kids playing at the park at that hour, and one of them was Josh and Dylan's across-the-street neighbor. He raced off, shouting, "I'll get your parents!" and Josh remembered the words that flitted into his mind in that moment.

No, don't! This is their fault!

287

Words he'd never said aloud. Words he'd pushed aside when his father wrote a whole new script for the day's events.

"I believed you," Josh said now, horror building up like bile at the back of his throat. "You said it was me."

He locked eyes with his father, and he knew no other explanation was needed. They were both back in that old house, in that quiet neighborhood park. They were both reliving the moments leading up to Dylan's death, and they were standing on opposite sides.

"Don't try and rewrite history," his father shouted, closing in on Josh. "You and I both know the truth. You come in here all high and mighty like you're so much better than the rest of us, but you know what you are." His father loomed in front of Josh, as if daring him to lash out, as if begging him to engage.

Josh's hands turned into fists at his sides. He clenched and unclenched them, anger coursing through his veins.

His father gave Josh a once-over, then a heavy push on the shoulder.

Josh shrugged him off, shaking away the angry thoughts building in his mind.

"You wanna hit me—then hit me," his father antagonized.

Josh wanted to hit him. He wanted to pummel his father until he was so bloody he lay limp and lifeless the same way Dylan had.

He took a step back and for a fleeting moment, it was as if he'd left his own body—and as he floated overhead, he could see a clearer picture of the scenario in which he now found himself.

"You're a bully," he said quietly and without thinking. He glanced at his mother, folded into a ball of timidity. He glanced at his father, whose face had reddened in his anger.

And for what?

"Is this what you think a real man does?" Josh moved away from his father. "You think a real man beats his wife and kids? Does a real man convince his son he is the reason his brother is dead?"

"Joshua, please." His mother reached for him, but he tore his arm away.

"No!" he shouted. "You were a part of this too. You knew what it did to me—thinking it was my fault, what happened to Dylan. You knew—" His voice broke and tears flooded his eyes. "And you did nothing." He choked out the last words, wishing he were stronger, wishing he were emotionally detached the way he'd worked so hard to be.

"Are you *crying*?" His father faced him.

Josh pressed the heels of his hands into his eyes and forced himself to pull it together. He shook with anger, with disbelief. He'd lost everything because of a lie. He'd lost Carly because he'd convinced himself he was exactly like his father—because what he'd done to Dylan proved it. Because he didn't want to risk hurting his own son the way he thought he'd hurt Dylan.

And it had all been a lie.

He glared at his father. "For as long as I live, I never want to see you again." He looked at his mom. "Either of you."

And he stormed out of the house and into the street, back to the safety and quiet of his truck, but he found no peace there.

Would he ever find peace again?

Chapter Thirty-Five

J osh wasn't responding.

Not to her texts. Not to her phone calls. Not to her voicemails.

It had been hours since she'd left Sunday dinner, and now Carly's mind had turned into a jumbled mess.

Why had she defended him at all? It was obvious that if Josh really reentered her life, she'd spend it wondering if this disappearance was his final goodbye.

It was no way to live.

Maybe that was why she'd spent the evening Googling jobs in Colorado.

Now who's the one running?

She shoved the thought aside, then picked up her phone and scrolled through her messages to Josh. If anyone found his phone, they'd think she was a crazy stalker—she'd even driven by Josh's parents' house. Twice.

But nothing. No sign of him anywhere.

Had he left for good?

She took a long breath, like a drag on a cigarette, and her nerves settled for a moment. "God, I have a really bad feeling something's happened. Please let him come to us if he needs us—he needs to stop running." *And please let him be okay.*

She'd just popped a bowl of popcorn when there was a faint knock at the back door. She pulled the melted butter from the microwave and listened—unsure she'd heard the knock at all. It was rare for anyone to enter her house through that door.

Seconds later, another knock. This one a bit louder.

She set the butter on the counter, walked to the door, flipped on the outside light and found Gloria standing there.

The older woman wore big sunglasses and a coat, and something seemed decidedly off. In her entire life, Gloria had never paid Carly an unannounced visit. In fact, Gloria had only ever been in Carly's house a handful of times, and usually for some family gathering celebrating Jaden.

"Gloria?" Carly opened the door. "Is everything okay?"

Slowly, Josh's mom drew her eyes upward to meet Carly's. Her face and neck were red and splotchy, the same way Jaden's got when he was nervous or upset.

"What's wrong?"

"I'm sorry to bother you." Her voice shook. "I thought the back door would be safer."

Carly frowned. "Safer?"

Gloria removed the sunglasses to reveal not one but two darkening bruises, one around each of her eyes. There was a cut above her right eye so deep it looked like it might need stitches.

"Gloria." Carly sighed her name, pushing the door open to let the woman in.

"Is Jaden here?" she asked.

"No. He went to the training center with Grady," Carly said. "Come in. Please."

"I don't want to impose."

"You're here for a reason," Carly said.

Gloria met her eyes. "I'm here because you're the strongest woman I know."

Carly's mind worked for a response, but the words had caught her so off guard, nothing came. She'd felt so weak and helpless lately—how ironic.

"And because you have medical training." Gloria passed through the door and into the kitchen.

"Here, sit." Carly pulled one of the kitchen chairs away from the table and Josh's mom set her purse down and sat. "You really need to go to the emergency room and have that checked out."

Tears streamed down Gloria's already stained cheeks. "You know I can't. What would people say?"

"This is about more than your family's reputation. You might need stitches—that cut above your eye looks pretty bad."

She gingerly pressed at the cut, which oozed red. "Can you just help me clean it up? It's been a long time since he hit me anywhere anyone would be able to see."

The sadness of that statement settled on Carly's shoulders, and she chided herself for not trying harder to help Gloria over the years.

The few times she'd even hinted that something might be wrong, Gloria had brushed her off. Should she have pushed harder?

"Have you called Josh?" Should *she* call Josh? His mom was sitting here, battered—wouldn't he want to know?

Gloria's tears fell more quickly now. "He doesn't want to speak to me. Maybe ever again."

Carly walked to the cupboard and took out a first aid kit. "I can't imagine that's true."

"No," Gloria said. "Those were his actual words. And I can't blame him."

Carly got to work cleaning up Gloria's cut, then her eyes fell to the older woman's lip and saw that it was split and swollen too. "What happened?"

Tears pooled in the woman's eyes, sliding in an already marked trail down her cheeks. "Josh loves you so much, Carly."

Carly stopped dabbing and found the woman's eyes.

"He loves you and we ruined that for both of you."

Carly went back to cleaning the wound. "That wasn't your fault."

Gloria wrapped a hand around Carly's wrist to stop her and met her gaze. "It was. I'm telling you."

Carly shook her head. "Josh chose to leave us. It was hard and he left. End of story."

"I know it's hard to give second chances, Carly—goodness knows I've given them when I shouldn't have. But would you consider it this time?"

Carly took a step back. "He's not sorry for leaving. He doesn't regret it at all. Said he did what was best for me and Jaden." A lump grew in Carly's throat. Josh's words had wounded her more than she'd realized.

Carly dabbed at the gash above Gloria's eye with a cotton ball soaked in hydrogen peroxide. Gloria grimaced at the touch.

"Sorry, I know it hurts."

"The night he left—what happened?" Gloria's voice shook as she spoke.

"To make him leave, you mean?" Carly patted Gloria's cut dry with gauze.

The older woman nodded.

"He told me to go out with my friends, and when I got home, I found Jaden screaming and Josh beside himself." Carly's mind whirled back. "He was so angry, as if it was somehow Jaden's fault—or mine—that Josh couldn't figure out why he was crying."

"Where was Jaden when you got home?"

"In his crib," Carly said, unsure why Gloria would ask that.

"And Josh?"

"The living room." Carly frowned. "Why?"

"I remember once when Josh was a baby." Gloria's voice hitched. "I'd run out to the store and left Josh with Jim. He'd been asleep and should've slept for another hour, but he woke up screaming." Her eyes went glassy. "When I got home, Jim was so irate for leaving him alone, for taking so long at the store." Her words faded away, as if she was remembering something painful.

"He hurt you?"

"I thought he might've hurt Josh," Gloria said. "I was so panicked, so worried that Jim had taken his anger out on my baby."

"Did he?" Carly carefully affixed Steri-strips over the wound.

She shook her head. "No. Not that time anyway."

"Gloria, why do you stay?" Carly sat down across from her. "I know Josh has asked you to leave."

Gloria nodded, turning away, shame clear on her face. "I was afraid."

"More afraid to leave than to stay and risk getting seriously injured?"

She shook her head. "You don't understand. I'm not strong like you are. I've only got a high school diploma, and I've never had a real job in my life. Where would I go? What would I do? I can't live so freely on my own."

Carly reached over and covered the woman's hands with her own. "Yes, you can. And you wouldn't be alone. You've got me and Jaden and Josh."

Gloria's eyes found hers. "The night Josh left, something was wrong with Jaden."

Back to this. Why was Gloria so interested in ancient history? "Yes. He had a fever. A bad one."

"And Josh didn't realize it?"

She shook her head.

Gloria stilled. "Carly, how much do you know about Josh's little brother, Dylan?"

Carly had never known Dylan, so sometimes it was easy to forget Josh had ever had a sibling at all. "I know he passed away before you moved to Harbor Pointe."

"Is that all?"

Carly folded her hands in her lap. "Josh never liked to talk about Dylan."

Gloria covered her mouth with her hands and looked away, eyes welling with fresh tears.

Carly sometimes wondered if Dylan's death was the reason Jim was the way he was. Surely the death of a child took a terrible toll on parents.

"I think I understand it all now," Gloria said.

Carly stilled. "Understand what?"

"Why Josh left."

Carly had been waiting for an answer to that question for sixteen years. She'd been waiting, but the other night, Josh had made it clear—his reasons were thin. He had no regret over leaving. "He left because he couldn't handle it," she said simply. He'd done the cowardly thing and left her alone to pick up the pieces.

"Carly, Josh left because he was scared," Gloria said. "And that was our fault."

"Isn't everyone scared when they have a child?" Carly asked, certain the answer was yes. "At some point, you have to grow up. Josh just wasn't ready. He took the easy way out."

"And you've never forgiven him."

"No, I have," Carly said.

Gloria's brow furrowed.

"You don't believe me?"

"Why aren't you together?" she asked.

The memory of Josh's kisses invaded her mind.

"It's obvious you love each other," she said. "So, what's holding you back?"

After a long beat, Carly saw no sense in pretending. "I'm afraid he'll leave again."

"He didn't leave because he wanted to. He left because he thought he was protecting you."

Carly frowned. "He said something like that, but it makes no sense. Protecting me from what?"

"It's true, Carly," Gloria said. "Look at me. He had good reason to fear something like this would happen to you."

"But Jim would never hurt me."

"Not Jim, sweetheart. Josh." Tears spilled from Gloria's eyes.

Carly shook her head. "Josh has a temper, but nothing like this—he was never violent or even physical."

"But he was scared he would be." Gloria paused. "I need to tell you something, Carly. And you're not going to like it."

The dark feeling of dread nagged her from the inside out. "Okay."

Gloria's eyes fell to her folded hands in her lap. "Josh has always blamed himself for Dylan's death."

Carly frowned. "Why would he do that? I thought it was an accident."

"Because we made him believe it was his fault." Her lower lip trembled, and her eyes fluttered shut, a shaky dam struggling to hold back the floodwaters.

"What do you mean?"

"Dylan died as a result of a hemorrhage in his brain. The kind you get when there's trauma to the head." Gloria wouldn't look at Carly.

Dozens of questions raced through Carly's mind.

"It was an accident," Gloria said. "Dylan was trying to protect me and got caught in the crossfire." She pulled a tissue from her pocket and dabbed the corners of her eyes. "Jim was so worried someone would find out what had happened, he told the police Dylan had fallen while he and Josh were rough-housing at the park."

Carly's heart sank.

"I think we told the story so many times we all believed it— Josh especially. I had no idea he was carrying around that kind of pain all these years. We told ourselves we did what we had to, to keep our family together, but today I realized the price we paid for our own comfort." She inhaled. "The price Josh paid."

Carly's mind spun. Josh had spent all these years believing he was the cause of his brother's death? How had she never known this before? How had he kept that secret from her of all people— she thought she knew everything about him.

"He came by this afternoon, Carly. He asked me to go with him. When Jim heard him, they fought and—"

"And what?"

"I watched my son remember what really happened. Not the version of events we told him, but the truth. He'd been bearing the weight of his father's sins all these years and it cost him everything. It cost him you and Jaden."

Carly's pulse quickened. She'd been so quick to write Josh off when he left. She'd been so angry, so bitter, that she wouldn't even entertain the idea that maybe Josh had a reason for running.

He didn't want to be the cause of any more pain. When he held his sick, screaming baby, did he see his brother's face? Did that moment close space and time in his mind, becoming the moment his brother died?

Carly had met Josh not long after Dylan's death—she could still picture his eight-year-old face, and now the line of worry that always laced his brow made so much more sense.

"He didn't leave because he didn't love you, or even because he didn't want to deal with having a child," Gloria said, interrupting Carly's thoughts. "He left because you and Jaden mean everything to him—and because he was afraid if he stayed he would subject you to the same kind of life he'd had. He was protecting you—from what he feared he might become."

The words nicked the edges of Carly's heart. Her eyes filled with tears and she shook her head. It couldn't be true. Josh never would've hurt her or Jaden—he was one of the kindest people she knew.

"Carly, if you love him at all, go find him. I don't think he's okay."

No, how could he be? How would he ever be?

"And you?"

"What about me?"

"What are you going to do now?"

Gloria's face fell. "Pray that he changes his mind and agrees to talk to me again." She pressed her lips together. "There is one thing I can do for Josh, if you'll help me?"

Carly stilled. "Name it."

"Would you mind calling your father and having him come over here?" Gloria drew in a long breath. "I think it's time to press charges against my husband."

Chapter Thirty-Six

If the frantic knocking on the cabin door was any indication, Carly wasn't going to leave him alone. Her timing was terrible. She probably wanted to yell at him about last night. Carly had a way of going home and stewing, thinking of all the arguments she should've made.

Had she come to tell him what a terrible mistake she'd made in letting him kiss her? Had she come to reiterate that he'd abandoned them when they needed them most—a fact he was most certainly aware of?

A fact that had become his life's greatest regret.

He'd been carrying around the guilt of a lie—it had altered the course of his life and there was no turning back. His mistakes were his own, regardless of why he'd made them, and he didn't need Carly to point them out.

The knocking continued. Nobody could ever accuse her of not being persistent.

He opened the door but refused to look at her. How could he, knowing the truth? It should exonerate him, make him feel vindicated—but instead, it had paralyzed him—it had made his choices that much clearer. That much more painful.

"Are you okay?"

He met her eyes. What did she know? Why was she asking? "Not great, Carly."

A nervous ripple washed across her face. "Your mom came by my house."

Josh scoffed. "She's got a lot of nerve."

Carly studied him through a long pause. "She's with my dad right now."

He frowned. "Why?"

"She was in bad shape, Josh. He really hurt her this time."

Anger rose like a fire in his belly, and it took everything inside him not to rush out and find his father—put an end to him once and for all.

"My dad was getting an arrest warrant when I left."

Josh's breathing turned quick and labored at the thought of his father finally—finally—paying for his sins, sins Josh and his mom had been paying for all these years. Sins that had led to Dylan's death.

He struggled for oxygen, and his stomach turned hollow. "Are you sure?" His eyes clouded and he gripped the door to keep from collapsing.

"I'm sure." She reached for him, but he moved away. Her touch on his skin would send his mind reeling. He couldn't get used to it again, the way it felt to hold her, to have a right to her.

And yet, it was the thing he wanted most of all.

He turned toward the living room, aware that she followed, the memory of his lips on hers still so fresh in his mind.

"I hate him, Carly. I hate them both."

She didn't respond.

He sank onto the couch. "There's a lot you don't know—"

She sat on the other end of the couch. "Your mom told me," she said quietly.

His eyes darted to hers. "She did?"

Carly nodded.

"About Dylan?"

Her eyes fell. She knew. She knew the truth—all of it—a truth he'd only just learned himself. He was no longer alone in carrying it. But what did she think of him—of his family—now?

Josh buried his face in his hands and let the sobs come. He'd refused them for years, but they were too strong now.

Seconds later, she was at his side, her hands on him, comforting and kind.

"I left you," he said. "I'm so sorry I left you."

"I think I understand now," she said.

He looked at her. "You do?"

She turned into him. "Dylan's death wasn't your fault, Josh."

The words hung in the air, their gravity pulling them to the ground, unheard.

She took his face in her hands. "Did you hear what I said?"

He closed his eyes.

"Do you believe me?"

He clung to her, pulling her closer. "I want to." But how did he forget what he'd always believed to be true?

He opened his eyes and found concern on her face. "That night—with Jaden. Carly, I was so angry. I was beside myself. I couldn't call you, and I—" He nearly choked on the words. "I wanted to shake him, to do anything to make him stop screaming."

She swallowed, her gaze intent on him.

"I had no idea something was actually wrong with him, but when the doctor said it was serious—" He broke, willing away the feelings of guilt and powerlessness. "All I could think of was Dylan. How it was my fault he was gone. I can still imagine his face, holding his body after he collapsed on the ground."

She wiped his cheeks dry.

"They told me I blacked out. They said it was a fit of rage." He pulled away from her. "I thought I was a monster, just like him."

She moved to the ground, on her knees in front of him so their faces were level, forcing his gaze. "Look at me."

He didn't want to. He didn't want her to see him like this.

"Do you agree that I know you better than most people know you?"

He nodded.

"Then my opinion matters more than most people's, right?"

Another nod.

"In all the years I knew you, I never, ever once thought you were anything like your dad. He's vicious and mean and you've always been tender and good and kind. That's why it hurt so much when you left, because we were meant to be together, Josh. You and me."

He reached up and touched her cheek, cupping her face with his hand. "I don't deserve you."

She shook her head. "You're not your dad. You're nothing like your dad."

"Then how do you explain the anger I felt that night?"

Carly let out a wry laugh. "I explain that as being human."

"You would've never felt that way."

"Are you kidding? Josh, a baby crying has got to be one of the worst sounds on the planet. I think it could be considered torture. What you felt was normal. The difference is, you protected Jaden that night. You laid him down and walked away."

He shook his head, unsure how to reconcile the person he'd always believed himself to be with the person Carly was telling him he was.

Josh held her hands in his own, drawing them to his lips then his forehead, where he quietly willed away the pain of the past.

"What's going to happen to my dad?" he asked.

Carly straightened. "I think they'll arrest him."

"It won't stick," Josh said. "She'll never go through with it."

"She might, with our help. She's going to stay with me for a few weeks, just until she can figure things out."

He shook his head, pulling away. "No, this is not your problem. You've got enough to deal with. You don't need this too."

"What if I want to deal with it?" she asked softly. "What if I want to be here for you while you sort it out?"

He stood and moved across the room, staring out the window at the lake. He didn't belong here—how could he when everything had turned upside down? He couldn't stand by and watch his mom lose her nerve or his father smugly get away with what he'd done—again.

He couldn't stomach it. And he didn't want Carly or Jaden anywhere near it either.

Jaden—oh no.

"Does Jaden know?"

Carly shook her head. "No. Not yet anyway."

Josh rubbed his temples. He never wanted his son to know any of this—where he'd come from, the kind of life his own father had lived. He didn't want Jaden exposed to it or embarrassed by it. It was humiliating. It was why they'd all kept it a secret all these years.

Some shame is simply too heavy to speak out loud.

Carly was at his side, in the exact place he'd been longing for her to be for years, but it all felt wrong. She deserved to be free of this dysfunction.

She slipped her hand into his. "He'll be okay, Josh. He's a strong kid with a strong faith."

Josh shook his head. "I don't want him to know any of this."

She faced him. "Josh—"

"I have to go." He spun around, suddenly needing space and air.

"Where are you going?"

"I just need to do something," he said, unsure what that was exactly. Knowing only that he needed to be by himself, away from her. She confused him. She made him feel like he was better than he was, like he was stronger than he was. Carly made him wish for things he could never have, and the pain of acknowledging the truth would be too great to bear.

He'd spent most of his life on his own, and while he regretted it more than anything, maybe it had been for the best. He'd only ever brought Carly shame—ruining her reputation, getting her pregnant, leaving her with a newborn baby and now this? Didn't she deserve better?

He'd hoped he was good enough for her. He'd hoped he could become the kind of man who deserved her, but he wasn't sure he'd even scratched the surface on who he needed to be for that to happen. Especially now, with the bombshell of abuse about to explode.

Would his mother tell the police everything? Would she go back all those years? And even if she did, could they ever prove what his father had done? It had been too long. The man would get off scot-free—again.

But not before dragging them all down with him.

How was Josh supposed to stand by and watch that happen?

"Josh, wait." Carly followed him out onto the porch.

He spun around and faced her. "You should go."

Her expression faltered. "What?"

"I know you were talking about moving away. You should do that."

Her eyes turned glassy, and Josh wanted so badly to pull her close, to take it back, to tell her to stay with him forever, that he'd never leave again.

But he couldn't make that promise. He couldn't bring more shame to her, and that's all his family had to offer.

"What do you mean?" Her voice broke.

"Take Jaden and get out of here."

"You don't mean that."

He looked away. "I think it would be better for everyone if you weren't here."

"Stop doing that, Josh." She raised her voice.

"Doing what?"

"Thinking you're protecting me by pushing me away."

He touched her face. "Carly, you mean everything to me. You always have. If you care about me at all—you need to get out of here. It's about to get really bad, and I don't want you anywhere near this."

A tear slid down her cheek. "It's funny, your mom said I'm the strongest person she knows. You obviously disagree." She pulled away from him.

"The doctor will give you a good life." His eyes dipped to her mouth—full lips that tasted sweeter than anything else in the world. He'd never know that taste again if he pushed her out of his life now. "I have something to take care of."

"Where are you going?" she asked.

"Go find Jaden," he said. "Please. Make sure he hears about this from you first."

He rushed to his truck, not daring to look back. On the porch stood the only good thing in his life, and he was running the other way.

Because that good thing deserved life's best things—and it was pretty obvious he wasn't going to be able to give them to her.

Chapter Thirty-Seven

The neighborhood felt stale in the thick summer heat. Josh sat in his truck, nearly a block away from his parents' house. So far, there was no sign of life inside. His father was likely holed up as if nothing had happened and with no idea his mother had gone to Gus.

He was completely unaware of what was coming.

Josh had been sitting in the truck for nearly forty-five minutes when the first squad car pulled into the driveway. He sat up straighter in the seat, thinking of all the nights he'd hid from his father—and later, the nights he was caught up in the mess of the man's anger.

This terrible secret had been eating away at him all these years —a secret so impossibly painful he'd blocked some of it out—but the truth had always been there, just beneath the surface.

Another squad car rolled up and parked in the street. An officer got out of the first car and walked toward the front door of his parents' house.

A few of the neighbors materialized on their porches, watching with morbid curiosity, the way small-town neighbors did. Josh's stomach rolled over as his father pulled the front door open.

He got out of his truck and shut the door, leaning against it with his arms crossed, watching in anticipation.

His father let out a hearty laugh, then said something Josh couldn't hear.

His face heated.

An unmarked cruiser pulled up. *Gus.*

Carly's dad exited his car and strolled to the door. He said something Josh couldn't hear, then nodded at the deputy, who motioned for Jim to turn around.

Josh's father was visibly agitated, and possibly drunk. He swore, but the two deputies wrangled the large man in, cuffed his hands behind his back, then turned him around. They walked him over to the squad car parked in the driveway and pushed him into the back seat.

One officer got in the driver's seat and started the engine as Gus turned around and headed back toward his car. As he did, he spotted Josh, still frozen in the street.

The older man held his gaze for a three-count, then continued on toward his vehicle.

The squad car with Josh's dad in the back pulled out into the street, slowly. Josh watched intently, eyes searching the back seat until they found his father—watching him through the glass. The car passed by slowly, and a shadow crept across his father's face. He latched on to Josh's gaze, and Josh forced himself not to look away.

A chill ran down his spine, and he felt like an eight-year-old all over again, under the watchful eye of a monster—the monster who'd stolen everything from him.

The image of Dylan's face lying in the dirt next to the merry-go-round rushed back, taunting him.

He needed air. He needed to escape. He needed to run.

* * *

Later that night, Carly prepared dinner while Gloria rested upstairs. Jaden was on his way home, and she'd been struggling to figure out how to explain this situation to her son.

Her nerves had been shot since leaving the cabin earlier. Josh wasn't answering her calls or texts, and frankly, she was worried about him.

He'd practically begged her for a second chance only a few weeks ago, and now he was pushing her to move away? It didn't make sense. Surely he didn't mean it.

Her phone buzzed.

Jim has officially been arrested.

Her father's text sent a shiver down her spine. Okay, so Jim knew Gloria had turned on him—what would come next?

Maybe she *should* move away, and maybe she should take Josh's mom with her.

The back door popped open and Jaden walked in. "What did you do?"

Carly turned away from the stovetop and stared at him dumbly. "What are you talking about?"

"Did you tell Dad to go back to Chicago?"

Carly wiped her hands on a kitchen towel. "No, and I don't appreciate your tone."

He handed his phone to Carly. She glanced down and found a text from Josh.

Hey, kid, I'm heading back to the city—work is calling. I'll be back in a week for your appointment, and then we can figure out a time for you to come stay with me for a few weeks if your mom is cool with it.

Carly's heart dropped. He was leaving? In the middle of all of this? What was wrong with him?

She thought about Gloria, likely terrified out of her mind. She needed her son.

Was Josh so angry he couldn't do the right thing?

"So was it you? Did you push him to do this?"

Carly glanced up and found Jaden's eyes drilling into her. She shook her head. "Jaden, there's something I need to talk to you about."

"If it's you telling me that Dad's no good, I don't want to hear it."

"No," she said. "That's not it at all. Your dad is actually very, *very* good."

She kept her promise to Josh. She told their son the truth about his grandparents, about the way his father grew up. She told him about all the times Josh would show up at the back door, bruised and bloody, the nights he would sleep in the shed so nobody ever found out.

"Why didn't you tell anyone?" Jaden asked.

Carly's mind spun back to a night it had gotten so scary she went to her father, and though she'd promised Josh, she knew keeping his secret was only hurting him and his mom.

But Gus didn't give her a chance to explain. It only took a few minutes of discussion for him to clamp down on Josh and everything that was wrong with him—Jim was, after all, well respected in their small community.

Nobody would ever believe me. That's what Josh had told her. And he was right. Nobody would've believed him. And if he didn't tell someone who would get him out of there, wasn't he risking making everything worse for everyone?

"I was scared," she told her son. "I was scared of putting them in more danger. I was young, Jaden. I didn't know how to help them—and then your father left. One time I tried to ask your grandma how she was and she pretended she didn't understand what I meant. Glossed right over it, like I wasn't making sense."

"So, what? Dad's just running away?"

"I think he's trying to sort through quite a bit right now, Jay," Carly said. "Let's just try to be patient with him."

But inside, Carly's head was spinning. How could Josh just leave? Again.

Maybe it was time she realized that he'd never really changed at all.

Chapter Thirty-Eight

The following morning, Carly woke up late, the smell of coffee tickling her nose. While she wished the night before had all been a terrible nightmare, it took only seconds to remember it wasn't. It was real life. And her heart was unsteady because of it.

She told herself to be strong—for Gloria, for Jaden. But she didn't know how to stand up under the weight of her emotional turmoil.

She loved Josh. She'd been vehemently denying it—even to herself—but saying goodbye to him had nearly done her in.

Downstairs, she found Gloria standing at the stove, making pancakes and bacon. The smell wafted toward Carly's nose, reminding her how long it had been since she'd had a proper breakfast.

Josh's mom looked up. "Oh, hon, you don't look so good."

Carly pushed the hair out of her face and tied it back with the elastic from her wrist. "I feel even worse." Her stomach growled as she poured herself a cup of coffee.

"Did you see Josh?" Gloria asked. "Will he talk to me?"

Carly didn't want to be the one to break the news to her that her coward of a son wasn't sticking around. He didn't care enough about either of them to muddle his way through the messy stuff.

Carly didn't know why she should stick around to muddle through it herself.

"Gloria, I was thinking," she said. "What if we leave Harbor Pointe?"

The older woman's brow furrowed as she turned her attention back to the pancakes. She flipped them, one by one, shaking her head. "I could never leave Harbor Pointe. It's my home."

"I know." Carly poured a dash of creamer into her coffee and stirred. "It's my home too, but I wonder what a fresh start might look like—for both of us."

Gloria pressed the pancakes with the silver spatula. "So he won't see me, then?"

Carly took a sip of coffee and leaned against the counter, facing Gloria. "He's going back to Chicago."

Gloria's expression faltered for a split second, and she looked away. The bruises around her eyes had darkened into a deep purple. Her lip was visibly swollen and the Steri-strips above her eye were covered with dried blood. Carly wondered if she'd looked in the mirror at all this morning. Did she know how badly she needed a fresh start?

Carly checked her phone, stupidly, it turned out, because Josh still hadn't responded to her calls or texts. Did he know his father had been arrested? Did he know how badly his mother needed him?

Did he know Carly loved him?

She picked up a pancake, tore it in half and ate a bite and stood at the window overlooking the backyard. At her side, Gloria hummed, and Carly wondered if she felt free as a bird or terrified of what was in store.

The sound of a small engine at the side of her house drew her attention.

"Is Jaden up?" she asked Gloria.

"It's been a long time since I've had a teenager in the house, but by my recollection, they don't stir before eleven in the morning during the summer." She smiled. "You're eating, aren't you?"

"One second." Carly walked through the kitchen and out the back door, the bright summer sun forcing her to squint.

And sure enough, there in the yard, pushing her *state-of-the-art* lawn mower, was Josh. Not in Chicago. Right here.

At the sight of her, he killed the engine.

"What are you doing here?" She walked toward him.

"Mowing your lawn," he said simply, as if the answer was obvious.

"What about Chicago?" she asked.

His eyes dipped to her lips, then latched on to her gaze. "You're not in Chicago."

She studied his face. "You didn't go?"

He shook his head. "Nope."

"Why not?"

He shrugged. "Realized everything I want is right here."

She pressed her lips together, unsure what else to say. "They arrested your dad."

He nodded. "I saw."

She wouldn't make him talk about it—not if he didn't want to. But she said a silent prayer that he would know he could if he needed to, that he knew he was safe with her—no matter what.

"Your lawn isn't going to mow itself." He pulled the cord and the engine roared back to life. He gave her a wave, then pushed the mower to the other end of the yard.

"I don't care what you think, Joshua Dixon," she said to herself. "You are a very good man."

* * *

Gus walked into the small office at the Harbor Pointe sheriff's headquarters where Josh had been waiting in a creaky wooden chair next to the older man's desk.

He gave Josh a once-over. "Been quite a couple of days for you, young man."

To say the least.

Josh knew Gus didn't like him. Carly's dad had made no bones about it. Convincing Carly to give him a second chance was one thing, but it would be nearly impossible to win over this man.

Still, he had to try.

The past few days' events had shown him what was important —and he wasn't about to lose them again—no matter how much easier it would be to run the other way.

"You know this is going to be all over the news." Gus turned off the small television overhead and sat in the chair behind the desk. "Could get ugly."

"I know." Josh had already thought about that. Small-town gossip could be hard to stomach—it was the last thing he wanted for Jaden and Carly.

"You won't like what people have to say."

"No, sir, I don't expect I will." Josh surveyed Gus's weathered face and found a fatherly concern knitting his brow. "And I don't think people will like what I have to say either."

"Ran into Linda Martin yesterday."

Josh leaned back in his chair and met Gus's eyes. "And?"

"She told me about the office space you leased."

Josh thought about the space he'd found a week ago—a loft right above a coffee shop downtown and only a few blocks from the Harbor Pointe hospital. He'd stupidly imagined meeting Carly for lunch on the days she worked. In fact, he'd worked out a whole life for himself, and every inch of it involved her.

A lot had changed since the day he signed that lease.

But his desire for Carly remained.

Still, he needed her father's approval. It was important to him to do things the right way this time.

"Seems like a pretty good spot." Gus ran a hand over his bushy white mustache, and Josh couldn't be sure, but he thought he might've even smiled.

Gus was making this much more difficult than Josh had expected simply by being unpredictable. Because instead of being his usual brusque self, Carly's dad was being kind, and Josh didn't know how to accept kindness from him. He'd planned out his whole speech to convince Gus he was worthy—but Gus wasn't giving him the cold shoulder, so Josh wasn't sure where to begin.

"You're not here about your father, are you?" Gus eyed him.

"Partly," Josh said. "I want to make sure he's behind bars."

Gus cackled. "Between me and Judge, that man is going to be locked down as long as we can legally keep him inside."

"I need to make sure he doesn't hurt her again," Josh said. "Because he will try."

"She filed a restraining order before the arrest. We can put a GPS tracker on him, monitor his whereabouts. If he comes within a certain distance of your mother, the tracker will alert us, and he'll be arrested again."

"So she wears a tracker too?"

"Or carries it with her, yes," Gus said.

"What about Carly and Jaden?"

"Them too." Gus leaned forward and looked at him across the desk. "We're on the same page, son."

Josh nodded. "You think they'll be okay?"

"Are you going to stick around and make sure of it?" Gus's forehead crinkled as one of his bushy eyebrows raised above the other.

Josh cleared his throat. "That's the other reason why I'm here, sir."

Gus leaned back in his chair, folding his hands across his belly. "I figured as much."

"And you're not going to shut me down?"

"I'd like to hear what you have to say."

Josh stood, circling around the chair. "I had this all worked out in the car on the way over here." He glanced at Gus. "But you were a lot meaner the way I played it out in my head."

Gus gave a soft shrug. "If you want me to be meaner, I can."

A nervous laugh slipped out and Josh shook his head. "No, that's okay." He mustered his courage. "I came to tell you that I love your daughter."

After a beat, Gus said dryly, "I'm so surprised."

"I'd like your blessing, sir," Josh said.

"For what?"

"To marry her."

Gus cocked his head to one side, taking him in. "You know that nothing about marriage and kids is easy."

"I understand that."

"So what happens when you want to take off?"

It was a fair question, but an upsetting one. "I won't."

"How do we know that for sure?"

"I tried running once," Josh said. "Biggest mistake of my life."

"And you're a different man now?"

Josh pondered the question a moment. "Yes, sir, I believe I am. Smarter. And I know what's important. I know who I am now." He met the man's eyes. "And I know *whose* I am."

"That right?"

Yeah, the last few days had worked him over. Letting go of everything he thought he was hadn't been easy, but when all the rubble had been cleared away, one truth remained—God loved him as much today as he'd loved him a week ago. There was comfort in that.

The awkward lull in the conversation sent Josh's mind whirling. He wouldn't leave again—he knew it. The only thing he wanted in the world was to love Carly for the rest of his life.

"What are you thinking?" Josh asked.

"I'm considering what you said," Gus replied. "I think a few things need to happen before I can give you my blessing."

Josh wasn't sure he wanted to know what those things were.

"First, I think I owe you an apology."

"That's . . . unexpected." Josh relaxed a little.

"I always liked you when you and Carly were kids," he said. "You looked at her like she was the most beautiful thing in the world."

"She is," Josh said quietly.

"But when she told me she was pregnant, I was shocked." Gus ran a hand over his chin. "Did not see that coming."

"Yeah, you and me both."

He fidgeted with a pen, eyes on his desk. "I thought I'd failed. I must've done something wrong as a father. The girls needed a mother, and I was lousy at that."

Josh decided not to disagree. Not because he didn't disagree, but because it sounded like Gus had things to get off his chest. Did he tell the old man that his daughter felt like a failure too? That they had that in common?

"And when you left—I guess I took all that anger I felt toward myself and directed it at you." Gus sighed. "I understand now why you did what you did, and I have to tell you, there was something honorable in your choice."

"We really don't need to talk about it, Gus—"

"I need to talk about it," Gus said firmly.

Josh watched the older man gather his thoughts. "Okay, if we're really doing this—You said I was a coward."

"I said that without all the facts, son," Gus said. "And I was wrong. I'm pretty sure you're the opposite of a coward."

Josh hung on the end of those words for longer than he should've. He drew in a long breath. "It doesn't matter anymore."

"Oh?"

"It's ancient history. Can't rewrite the past."

Gus frowned. "No, but you don't have to let the past write your future."

"You sound like a fortune cookie." Josh felt a grin prickling the corner of his mouth.

Gus didn't look amused. "Look, I misjudged you. I made a mistake. You had a hard life, much harder than any of us knew. Carly tried to tell me, but I'd had your dad in my ear every week. And by then, I'd seen some of the choices you were making. Not exactly a stellar record."

Josh didn't want to talk about this—not with Gus. Not with anybody. He wanted his dad to stay behind bars and he wanted to move on, hopefully with Carly and Jaden. The rest of it he wanted to bury.

But when he looked at Gus, he knew that this man's opinion of him mattered too. More than he cared to admit.

"I'm sorry I didn't help you back then, son," Gus said.

Josh shook his head. He hadn't come here for Gus's apologies. He wasn't prepared for it.

"I understand now that you left because you thought you were protecting them," Gus said. "You gave them up because you really believed it's what was best."

"All I've ever wanted is for Carly to be safe. For Jaden to be safe," Josh said. "Even if it meant I didn't get to be with them."

Gus nodded. "That's a very unselfish thing you did."

A lump formed at the back of Josh's throat and he willed it away. The last thing he needed was to fall apart in front of Carly's dad. "Carly is the most amazing woman I've ever met."

"If you really believe that, you'll do everything you can not to let her go this time."

"Does that mean—" He looked up hopefully.

Gus picked up a pencil and tapped it on the desk. "I really don't like being wrong."

Josh didn't move.

"But when you're wrong, you say you were wrong," Gus said. "And then you move on."

The words lit up the air, pulsing overhead like a neon sign.

"You got a bum deal having Jim for a father." Gus leaned across the desk, hands folded in front of him. "But having a bad father doesn't make you a bad father."

Josh looked away. He'd come here to ask for Gus's blessing. What he'd gotten was so much more. And it felt good to have it all out in the open—no more living in the shadows.

"Thanks, Gus," Josh said.

"You're a good man, Josh," Gus said. "I see that now. You always were a good man, just a little misguided. And—" he made sure he had Josh's full attention now—"you're nothing like your father."

The words melted into the broken spaces of Josh's heart, winding their way deeper and deeper, warming and mending and healing as only love and forgiveness can.

"I know that now, sir," Josh said.

"Good. Now comes the hard part."

Josh frowned.

"Getting Carly to take you back." Gus laughed. "She's awfully stubborn, that one."

Josh stood. "Yeah, I wonder where she gets that."

Gus met him near the door and pulled Josh into the only fatherly hug he'd ever had, clasping his arms tightly around him and clapping him three times on the back.

When Josh pulled out of the embrace, he saw tears in the corners of Gus's eyes. So different from his own father, who had never shown a single sign of remorse, even after Dylan's death.

"Good luck, son," Gus said. "I hope she'll give you a second chance."

Josh walked out to his truck and glanced down at the set of keys in the drink holder.

You don't have to let the past write your future.

The words pricked at the edges of his heart, and Josh began to imagine a different future. Not the one where he came home from work to an empty apartment in the city. Not the one where he walked around with vows written in faded ink in his pocket. The one where he made good on his promises, where he put action to the words he'd written all those years ago.

He started the engine and exhaled a long, slow breath.

Could Josh ever be the person Carly made him want to be?

Could he figure out a new way to write his future?

He'd taken the first steps—but Gus was right—this is where it got hard. He pulled away from the curb and prayed that Carly would give him that second chance.

Chapter Thirty-Nine

I t had been four weeks since Jaden's surgery, and his follow-up visit with Dr. Carroll could not have gone better.

Carly may have lost her promotion, but Jaden gained a first-rate doctor who was up on all the latest treatments for his particular condition.

The trade was more than fair.

Now she sat at the indoor training center, which was terribly cold, she realized—was Grady trying to create the atmosphere of winter for everyone who walked through the door? If yes, he'd succeeded.

She shivered as she watched Jaden move onto the simulator. His first practice back since surgery, and there was no way she was going to miss it.

Coach Ted Myers caught her eye and waved. "You're Jaden's mom?"

"I am," she said.

"We've got high hopes for your son."

She glanced at Jaden as he moved to the top of the indoor slope. "So do I."

"Was awfully glad to hear his new doctor cleared him," the

coach said. "Our team will be stronger for it. Jaden's passion is infectious."

Ian Dobson moved toward the top of the simulator and fell. The machine, which was like an oversized treadmill set on a steep incline, hadn't even been turned on yet. Jaden laughed.

"His dad is pretty passionate too," the coach said. "At least about Jaden."

Carly looked at Ted. "What do you mean?"

"Just the way he barreled into the office about a month ago. Made it pretty clear nobody was going to count his kid out—not yet anyway."

Carly smiled. "Is that right?"

"Jaden's lucky to have a dad who loves him so much." The coach gave her a nod and walked toward the boys on the simulator. "All right, team. Let's do this."

She sat back and watched the entire practice, not to keep tabs on Jaden, just to relish the fact that he was back out there, defying the odds.

And one thought ran through her mind—*Luck has nothing to do with it.*

* * *

After ski practice, Carly took Jaden home. She sat on her porch, admiring her freshly cut grass, aware that mowing her lawn had become a weekly ritual for Josh.

She wasn't complaining.

Gloria and Jaden were inside, and last she heard, Jaden was teaching her how to play Josh's video game.

She'd escaped out here because she was secretly hoping he'd return, and frankly, she wanted to be the first one to see him when he did.

Freida Jenkins strode down the sidewalk, Elmer on a leash at her side, stopping in front of the house.

"Well, good afternoon," the old woman said. "Your lawn looks mighty nice."

Carly glanced up over her magazine and smiled. "Doesn't it?"

"I've seen that handsome man out here taking care of things. You two are the talk of the town."

For the first time, Carly didn't mind that one bit. Let them all talk. Let the rumors spread that Josh Dixon had returned and that he'd kept his promises and found a way to take care of his family. Let them admire how dutiful he'd been. How dependable. How loyal.

She certainly admired those things about him.

No, he wasn't perfect, but then, neither was she.

Freida waved and continued on, Elmer happily prancing along beside her.

"Jaden," she called, "have you heard from your dad?"

"Nope," Jaden yelled back. "Said he had some errand to run."

An engine roared toward the house, and she turned toward the street just in time to see Josh's truck pulling into her driveway, the sight of it causing a hitch in her breath.

He opened the door but didn't turn off the engine, got out and looked at her.

Why did he have to be so handsome? And why did he have to be so kind? He'd been putting Carly first since the day they met—something told her he'd do that for the rest of his life if she let him.

If her heart had been torn before, it was shredded now.

Behind him, the dipping sun created an orange glow, bathing him in perfect golden-hour light. "Will you go for a ride with me?"

She frowned. It wasn't what she'd expected him to say. "Where?"

"It's a surprise."

"But Jaden—"

"Is he alone?"

She glanced back at the house. "Actually, no. He's with your mom."

Josh nodded. "I think he'll be okay."

"And your mom?"

"There's no way my dad's getting out tonight," he said.

It was true. Right now was perhaps the safest they would be until his father's trial.

"Okay," she said.

"Yeah?" His face brightened, reminding her of the Josh she used to know.

"Should I tell them where we're going?"

"You don't know where we're going." There was mischief in Josh's smile.

She looked away to hide her own smile. "Then should you tell them?"

"I'll text Jaden."

She got in the truck and closed the door. "Everything okay?"

He reached across the seat and squeezed her hand. "Everything's good."

He pulled out of the driveway but didn't let go. She looked down at their two hands, still entwined, and her insides filled with warmth. She didn't know where things stood between them, and while she wanted to label and define it, she chose to let it just be— for now anyway.

"Where are we going?"

"You'll see." He smiled at her.

They drove through town and then along Bend Road, which had spectacular views of the lake.

His dad had been in court earlier that morning. Had Josh gone? Was that the errand he needed to run?

She ran her thumb over his hand. "You're okay?"

He glanced at her. "I think I will be."

She nodded, knowing it would take time to heal what was broken inside him and time to heal what had been broken between them. She only prayed it was time they had, that maybe they'd get that second chance, after all.

He veered onto a gravel road, which turned out to be a private driveway.

"I think we're trespassing," she said.

"It's fine," he said. "I promise."

She eyed him suspiciously, searching for any hint of what he was up to, but found nothing but amusement behind his eyes.

They rode up over the hill and a sprawling white, two-story house came into view. With a large wraparound porch and direct view of the lake in the backyard, the cottage could've been photographed for magazines—and probably had. It had a distinctly upscale cottage feel, with a bright red mailbox, black light fixtures and a sweet little playhouse off to one side.

"Do you know Gerard Thomas?"

"Who?" Josh laughed.

"This is his house. He and his wife, Winnie, built it when he retired. I think all of their kids got married in the backyard, and one of them moved back in with her baby a few years ago."

"I had no idea," Josh said. "Pretty, right?"

Carly was perfectly happy in her quaint little cottage, but this house made hers look like a shanty. Josh pulled up into the driveway and Carly admired the giant hydrangea bushes flanking either side of the stairs leading up to the porch.

"Are we here for a dinner party or something?" Carly asked. "I'm not really dressed to see anyone." She glanced down at her cut-off jean shorts and loose red tank.

He opened the door. "Come on, let's go look around."

She frowned as he got out of the truck, stopping in front of it and peering at her through the windshield. She opened her door and slid out, trying to make sense out of the scene.

"Come on!" He motioned for her to follow him, which she did, realizing it was the only way to figure out what he was up to.

He led her up the steps and onto the porch, then he pulled a key from his pocket and inserted it in the lock.

"What are you doing?" she hissed. She tossed a glance over her shoulder, as if Gerard and Winnie could show up at any moment.

"It's fine, there's no one here."

"Is it, like, an Airbnb?"

"You ask a lot of questions." He pushed the door open and smiled at her.

She walked through the door and looked around. "Wow."

"Nice, right?"

"Josh, this house is amazing." They stood in a wide entryway, and Carly admired the high ceilings that drew her eyes up to a second level. On one side of the staircase was a large family room and on the other, a formal dining room.

She followed Josh past the stairs to the back of the house, where there was a large, farmhouse-style kitchen with a breakfast nook and a big wall of windows that looked out across the lake. She moved toward one window, staring down at the private dock and a guesthouse off to one side.

"Do you like it?"

She turned and saw Josh leaning in the doorway of the kitchen, watching her.

"Are you kidding?" She faced him. "This place is incredible."

"I was hoping you'd say that."

Okay, now this was just getting weird. "Why?"

"Because it's yours." He held up a small set of keys and jangled them in the air.

"I don't understand."

"I mean, I was thinking my mom could live out in that little guesthouse," he said. "It's kind of perfect since she's going to need some help, but she'll also want her own space."

Bewildered, she shook her head. "Josh, what are you saying?"

"Look, I know things have gotten really crazy, and they're only going to get worse the more people find out about my family. It's a lot to take in."

She didn't respond. It was true—it was a lot to take in—and yes, it was only going to get worse.

"But I'm not going anywhere." He closed the space between them. "Even when things get hard." He took her face in his hands and searched her eyes, but she was certain all he'd find there was confusion.

"Stay with me," he said. "I know you like things in order. I know you want everything to fit neatly into all those little boxes you have to check off. You want stability and assurances and guarantees. But life doesn't give us those things. Life is messy and chaotic and hard."

"Josh—"

"Let me say this, Carly, please." His hands slid down to her shoulders, then rested on her arms. "I won't lie. I thought about leaving. I wanted to run. After I found out the truth about my brother—after I realized what my parents had done—I packed a bag and I sat there, trying to go."

She exhaled a slow breath. "What stopped you?"

He brushed his thumb across her cheek. "Do you really need to ask?"

She shrugged. "Maybe."

"I couldn't leave you again," he said. "I kept thinking about you—about Jaden. I kept thinking about that kiss, the night you came over to the cabin. That one kiss wrecked me—made it clear that there was still so much between us."

Her eyes misted as she struggled to wrap her mind around the words he spoke.

He fixed his gaze intently on her, looking for a moment like he was holding his breath. Slowly, he reached into his back pocket and pulled out his wallet, opening it and sliding the faded sheet of notebook paper out.

He knelt down in front of her. "Carly Raeanne Collins—" He unfolded the sheet of paper.

"Josh—"

He smiled up at her, then glanced down at the page. "I promise to love you the way I loved you the first time I ever saw you when we were kids. To remember the way my heart jumped the first time we held hands. To reinvent ways to kiss you like it was the first time we ever kissed. I promise to be faithful to you, to protect you, to listen to your advice and sometimes even take it."

A soft laugh escaped and she swiped a tear from her cheek.

"I promise to cherish you. To take care of you. To do what's best for you and to always put your happiness before my own. I promise that in all things you will forever be my *always.*"

The words brought her to tears the way they had the first time she'd heard them. For the briefest moment, they were those same two kids who loved each other beyond reason, the pain of the past a distant memory.

He reached into his pocket again and pulled out a small box, opened it and held it out to her. "Carly, I know you feel like you and I are a risk, but we're a risk worth taking, I promise. I'm going to love you every day for the rest of my life if you'll let me."

She sniffed. "I'll let you."

"Yeah?"

She nodded. "If you'll let me love you back."

He stood, wrapped his arms around her and pulled her toward him. He studied her face, as if memorizing every line, each one a moment he'd missed and needed to make up for. "I've loved you for as long as I can remember."

She inched up on her tiptoes, drawing him closer, and her kiss became a promise to love and honor and cherish him in return.

His lips searched hers with all the familiarity of the years they'd been together and the curiosity of the years they'd been apart. She didn't have guarantees—nobody did.

But this—she and Josh together—it was right.

And whatever came, they'd face it together. Carly, Josh and Jaden. A real family.

He pulled away, his breath short. "Man, I can't wait to make you my wife."

"'Bout time you made an honest woman of me," she said with a grin.

He smoothed her hair away from her face and kissed her softly. "Do you want to see the rest of the house?"

She nodded and followed him to the top of the stairs. "We might have to wait until after Quinn's wedding. I don't want to steal any of her thunder."

"We could elope?"

"My sister would kill me."

"Then we'll do it up big—anything you want."

She tugged his hand and he faced her. "I don't want anything but you, Josh. You and Jaden are really all I need."

"And maybe another couple of kids down the road?" He pushed open the door of the bedroom they stood in front of.

Inside, she saw a perfectly decorated Peter Rabbit nursery and her heart leapt at the idea, one she'd stopped entertaining years ago.

"It's our second chance," he said.

She wound her hands up around his neck and leaned into him. "Better than anything I could've ever hoped for."

And as she fell into his warm embrace, drinking in the sweetness of his kisses, her mind fluttered not back to the past but forward to the future—a future they got to write together.

Forever and always.

THE END

A Note From the Author

Dear Reader,

It doesn't escape me how very blessed I am to be able to share my stories with you. I count it among my life's greatest joys, and it is something I'll never take for granted.

When it came time to write a new novel, I found myself thinking (constantly) about Carly and Josh. About first love. About second chances. I wondered if I could make Josh lovable after what he'd done, and then I realized, we're all unlovable after what we've done.

And that's where grace comes in.

I am so thankful to have had the chance to explore this relationship, and especially to look at the whole idea of forgiveness and unconditional love. I especially loved the opportunity to put this family back together again.

I know you have a plethora of reading choices. There are so many wonderful books out there for you to read and love, and I want to personally thank you for choosing to make mine one of them.

It means the world to me.

Of course, I would be so grateful if you had time to share with your friends about Just One Kiss, whether by leaving a review, posting about it or simply letting someone borrow it. That is greatest gift of all.

I truly hope you enjoyed Carly and Josh's story. As always, I love to hear from my readers (and I really love to make new friends!) and hope you'll find me online at one of the places listed below, and drop me a note via email at courtney@courtneywalsh-writes.com

It would brighten my day!

With gratitude,
    Courtney Walsh
    www.courtneywalshwrites.com

Acknowledgments

To Adam. Always and forever. Me + You. Thanks for not letting me give up.

For my kids. I'm so thankful you're mine. I don't consider being your mom a job, but if I did, it would be the best one ever.

My Parents, Bob & Cindy Fassler. So grateful for your love and wisdom in my life.

Charlene Patterson. Thank you for helping me make this book stronger. I'm so grateful for your wisdom.

Stephanie Broene, Danika King & the Tyndale team. For being amazing humans who just happen to be incredible at their jobs. I'm grateful for every day I get to work with you both.

Carrie Erikson. For always, always making me laugh.

To Natasha Kern, my agent. Thank you for challenging me to be better and write stronger. I am so thankful for your wisdom on this journey.

To Deb Raney. Always my mentor and always my friend. For all you've done to help me understand story—I am grateful.

To my Studio kids and families. For the support and joy you bring into my life. You are such a gift to me.

And especially to you, my readers. I hope you know how special you are. I hope you know that your kind words (either directly to me or via a review or social media) are so greatly appreciated. I hope you know that these stories are my way of sharing my heart with you, and I am so grateful to have that opportunity. You mean the world to me.

About the Author

Courtney Walsh is the author of *Just Look Up, Just Let Go, Things Left Unsaid, Hometown Girl, Paper Hearts, Change of Heart,* and the Sweethaven series. Her debut novel, *A Sweethaven Summer,* was a New York Times and USA Today e-book bestseller and a Carol Award finalist in the debut author category. In addition, she has written two craft books and several full-length musicals. Courtney lives with her husband and three children in Illinois, where she co-owns a performing arts studio and youth theatre with the best business partner she could imagine—her husband.

Visit her online at www.courtneywalshwrites.com